From the Author of *Dishwasher Safe*

M.J. ETKIND

The Witch of Wall Street

M.J. Etkind

Izzi House Books

1st edition 2025

Ebook ISBN 979-8-9907191-2-5

Print ISBN 979-8-9907191-3-2

Other Books by M.J. Etkind

Dishwasher Safe

For Dr. Treba Marsh and all the women who are witches in finance because of your dedication to our education.

Content warning

Warning, contains minor spoilers

In chapter 10 of this book, a secondary character overdoses on opioids and is given Narcan. She is ultimately survives, but there are detailed depictions of her time in the hospital and the decision she makes about future treatment. Take care readers, chapter 10 can be skipped without much impact on the story as a whole. This chapter was vetted by a professional who works with those struggling with addiction.

Prologue - 2009

THE POSTER BOARD MIRIAM was attempting to schlep to school caught in the wind, pulling her every which way down the sidewalk. Her once-pristine presentation was now a rumpled mess. Her hair, which she'd tried to tame that morning, had twisted into a curly bird's nest on top of her head. And despite the fact that she hadn't eaten breakfast because she'd feared spilling food on her clothes, the blouse she wore already had some mysterious grease stain on it; her mitigation efforts had clearly failed. She would've tried to magic everything back into place, but it was her attempt to straighten her hair with magic that had led to the disorder she was experiencing in the first place.

She felt chaotic. Not that that was anything new; she always felt chaotic, intolerant of the anarchy that battled to control her life. But today, she'd really, really made a concerted effort. Every decision had been coordinated, intending to control the chaos. She'd chosen to walk instead of ride her broom in an effort to avoid battling the wind. That hadn't worked. She'd avoided eating breakfast in order to prevent stains—now a moot point. And her hair . . . well, trying to do anything for her hair was obviously pointless.

"Heya," a buttery-smooth teenage voice sang from her side. She couldn't see the speaker over her unruly poster board, but she knew who it was. Also, what teenager used the word *Heya*?

"Nelson." There was a bitter edge to her voice, and she hoped the single word conveyed what she was feeling, which was the standard *fuck off* she had always reserved for Nelson.

"Do you need help?" he asked, so cheerfully she was sure he'd meant it to get on her nerves.

"I'm fine," she snapped as she wrangled her poster board below her face so she could see him. As she did, she heard the distinct sound of cardboard ripping. "*Shit.*"

Scowling, she lifted her eyes to Nelson, who stood straight and tall, his dark, glossy hair shining in the spring sun and his smile just crooked enough to feel annoyingly sincere. He held his own poster board, which, unlike Miriam's rumpled mess of a project, was perfectly pristine. The red, white, and blue construction paper he'd used to detail the three branches of government was cut perfectly straight and neatly glued down. Miriam's looked pathetic in comparison, all the corners of the construction paper coming unglued and turning up at the edges.

Miriam knew all of the information on her poster board was correct and that she'd do well with her presentation. But this was the last grade in her AP Government class, and she really needed a good score to bring her grade up from a B+ to an A. It could mean the difference between valedictorian or salutatorian, which would affect the scholarship money she was offered. Nelson, with his perfect presentation, was her competitor.

"I could help," Nelson offered, looking around to make sure there was no one else on the sidewalk. Miriam and Nelson were just two of a handful of magics at their high school, and keeping the secret about their magic was important.

"It would take a small miracle to fix this mess," Miriam responded, and then choked a little on the words.

Nelson gave her his signature smile and then a wink. There was the subtlest of changes in the air, and Miriam looked down at her poster. The rip was gone, the construction paper was firmly stuck onto the poster board, and even the glitter glue she had attempted to use shined a little brighter and no longer looked patchy.

Miriam groaned at the now-flawless presentation. She didn't know if it would get her the grade she wanted, but at least she now had a fighting chance at the valedictorian spot and all the scholarship money she desperately needed to afford Harvard in the fall.

Even still, there was something so infuriating about Nelson's golden boy act. When Nelson was around, good things happened, because of course they did. His magic was all about performing small miracles. Most of the time, he couldn't even help it.

Miriam's magic, on the other hand, was chaotic, just like her.

"Why did you do that?" she asked, groaning again.

"To even the playing field," Nelson responded with another wink, and all the stray hairs suddenly stopped whipping in Miriam's face.

"I can take care of myself," she grumbled as she shifted the poster board into a more natural position now that the wind seemed to be working for her instead of against her.

"If you say so," Nelson said, his tone patronizing.

Miriam could feel frustration pooling in her stomach, and even worse, it was threatening to morph into anger. "I'm not some charity case."

"You needed help," Nelson replied casually, easily, as if it were his responsibility to save Miriam from her own dumb chaos magic.

"I was handling it just fine," Miriam snapped.

"You deserve—"

"I *deserve* to do things on my own." Miriam stomped away with finality. Just a few more weeks and she would graduate from high school, and then she would never have to see Nelson Copperfield again.

Chapter One –
Present Day

M IRIAM LEANED BACK IN her chair and rubbed her eyes, careful to avoid smearing the remnants of the eye makeup she had applied that morning. She dug her bare feet into the scratchy, short industrial-blue carpet under her desk, her pointy black stilettos having been discarded hours ago, and with a tired sigh, she glanced out the open door of her office. The sun had long since set, and it was nearly midnight, making the fluorescent lights out in the bullpen feel jarring and much too bright. The light's harshness matched the staccato clacking of keyboards and clicking of mouse buttons from the other room as well. With another sigh, she looked back at her computer. Maybe she should turn all the analysts' computer mice into *real* mice. They wouldn't know what had happened, but it would be a good way to get them using keyboard shortcuts in Excel like they should rather than just click-click-clicking with their computer mice. Kids these days were bad at learning keyboard commands. Besides, an impromptu mouse infestation would also make a good excuse to call it a night and . . .

There was a gentle warning knock on the doorframe of her office, and Miriam looked up from her computer, surprised to see Charlie walk in. Charlie was the middle-aged managing partner of Alchemy Partners, the midsized investment bank where Miriam had worked for the last decade. Even though it was well past working hours, and he usually wasn't around this late, Charlie was still dressed in a bespoke suit, his tie was still straight, and his buttons were done up all the way to the top. His salt-and-pepper hair was pristine. Miriam could barely pull off such a look with magic at her disposal, but Charlie, who was as non-magical as possible, accomplished it with what seemed like ease. *Men.*

"Hey, Charlie," Miriam greeted. "You still here?"

He ignored the comment, closed the door, and took a seat on one of the free chairs opposite her desk. He made himself comfortable, with his legs spread wide, taking up an immeasurable amount of space in her small office.

"I want you to take the lead on Pentacle," he said, blunt with the delivery.

"Pentacle? But that's . . ." Miriam trailed off, trying to maintain her composure.

"Robertson's," Charlie finished for her, referring to Gregory Robertson, one of the other senior vice presidents at Alchemy. Charlie always called the male employees he liked most by their last name, as if they were on the same lacrosse team. Miriam tried to ignore it, even though it often felt like she was missing out on a secret fraternity she would never be invited to. Charlie continued. "Robertson is stretched thin, and this is a big deal. Could make or break us."

"We're in a good place on it," Miriam mused.

"You know this client backwards and forwards." Charlie gave her a knowing look as he added, "And the bonus when you close is sizable."

Miriam paused. The bonus for taking the lead was a large sum of money. She already did well, but what she could do with this amount of money would be . . . well, it would be life-changing, even for her. It would mean knowing she could take care of her parents into their retirement. It would mean no more worrying about what she was going to do as they got older.

She had worked hard on Pentacle, but taking the lead would mean putting her entire career on the line. If she did well, besides the bonus, it could mean a big promotion, a big step up, a reward for everything she'd been working for the last decade. Yet, if the deal failed, it would be her responsibility. Staying on as second-in-command would mean she could bow out after it was done, but taking the lead was something else entirely. It would give her a real stake in the game, a responsibility that would affect other people's lives.

"We're not meeting with the client for another few weeks to present the options." Charlie continued on, as if his offer wasn't a huge bombshell. "Think about it this week, and then we can talk first thing Monday."

"Sure," Miriam agreed casually, though she immediately second-guessed herself. Had it been too casual? Would Charlie think she was uninterested in the position? No, she decided, her aloofness was probably the sort of reserved attitude that Charlie was expecting from a future partner, a cool unattached-ness that all the partners seemed to carry themselves with. She turned her attention back to her computer, as if there was something urgent she needed to work on.

"You want this open or closed?" Charlie asked, and she glanced up to see him standing in the doorway with his hand on the doorknob.

"Open's fine." Miriam waved him off and then looked back at her computer. When she was sure he was gone, she rubbed her eyes again. Then she snapped her fingers and waited for the synchronized shriek of the newly minted associates out in the bullpen as their computer mice all suddenly transformed into real mice.

Miriam gave a quiet cackle at the reaction. They were mostly the sort of young guys who had gone to fancy schools and rowed crew or played rugby in school. They carried themselves with a sort of inscrutable upper-class masculinity, and there was a joy in unraveling that, even if just for a moment.

The chaos created by a dozen or so mice running all over the office seemed to be enough to send everyone home for the night, finally concluding a very long workday. Once the office had cleared out, she snapped her fingers, turning the live mice back into the computer type. The last thing the office needed was a rodent infestation, and though she was having a little fun now, changing the mice back was a crucial part of the prank.

She slipped on her stilettos that were lying under her desk and packed up her bag. Then, with another snap of her fingers, the floor-to-ceiling window in her office disappeared. She pulled out a compact, lipstick-sized canister from her purse, and with just a flick of her wrist, it extended into a full-size broomstick.

The broomstick was a classically made wooden one, with twigs at the end forming the bristles and smooth knots lining the long handle. It was widely impractical for cleaning, but it was perfect for a late-night ride over the Hudson.

Miriam lived close enough to her downtown office that walking home was more practical, but she wanted the opportunity to put distance between the office and her apartment. And so she took to the skies.

It was still cold out, just past the spring equinox, and the air was icy. Miriam took a deep breath in, letting the briny air of New York Harbor fill her lungs. She juked and jived through the clouds and then around the Statue of Liberty. She wove through the coppered green spikes of Lady Liberty's crown. As she did, she thought of all the people this statue had welcomed to the shores of New York and the country.

Give me your tired, your poor . . . She read the poem engraved on the statue and laughed sardonically, wondering how well those tired and poor were doing now. The Pentacle deal wouldn't help, either, and maybe that was getting to her. It was a big deal for the firm, but the implications for the city were troubling, and alarm bells were going off in her head, reminding her of the ethics classes she'd been required to take during her MBA program. Could she really get on board with it as *the lead*, knowing what she did? Knowing how it would affect the most vulnerable populations in the city?

She shivered a bit as she paused in the clouds. She'd put on her jacket over the suit she was wearing, but it wasn't enough to beat the early spring chill. The breeze up here, high above the water, only made her colder and ruffled the tight curls of her hair, which she'd worked so hard to learn how to tame. Being employed at her level meant keeping up a certain appearance, and it always felt like her body was working against her, hair included. Not to mention she was small-chested and flat-hipped but also a smidge larger than average size, making her awkwardly out of proportion. And in the moonlight, her pale skin nearly glowed. It definitely didn't help her fit into any mold that could be labeled as "normal." But then again, she was also floating hundreds of feet up in the air on a broomstick, and that was about as "not normal" as things got.

The cold finally got to her, and she headed towards the alleyway just outside her apartment building. This was her go-to spot. It always smelled vaguely of French fries from the plant-based burger place that had moved in three years ago to the ground floor of her Finance District apartment building.

"Ms. Blum," the doorman greeted with a curt nod, opening the door. "Working late again?"

"Always, Bruce," Miriam replied. She paused, giving Bruce, her sixty-five-year-old doorman, a smile. He worked hard, had a tough job, and still always greeted her with a smile. He was about the only person who did. She could have flown straight into her apartment, bypassing the front door all together, but she enjoyed seeing Bruce every night when she got home.

Miriam made her way through the building's lobby and then rode the elevator up to her floor, and the moment she opened the door of her small but modern apartment, there was a loud yowling.

"Larry," Miriam said lazily, reaching down to pat the seventeen-pound black cat that was making the ruckus. "I know you ate dinner; I got an alert on my phone." She'd set the fancy self-feeder she'd bought for Larry to take a picture of him eating his dinner and send it to her. It was the one thing that connected her to the world outside her office each day.

Larry just stretched long, sticking out a leg in front of him, and then started yowling again.

"Wet food?" Miriam asked, as if Larry would answer back. Larry couldn't talk, and it was doubtful he understood much of what she was saying. Magical cats might exist (Miriam was skeptical), but if they did, Larry was definitely *not* one of them. Larry was a rescue Miriam had adopted five years ago, back when he was a small kitten. Miriam found it hard to remember there was ever a time Larry was small. And it wasn't that he was fat. No, he was just a very, very large cat.

After slipping off her shoes, Miriam went into the kitchen, where she opened a new can of wet food. She scooped half of it out and plopped it into Larry's food bowl. He would get the other half of the can before she headed to work in the morning.

Miriam pulled off her clothes on her way to her bedroom and then headed into the bathroom. There were plenty of magical people who could snap their fingers and suddenly be made up for bed with no effort at all, but Miriam was not that kind of witch. If she were on her game, she might have been able to do something passable, but her chaos magic meant that she was more likely to spill mouthwash all over her bathroom than to do anything productive.

She spent a few minutes getting ready for bed, then climbed under the covers, exhausted. She usually went to sleep fast once she was in bed. Long days at the office meant that there was no time to waste trying to fall asleep. Tonight, though, her mind was spinning with thoughts on the Pentacle deal. She knew she needed to make a decision about it, but she wasn't sure what. The promotion was huge for her career, but she wasn't sure if she could live with herself if the deal was successful. The impact on the community would be too devastating.

Needing a distraction, she rolled over and picked up her cell phone, her fingers instantly tapping the screen to take her to her email, even though she had left work late and it was unlikely anyone was still emailing at this hour. When she saw nothing new in her inbox, as expected, she turned her attention to her calendar, only to see an event she had almost forgotten about. Housing Magic's annual fundraiser.

The firm had bought seats to the fundraiser months ago, way before the Pentacle deal landed on her desk. It was ironic that the weekend she had to make a decision about taking the lead on the deal was the weekend she was supposed to go to Housing Magic's fundraiser. She'd be headed directly into the epicenter of her moral conundrum.

Maybe, though, she considered as she drifted off, maybe this was how she was going to make everything work out. Maybe there was a way to clear her conscience while still getting the biggest promotion of her career.

Maybe she could have it all.

***

"I need a check for a hundred thousand dollars," Miriam demanded a few days later while standing in the doorway of the controller's office. The request was directed towards Hannah, the controller at Alchemy Partners and the only other person at the bank who was also magical. She, along with Hannah's wife, Maddy, were also in Miriam's coven, a group of highly successful New York witches. Collectively, they were the "Witches of Wall Street."

"What?" Hannah asked, as if she hadn't understood Miriam's words.

"I'm going to the Housing Magic fundraiser tonight. I need a donation to bring."

"We already donated 10K," Hannah replied, continuing to click away at her computer.

"For the tickets," Miriam challenged.

"We paid 3K for the tickets and 10K for the sponsorship," Hannah corrected. "I can't just write a check for a hundred thousand dollars. That has to be approved by one of the partners."

"But . . . do you know how much this firm makes each year?" Miriam pleaded.

"Intimately." Hannah rolled her eyes. "But if I write you a check without approval, then I'd lose not only my job but also all future accounting jobs. And Maddy would literally kill me."

Hannah got up from behind her desk, shut the door, and motioned for Miriam to sit. "What's going on?" Hannah asked softly after they both sat again.

"It's nothing," Miriam said, squirming under Hannah's scrutiny. She was looking at Miriam as though she could see straight through her guise, revealing all the emotions Miriam was trying to keep hidden. Hannah knew what the bank did, but she rarely knew the details of the deals until they were closed and the press releases went out. Usually, the deals were boring, and Hannah had little interest in knowing the specifics. Usually, the terms were about selling a company owned by some really rich people to some other really rich people. This deal was different. The implications were different.

"It's not *nothing*," Hannah pushed.

"It's the Pentacle deal," Miriam admitted. "Charlie wants me to take the lead."

"That's great." Hannah smiled at Miriam enthusiastically. "That means . . . Oh! Does that mean you'll be up for partner?"

"Maybe . . . I don't know." Miriam was hesitant to sound excited, for more than one reason.

"You're worried about your chaos magic?" Hannah guessed.

Miriam didn't take the opportunity to tell the truth about what was really bothering her concerning the deal. "Yeah, I'm just worried I'll mess it up."

Hannah shook her head. "You are the most in-control witch and person I have ever met, and I am literally a controller. I promise you won't mess it up. You've got this, and you deserve this." Hannah was well into the pep talk, and Miriam could tell she was using that as an excuse to no longer talk about the deal itself.

Miriam nodded. She couldn't tell Hannah the truth. Partly because of Miriam's own reservations, but it would also be unfair to Hannah. Hannah was a good person, and she worked this job because she was a talented accountant who needed to pay her rent. It was unfair to pull Hannah more into the morally gray world of investment banking, especially when Hannah didn't make any decisions around the deals the firm took or how they were executed. Hannah was also the one who kept them all honest, no matter what, and Miriam was happy to keep it that way.

"So the check." Miriam brought the conversation back to why she'd originally come into Hannah's office.

"Get Charlie's approval, and then we can talk. He'll have to sign it too," Hannah reminded Miriam.

"But—"

"I'm not losing my job over this," Hannah said, cutting off Miriam's protest with a finality that Miriam couldn't dispute.

"Fine," Miriam finally acquiesced, yielding her time in Hannah's office.

Hannah was right about the check, and not just about the ethics of using company funds without proper approval. Miriam had known it was a long shot, anyway—asking for such a huge sum of money as a means to offset her own guilt around the Pentacle deal. And Hannah's reminder just meant she'd have to find a different way to get her promotion, guilt-free. If she'd learned one thing about working in finance, it was that there was always a solution to every problem. She just had to dig deep enough to find it.

***

Later that day, the senior members of the team assigned to the Pentacle deal were gathered in a conference room for a strategy meeting, and Charlie was explaining the Pentacle deal in full. Miriam had gotten the overview that had sent her on her initial spiral a few days ago, but now she was getting all the details.

"This deal is contingent on being able to get the land rezoned," Charlie explained, going over information from his initial meeting with the client—the one where they'd formally accepted the deal. It would be another few weeks before the bank's team would meet with the client and present them with a full outline on how the bank would help them accomplish their goals.

"We'll need legal," Miriam muttered despite herself. "It's going to be expensive."

"And we're in a bidding war," Gregory reminded the group.

Miriam could feel sweat forming on her palms. She didn't mind the bidding war itself; she was a seasoned pro, after all. But it was *who* they were in a bidding war with that made her stomach turn.

"It should be easy," Charlie said, brushing her off. "It's some nonprofit, and their budget is set. We just need to come in above them. Once we get city council to agree to rezone the building for luxury condos, we'll get the bid in before anyone else finds out. It'll be ours for a steal, and it'll all work in our favor. No one wants affordable housing in the neighborhood, anyway. It brings in the riffraff and lowers property values. Once we start to get the locals involved and let them know that there's an alternative, this will be easy."

"Nonprofit?" Norman, a mostly retired partner who still showed up to these meetings, seemingly just to meddle, huffed and then laughed a bit. "I'm not even sure why we should be worried. Are they big?"

"Housing Magic," Miriam said, the words escaping her mouth before she could stop them. "They have a housing-first approach for the homeless." Charlie and Gregory looked at her like she had two heads. So, she was apparently the only one concerned with the ethical implications of this deal. Of course.

"Okay." Charlie shook his head at Miriam, as if she'd said the wrong thing. She wanted to fire back at him how it was the truth—and an important truth—but she held her tongue. "Now, I have the deck that the client shared with us. They want us to manage the acquisition and the rezoning. It's currently five hundred residential units. Given the nature of this deal, we need to keep things more confidential than usual. We're going to redact the information that's going to the associates. If this gets out, the deal will be over."

"Why? It's just a real estate deal?" Gregory asked. "We've done similar deals before."

Miriam sucked in her breath. She already knew some of the details about why this was more sensitive than many of the other deals Gregory had probably helped to broker.

"Housing Magic did a big public fundraiser to buy these buildings," Charlie explained, his tone matter-of-fact. "They got all sorts of grants, and the mayor has even spoken publicly about how great this project is."

"So . . . ?" Gregory arched his eyebrows in confusion.

"So," Miriam continued, trying to act as cavalier about the situation as Gregory and Charlie, "this is five hundred apartments for unhoused people, including families, no questions asked, no requirements for sobriety or a job. Just a safe, free place to live. They struggled initially to even get government funding because they promised housing with no strings attached, but a high-profile congresswoman went to bat publicly for them. It was a massive effort to lock down the funding, and now, we're going in to buy it up so our client can turn it into luxury apartments that start at a few million apiece," Miriam explained, attempting to keep her voice calm. Perhaps she'd gone down a bit of a rabbit hole when this deal had first come across her desk. She was the sort of person who was always listening to podcasts, and there was a period when she'd gotten way too caught up in a series of podcasts on housing justice. Housing Magic's efforts had been at the forefront of many of those podcasts.

Gregory gave a low whistle. "That would be a PR nightmare. We'd lose the deal to public scrutiny and lose a lot of future clients at the same time."

Charlie nodded along and then turned to address Miriam. "Exactly, which is why I need the two of you to handle this with discretion. And we need to get this job done. The reputation of our firm depends on it."

"Of course," Miriam agreed, working to control her expression so she didn't show what she was really thinking. Miriam had done plenty of deals since she'd been hired at Alchemy years ago. Some had even been real estate deals, large portfolios of commercial land, or established apartments that had been sold from some family-owned business or from one private equity firm to another. They'd been . . . well, harmless wasn't exactly the word, but they'd been no better or worse than anything else that happened in business. Now, however, this deal was threatening to derail a nonprofit that was providing free housing in a city where housing was nearly impossible to secure. Miriam had accepted she was the harbinger of capitalism years ago, but she'd always been far enough removed from the worst implications of the construct. She'd been able to separate herself from any harm that might have come from the deals she'd been involved in. This was different, however. This deal was one she was firmly in the middle of, and if she were to be successful at her job, it would mean that many, many people would lose out on free housing.

The meeting carried on as Miriam took notes in her scratchy handwriting on the printed-out slide deck. The notes included both the address of the property and the name of their client, as well as all the other details that Charlie said would instantly tank Alchemy for shady dealings. The deal wasn't illegal, but it was definitely in a morally gray area, and if any of the details got out . . .

When the meeting concluded and Miriam had finished her work for the day, she packed up her bag, stuffing a file folder with all the pages of printouts and notes she wanted to look at later. She'd review them at home, away from the distracting dings of her computer, the constant notifications of emails and other messages. She'd head back to the office at some point tomorrow, but for now, she only wanted to take the files with her and get home. At a minimum, she'd get some review work done after the Housing Magic fundraiser.

She pulled open her sleek, black designer bag, double-checking that her pocketbook and broom, neatly stowed in its lipstick-shaped canister, were packed. Then she slipped in the thin manila file folder with all the details of the Pentacle deal.

She peeked out her office window. The alleyway was clear, and she should have no trouble sneaking down there once she was out the front entrance. Then, she could make her way to the Housing Magic fundraiser without having to worry about public transportation, hailing a cab, or the unpredictability of a ride share.

The receptionist had already left by the time Miriam made it to the elevator, and the security guard at the front door waved her out. She slipped easily into the alley and cast an invisibility spell on herself so she could fly through the city without being spotted.

Miriam stayed focused as she flew through the city. Her chaos magic fought against the need to remain hidden, and it had taken her years to master it enough to fly undetected. When she was a kid, her mom used to take her up high over the Long Island Sound and work with her on all the enchantments she would need to successfully fly without detection. There were other ways witches got around, of course, but brooms were a classic and the type of magic she had gotten used to. It was what her mom preferred, and it seemed as though Miriam had inherited that preference. It was also what worked best with her chaos magic.

But mastering the skills she had needed had been painstaking work. While her few magical friends had all mastered transportation quickly, Miriam had spent hours upon hours fighting against her magic, which had wanted to blow away cloud cover or redirect her to populated beaches on a clear day. Once, it had even released a bunch of fireworks in the middle of September.

Now, Miriam was glad for all the time she'd put in learning to control her chaos magic. Her ability to fly meant that she reached Williamsburg in a matter of minutes, just in time for cocktail hour, with everyone none the wiser.

But as she landed, still using her invisibility spell to conceal her presence, Miriam couldn't help thinking about magical secrecy and how nothing was really black-and-white. Magical secrecy and the need to maintain it were such odd concepts that existed in a sort of unscientific, subjective curve. Magic could not be too obvious, or it needed to be so ridiculously obvious that it was so beyond belief, no one could reconcile what was happening. Flying on a broomstick through the New York skyline fell firmly in the middle of the curve. Turning computer mice into real mice, however, was far enough on the absurd end of the curve that Miriam felt safe risking secrecy to have her little bit of fun.

Chapter Two

THE FUNDRAISER WAS IN a converted warehouse turned event space in Brooklyn. Fairy lights had been spread across the ceiling, and standing tables were dotted across the exposed concrete floor. Banquet tables had been set for the standard three-course meal on the far side of the room.

Miriam was overdressed in her casual Friday dress. Most attendees were wearing smart-casual jeans and dressy sneakers, giving away the fact that they worked in tech or some other industry that paid well but no longer required the formalities of business wear.

The bank had purchased an entire table, but most of the tickets had been given away to clients and partners—folks that Miriam was supposed to entertain. Typically, there would be more of a presence from the actual firm, but the fundraiser was in Brooklyn, and no one was willing to go that out of their way on a Friday evening. That meant Miriam was the sole representative from Alchemy. She'd agreed to it anyway, in large part because of her own guilt over the Pentacle deal, although her ambition had also played a part. Being a woman in investment banking meant doing twice as much as her male counterparts to get half as far.

As Miriam walked through the venue looking for her table, she tried to ignore the extra bulk of her bag. But the weight of the files she'd stuffed in there—the slide deck and all her notes—was just another reminder of how her actions were going to derail Housing Magic's newest project.

She passed the bar on her way to find her table. The line was long already, full of folks who had just left the office and were looking for a drink to kick off the weekend. She got in line, deciding she'd need something to get through the next few hours, but then she noticed several servers walking around with flutes of champagne. That would do, and would save her from having to wait.

She turned quickly, not wanting to miss the server she saw walking the other direction, and she knocked right into another server carrying a full tray of champagne flutes. She jumped sideways, gasping, as the server stumbled back, the glasses on his tray starting what would no doubt be a very messy, very loud descent. Then, in a moment that could only be described as a small miracle, the server righted himself, and the glasses tipped back into place.

"Woah, that was close," the server said, wide-eyed. "I guess those yoga classes have been paying off."

"That or a small miracle," Miriam replied dryly. She was used to chaos, but what she wasn't used to was it righting itself right in front of her face. It had been a long time since she'd seen this sort of magic, but it had a familiar feeling. Magic was like that. Everyone had their own mark, their own take, even on common magics that a lot of witches shared.

Miriam looked over the server's shoulder and was unsurprised to see a familiar face. Nelson Copperfield. She'd seen him periodically over the years. Miriam's parents and Nelson's mom had been in the same coven on Long Island until Nelson's mom had moved to Westchester a few years ago. But they had mostly avoided each other since high school. They didn't like each other then, and they hadn't cared to remedy that over the years.

Nelson had grown into his gawky teenage frame. Now, he was tall and lean, with dark hair that fell over his forehead. In high school, he'd looked like he was auditioning for that week's latest emo band, but now, he looked artfully sloppy. Messy, alive. Perched on his nose were a pair of thick, black plastic glasses. They were officially out of style, but Nelson still made them work. If anything, they made him appear softer, more approachable. The finance guys she worked with would never allow themselves the vulnerability of glasses. They insisted on contacts.

Nelson gave Miriam a knowing smile. "A small miracle indeed . . . How are you, Miriam?"

Miriam rolled her eyes. Nelson's magic almost exclusively worked in small miracles. He was the entire reason the glasses of champagne hadn't crashed to the ground.

"What are you doing here, Nelson?" Miriam asked with a huff, ignoring Nelson's question. Of all people, Nelson was exactly the one person she was uninterested in talking to. It had already been a long week, and the last thing she needed was Nelson's do-gooder, golden-boy act.

Nelson shrugged. "I know the organizers."

That tracked, maybe. At least, given how Nelson was dressed—much more formally than the rest of the attendees. He was wearing a white button up and a pair of gray slacks, and he filled out the outfit nicely, the shirt highlighting his well-built arms. Going without a jacket had been a smart move, at least in Miriam's opinion.

Miriam gave a loud "uh-huh" and a nod, but she realized she didn't actually know much about what Nelson was up to nowadays. She'd heard from someone or another that he'd ended up in the city, but a lot of the people she'd gone to high school with had ended up in the city, at least for a few years. Apparently, he was still here, and apparently, they'd both found themselves at this fundraiser.

"Nelson! Nelson!" a woman wearing a sleek purple jumpsuit called out from a few feet away. She was holding a clipboard, and she had the look of someone who was on the organizing committee.

"I gotta go, but catch you later?" Nelson asked Miriam, as if she would actually want to talk to him again. As if whatever relationship they had was important enough for a second round. She hardly knew Nelson, at least not anymore.

So she waved him off, stepped back into the line to the bar, which was now much shorter, and waited. Better to be safe than try to hunt down one of the servers handing out champagne and risk another mishap. Besides, she reasoned, rubbing her temples, a glass of red might be in order now. She could already feel a small headache forming, and she hadn't even made it to her table yet.

The table the bank had purchased was prominently featured in the middle of the room. As a title sponsor, the bank had been given prime real estate. More importantly, they would be front and center as folks spent the evening walking around asking for additional donations. Miriam already knew she would open her own pocketbook, but whatever she could give would be nothing compared to the amount she'd asked Hannah for that morning.

Despite it taking Miriam a long time to finally make it to the table thanks to the line at the bar and the near disaster Nelson had prevented, the table was only two-thirds full, occupied by Robert Dowling, Harvey Cobbler, and their wives. Robert and Harvey were two VPs at Ablesworth Capital, a private equity firm that had worked with Alchemy on a few deals, though notably, not the Pentacle deal. Which made sense. It would have been particularly sinister for representatives from Pentacle, who were planning to directly undercut the nonprofit, to attend. Alchemy was really just a broker, the facilitator of the deal, Miriam reminded herself as she approached the table, forcing a smile. There was no reason for her to feel as guilty as she did. It wasn't like she was the one making the decision.

"Robert, Harvey," Miriam greeted, giving them each a firm handshake. She was especially forceful when she was met with Harvey's weak grip on her fingers. If there was one thing she hated, it was the handshake men sometimes used specifically for women. His fingers curled over the side of her hand, limp, and so, Miriam returned a firm squeeze, repositioning her hand in his so that she could shake it firmly.

Both men introduced their wives, blonde, primed, and over-made, who were seated alongside them at the table. Robert's wife, Charlotte, looked as if she hadn't worked a day in her life, and Harvey's wife, Emily, looked no different. They'd probably both been swept off their feet by their men before they'd ever learned such a simple thing as how to use Excel.

After all the introductions were made and Miriam had given enough fake smiles to last a whole year, she took her seat, glancing at the extra chairs positioned at the table. She doubted anyone else was going to show up. They never could get people to commit to these sorts of things. Usually, they would pull associates to fill the seats, but the office had been chaotic after the spontaneous rodent outbreak the night before. That meant the associates were all stuck making up missed time ahead of the weekend, and it was unlikely they'd be showing up here. Miriam almost wanted to kick herself for not being more mindful. Even when she was in control, she seemed to always be making life harder for herself.

"So, Miriam," Charlotte started, her coifed blonde chignon bobbing as she spoke, "are we waiting for your . . . husband?"

"No," Miriam answered firmly. "I'm flying solo tonight."

"Is your husband out of town?" Emily asked.

"No," Miriam answered. "I'm not married."

"You work with Robert?" Charlotte asked, as if she could not comprehend that a woman might work in finance. Or perhaps she felt threatened by the fact that Robert might work with women. There were plenty of other women who worked at Alchemy, including a few associates. At Miriam's level, though, the majority of employees were men. She wasn't surprised, of course. This is how conversations always were with the wives of the upper-level executives Miriam worked with. It was 2025; plenty of women worked in finance. Hell, Miriam had even done a deal late last year where the majority of the team had been women.

"Alchemy, the bank I work at, does a lot of business with Ablesworth," Miriam explained bluntly and then took a sip of her wine. Miriam had never smoked a cigarette in her life, but in that instant, she felt a strong urge to take a long drag from a Marlboro Light. She could picture it now—her standing outside, leaning against the building, letting out a long, frustrated stream of cigarette smoke in that battle-scarred way people in old movies would. She struggled not to laugh at the absurdity of it, and instead, she let out her frustration in another lovely, fake smile.

It was always so weird being paired with the wives. Miriam could not fathom what they did with their time. Though, she guessed, they probably organized functions much like this one. Perhaps they had children, or maybe they spent hours at med spas, undergoing treatments that were meant to make them look younger than their age. And even that, Miriam couldn't understand. But then, her own beauty routine was quite simple. Donavan did her hair every six weeks, and Kerry at the Clinique counter at Macy's walked her through new products every six months and showed her how to use them. Miriam had little patience for makeup, but it was something she'd had to learn, something to achieve and control, just like everything else. Each morning, she slathered on thick foundations and powders to make herself look put together. It was a necessary evil for her, not something she enjoyed. These women, though, probably had much different opinions of the stuff.

"Oh." Emily nodded demurely as she swirled her glass of chilled white wine. "We just don't meet that many women who work in finance."

"It's not that uncommon." Miriam gave another pinched smile, already over having to defend her career.

Charlotte opened her mouth to add to the conversation, but before she could say anything, the lights in the venue dimmed and a voice boomed over the speaker. "Welcome to the Housing Magic Annual Benefit. This is our twenty-fifth year in operation, and to date, we have housed over twenty thousand people in our two thousand units across the city, many of whom have gone on to find jobs and permanent housing. We are pleased to announce that dinner and the show will start soon, but for now, I would like to introduce Nelson Copperfield, Housing Magic's executive director."

Miriam groaned inwardly. How had she missed this? In all her research on how the Pentacle deal was going to affect Housing Magic, Miriam hadn't noticed that *Nelson*, of all people, was the executive director.

"Good evening!" Nelson boomed from where he'd taken the podium. He paused for applause. It was smooth without feeling overly contrived or rehearsed. The glasses perched on his nose gave him an earnestness that made Miriam roll her eyes. "Welcome to a night of magic. In a moment, my good friend

Meyer the Magnificent is going to take over, and I promise he's a lot more entertaining than me." He paused as the crowd gave a polite chuckle. "We also have dinner as well. But, before everything gets started, I wanted to thank each and every one of you for your support. Housing Magic would not be here without our donors." He paused again, and the patrons golf-clapped for themselves. He then continued. "Over sixty percent of Americans live paycheck to paycheck, which means they're at risk of falling into homelessness after just a couple of missed rent payments. Layoffs, injury, or even just a single emergency can put people at risk of homelessness.

"Although we need systemic changes, Housing Magic provides an interim solution, giving people housing without conditions. While we provide access to job training, social workers, and substance abuse counseling, we believe these services only work if people have a safe, guaranteed place to lay their head each night. We are not a homeless shelter. Our residents have permanent apartments that they can move about freely in. But we need more housing. We have identified five hundred units, and we are in the process of making a bid on the property. We are so thankful that you have already opened your pockets tonight, but to be blunt, we need more. Tonight, our social workers will be walking around, sharing some of their stories, and we encourage you to pledge your support and your money to make tonight successful. First, though, I want to introduce Talia, one of our residents, who has agreed to speak to you tonight."

Nelson yielded the stage to a white woman somewhere in her mid-twenties or early thirties. She was worryingly thin, with long, stringy blonde hair that seemed patchy. Her dress was a bit too big, and the fabric was stretched in weird places, giving the appearance that it had been worn and washed many times before.

"Hello . . ." she started. The mic let out a loud screech, and Talia stepped back, a look of panic plastered on her face. A woman wearing all black quickly ran out to the stage and adjusted the mic so that it was closer to Talial's face. "Hello . . . My name is Talia. I have lived in a Housing Magic building for the past year. For a lot of my life, I have been an addict. I was out on the street and had nowhere else to go. I was a foster kid, and a lot of bad things happened to me that I don't like to talk about. The shelters are dangerous for women and fill up fast. The one time I got an apartment, I was required to be sober to live there, and that only lasted a couple of weeks before I got kicked out for using again." Talia paused and let her words fill the room. She was by no means a gifted orator, but she seemed to know how to hold a crowd for a moment.

"If you have never been truly addicted to something, it's impossible to understand how hard it is to stop. I was so incredibly lucky when Housing Magic was able to offer me housing. I had been living on the streets for years. I was still using when I moved in. I was not required to go to a treatment program, but Housing Magic had safe injection sites and people who started talking to me about really getting clean. I am officially four months sober, as of yesterday." She paused as the crowd clapped.

"It took a lot of work, and I relapsed three times. But Housing Magic let me stay, and they let me keep trying. Last month, I started the first job I've had in a couple of years. It's still going to be a long journey to truly get back on my feet, but having a place where I can do that has made an enormous difference." The crowd cheered her on as she stood, soaking it all in.

Miriam had felt her stomach churn at Nelson's speech, but Talia's story had it churning even more. Five hundred housing units was a big deal for this organization, and all these people had come out to help make it happen. Miriam could feel her bag leaning up against her ankle under the table, the deck with her notes in its neat file folder like a lead weight. Heavy and real. She had no idea how she was going to detach herself from the moral dilemma and do her job. The wall between client and facilitator had never felt so thin.

Another speaker had taken the stage, but Miriam was having a hard time focusing as the speaker shared anecdotes about the great work Housing Magic had done for their residents—helping them become independent, procure jobs and housing on their own, get clean. None of it helped her feel any better about herself.

Almost as soon as the speeches ended, a server set down a plate with a bland-looking piece of chicken coated in some sort of soggy breading, along with blanched potatoes and green beans. It was the familiar rubber chicken dinner served at all of these events. The magician that Nelson had promised in his intro speech made his way onto the stage, followed by a few stagehands and an assistant, who pushed a large prop onto the stage as well.

Miriam nodded as another server filled her wineglass. At least she didn't have to make conversation with Charlotte and Emily throughout dinner. She had a feeling that Robert and Harvey had been more than happy to pass Miriam off to their wives while they talked about their golf game or where interest rates were headed, as if Miriam couldn't keep up. The magic show provided a pleasant distraction from the requisite small talk.

When a social worker came around with a clipboard and a pen a few minutes later, Miriam was driven by guilt to pledge a hearty four-figure amount out of her own pocket. She'd have to pay up next week, but the free-flowing wine and the fact that the money could be paid at a later date made the entire thing easy to do.

Meyer the Magnificent finished his set by cutting his assistant in half and then putting her back together. Weak applause ushered him off the stage and dessert onto the tables. Miriam, however, had no interest in dessert. So she picked up her wineglass as well as her jacket and her bag and went to find the bar. She was still technically supposed to entertain Alchemy's business partners, but she really wanted to be anywhere else right now. The businessmen had no desire to include her in their conversations, anyway. She already knew that much.

"Vodka soda?" Miriam asked the bartender.

He gave a curt nod and poured a finger of vodka into a rocks glass. He then reached down to open a fresh can of seltzer. Just when he popped open the top, however, the seltzer burst out, spraying all over the bartender, the bar, and Miriam.

"I'm so sorry," the bartender said, apologizing profusely while wiping up the bar and attempting to hand Miriam napkins.

Miriam gave a smile. She was used to outbursts of chaos, especially when she allowed her focus to slip a bit. "It's really okay, it's just water," she reassured him.

"And thankfully, the night is almost over," Nelson's buttery-smooth voice said from behind where Miriam was standing.

Miriam turned around; her jacket still wet from the seltzer, and she casually swiped at the wet spots. "Hey *again*," she said, trying not to let her suspicions get the best of her. But she couldn't help think it odd that she'd run into him twice in one night. Wasn't he supposed to be out wooing donors?

"Ma'am?" the bartender asked. She glanced back at him to see him waiting with the rocks glass, despite his shirt still being wet.

"I'm okay. This is probably a sign I should get out of here, anyway," Miriam replied. She reached for her pocketbook to offer the bartender a tip, but before she could take it out, Nelson placed a crisp ten dollar bill on the bar.

"Thanks," Nelson said, and then nodded for Miriam to follow him to a nearby empty table. She obliged, despite herself.

"I didn't realize this was your organization," Miriam said as they settled into their seats.

Nelson shrugged matter-of-factly. "It's not my nonprofit. I'm just the temporary steward. The leader for a moment."

Miriam gave him a glare, unamused by his response. "You know what I mean."

"I'm surprised to see you here." Nelson changed the subject as if he didn't want to talk anymore about the nonprofit. Miriam was unsure if it was his own humility or something else that took the conversation in a different direction. "I'd heard you were an investment banker."

"I am. My firm's a sponsor."

Nelson nodded and then said, "It's been a while."

"We've been out of high school for a while," Miriam quipped, though she knew it was a weak reply.

Nelson had drifted closer to her, their faces now just inches apart. It felt intimate, even though they were in a crowded room, music and chatter going on around them, drinks flowing freely. And she felt Nelson's intention. It was clear he was looking for something. Miriam was not uninterested. She'd been working a lot lately, and she knew that was only going to increase if she took on the Pentacle deal. His unspoken offer was a good opportunity. Besides, Nelson would be an easy person to sleep with once. She knew him well enough that it wouldn't exactly be having sex with a stranger, but she also didn't see him regularly, so it wouldn't be weird. They were unlikely to run into each other again anytime soon.

Her mind made up, she gave herself permission to let her eyes wander. His arms filled out his shirt nicely, and there was a part of her that wanted greater exploration of the thick biceps that flexed under his shirt. She was by no means drunk, but the couple of glasses of wine she'd had definitely made her more amenable to the idea. It was practical, more than anything. She could have her own needs met with someone she'd deemed safe.

"You want to get out of here?" Nelson asked, as if reading Miriam's mind.

"Don't you have to clean up?" Miriam asked.

Nelson shrugged. "There's an entire volunteer team that organized this. This is their show. Anyway, I'm starving, I didn't get a chance to eat dinner. Do you want to get ice cream?"

Miriam laughed, raising her eyebrows. Had Nelson really just asked if she wanted to get ice cream?

"That's . . . Yeah, I do," Miriam answered. It was unexcepted. She'd anticipated an invitation straight back to his place. She was used to that. The people who ran in her circles tended to be efficient and straight to the point. There was rarely romance, and if there was, it was more about going to the most-expensive restaurants with the hardest-to-get reservations. It was for showing off more than anything else.

"You ready to go now?" he asked. His hand was already in his pocket.

Miriam nodded, grabbed her bag, and swung it securely over her shoulder.

Nelson reached out, placed a hand on her shoulder, and took a quick glance around the room, making sure no one was paying attention. Then, in less than a blink, they were standing outside a small ice cream shop somewhere in Brooklyn.

"You still have that taxi medallion your uncle and grandfather made for you?" Miriam asked. She'd figured that had been the case, but this confirmed it.

Nelson gave a toothy grin, and Miriam was starting to feel even better about her decision to sleep with him. He took out a palm-sized metal shield from his pocket, gave it a quick flip, shined it on the hem of his shirt, and handed it to Miriam to examine.

Miriam remembered when Nelson had gotten it. It had been on his bar mitzvah, his thirteenth birthday. The Manhattan Taxi Medallion was enchanted to take the user anywhere they wanted to be in just a blink of an eye. Before ride shares had destroyed the taxi system, the medallion, even without the enchantment, had been worth a small fortune. Taxi cabs were required to have a medallion, and their supply was fixed. There was an entire secondary market where they often sold for seven figures.

"It's pretty handy," he said with a wink. "Ice cream?" He held the door open for her to enter.

"You're sure committed to this bit," Miriam goaded even as she entered the shop ahead of him.

There didn't seem to be anything special about the place. There was a sign announcing they served Hershey ice cream, and the menu seemed standard—chocolate, vanilla, mint chip, and a few other staples. The shop itself was small and shabby. Linoleum tiles and a couple of lopsided tables sat to one side. A pimply faced kid watched them from behind the counter, not looking particularly interested.

"Hey, Jack." Nelson waved to the guy standing behind the counter while Miriam peeked in at the flavors. "I'll do the usual," he said, and then turned to Miriam. "Miriam, what are you thinking?"

"You have a usual at an ice cream shop?" Miriam couldn't help but comment. It was absurd, after all. The man was like something out of a children's book. She would have long stopped trusting him this evening if not for the air of sincerity with which he carried himself.

Nelson shrugged. "They have this great fudge peanut sundae, and their malts are out of this world," he explained. "But"—he paused and smiled as Jack placed a banana that had been split into two in a long plastic bowl—"I'm partial to the banana split."

Miriam laughed inwardly, thinking how that, too, seemed very much like this new picture she had of Nelson. Then, while Jack continued making Nelson's banana split, Miriam looked at the very standard menu and eventually decided on a single scoop of mint chip.

"This isn't exactly what I had in mind," Miriam admitted once they both had their ice creams and were standing awkwardly in the middle of the store.

"Me neither." Nelson gave a smile. "Do you want to come up to my place?" he said, and he motioned to a door at the back of the ice cream shop. She followed, figuring he was taking her to some broom closet he used to make a less-conspicuous exit. Instead, when he opened the door, he waved her forward towards a fluorescently lit staircase.

"You . . . live above an ice cream shop?" Miriam asked as they began walking up the stairs.

"The rent was cheap-ish, all things considered. It's close to work." Nelson shrugged.

"Does location really matter when you can be wherever you want in a matter of seconds?" Miriam gave a good-natured jab as Nelson pulled out his keys and unlocked his apartment.

"It's still nice to be part of a community," he explained, his eyes softening as if to convey how important the community was for him. He pushed the door open and flipped on the lights, motioning her inside.

The apartment was all warm colors—reds, oranges, yellows. It was cozy without feeling cluttered. There were shelves with mismatched, well-loved books, and the whole place looked and felt lived-in and smelled fondly of used books and worn leather. Most of all, it was warm against the still-cool early spring weather. She immediately felt at home.

Miriam nodded. "I guess that's important, if you run a nonprofit," she said. She pulled her phone out but left her bag by the door. Nelson emptied his own pockets, including his taxi medallion, and set everything on a table by the door.

Then he slipped off his shoes, took a seat on the sofa, and indicated for Miriam to join him. She discarded the heels she'd been wearing and sat next to him, curling her feet up underneath her.

There was something that quickly felt intimate about the interaction. Perhaps it was because Miriam had known Nelson her entire life, even if she'd never particularly liked him. Or maybe it was just because she was near someone else who was magical. Besides Miriam's coven and her parents, she didn't actually spend a lot of time with magical people. Casually sleeping with anyone in her coven was a bad idea, though there were a few long-term relationships that had formed—Hannah and her wife being one of them. But everyone in her coven was already coupled up by now, so the coven option wasn't viable anyway.

"Do you want an actual spoon?" Nelson asked as Miriam plunged the cheap plastic one from the ice cream shop into her ice cream.

"This is fine," Miriam replied, licking a bit of mint chocolate chip off the back of the spoon. She sank back into the plush cushions of Nelson's oversoft couch, and it enveloped her as if it were made for her. It felt comfortable, like she were putting on a familiar pair of cozy pajamas.

"It's been a long time, Miriam Blum," Nelson said, gazing at her as he took a small bite of his banana split. He'd already said similar words at the benefit, but there seemed to be something else in his tone this time.

Miriam shrugged. "We've had different lives. It's not like we were actually friends in high school."

"We had a friendly rivalry," Nelson said.

"We were straight-up enemies," Miriam argued, realizing she maybe had a very different memory of their time in high school than Nelson. She and Nelson had always been competing for the top spot—in school, in the junior coven they'd both been a part of, even in Hebrew school, where there'd been no grades or rankings. Nelson, whose magic was all about performing small miracles, had seemed to breeze through it all. In contrast, Miriam had been constantly fighting to control her chaos magic. They'd always been coming from different places, and Nelson had spent so much time trying to one-up her, much to Miriam's frustration. By the time she'd finished high school, she hadn't wanted to see Nelson ever again.

"We . . . were friends." Nelson seemed confused, his eyebrows pinched together and his expression tight.

"We were forced to be in the same place a lot of the time, but we weren't friends." Miriam was insistent. She and Nelson had never been anything even close to friends.

"But . . ." Nelson stepped into the beginnings of an argument, but before he could make his opening statement, Miriam's phone vibrated with a notification.

By habit, Miriam picked up the phone, looked at the screen, and then threw it back on the sofa.

"Anything important?" Nelson asked. "Big bank business?" Miriam flinched at Nelson's question. She'd almost forgotten about the pages in her bag, the ones that detailed Alchemy's entire plan to undermine Housing Magic's latest project.

"Just Larry," Miriam brushed off.

"Larry?" Nelson asked, his eyebrows raised. He quickly scooted a few inches away from Miriam, putting space between them again. They'd drifted close during the prelude to their argument, which had almost felt more like foreplay than a true disagreement.

"Yeah, just Larry," Miriam repeated, this time holding up her phone to show Nelson the picture of Larry's blurry little cat face, mostly black but with a little white chin, frantically munching his dry food. "I get a notification from the self-feeder with a picture of him eating."

Nelson's fingers gently wrapped around Miriam's wrist, and he brought the phone closer so he could get a better look at Larry eating his dinner. A tremor ran through her body at his touch on her bare skin, even though his fingers were deliciously warm. She resisted another shiver of anticipation, wondering what his warm fingers would feel like touching other parts of her body.

"Just Larry," he agreed with a laugh, scooting closer to her again. "And it's just you and Larry at home?" he asked. He placed his half-eaten banana split on the coffee table.

"Just me and Larry," Miriam confirmed, placing her own ice cream bowl next to Nelson's. "And how about you? Do you have a golden retriever I haven't met yet?"

Nelson gave a rough laugh, his smooth public-presenting facade finally showing some cracks. "No, it's just me. I work a lot. It makes dating hard."

"I understand that," Miriam replied, just as Nelson placed a hand on her exposed thigh, where her dress had ridden up. This was easy, comfortable. She looked down at where Nelson's hand was now slowly inching upward, and that shiver she'd fought back earlier coursed through her, hot desire pooling in her belly. "No strings attached?"

"Just friends." Nelson gave a sloppy smile, suddenly appearing more earnest and open. His eyes crinkled behind his glasses, and Miriam felt her entire chest contract. He was gorgeous. And she wanted him.

"Only tonight?"

"For tonight," Nelson agreed. "Come here," he said, standing up and offering her his hand. When she joined him, he pulled her close, and his breath was hot on her ear as he whispered, "One night, old friends, taking care of each other. That's all."

It felt right, like she knew she could trust this. True, Nelson might be able to work small miracles, but she knew that didn't extend to controlling the free will of others, and Miriam knew she'd be able to offer her own consent. And anyway, it was Nelson. She trusted him.

She could already feel the heat forming between her legs, the excitement of abandoning the carefully composed front she put up every day. It felt good to do something spontaneous, chaotic even. She thrived on the chaotic, but it was a part of herself she had to constantly push down and control. Now, she didn't have to. She could be herself, even if just for one night.

Her decision made, she moved, shifting in Nelson's arms to kiss him. His lips were soft and full and comfortable. She sank into them just like how she'd sunk into the overstuffed pillows on his sofa. She fit so easily.

They stumbled backward together, Nelson directing them, and after only a few more steps, they ended up in his bed.

Chapter Three

M IRIAM WOKE UP WITH a start, naked and disoriented. She turned her head to see Nelson next to her, sprawled on his back across the bed. He was shirtless, and the only thing covering him was the thin bedsheet, leaving little to the imagination. The glow from the city streaked across his body, painting him with a yellow radiance that revealed just enough—the outline of his chest, his thighs, and what lay between.

She quickly realized she must have fallen asleep, too limbless to get out of bed after they'd finished. Nelson must have fallen asleep too, which wasn't surprising. He'd been every bit as considerate as she'd expected, making this one night of irresponsibility far from regrettable. Even so, she reminded herself, this was a single, one-time thing. They'd made sure to take care of each other's needs, but their passion had been limited to the transactional. It had been a particularly enjoyable transaction, at least, but she expected the evening would soon fade into her memory as little more than a single night with an old acquaintance.

Now, though, she needed to get home. Larry would be yowling for his second dinner, and Miriam needed to put in some hours at the office in the morning.

As quietly as possible, Miriam found her clothes and re-assembled herself enough to make her way home. She padded out to the living room in her bare feet and then put on her shoes, which had been discarded in front of the sofa. Her phone was still on the coffee table, where she'd left it after she'd shown Nelson the photo of Larry eating his dinner. She now only needed her bag, which contained her neatly stowed broomstick, and then she would be on her way.

When she'd entered the apartment a few hours ago, she'd dropped her bag by the door, under the small table where Nelson kept his wallet, keys, and prized taxi medallion. So Miriam rooted around in the dark, attempting to feel for her bag, but came up with nothing. She took out her phone, turned on the flashlight, and rotated around, but she still saw nothing. Teeth worrying at her bottom lip, she pointed her phone's flashlight at the door. It appeared to still be locked and deadbolted closed, just like it had been when they'd gone to bed hours ago.

Where had her bag gone?

"Hey," came a sleepy voice from behind her. She turned around to see Nelson wearing nothing more than a pair of gray sweatpants. He shielded his eyes to block the light coming from Miriam's phone flashlight. "Come back to bed."

"Nelson," Miriam started, needing to remind him that their agreement hadn't included her staying the night, "we promised this would only be a one-night thing."

"You're leaving?" Nelson seemed disappointed but accepting.

"Trying to, but I can't figure out where my bag went. Did you move it?" she asked.

Nelson snapped his fingers, and the lights magically turned on, illuminating the room fully. Miriam did another sweep now that she had more light to see by. Her black designer bag, which contained her broomstick *and* the information that could derail the entire Pentacle deal, was missing.

"No, I fell asleep after . . . you know," Nelson said sheepishly, as if he hadn't been an active participant. "I'm sure it's here somewhere."

Nelson spun around the room, looking at the door. He then walked to the coat closet, opened it up, and looked around. He shook his head.

"I'll try a finding spell," Miriam decided. She waved her hand and *nothing*.

"Let me try. It's my apartment. I might have better luck." He waved his hand in the same pattern Miriam had used, but again, *nothing* happened. That was surprising. Miriam's finding spell not working in an unfamiliar location was one thing, but Nelson's, in his own apartment, was another.

"Are you sure you didn't leave it at the fundraiser? We could go back and look," Nelson suggested.

"No, my phone was in my bag, and I remember taking it out when we got here, and then I set it down right here, by the table," she insisted.

"Let's check, anyway. It'll take just a minute," Nelson said as he walked purposefully to the table near the front door again and froze, his eyes wide.

"What?" Miriam asked.

"My medallion is missing."

"No, it has to be here," Miriam replied. "You brought us back here using it, and I saw you take it out and put it on the table last night."

"Miriam?" Nelson asked seriously. "Was your broomstick in your bag?"

"Yeah, why?" Miriam asked.

"And your chaos magic last night . . ." Nelson trailed off and then shook his head as he continued. "It wasn't under control."

"I . . ." Miriam didn't know how to respond. It was true. She'd dropped her careful control for just a little while, allowing herself a tiny bit of fun. After all, it was hard to do something chaotic, like sleep with your former high school rival, and still maintain control.

"I think your broomstick stole my medallion."

"Or they ran away together," Miriam proposed, even though semantics were not the point at the moment.

"My medallion has never done such a thing. It must be your chaos magic," Nelson accused.

Miriam wanted to counter, but then she remembered the one time in college when her broomstick had jetted out of Harvard Yard and up to Salem. It had been both Halloween *and* a full moon, and she'd located it pretty quickly. But still . . . There was also the time it had taken her all the way to Montauk, to an entire school of Mer people sunning on the beach, and she'd had to get the local coven, the Mages of Montauk, to help her get it back. She was usually in control, but sometimes her broom had a mind of its own.

Nelson sighed. "I should have known this would happen."

"That your medallion would run away with my broomstick, or rather, my entire bag?" Miriam was unamused.

"That something would go wrong with your chaos magic, and I would need to save you, yet again," Nelson explained. He seemed frustrated with the situation, but in a way that made Miriam think he was frustrated with himself more than with Miriam. Still, she couldn't help but feel her blood start to boil.

"What do you mean, *save me*? I have never once asked for you to save me." Suddenly, all the reasons she'd disliked Nelson Copperfield, her high school nemesis, came whirling back. No longer was she looking at the mature adult who'd wooed her into spending the night. He'd been replaced with the brownnosing golden boy who could do no wrong, and his smug air of superiority drove Miriam crazy. She could see it plastered across his face now. That genuine smile that crinkled around his eyes had turned into a scowl bursting with arrogance that only served to fuel Miriam's temper.

"Miriam," Nelson said, "you were a mess in high school. You could never find your assignments. Your textbooks were always half destroyed by the end of the year, and you would have been late to nearly every class if I hadn't reminded you what time it was." Nelson lifted one eyebrow. "I'm probably the only reason you made it into Harvard."

"*Excuse me*?!" Miriam was inflamed. She could feel the hair on the back of her neck sticking up, and she knew it was only a matter of time before her feet lifted off the ground. It was the middle of the night, she'd allowed her control to slip, and now Nelson's whole thing was turning her into the chaotic mess she fought against every day. "You aren't the reason I got into Harvard. I worked for that spot! I learned to control my magic, I figured out how to pay for school." Miriam could feel her hair standing up straight on her head now, but she didn't really care.

"Miriam," Nelson cut in, attempting to interrupt her, but she shook her head.

"No! And my broomstick would never have run away with your medallion if there hadn't been additional magic involved. You can't pin this on me. You don't get to act like I'm the only one with some weird magic thing. That medallion is probably unstable—it's ancient, and it was never built to hold that much power."

"Miriam!"

"And another thing—"

"MIRIAM!"

"What!"

"You're floating."

"Dammit," Miriam swore, taking in a deep breath and calming herself down enough for her feet to touch the ground again. She reached her hand up and smoothed down the curls that were still floating in the air above her head.

"Does that happen often?" Nelson asked.

"No," Miriam snapped. She turned back towards the front door, towards where her bag had been the night before, and her stomach sank. "Shit," she cursed as the realization hit her. Her bag, with the papers about how Pentacle was going to derail Housing Magic's project, had gone missing along with Nelson's magical taxi medallion.

"Now what?" Nelson asked, shuffling over and collapsing onto the sofa. He looked exhausted as he scrubbed the sleep from his eyes.

"We need to find my bag and your medallion," Miriam answered, exasperated.

"I know that," Nelson retorted. "I mean, how do we do this? You seem to have some experience here."

"I thought you were the one who always had to rescue me," Miriam snapped back.

Nelson ignored her comment and asked, "How have you found your broom in the past?"

"Why do you think this is a common occurrence?" She scowled at him with her hands on her hips. It didn't matter that he was right about this sort of thing happening on a semiregular basis.

"Well, my medallion has never run away before. So, I have to assume that this is your magic making this happen."

"*My* magic," Miriam huffed, though she didn't actually counter his statement. "You *assume*."

"Am I assuming incorrectly?" Nelson asked, that hint of superiority in his voice again.

Miriam rolled her eyes but then grumbled, "No."

"Ah, see. So what happened before?" Nelson goaded her now, sitting up straighter and watching her with a knowing grin.

But Miriam was over it. "Why should I tell you?" Sure, it might have been in part her magic, but Nelson's medallion had run away just the same.

"Because we need to work together to get our things back. It's both of our magics," Nelson reminded her.

"But I know how to do this alone." Miriam stuck out her chin in defiance. She would not be belittled by Nelson Copperfield for her magic.

"Come on, Miriam, you know that this will be easier if we do it together."

Miriam rolled her eyes, but she knew he was right. Their magical objects were both so entwined with their actual magic that they would need to work together to find them. Magical objects were good at hiding themselves from everyone but their owners.

"I have to get my scrying stuff," Miriam conceded with a sigh. "It's at my apartment." Miriam looked at her phone and quickly realized she had no good way to get home. It was nearly 3:00 a.m., and she wasn't exactly sure where she was in relation to her apartment, given Nelson had transported them here from the fundraiser.

"I'm coming with you," Nelson declared, and he stood up abruptly, crossing his arms over his bare chest as though in some heroic defiance.

But Miriam could only blink, her cheeks heating at the sudden reminder that he was still wearing his pair of gray sweatpants and nothing more. His chest was exposed, revealing an expanse of smooth skin and a tempting trail of hair leading from his belly button to parts unseen. She stared for a long second, then coughed to clear her throat and shook her head.

"No. It's late. I'll get my stuff and then come back in the morning," she said. She definitely didn't want him with her because she fully intended to take the opportunity to find their things on her own. No reason to give Mr. Golden Boy an excuse to say he got to "save her" once again.

But of course he argued with her. "Maybe you stay here," he suggested, "and then we can start again in the morning."

She shook her head. "I need to go home. Larry needs to be fed."

"I thought he ate with his self-feeder thing already," Nelson countered.

"He gets wet food around midnight, before I go to bed," Miriam said as she looked down at her phone and pulled up a ride share app. The only time she used it was when she had to go to a client meeting with other people.

"Then I'm coming with you," Nelson insisted. "That way, you aren't making two trips. We get to your apartment, figure out where our things went, and then this is done. No reason to drag this out. Let me just put some clothes on."

Before she could respond, Nelson slipped back into his bedroom.

Miriam let her head fall back and scrubbed her hand through her tangled mess of curls. Of course Nelson wouldn't let this go. He did have a point, though. It made sense that they should stick together to get this figured out. Having their magical items somewhere out there on their own was really not ideal.

Not more than a moment later, Nelson reemerged from his room dressed in a pair of jeans and a blue sweater. His feet were sock-clad, ready for the leather sneakers waiting by the door. He had put his glasses back on, and Miriam could almost forget how smug he'd seemed without them. It was like some opposite superhero effect. He seemed all earnest behind them, and once he took them off, he became superior and self-righteous.

"I called a car," Miriam explained, holding up her phone. "It'll be here in a few minutes."

"Thanks," Nelson replied shortly. He seemed frustrated or maybe even angry and was likely exhausted. Having to track down their magical items in the middle of the night after the big fundraiser for his nonprofit obviously wasn't what he'd had planned.

There was something refreshing to Miriam about seeing his golden-boy persona crack, even just a little, and for a moment, she disregarded her empathy and allowed herself to bask in the glee of it all.

Together, they made their way to the curb, the street much emptier than it had been when they'd gone up to his apartment. The ice cream shop was dark, and the city felt still and almost quiet so late at night. There were parts of Manhattan that would be awake all night, but this sleepy street somewhere in Brooklyn was not one of them.

The car arrived, and Miriam and Nelson each climbed into their respective sides. They were lucky. It was the sort of ride share where the driver was considerate of their passengers. There were little water bottles in the back pockets, an array of charging ports, and most refreshingly, the music was a breezy pop song played at a comfortable level.

It was only a few minutes before they were crossing the Williamsburg Bridge, the city lights illuminating the car and casting a yellow glow across their faces.

Miriam stifled a yawn. The late nights at work were more than catching up with her, and now she was on this inane mission with Nelson, hunting down a broomstick and a medallion that could be anywhere in the Tri-State area. At least, Miriam was *hoping* they'd stayed in the Tri-State area. Any farther and this task would be nearly impossible. Her broom had almost always stayed close, but if it had paired up with Nelson's medallion, she feared their things could be anywhere.

The car smoothly navigated through downtown to Miriam's apartment building. Unlike Nelson's shabby, quaint place over the ice cream shop, Miriam lived in a forty-six-story behemoth of a building in the Financial District.

The car slowed as they reached the front door, and Miriam felt a slight pull of self-consciousness at the building. It was an odd feeling. Her coven all lived in equally appointed properties, given they were the Witches of Wall Street. Her investment banking coworkers never struggled with finding an apartment, and so Miriam's entire social circle lived in the more desired locations in the city. Nelson, in comparison, seemed too humble to even be in this neighborhood.

Maybe it was just Miriam's ongoing guilt about the entire housing development thing. Not to mention the fact that the files in her bag were missing—files that could expose the entire deal and put her job at risk.

"Christ, you live here?" Nelson exclaimed once the car came to a stop and Miriam unclipped her seat belt. "I should have asked for a donation," he muttered.

"Just come on, the quicker we get this over with, the sooner we can pretend none of this ever happened," Miriam grumbled as she jumped out of the car. She hurried up to the front door, not waiting for Nelson, and right on cue, Bruce opened the door to welcome her into the lobby.

"Ms. Blum," he said, "and your gentleman friend." He waited for Miriam to give a confirmatory nod that they were, in fact, together. It was one advantage of having a doorman. He knew what questions to ask and how to send unwanted guests away. Miriam didn't exactly make a habit of bringing men home in the middle of the night, but Bruce was one for discretion.

By the time they got off the elevator on Miriam's floor, she could hear faint yowling from Larry, who was obviously disappointed his second dinner had not yet been provided. When she opened her apartment door, the cat was standing on the other side, wide-eyed, as if he had not been screaming for dinner just a moment before. As Miriam entered the apartment, he circled her ankles.

"Alright, friend, what do you want to eat tonight?" Miriam asked, bending down to run her hand over his smooth fur. He didn't answer, of course, and she straightened back up and moved from the entryway into her kitchen. It was a sterile white, so different from the warm colors in Nelson's apartment, and she tried not to flinch at the contrast, especially when she set her hands on the faux marble countertop. "How about salmon?" she asked, distracting herself from the guilt still wanting to bombard her. She took out a can of cat food about the size of a hockey puck and pulled back the tab.

Nelson just stood in her kitchen, gazing around at her apartment as Miriam scooped the contents of the can into a small dish and placed it down for Larry to lap up.

"I'm going to get my scrying stuff," Miriam said, leaving Nelson at her kitchen island. She headed back to her bedroom to sort through her closet for what she needed. She knew her scrying stuff was in a box at the top of her closet, but she couldn't remember exactly where she'd left it. She slipped off her shoes and then stood on her tippy-toes so she could start pulling boxes down.

Almost immediately, a couple of old shoe boxes fell with a clatter to Miriam's bedroom floor. "*Shit*," Miriam swore quietly.

"You okay?" Nelson called out, his voice echoing through the otherwise silent apartment.

"I'm fine," she said, and she reached down and found the box she was looking for.

When Miriam walked back out into the open-concept kitchen/living room area, Nelson was fidgeting with her fancy pod coffee maker, one cup already completed and another brewing.

"What are you doing?" Miriam asked as she dropped the box on the kitchen island.

"It's going to be a long night. I figured I would make us some coffee," he replied with a golden smile that lit up his entire face. With his glasses still firmly affixed, he seemed way too earnest again, and she was quickly starting to hate that smile. It had been the most annoying thing in high school, and now that he was standing in her apartment in the middle of the night, making her coffee, using her coffee machine, it was even worse.

"I mean, what are you doing in my kitchen?" Miriam knew she was being too snappy, all things considered, but she was frustrated enough with Nelson. Getting a verbal punch in felt satisfying.

But he didn't take the bait, and instead, he just repeated, "I'm making coffee." He opened her refrigerator and rooted around, presumably looking for milk.

Miriam shook her head in disbelief at the whole coffee service as Nelson placed a mug in front of her and held out a carton of almond milk. She conceded, accepting the coffee with a nod of her head. With another of those annoying bright smiles, Nelson tipped some coffee into her cup and repeated the process with his own mug.

Now resigned to both having coffee and working with Nelson, Miriam opened the box and pulled out a worn tea towel with a map of Manhattan on it, the major tourist areas, including Central Park, Times Square, and the Empire State building, highlighted with large, illustrated images. In addition, she placed a snow globe with the Statue of Liberty inside next to the tea towel on the counter. The snow globe was so old that the glitter had broken down, turning the liquid inside foggy.

"What's all this?" Nelson asked, confused, as he looked down at the items Miriam had placed on the counter.

"My scrying stuff," Miriam said, defensively.

"How does this even work?" Nelson picked up the snow globe and examined it, maybe trying to assess whether he could deconstruct the magic right then and there.

"If you give me a chance, I can show you." She took the snow globe from Nelson and placed it back on the counter. Then she carefully spread the towel out so that it lay flat on the table. She placed the snow globe in the middle of the towel and snapped her fingers. The lights in her apartment immediately went out.

Next, she placed her hand on top of the snow globe. It glowed, the light concentrating on a single spot on the map.

Miriam looked down and studied the map for a second. "Chinatown," she mused, noting the general area on the map. "Now we just need to cross-reference with a map of Manhattan and—"

Before Miriam could continue, Larry jumped on the counter, crashing into her cup of coffee. The coffee cup tipped and fell over, and coffee sloshed all over the tea towel. The light from the snow globe blinked out.

"Larry!" Miriam exclaimed. Frustrated, she picked him up and placed him back on the floor, and she snapped her fingers again to turn the lights in her apartment back on.

Next to her, Nelson sucked in a breath. "So . . . what now?" he asked.

"Have you never done this before?" Miriam placed her finger where she thought the light had hit, ignoring the puddle of rapidly cooling coffee.

"I rarely lose my things." Nelson was a bit too smug for Miriam's liking, and she groaned inwardly at him. "So, where do you think this is?"

Miriam let out an annoyed sigh and then reached back into her shoe box and pulled out a ragged paper map of the city. She unfolded the map and held it over the tea towel, careful to avoid the spilled coffee.

"There," Miriam said, pointing to a location on Doyers Street.

Nelson pulled his phone out of his pocket. "Tao Tie. It's a dim sum restaurant, but they don't open until 10:00 a.m. tomorrow."

"Great, then we meet at Tao Tie at ten," Miriam decreed as she picked up the tea towel, turned around, and wrung out the excess coffee into the sink.

"It's almost four in the morning now. Are you really going to make me go back to Williamsburg tonight?" Nelson asked, his tone pleading. "I don't even have a way to get there." His eyes looked almost too big under his thick-rimmed glasses, and it was so easy to agree to let him stay. Miriam didn't exactly like the man at this moment, but whatever had convinced her to sleep with him just hours before had not entirely worn off, either.

"Fine, but you sleep on the sofa. I'm still mad at you," Miriam said. She turned and started to finish cleaning up the coffee Larry had spilled.

"You're mad at me? I'm the one who should be mad at you. It was your broom that ran away with my medallion."

"That's an assumption," Miriam grumbled, even though she knew he was probably right. She really was not in the mood to argue. "I'll get you a blanket."

"Thanks," Nelson said, and he slipped off his shoes and headed over to sit down on the sofa as if to stake his claim.

"And, by the way, Larry snores," Miriam tacked on, tossing a couple of paper towels in the trash. "So have fun with that."

Nelson glared at her, but when Miriam returned his look with a menacing look of her own, Nelson backed off. She let out a hearty cackle and then turned on her heel to find bedding for the sofa.

Once Nelson was settled, she made her way to her own bedroom, shutting the door behind her. To her credit, she made sure Larry was inside with her rather than left out to terrorize Nelson all night.

She quickly changed and slipped into bed, but even though she was exhausted, sleep was impossible to find. Her mind raced, guilt and fear swirling around in equal mixture. She hadn't told Nelson the entire truth about their trip to Chinatown—particularly why she really, really needed to find her bag as much as she needed to find her broomstick—but as long as they recovered *all* of their missing items, he never needed to know the truth. As far as Nelson was concerned, their items were certainly in Chinatown. Miriam was sure that was where they would turn up.

She snuggled into Larry, who had taken up residence on the empty pillow next to her head, and she kept repeating the same mantra over and over. Nelson never needed to know the truth because everything would be right there in Chinatown. And everything would be fine.

Chapter Four

I**T WAS NEARLY ELEVEN** by the time they made it to Chinatown, even though Miriam only lived about twenty blocks away.

They had both overslept, sure that they would wake up in time to make it to Chinatown by ten without an alarm. And then Larry had needed breakfast, and Nelson had insisted on making more coffee.

The walk had been refreshing, though, and Miriam was ready to get this debacle over with. She stopped in front of the restaurant Tao Tie, Nelson at her heels.

"So, this is it?" Nelson asked, looking up at the green, scaly tiger-like creature between the "Tao" and "Tie" on the neon sign above the door. It appeared as though a tiger and a dragon had been merged in some magical experiment.

"Yup," Miriam confirmed as she reached out to push open the door.

"Wait, what are you going to do?" Nelson asked, stopping her with a hand on her shoulder. "You can't just walk in and ask if a magical taxi medallion has been seen with a broom."

"I was going to ask to use the restroom. That should give me the opportunity to look around a bit."

"Oh," Nelson replied lamely.

Miriam shrugged his hand away and pushed open the door.

Even though it was Saturday morning and even though the other dim sum places on either side of the street were already busy, with lines out the door, Tao Tie was nearly empty except for a group of older women at a table near the back. One elderly man was pushing around a clanking cart full of bamboo steamer baskets and covered crocks full of dumplings and other foods.

The restaurant itself was enormous, defying all the rules that governed New York real estate and the requirement to fit as much into as small a space as possible. Large banquette tables covered in pink nylon tablecloths were spread out around the room, with enough space for the dumpling cart to roll around the frayed red carpet.

The host stand at the front of the restaurant was occupied by a bored-looking teenager who wore a polo shirt sporting the green dragon tiger logo embroidered with sequins. Attached to the host's stand was a little sign that read "Restrooms for customers only."

Nelson gently nudged Miriam on the shoulder and nodded at the little sign.

"Two?" the teenager asked.

"Yeah . . . sure," Miriam agreed, her eye catching Nelson's. She instantly switched strategies. They would sit down at a table, order a few things, and then, once they were left alone,

Miriam could excuse herself to the restroom and look around the back of the house for their things.

The host showed them to a large table in the front of the dining room. If the restaurant were fuller, it would have been a shared table with other groups of diners, but given how empty the restaurant was, they had the table to themselves.

"I'll bring some tea," the host said, walking away to leave Miriam and Nelson alone for a moment. The dumpling cart rattled around the empty dining room, heading to their table, but Miriam figured she had enough time.

She leaned over closer to Nelson and whispered, "I'm going to use the restroom." But before she could get up from her seat, the man with the dumpling cart seemed to materialize in front of their table. He'd arrived so quickly, in fact, that Miriam had to wonder if there was magic involved.

This was a significant sign—proof that their things had likely taken up residency somewhere in the restaurant. A broom closet, perhaps. Unironically, her broom liked to hide in broom closets. In high school, she used to always find it in one particular maintenance closet on the second floor, near the library.

"What can I get you?" the man behind the dumpling cart asked, pulling the tops off the steamers to show Miriam and Nelson their contents. "Our shrimp dumplings are the best in the city." He gave a forced smile.

"I *am* hungry," Nelson confessed, giving Miriam his own apologetic smile. When she scowled at him, he frowned. "I only ate ice cream for dinner last night. Remember?"

"Fine, I could go for some of those squishy pork buns," she conceded, realizing she didn't know the actual names of the dumplings. The man nodded and set a crock full of pork buns on the table. Nelson pointed to a few of the other crocks, picking out a variety of dumplings for them to share. At the same time, the teenager returned to the table with a large teapot and two little handleless white ceramic cups. She set them on the table and then poured them each some tea.

As Miriam took a sip, Nelson finished ordering for them, and within what seemed like seconds, their table was suddenly full of food. They'd come simply to use the restroom, and now they were committed to a full morning of dim sum.

"This looks amazing," Miriam said despite herself. Nelson was right. It had been a while since the rubber chicken dinner from last night, and a lot had happened since then. Not to mention they'd spent plenty of time and energy on physical activities the night before. She wasn't exactly excited to be eating brunch with Nelson, all things considered, but it would just be one meal and then they could move on.

Miriam opened the package of wooden chopsticks sitting on top of her napkin and then carefully extracted a steamed crescent-shaped dumpling from a nearby crock. She brought the dumpling to her mouth and took a small bite. Immediately, she let out a moan.

It was unexpectedly phenomenal.

Sure, she liked dumplings well enough, but these were next-level and significantly better than not only anything she had gotten from a grocery store but also every one of her rotating take-out places. The wrapper was tender without being soggy, and the inside of the dumpling burst with flavors of scallions and ginger without being overly greasy.

"This place is amazing," Nelson said, echoing Miriam's thoughts. "I wonder why it's so empty?"

Miriam selected a pork dumpling wrapped in pillowy white bread. "Probably because it's a hotbed of magical activity," Miriam said as she took another bite.

"Really?" Nelson asked, looking around as if there was some visual clue revealing the magical nature of the restaurant that he hadn't seen. "How do you know?"

"Oh . . . well . . ." Miriam swallowed the bite she'd taken. "Our objects came here, so obviously there must be magic that drew them here." It wasn't exactly a lie; the statement was just backwards.

"Our stuff," Nelson said, as if suddenly remembering. "You were going to go look for it."

"I will," Miriam replied, a little surprised at her own response. But there was no rush, really, and they'd ordered so much food, they might as well finish it first. She selected another dumpling from a crock. "These are fantastic," Miriam repeated. "I think I want to do a coven meeting here."

"My coven is mostly vegan," Nelson said wistfully, and Miriam wondered if there was more to the statement. "I love them, don't get me wrong, but it makes potlucks really boring."

"My coven eats vegans for breakfast," Miriam said sardonically.

Nelson rolled his eyes. "They all do fantastic things for the city—librarians, schoolteachers, social workers," he explained, finishing the last of the dumplings in one of the crocks. There was something that Nelson wasn't saying, but Miriam didn't press him on it. She and Nelson were going to go their separate ways after this was over, and she had no desire to hear about any coven drama. All covens ended up with drama at one point or another. It was just the nature of that sort of thing.

"And your nonprofit," Miriam reminded him as she took the last dumpling from another steamer basket.

"It's not my nonprofit," Nelson said, repeating his words from the night before. "I just work there."

"How'd you end up there?" Miriam asked. She took a bite of her dumpling.

"I'm a social worker," Nelson explained, and as soon as he popped the last dumpling into his mouth, the dumpling cart was suddenly back at their table.

"We have fresh xiao long bao, based on a two-hundred-year-old recipe, and crispy spring rolls," the man said, already picking up the crocks to place on the table. Neither Miriam nor Nelson rejected the dumplings or spring rolls.

"So, a social worker?" Miriam asked, as she crunched into one of the spring rolls, not exactly sure why she was having this conversation with him. They'd ended things in an argument last night, and she'd never really liked him anyway. Sleeping with him had been a momentary weakness, brought on by working too much. Maybe she just needed to buy a better vibrator. That was probably healthier than randomly hooking up with men she hardly knew.

"I started with Housing Magic almost ten years ago. I'd worked for child and family services for a while, doing foster home placements, but that work wears on you fast, even when you can perform small miracles. Housing Magic was looking for a case manager, and I took the job. I was good at it, and I moved up." He scooped a soup dumpling onto a wide-bottom spoon, then paused, expertly piercing the dumpling skin and slurping up the steaming broth.

"Is that what you do with Housing Magic?" Miriam asked as the guy pushing the dumpling cart came back around and displayed a basket of something fried that looked like a bird's nest and another basket with sweet sesame balls. Miriam nodded in agreement, and the man placed the baskets on their table and walked away.

Nelson nodded. "I help people. Getting housing when they otherwise can't is already a small miracle, but sometimes they need a job application sent to the top of a pile, or an overly busy social worker to pick up the phone, things like that." Nelson picked up an egg tart that had arrived at their table at some point, though Miriam had no recollection of when that had happened. The man pushing the cart clanked around the near-empty dining room, every so often stopping at their table. Each time he did, something else appeared, and Miriam and Nelson kept eating.

"How about you, Miriam Blum?" Nelson asked. "You have a big, fancy downtown apartment, working for the firm that sponsored the fundraiser. You've done well for yourself?"

"I'm a banker," Miriam muttered. It was what she said when she really didn't want to talk about what she did for a living. She let people assume what they wanted. If she were out and about with strangers, she sort of hoped they assumed she meant she was something like a teller at a commercial banking branch. However, the type of banking she did had nothing to do with the institutions that actually provided personal banking services.

"I know that, but you're not just some analyst," Nelson commented as he dug into a bowl of soup—yet another dish that had been added to their table when she hadn't been paying attention.

Miriam felt her extremely full stomach flutter at what should have been little more than small talk. At some point since they'd sat down, she'd forgotten about the information in the files in her bag and what that information would do to Nelson's nonprofit. She'd forgotten a lot of things, she realized.

"What . . . what are we doing here?" Miriam asked, suddenly unsure. They'd been eating for so long, and time had slipped away. What time *was* it anyway?

"Having lunch with an old high school friend," Nelson said easily, unperturbed. He took a sip of his tea as if all was right in the world.

"But we were never friends," Miriam replied suspiciously, looking out over the enormous banquet table meant to fit ten. Dishes, baskets, bowls, and crocks littered the entire table.

Nelson's face fell. "We . . . we were friends," Nelson repeated, as if surprised.

Miriam brushed it off. His confusion was merely a result of whatever spell they'd fallen under. He'd forgotten their history. He obviously needed them to be friends for the mental gymnastics to work to explain why they were here. And that was the part Miriam needed to figure out.

"Nelson, do you remember why we're here?" Miriam asked again. A fuzzy recollection of something was floating in her brain, but she was having a hard time pinning it down.

"Lunch?" Nelson questioned, but this time, he seemed unsure, just as confused as Miriam.

"Why here, why now?" Miriam asked. "How did we end up here?"

"We walked from your apartment," Nelson replied as he took in another spoonful of soup.

"Why were we at my apartment? And why did we walk here?" Miriam pushed through all of her questions. That was a big part of her job, to keep asking questions. She had spent years and years and years asking every single question she could think of, much to the annoyance of the people whom she'd been questioning. This was how she did deals; this was how she found that one thing she could use as leverage, that one little secret the company had and was trying so desperately not to disclose.

"We were at your apartment because . . ." Nelson paused and then recounted, walking backwards through the evening. "We"—he motioned with his head to hint at what they had done—"um, at my place, and then we took a ride share to your place to . . . feed Larry."

Miriam shook her head. "Larry has a self-feeder. Sure, he wanted a second dinner, but he's fine without it, and I can always give him another helping with my phone. So . . . why did we take a ride share?" It seemed wrong, like there should have been another way to get to her apartment.

"Why did we take a car?" Nelson contemplated, repeating Miriam's words, as if he couldn't quite get to an answer either.

"How did we get from the fundraiser to your apartment?" Miriam fired back at him.

"My medallion," Nelson answered easily.

"And why didn't we use your medallion to get to my apartment?" Miriam paused and took a bite of a fresh bao bun that had been dropped off at their table while they were going through the facts.

"We . . . It went missing," Nelson realized. "Your broom ran away with it." He let out an angry grunt, his own fury at the situation returning full force.

Miriam nodded. "And we needed to go look for it," she started, putting the foggy pieces back together. "And now we've been here all day, and we can't seem to escape," she reasoned, even as she opened another new steamer basket. She examined the contents and dove in, starting into a round of fresh dumplings. She could feel how distended her stomach had become while she sat there with no choice but to keep eating.

"We're trapped," Nelson said, verbalizing what Miriam had already realized. "Unless, that is . . ." Nelson trailed off slyly, a pleased gleam in his eye. "There's just maybe some sort of a small miracle that gets us out of this." He finished by biting into a crab rangoon.

The menu was apparently as extensive as the length of the meal, Miriam realized, as a large noodle dish was delivered to their table—one Miriam was very sure they had not ordered.

"Work your magic," Miriam huffed with an eye roll. It was an inside joke from when they were kids, something Miriam's dad always used to say whenever they were working on something magical. Miriam was older when she'd realized it was an actual metaphorical turn of phrase used by non-magics.

Nelson gave his signature wink and then paused, as if waiting for something.

"Is the spell broken?" Miriam asked sardonically, taking a bite of a shrimp roll even as her stomach protested against more food. When they made it out of here, Miriam wasn't sure she'd be able to eat for the rest of the week. It was a shame, because this dim sum was fantastic, and, as a lifelong resident of the Tri-State area, she'd had her fair share of dim sum over the years. She hated the sensation of being sick on it.

Nelson looked confounded as he considered the possibility that his magic had failed him. "Let me try something else," he said, and then snapped his fingers and picked up a shumai that had been sitting on the table for a while.

"We need to figure out how this spell or curse or whatever it is works"—Miriam dipped her chopsticks into the noodle dish she'd served herself—"before my stomach explodes."

"What do you mean 'figure it out'? Magic just . . . works," Nelson replied, confused. "It's not like a computer that actually works in a specific way."

"Magic isn't technology," Miriam agreed, "but all magic works in specific ways. You perform small miracles. You make the train come on time or make time slow down just a little to be on time for a big interview. All of these little things make a difference. I, on the other hand, make a bag of flour explode or cause a small power outage right before a big client meeting. We don't know how this works mechanically, but we know it works in specific and patterned ways. I can't make small miracles happen, and you're too in control for chaos."

"I never thought of that before." Nelson cocked his head to one side.

"You never . . ." Miriam trailed off. Now wasn't the time to question how Nelson had gone his whole life without noticing the very specific and obvious patterns around magic. Instead, she needed for them to recalibrate, get on the right page, look for patterns. Her mom had taught her that. She had inherited her chaos magic from her mother, and her mom had always insisted that looking for patterns was the key to staying in control. "Alright, so, what do we know?" she asked, setting down her chopsticks and focusing fully on Nelson.

"We're at a dim sum restaurant," Nelson replied, densely stating the first obvious thing.

Miriam shook her head. She needed more than that. "We know we can break through, because we did that earlier, when we remembered why we were here."

"Why *are* we here?" Nelson asked, confused again.

"To find your medallion and my broomstick," Miriam reminded him as she dug through the backup bag she'd picked out that morning. She pulled out a ballpoint pen and tested it against the back of her hand, making a quick scribble. Then she looked around the restaurant. No one seemed to be paying them much attention. Though, she assumed, the guy with the food cart would be back around soon.

She jotted a few words down on her wrist.

Looking for broom and medallion
Cannot stop eating dim sum

Need to break the spell

She showed it to Nelson. "So we don't forget."

He nodded his approval at Miriam's plan, realizing what she was doing. "Now what?" he asked.

"What else do we know?"

The dumpling cart clanked by their table again, and the man presented them with more pork buns. Nelson nodded his approval, and the man set down the basket.

"So?" Nelson asked as he indulged in another hot, soft pork bun.

Miriam shook her head. There was something she was supposed to remember. They were talking about something, and then suddenly, her train of thought was gone. There was a pen in her hand and a slight smarting on her wrist, so she looked down. Words she had to have scribbled just a few minutes ago were written on her skin.

"We're looking for my broom and your medallion, and we're stuck here and can't figure out how to get out," Miriam said, and the facts came rushing back to her just as the dumpling cart clanked across the red carpet to the other side of the restaurant.

"We forgot again." Nelson seemed to be lagging a little behind Miriam.

"But only when the dumpling cart got close to us."

"So, the spell is in the dumpling cart?" Nelson asked.

"Or the man moving the cart," Miriam realized.

"So what do we do?"

Miriam watched as the man served the only other table, occupied by a few elderly people. Miriam couldn't help but wonder if they'd been young when they'd started eating dumplings.

"Chaos and timing," Miriam answered, though she was anything but sure of herself. She usually kept her magic under tight control, which was necessary when she had the sort of magic that was always derailing everything. Right now, however, the entire situation needed to be derailed. With a subtle wave of her hand, the dumpling cart squealed to a stop, and the crocks and baskets spilled out, creating a mess all over the floor. Piles of dumplings tumbled across the carpet, making greasy stains where they exploded. Meat and vegetables oozed out of doughy cages, and the flaking wrappers of the spring rolls shredded and burst open.

Miriam could almost feel the confines of the spell releasing her, a sudden clarity breaking through the haze. The fragments of memories she'd been fighting for came back in full, overwhelming force.

"I'm going to look for our stuff," Miriam announced. Nelson just nodded, still seeming a little shocked at what had happened, but she was happy to ignore him now that she had her full faculties about her.

She was, in fact, able to leave their dumpling feast behind and make her way to the narrow staircase that led down to the bathroom and the restaurant's storage area. If she knew anything about her broom, it would have happily settled into a cozy broom closet near a source of great magic. There was certainly a great magic here. It had to be great to have captivated her and Nelson so subtly and so quickly. It was an elegant spell that must have been worked by an entire coven. They'd unknowingly stepped into something far bigger than she'd expected.

She waved her hand, performing a close-range finding spell that should be able to reveal the existence of her broom. She waited just a moment, but the spell didn't seem to work. No rattle of a closet, no glowing light to indicate she had done it. She sighed, recognizing that whatever was going on with the dumpling cart was probably interfering with her minor spell.

With a scowl, she stepped up and opened the first door, which read "Staff Only," and to her relief, it was exactly the sort of place her broom liked to hang out. There was a mop cart with a couple of mop handles sticking out of the top. In addition, there was an old Electrolux vacuum that could only be described as vintage, and there were a couple of brooms with worn plastic bristles. Miriam turned on the flashlight on her phone and scanned the room, hoping to see a glint of a reflection from either Nelson's medallion or the lipstick-sized canister she kept her broom in.

She moved the mop bucket, the vacuum, and the brooms, but there was not even as much as a hint of a reflection or movement or anything of the sort that would indicate their things were there. For good measure, she cast a second finding spell. Again, nothing.

"*Shit*," she swore quietly. This usually worked when her broom went missing. Now, the one time it didn't was the one time she'd lost someone else's stuff as well. Of course her magic got more unpredictable when another element was added.

Her usual approach was obviously not going to work in this case, not when there were more variables than she was used to accounting for. Not one to just give up, even in the face of clear logic, she stepped back out into the hallway and then opened a few more doors, stuck her head through the threshold of the bathroom, cast another finding spell, and shined her flashlight around the unused part of the back of the house. Still, she found nothing. Their stuff was not here.

Resigned, Miriam walked up the stairs, readying herself to give the bad news to Nelson, only to be met at the top of the steps with an incredible commotion. The dining room was in complete chaos. Standing in the center was something that looked like a tiger with dragon scales, not all that dissimilar to the design on the shirt the restaurant's host was wearing. Not only was the dumpling cart still askew, but Nelson and Miriam's table had been flipped over, sending what was left of their grand feast across the room. The floor had turned into a river of spilled tea, soups, and noodles.

The man who'd been pushing the dumpling cart was nowhere to be seen, and Nelson was standing waiting for her at the top of the stairs.

"What *is* that thing?" Miriam gasped, her eyes locked on the creature pacing around in the middle of the room.

"The dumpling cart guy," Nelson explained simply, though his eyes were a bit wide.

Miriam stepped right up next to him. "Do we make a run for it?"

"We'll need a small miracle to make it across." Nelson gave his signature cocky smile once more, though it was a little strained.

"Go for it," Miriam said as Nelson extended his hand for Miriam to take.

"Here goes nothing." Nelson flicked a wrist, and the dumpling cart rolled into the creature, creating a temporary but clear path to the door.

"Now!" Miriam yelled as she pulled Nelson with her and sprinted through the mess towards the door, keeping one eye on the creature. The creature saw them just as they reached the exit, and it roared and leaped over the dumpling cart.

Quickly, they both reached out and pushed the door open at the same time, light and fresh air hitting them as they stumbled onto the busy Chinatown sidewalk. There were still people milling about, but the sun was low in the sky and the other dim sum places had already closed for the day.

Miriam waved her hand, casting one more finding spell. This time, her backup bag she'd packed for the day flew gracefully out of the restaurant and onto her arm. It wasn't exactly what she'd wanted, but she was already missing one bag from this adventure, and she was not exactly excited about losing another.

"Come on," Nelson said, already looking down the street. Miriam agreed. It made sense to get as far away from the restaurant as possible.

Chapter Five

M IRIAM FOLLOWED NELSON FOR a couple of blocks until they finally ducked into a chain coffee shop.

"So, where's our stuff?" Nelson asked, dragging Miriam with him to take a seat at a table in a corner. One of the baristas glared at them for not immediately ordering, even though the shop was empty.

"Um . . ." Miriam trailed off, not really sure what to say.

Nelson sighed. "Do we have to go back to Tao Tie and go up against that creature or the dumpling guy or whatever?"

"No. Our stuff isn't there," Miriam said. She was calm. She had learned a long time ago how to deliver absolutely devastating news with little expression and no pity. That was the sort of thing she had to do all the time.

"Wait, what do you mean?" Nelson asked. "You said the scrying would work."

"It usually does," Miriam replied.

"*Usually*? That doesn't give me much confidence." Nelson's voice rose slightly in frustration, and the barista looked over in their direction.

Miriam smiled tightly at them, then turned back to Nelson and lowered her voice. "Usually, my broom goes to a great source of power, so I scry for places with a high concentration of magic. One time, it was Salem on a full moon during Halloween. Another time, it showed up at the birth of a seventh child of a seventh child in Westchester, but the Warlocks of Westchester were nice about it." Miriam grimaced at the memory. She'd ended up at a poor witch's home birth. When she'd knocked on the door, she'd been greeted by a harried grandmother attempting to wrangle her young grandchildren while her daughter gave birth in another room. She'd handed Miriam her broom with an annoyed shake of her head and sent her on her way.

"So, something big and magical has happened, and that's where our stuff is, but we can only guess which place of highly concentrated magic our things went to," Nelson recounted.

"Unfortunately, yes," Miriam confirmed with a sigh.

"So what now?"

"I need to go to the office," Miriam decided. "I was supposed to get a ton of work done for the . . ." She trailed off. *Shit*, she mentally chastised herself. With everything going on, she'd almost forgotten that her firm was working on a project that was going to destroy Housing Magic's new development. To make things worse, papers revealing all of that were also lost, having disappeared along with their things.

"For what?" Nelson asked.

"For a deal I'm leading," Miriam said dismissively. Technically, she wasn't leading it yet, but losing the files, including that slide deck with all the potentially incriminating information in it, meant she was the best person to take the deal. If things went to shit, then she'd be the one to take the heat. It was the best-case scenario given all the employees whose livelihoods were attached to the firm's success. Not to mention her own ethical conundrum.

Nelson let out a frustrated sigh. "Our powerful magical items are missing, and you need to go to the office?"

"With your medallion, they could be anywhere in the entire world," Miriam argued. "We may never find them. What I need to do is to be able to pay my rent, which means putting in time at the office."

"Well, not the entire world." Nelson gave a sheepish grin. "My medallion can only go anywhere in the New York metro region. I once made it to New Haven, but that was a stretch. Anyway, are you actually telling me you want to spend your life on the subway?" He raised his eyebrows skeptically.

"I can walk to work," Miriam replied, trying not to sound too defensive.

"How about all your other errands?"

"Delivery. Who doesn't get their groceries delivered?"

"Client meetings." Nelson seemed to know how to really get under Miriam's skin.

She gritted her teeth. "I can take a cab." There was nothing she disliked more than sitting in a stalled-out cab during rush hour. The only time she did anything so stupid was when she was out with coworkers. But she wasn't about to let Nelson know just how much the prospect of having to take a cab bothered her.

"Anyway, you know as well as I do that it's not exactly a good idea to just let our things roam around without us," Nelson continued. "We need to find our stuff."

Miriam threw her head back in frustration. "I know, I know," she conceded. "But, look, I can do this on my own. Then I can just return your medallion, and we can go our separate ways."

"We barely made it out of Tao Tie, and it took both of our magics combined. You've only had to find your broom before, and from what you told me, this is different than usual," Nelson argued. "Miriam, we need to do this together."

He was right, but Miriam was exhausted, and she really needed to get some work done. "I feel like I'm going to barf," she blurted out, which was not untrue, but was also not exactly what she'd meant to say. She had eaten more dumplings than her body was willing to tolerate by a large margin.

"Oh . . ." Nelson recoiled slightly, looking at Miriam with a mixture of concern and disgust plastered across his face, and he seemed unable to find the right words. "I . . ."

"Let's just take a break for today, okay?" Miriam offered.

Nelson nodded. "Okay. I'll—"

"I'll call you," Miriam cut in, standing up from her chair. She was done arguing with Nelson, and she was done with his attempts to save her, and she really just wanted to lie in bed and think about absolutely nothing.

"Yeah, okay," he agreed, although maybe he was only agreeing because he found it more acceptable than potentially seeing Miriam vomit all over a chain coffee shop. Plus, he was also probably just as exhausted as she was. His skin creased just at the corners of his eyes, and he looked like he'd aged overnight. At minimum, he definitely had aged from when she'd last really known him. He was no longer the boy from high school. Like her, he was a grown adult with an adult life and adult problems.

"I'll call you," Miriam repeated, definitively this time, putting herself firmly in control of the situation. She held out her phone, and he took it and typed in his number.

"We'll find our things. It'll work out." Nelson gave a hearty, wide smile, his weariness from before gone. It had morphed into some sort of personalized pep talk, as if Nelson were attempting to hide that there had ever been any concern at all.

Miriam gave a pinched smile in agreement and then turned her attention to the exit. A few seconds later, she stepped out onto the sidewalk, golden light from the setting sun casting long shadows around her. They'd been in the dim sum restaurant all day, and they'd made zero progress at finding their things. She refused to give up, though, and as she started on the walk back to her apartment, now blissfully Nelson-free for the first time in almost twenty-four hours, she found herself hoping this had just been a false start. It had to be. Things would start to look up in the morning.

There was no other option.

***

On Sunday morning, Miriam finally made her way into the office. She'd spent most of Saturday night flopped across her bed, taking small sips of Pepto-Bismol to alleviate the pain in her stomach. Her scrying items had stayed on her kitchen counter, untouched, and the New York tea towel was still stained from when Larry had spilled coffee all over it.

She didn't text Nelson, and although he'd given her his number, she hadn't extended the same courtesy. This all meant she was in control of the situation.

Miriam started her Sunday in her office, preparing for the week ahead. She had already decided to tell Charlie first thing Monday that she would take the deal, which would mean pulling the associates in and getting them briefed and working. It was a big undertaking, and there was a bunch of modeling they would need to do to calculate construction costs, timing, and so on. So she got working on that, almost immediately engrossed in spreadsheets and models, just as she liked to be.

It was sometime later when a light tap on her office door startled her out of her deep concentration. She looked up to see Hannah standing in the doorway, a paper coffee cup in each hand.

"Hey, what are you doing here?" Miriam asked as Hannah entered her office and then placed one of the cups on Miriam's desk and nudged it towards her.

"I had a feeling you would need this," Hannah said, taking a seat opposite Miriam and tapping her temple.

Miriam gave a little chuckle. Hannah was mostly clairvoyant, at least to an extent, so it wasn't completely surprising. However, Hannah didn't often work weekends, and for her to just show up, even if she'd suspected Miriam needed a chat, was maybe a little farfetched.

"You came all the way over to the office to bring me a coffee?" she asked suspiciously.

"I came over to finish audit requests, and when I was getting coffee on my way, I had a feeling that you would not only be here but that you'd also be in desperate need of a coffee," Hannah clarified. "Which makes me wonder what happened at that fundraiser. You've been MIA all weekend from the group chat." Hannah was also extremely detail-oriented. Miriam wasn't sure if that was her clairvoyance, her accountant mindset, just who Hannah was, or a combination of all three.

"I . . ." Miriam paused, trying to decide what she wanted to tell Hannah. With a grimace, she settled on starting with the dumbest, most believable part of the story. "I hooked up with someone at the fundraiser."

Hannah raised her eyebrows in surprise and leaned in closer, her expression filled with intrigue.

"An old . . . acquaintance . . . from high school." Miriam was still not ready to call Nelson her friend, and she was still angry at him over the whole *having to work together to find their stuff* thing, amongst other complaints.

"And what? You've been cuddled up together all weekend?" Hannah proposed, but there was something insincere about her tone, hinting to Miriam that Hannah suspected there was something else going on.

She ignored it and flashed Hannah a fake smile. "Hey, I decided I'm going to accept the lead on the Pentacle deal," she declared, attempting to redirect the conversation in a completely different direction.

"I'm glad to hear," Hannah said dryly. She took a pointed sip of her coffee and gave Miriam an unrelenting glare.

"The guy was nothing. It's over," Miriam said with finality. She had to get her broom back without telling her coven, and that included Hannah.

Magic left to its own devices was never a good idea. True, a non-magical person who found their magical items wouldn't be able to do anything with them. The magic, after all, came from the practitioner. The object just acted as a cipher. Even so, there were plenty of wild, uncontained magics that could glom onto these objects and make a magical mess of things. If her coven found out, then it would be an entire thing. Their objects had the potential to create a magical maelstrom through the city, especially considering that her broomstick was imbued with her own chaos magic.

"Okay, okay," Hannah conceded, but Miriam could tell she was not entirely interested in dropping the point. "Are you still coming to the coven meeting tonight?"

"I'm going to try to make it," Miriam replied, hunkering back behind her computer. "But I need to get through this mountain of work first."

"You've missed a few lately," Hannah reminded her, a gentle suggestion that she actually show up. Covens were important to witches. It was, after all, how they worked big magic, but Miriam had been struggling to find the motivation to engage with hers for quite some time.

"I'll be there. Promise." She gave Hannah a firm nod, which she hoped was convincing enough. And she would make it, at minimum. After all, it would be more suspicious if she was not there. The last thing she needed was for Hannah or anyone else in her coven to get suspicious about her missing broomstick.

Chapter Six

Miriam arrived at the cozy SoHo loft later than she anticipated. She was used to traveling to the meeting via broom, but today she had the option of an inconvenient crosstown subway or her own two feet. She elected to walk the entire seventeen blocks.

She probably wouldn't have bothered if Hannah and Maddy were not hosting this week's meeting, but Hannah had already goaded her into attending. Hannah had been her first friend in New York and how she'd ended up in this coven in the first place. It made saying no to her incredibly hard.

When she arrived, the other members of her coven were already spread out around the boho chic-styled loft. Derek, one of the founding members, and his husband, Craig, were picking at pieces of cheese from the same plate. Isabelle was helping Hannah in the kitchen, while her partner, Henry, was talking to Maddy in the living room.

Heather was busy typing away on her phone, no doubt preparing for a court case, while Franklin chased their two-year-old daughter Chloe around the loft.

"Babe, you made it," Isabelle called out with a dramatic flourish as Miriam entered the kitchen. "I thought you were going to be a no-show again."

Miriam smiled and shrugged. "I've had a few big deals at work," she explained. "So it's been busy." She knew she didn't really need to go into any detail.

Everyone in her coven knew all too well what that was like. Isabelle was a stock trader on Wall Street. She was literally one of the people running around the floor, yelling orders, and she'd worked hard to climb up the ranks in a mostly male-dominated field. The others in the coven had similar stories and careers, so they, too, would no doubt understand her half-explanation.

"Well, we're glad to see you." Isabelle pulled her in and gave her a peck on the temple. "Come here. We have so much to catch up on." Isabelle took her hand and led her into the fray.

Miriam followed willingly, allowing herself to bask in the familiarity of everything for just a moment. Covens had a very practical application, which was to work big magics together, and it was easier to work big magics with people you were comfortable with, your community. Another benefit for Miriam was that it gave her a community outside of the cutthroat investment bankers at work. But in addition to these more practical justifications, the other members of the coven had become her best friends, people she could always lean on, which was important when living in such a large, isolating city.

She took a seat with Isabelle on the edge of the sofa, but in no time, Henry and Maddy joined them, and Hannah came in from the kitchen. Then all the couples coupled up, leaving Miriam alone on her little edge of the sofa. And that warm, bright feeling she'd had of being back with her coven slowly faded.

"Alright, alright, coven business," Heather announced as she picked up Chloe and bounced her on her hip. "First, any magical news to share?"

"There was a Taotie loose in Chinatown yesterday evening," Craig announced. "It ate through half a dumpling shop before it could be contained."

Miriam pursed her lips. *That* was what she and Nelson had been battling at the restaurant.

"I'm sorry, but what's a Taotie?" Miriam asked, because except for the encounter yesterday, she actually didn't know much else about the creature.

Derek picked up where his husband had left off. "A Taotie is a Chinese immortal magic that thrives on gluttony and loves to eat its way across a city. This one was bound to a dim sum place," Derek explained.

That was important information, but it didn't answer why the creature had kept feeding her and Nelson and why they'd gotten stuck all day thanks to some strong enchantment.

Maddy raised her hand. "How'd this one get lost?"

Craig took the rest of the explanation. "Seems like there was some sort of magical interference—erratic, but masterful—hard to trace."

Miriam was careful to school her face. She had never heard her magic described like that before, but she liked it. *Erratic but masterful.* That had a nice ring to it. She'd spent so much time controlling her magic that it often felt weak and timid. Letting it out like that had felt good.

"But it's contained now?" Heather asked, clutching Chloe a little closer.

"The spell that binds it to the restaurant was recast," Craig assured. "It's not a big deal, really. New York is home to all sorts of creatures from all over the world. This one is safe and sound, right where it belongs, and no one should have an issue with it as long as magics leave it alone. My cousin's coven in Chinatown checks in on the spell from time to time."

Miriam's stomach twisted painfully, and she clenched her jaw. *Erratic but masterful*? No. *Erratic and harmful* was more like it. They were not meant to have ever wandered into the restaurant. The other table and the teenage host were likely just illusions, part of the spell to keep the creature contained and happy, and when Nelson and Miriam had walked in, they'd gotten caught up in the same enchantment. The Taotie had continued to serve them food, just like it did every day to the single table of guests. They had meddled with something they shouldn't have. In fact, no one should have been in that restaurant except the Taotie, certainly not Miriam and Nelson, who had landed there in search of her broomstick.

She'd been so sure she'd broken all of her dumb, chaotic habits by schooling and training and working on every single thing about herself. But then she'd walked right into an enchanted dim sum restaurant, and everything had gone to hell.

Now she was even more motivated to not tell her coven about her missing broom. Not to mention the monster she had inadvertently released in New York and had not bothered to clean up after.

"No other magical business?" Hannah asked the group, pulling Miriam from her thoughts as the chatter about the Taotie died down. "How about big magics?"

This was when Miriam was supposed to speak up and ask for help to find her broom. Big magics were things that needed working but could not be done alone. Sometimes it was a ridiculously practical task, like attempting to hoist a piano up a fourth-floor walk-up. Isabelle and Henry had needed help with that some months ago, and it had been much cheaper than hiring a crane. But sometimes it was more nuanced tasks. When Chloe was born, the coven had sealed a broom for her, as was custom, so that when she was old enough, she would have a magical object already bound to her magic. Brooms were typical.

Frowning, Miriam wondered how Nelson had gotten his medallion, which likely had *not* been bound at his birth.

No one spoke up in response to Hannah's question, and so, she moved on.

"Any non-magical announcements?" Hannah asked.

Craig beamed as Derek took his hand. "We got matched with a child. We're officially adopting!"

"That's amazing!" Maddy squealed, moving in to hug the happy couple.

"Actually, we have news as well," Isabelle said, patting her stomach. "I'm due in September."

"We're going to raise our kids together," Heather said, even as Hannah and Maddy shared their own secretive but not-so-subtle look.

Miriam allowed herself to fade into the background, which wasn't too difficult since she was already sitting alone at the very edge of the couch. When the coven had first formed, everyone had been in their early twenties, all fresh in their big careers. Miriam had fit in then. They were all single. Hannah and Maddy were in the accidentally-always-sitting-next-to-each-other phase, and Derek hadn't yet met Craig, who had actually still been in another coven. Cathrine had also been with them, but then she'd married her partner and left to join their coven.

Now, Miriam was the only one not in a committed relationship and apparently the only one who was not a parent or imminently about to have a child. She wasn't sure if she even wanted kids or a partner, but regardless, it sure felt like her coven was moving on without her.

Who would she be, in this coven, without a partner? She didn't really want to find out. It was a depressing question because she loved her coven. They were more than friends. In so many ways, they had become her family.

But finding someone wasn't exactly at the top of her to-do list, and it was unlikely that some perfect man was just going to fall into her lap. Not that she really wanted that, anyway. Her single life was just fine, and dating sucked. She would much prefer to live a fulfilled life than spend every free moment meeting men at bars, or worse, on dating apps. Nothing about that was fun.

As the chatter went on around her, Miriam tried to keep her spirits up. But after a few more minutes, she knew she had to get out of there. It was easy to sneak out quietly; she just briefly caught Hannah's eye with a small wave and then slipped out into the chilly early spring evening.

It was golden hour again, the city sparkling with the amber hue of the sun fighting for time in the sky. A reminder that summer was never that far away. Miriam made her way back to her apartment on foot. When she got there, Bruce was waiting, holding the door open as he always was.

"Good evening, Ms. Blum," he greeted with an easy smile.

"It is, isn't it?" Miriam smiled back. The sun had gone below the buildings now, making way for dusk. She got on the elevator that would take her to her apartment and pushed the button for her floor. A moment later, she unlocked her door, and Larry was there to greet her as she entered her apartment. *This is nice*, she thought, and she pushed any lingering feelings of loneliness away and let herself be grateful for her life, just for a moment.

She pulled off the dark-wash jeans and spring boots she'd worn to the office and changed into a pair of stretchy yoga pants and a comfortable, worn Harvard sweatshirt. Her scrying stuff was still on her island, but she needed a few minutes before she went back to it.

So instead, she pulled a pint of her favorite ice cream from the freezer and settled into her sofa, turning on some trashy reality show about a man who had to simultaneously date six women and then pick one at the end.

Larry hopped up onto her lap, making it hard to navigate the spoon into her mouth, but she managed. This life she had built for herself was nice and calm and as unchaotic as she could possibly make it.

She couldn't imagine having a baby to care for every three seconds or a partner who could hardly manage the microwave alone. She liked that she was only responsible for a single person, and Larry. Sure, she worked a lot, but she also liked her work, or at least she liked it enough as far as jobs went. And she was good at her job. She relished in the fact that it gave her the ability to take care of herself. Actually, she liked that the best. She liked that she didn't need anyone and, more importantly, that no one needed her. As the reality show playing on her TV cut to the different women, Miriam wondered why they even put themselves through so much stress. They could be happy, on the sofa, with a large black cat, watching trashy reality TV.

Once she'd eaten enough ice cream and Larry had moved elsewhere in the apartment, Miriam made herself get up and head over to the counter, where her scrying things were. She was sufficiently relaxed and calm, and with a little luck, maybe her magic would behave itself so she could finally find their items.

Concentrating, she hunched over the counter and waved a hand above the snow globe, waiting for it to glow on a singular point on her tea towel. That was what was *supposed* to happen. But instead, the light from the globe refracted into a million rainbow pieces, as if it were a prism. Rather than the light hitting one spot, small distinct pinpricks covered all of Manhattan. There were hundreds, if not thousands, of spots.

Miriam was unsure how to even identify them, let alone figure out what they meant. This had never happened before, but she couldn't say she was too surprised. Her magic was predictably unpredictable. There was a chance that the coffee all over her tea towel was the reason her magic was not working properly. She looked at the ratty paper map she kept for reference, but it was too worn and too unloved to be useful in the slightest. There was no way she could use that map for anything magical.

She'd need to change tactics all together.

She needed to find a solution, because really, she just wanted to be able to call Nelson and let him know she'd found their stuff and then it would all be settled. Easy as that. She wouldn't have to look at his smug face, or validate how right he felt this whole time about it being her fault their stuff had gone missing.

However, her own method of looking for their things had now failed *twice*. She still believed she could do this on her own, and she would. But she'd have to think. To regroup. To recharge. And right now, what she really needed was to get to bed, because tomorrow was a big day. Tomorrow, she was going to tell Charlie she'd take lead on the Pentacle deal, and then she'd be well on her way to making partner.

Chapter Seven

"WE TALK A LOT about confidentiality," Miriam started as she addressed the associates and analysts sitting at the conference table in front of her. They all had their laptops out and were flipping through a version of the slide deck that had gone missing with her broomstick and Nelson's medallion. "But this deal is even more sensitive than most. I don't want to get wind you are talking about this on elevators or in coffee shops or even to other people at the firm. Not this deal. Computers need to be locked every time you get up from your seat," Miriam lectured sternly. This would be a giant shit storm if the details got out before the deal had closed.

The associates nodded along as Miriam guided them through the deck, pointing out specific details and assigning tasks and projects. There was a flurry of excitement among her colleagues, which was good. The kick-off period was almost always like this; the long nights would be met with enthusiasm, and it would be a while before the staff started burning out. Miriam's excitement was further heightened by having formally accepted the lead position on the deal that morning.

As she watched the associates begin to talk amongst themselves about specific details and things, a soft knock came on the conference room door, distracting her. Miriam turned to the door and stuck her head out, expecting maybe to see Hannah looking for Charlie for something accounting related. She was pretty sure Hannah was the only person in the entire office brave enough to interrupt a meeting that Miriam was leading.

Instead, standing right in front of the room full of investment bankers discussing how they were going to undercut Housing Magic for a luxury condo development, was Nelson, the executive director of Housing Magic.

Miriam's eyes went wide. She peeked back at the conference room and then stepped out into the hallway, shutting the door behind her.

Without saying anything, Miriam grabbed Nelson by the wrist and dragged him to her office. "Hey, what was that for?" Nelson grumbled as Miriam shut her office door behind him.

"What are you doing here?" she hissed. She was trembling with some combination of anger and anxiety. The fact that Nelson was here could blow up her entire career and mean the end of Alchemy.

"You never called me," Nelson said, lowering his voice. He was apparently aware, just as she was, that the office walls were thin, and magic was one of those things that required discretion.

"I was getting to it," Miriam replied, and she leaned in closer and whisper-yelled, "But what are you doing here, in the middle of the workday?"

"It's after six," Nelson replied, as if that obviously meant work should be done, "and you weren't home when I stopped by, so I looked up your firm's name and came here."

"And you just walked into my meeting," Miriam muttered, not even trying to hide her annoyance.

"No one was at the front desk." Nelson shrugged. "Anyway, what are we going to do to find my medallion?"

"Right now, you're leaving, and I am going back to my meeting," Miriam stated.

"That meeting?" Nelson said, pointing towards the window in her office, which gave a clear view of the bullpen and everyone from her meeting—that he'd interrupted—streaming out of the conference room door to get back to their desks.

Miriam threw her head back with a groan. "This is an enormous deal. I really, really need for you not to mess this up, which means not being here right now."

"Help me find my medallion and I'll leave you alone." Nelson stood firm in the middle of Miriam's office, his arms crossed over his chest.

"There's nothing we can do right here," Miriam argued. "They'll throw us both out if we start staring at a snow globe and waiting for it to glow."

"Come on, Miriam, I spent all of Sunday trying to figure out how to find my medallion, but I came up short, and given that you never called, I'm guessing you haven't had much luck either." Nelson pushed a hand back through his dark hair.

Miriam let out a deep breath. Through the window to her office, she could see that Charlie was pacing back and forth, obviously waiting for her. She needed to finish this and get Nelson out of her office and as far away from Alchemy as quickly as possible.

She stepped up a little closer to him. "Okay . . . okay . . . So, how about you come by my apartment at eight and, uh, bring a map of New York City. On paper. It needs to be something we can spread out and see the entire city."

"For better scrying?" Nelson seemed to understand. "Okay, anything else?" he asked.

Miriam nodded. "A chicken Caesar salad from sweetgreen."

"Seriously? What does that have to do with finding our stuff?"

"I'm hungry, and I am not going to start this whole thing again before I eat dinner." Miriam shrugged. "Now, please, please get out of my office," she implored as Charlie stopped and glared at her through the window.

"Fine. I'll see you tonight," Nelson said, and he tipped his head at her and then left, heading in the direction of the elevators.

She had just enough time to release an exasperated sigh before Charlie pushed the door open and entered her office.

"Miriam," he said, his voice low with just a touch of anger. He looked menacing with his bespoke suit, slicked back hair, and impeccably shined shoes. All the bankers dressed this way, including Miriam with her severe black skirts and pointy stilettos. "What was that?"

"He's just a . . . friend." Miriam hesitated. *Shit*, she thought, realizing how the whole thing must have looked. She'd just had some weird guy show up during a meeting. That was not normal.

Charlie nodded and then gave her an examining look. "I'm trusting you to handle this deal, but if your . . . acquaintances are just going to show up willy-nilly, then I may need to reconsider. What if that had been a client meeting?"

Miriam shut her eyes and let out a breath. "I promise, that wasn't something he'd normally do. I'm not sure why he thought it was okay." She wasn't actually sure if it was something Nelson would normally do, given that she didn't really know him. But it seemed like the thing to say.

Charlie still wasn't pleased, though. "I don't feel like putting you in charge is a risk. You've been dedicated to this firm for a long time, and you do a good job. I know you can get this deal done. But whatever just happened right now," he said, frowning, "was a disappointment."

Miriam gave a pinched smile. "Won't happen again, I promise."

"These kids," he started again, motioning with his hand to where the analysts and associates were now heads down at their computers in the bullpen, "need you to set a good example. Understood?"

Miriam nodded. "Understood."

"Alright, let's get to work," Charlie finished with an upbeat wave of his hand, and he pushed Miriam's office door open and headed back towards his office.

Miriam moved over to her desk and collapsed into her chair. Then she set her elbows on her desk and lowered her head into her hands, pushing her fingers into her curls. Everything suddenly felt heavy. Leading the project was a major step in her career, but her success would come at a seriously high cost to a wonderful nonprofit with a seriously altruistic mission. And further complicating things was the fact that she'd just slept with the executive director and was on some insane quest to find their lost magical items.

She'd worked so hard for this job over the years, starting all the way back in high school, when she'd pushed to get accepted to Harvard. She'd stuck around while other analysts and associates working at her level had burned out and taken cushy tech jobs. She'd gone back to Harvard for business school. Hell, she'd even worked late hours on a truly vile deal with a meat-packer where she'd been required to visit a slaughterhouse as part of her due diligence to see the entire process, from tail to snout. And she hadn't eaten meat for nearly six months after that. The first time she'd been able to tolerate it had been when her mom had made brisket for Passover.

Now, the entire foundation she'd built her career on, what had felt sturdy and strong, was balancing on her own morality. She'd never really considered that she could be the villain in any story. Banking had always felt like a neutral career, the intermediary between owners. She was a facilitator, a broker. She'd never felt as if she needed to question whether a deal should even be made.

And it wasn't a fun place to be. It was uncomfortable to have to ask these difficult questions. Right now, however, she just needed to forge ahead and stay the course.

Miriam was about to turn her attention to her computer to get back to work when there was a light tap on her door.

"What?" she snapped, looking up. Hannah stood in the doorway. She didn't flinch at Miriam's outburst and instead made her way into Miriam's office without waiting for a formal invitation. She looked comfortable in her cozy knit top and cute dress, and for a brief moment, Miriam was jealous that Hannah's job wasn't client facing and so she was allowed a more lax dress code than the bankers who dealt with clients.

Hannah just shut the door and took a seat in front of Miriam's desk.

"You okay?" she asked, leaning her elbows on the white laminate surface of Miriam's desk and waiting.

"Yeah, I'm fine," Miriam said dismissively. She tapped on her keyboard, trying to refocus.

"Really?" Hannah asked.

Miriam rolled her head on her neck, disappointed when she did not hear the satisfying crack of her own bones as she stretched.

"No," she admitted, and she turned to face Hannah, frowning. "Do you ever wonder if we're doing the right thing here?" she asked. When Hannah didn't seem to catch on, Miriam continued. "I mean, do you think the sort of deals we do actually help the world?"

"No," Hannah replied bluntly.

Miriam was almost taken aback by how quick and certain her answer was.

Hannah backed up and started over. "I know for a fact they don't," Hannah explained. "But my job is to make sure our management and their bosses have the information they need to run this bank. I don't make the decisions, I don't do anything that could directly harm people. I report accurate numbers, even when they're bad. I do my job, I pay my rent. I would love to take some cushy nonprofit job, but those are hard to find. New York is expensive, and I need to buy groceries."

Miriam nodded, but she was unsatisfied with Hannah's answer, which made sense. They were in much different positions. Hannah had layers between the decisions the bank made and her job, whereas Miriam was barreling right towards being a key decision maker. No longer would she be able to just take her assignments and collect a paycheck. She would be part of the team, determining which clients the bank would take. Hannah was not wrong. It was hard to be ethical in a world where good jobs often came at the cost of working for questionable conglomerates. In a lot of ways, it meant doing what Hannah did, making sure she operated in the most ethical way she could within the context of her position.

But the context of Miriam's position was about to transform. No longer would she be a working stiff, just trying to pay rent. She would be the one who determined the fate of her coworkers.

And she would have to live with the consequences of every deal she worked on.

Chapter Eight

I T WAS CLOSER TO 8:30 p.m. by the time Miriam arrived back at her building. Bruce held the door open for her and nodded to where Nelson was sitting in the lobby, laden with shopping bags.

"Evening, Miriam. Does he belong to you?" Bruce asked.

Miriam let out yet another long sigh. She was losing track of how often she had done that in the last few hours. She really needed a more interesting expression before all she ever did was sigh. "Yeah. Thanks, Bruce."

Bruce gave a confirmatory smile as soon as Miriam had identified Nelson as her guest, and Miriam continued on her way in, motioning to Nelson to come with her as she walked by. He followed her into the elevator and up to her apartment. Larry met them at the door, just like he had last time, his eyes sleepy from his predinner nap, and he was quiet and curious about the unexpected guest.

"You seem to have gotten a lot done," Miriam said as Nelson placed the shopping bags on the kitchen island.

Nelson shrugged. "You can get a lot of places with just a MetroCard, it turns out."

He pulled out two familiar sweetgreen containers and an elongated cardboard tube. Next, he opened another bag, and out came three pints of fancy, expensive ice cream—the sort Miriam would choose for herself versus the more workaday ice cream Nelson got from the little shop below his apartment. Miriam was pleased when she noticed his purchase included her go-to, mint chip. Nelson must have remembered from the other night.

"This is my favorite," Miriam said as she examined the pint.

Nelson gave a smile but didn't comment on the ice cream. "So, what's the plan?" he asked, passing a salad to her.

Miriam opened the paper bowl as Nelson riffled through the drawers in Miriam's kitchen to find forks. Then she spread out the large map of New York City on the counter. All five boroughs and a bit of New Jersey and Long Island were on display.

"This'll work," Miriam said. "But we need to enchant it so I can scry with it."

Nelson's eyebrows arched. "I'm sorry, what?" Nelson asked, the plastic lid from his sweetgreen order in his hand.

"It needs to be enchanted to work. You know about making magical items, right?" Miriam cocked her head to one side as she asked.

"Do I know about working big magics, sure, but I didn't actually plan to perform one, on a Monday night, without my coven?" Nelson rebutted her suggestion.

"Okay, call your coven," Miriam proposed. She might not want to share with her coven, but perhaps Nelson had a better relationship with his own.

Nelson's eyes went wide at the idea. "That's . . . Look, maybe we can wait until this weekend, when your coven is free," Nelson backtracked.

"I thought we needed to find our stuff as soon as possible," Miriam countered. "My coven doesn't meet again until next Sunday."

"It's fine." Nelson seemed to clam up, shaking his head and looking back down at the map.

The entire thing made Miriam a little wary. She suspected there must be a reason he'd want to avoid asking his own coven. But she didn't pry. They weren't friends, and as soon as they located their things, they would be done with each other. It was none of her business, anyway.

"It's not a big magic, it's more like a medium magic, and we should be fine doing it together," Miriam explained casually.

"Miriam," Nelson whined, "we've already made a mess out of this. I heard that the creature we let out had to be wrangled by the Sorcerers of SoHo."

Miriam already knew this, of course, although she hadn't known that the local coven in Chinatown had been involved.

"Okay, then let's just go to your coven and tell them your medallion is missing," Miriam replied, and she turned and headed back into her bedroom briefly. A moment later, she came out with a briefcase that she placed on the counter.

"Miriam," Nelson protested for a second time.

"What?!" Miriam snapped. She certainly understood Nelson's reluctance to contact his coven, but he was also starting to get on her nerves.

"We can't do this," Nelson argued. "We need more people to work a big magic."

"It's not a big magic," Miriam repeated. "Really, it's just an easy binding spell. It just takes a bit of energy." She gave him a reassuring nod, even though she knew it was a reckless thing to do. But it would be fine. "We're not kids anymore," she said. "We know how to work this sort of magic, and we know how to do it safely."

"Safely would be with the assistance of an entire coven." Nelson sighed as though he knew his last attempt at arguing was a weak one. "But you're right. Binding a bit of magic to a map is not exactly a big ordeal. We should be able to handle it together."

"Perfect!" Miriam said. She pulled out an old jump rope and set it on the counter next to her still-untouched salad.

"This is what you use for bindings?" Nelson gritted his teeth at the idea as he picked up the jump rope.

Miriam took it back and placed it on the table. "I use what works," she explained. "Now, I think the best way to set this up is for you to set your hand on the map where you have power—where you live or where you cast a lot of magic."

"I know how to cast a binding spell," he insisted, placing his right hand on top of Williamsburg and his other on the far corner of Long Island, just before the map ran out and the suburbs of New York turned into small towns.

Miriam placed her right hand on Lower Manhattan and the other . . . She looked down at her left hand and paused. It belonged where Nelson's hand was sitting, on the place where she'd grown up. She still found so much power there, and her parents were still there. So much of what she knew about magic came from the same place he'd chosen.

"Oh . . . right," Nelson said as he realized why she was hesitating. He picked his hand up and reached out to take hers, interlacing their fingers. Then, he set their hands together on top of the map.

She could feel his magic, warm and bright against her hand. It was already flowing. She adjusted to the sensation, allowing just the smallest amount of intimacy. Nelson had been the last person she'd touched before this, and now, everything felt a little tingly and strange.

"We should get started." Nelson's voice was rough, as if he were as distracted as she was. As if he were having the same sorts of thoughts she was.

"Sure," Miriam agreed, but then she paused, feeling the need to be honest about the map. "I . . . I don't think this is actually going to show us where our things are," she confessed, and it felt good to tell him the truth. She liked that at least one thing was out in the open. "But with our combined magic going on the map, maybe we can find the sort of power that might attract our things. We just need to each bind enough force to fill up the map."

Nelson nodded, signaling to Miriam that he understood her vague instructions.

"On three," Miriam said, leaning over the map and bracing against the counter. There were no incantations to speak, just the desire to will something into existence. Plenty of witches used hand motions for small everyday magic, but for this, it was just concentration. "One . . . two . . . three . . ."

Miriam pushed her magic into the map. She could feel it flow out of her body, through her fingers, stream through the streets and subways, into the buildings, and across the parks. Her magic joined with Nelson's streaming uptown, down across the bay, into Staten Island, into Queens, and up through the Bronx. His magic was wonderful and wistful against her chaotic mess driving them forward.

She looked down at the map, but her vision blurred. Her eyes shut as she pushed even more of her magic, ignoring the pulse behind her eyes as she felt her magic spread through the entire New York metro area. She was in every borough, every bodega, every subway line, apartment, and office building. She was everywhere all at once, and yet they were still standing in her apartment in the Financial District. There was nowhere else for her magic to go.

"We did it." Miriam forced the words through an exhaustion she was only just starting to feel. She stood up straight and then swayed. Nelson placed a firm hand on the small of her back, and she fell into his shoulder, spent. She could hear his racing heart and his labored breathing, and she let herself linger there for a few seconds, her head resting just above his chest.

"Mmm," he groaned, and then, his words some weird combination of fatigued urgency, he added, "We never ate." He carefully reached across the island and grabbed the pints of ice cream and a couple of spoons. "Come here."

"I'm fine," Miriam murmured, but Nelson still gently pushed her over to the sofa on the other side of the kitchen.

They sort of collapsed onto the couch together, their legs giving up as soon as they were near a soft landing spot.

"Here," Nelson said, handing her the pint of mint chip.

Miriam took it, but the effort she needed to open the pint and then scoop out the ice cream all felt like too much. They had pushed a lot of magic into the map. It was a bigger magic than Miriam had expected, certainly more than her tea towel held.

She curled up in a corner of the sofa, and Nelson sprawled out on the other end. Larry jumped up and made himself a spot right between them.

"Come on, eat something," Nelson encouraged as he opened his own pint of ice cream and dug his spoon in to take a bite.

"I don't need you to take care of me," Miriam grumbled, but she copied Nelson and finally dipped her spoon into the ice cream.

Nelson pulled the spoon out of his mouth and then scooped up another spoonful of ice cream. "You obviously do."

Miriam sighed and let her eyes fall closed for a second. "I'm fine."

"Neither one of us is fine," Nelson countered.

"Which is why you don't need to take care of me." Miriam was tired of arguing. Actually, she was tired of talking all together. Her head was pounding, and it felt as if someone had drained every last iota of energy from her body. They had really dug deep.

"Fine," Nelson replied with finality. "Also, I think I'm going to have to sleep on your couch tonight. I don't think I have enough energy to even catch a cab."

"URGH," Miriam groaned. "Me too." Because she was unsure she even had the energy to get up and walk the few feet to her bedroom. "I'm too spent to try to scry tonight. It'll have to wait until the morning."

They each ate a few more spoonfuls in silence, and with each bite, Miriam could feel herself coming alive, the refined carbohydrates and fat reinvigorating and refilling her after she'd given all of her energy to the map. She would still need a full night's sleep, but she would make it to her own bed instead of spending the night squashed on the sofa with both Nelson and Larry.

"Miriam," Nelson said after a while.

"Hmm?" Miriam asked.

"I like taking care of you."

"Because it means you get to have the upper hand, be the golden boy, pity the chaos monster?" Miriam could feel rage pool in her stomach, weak as it was with her lack of energy. That had always been how Nelson was with her. He only saw her as something to be saved, no matter what.

"No," Nelson said simply, and when Miriam glanced over at him, she couldn't read his expression. It was schooled and impassive and maybe a bit pitiful. Miriam wasn't sure what he was trying to communicate. All she really knew was that she was exhausted and that it felt like every bone in her body was about to turn to Jell-O. She didn't have the energy or desire to argue with Nelson.

"Look, I'm going to go to bed," she said, and then she paused, looking at his rumpled, pathetic form on her sofa. "You're welcome to sleep on the couch. I'll get you a blanket." Mustering up as much energy as she could, she picked up the remains of the ice cream, stood, and made her way into the kitchen. Then she put the partially eaten ice cream in the freezer and shuffled off to the closet to get Nelson a blanket.

There was something she liked about this vulnerable version of Nelson, she thought as she dug lazily around in the closet and pulled out a thick, warm blanket. She turned back to face him and her breath caught. He looked . . . soft and approachable, and that vulnerability was so different from what she was used to. The finance guys she worked with spent their entire lives avoiding any show of weakness. But here, right on her sofa, was Nelson, honest and open as he'd always been. There was a part of Miriam that wanted to sit back down on the sofa and curl up next to him. She wanted to feel his arms holding her close, the touch of his lips on her temple, the warmth from his body pleasantly enveloping her. She wanted . . . She shook her head. She *needed* to get a hold of herself. She needed to leave Nelson alone for all the obvious reasons.

She stepped over to the couch, managing a tight smile. "Here you go," she said as she handed him the blanket.

Nelson took it from her with a weary smile of his own. "Thanks." He looked like he was going to say something else, like maybe his thoughts had strayed in the same direction hers had. But instead, he just nodded and patted Larry's head.

It was for the best, she knew. Even if he had been thinking the same thing as her, even if he wanted her to join him . . . maybe that was an avenue best left unexplored.

"Get some sleep," Miriam said, forcing another smile. She quickly picked up Larry from the sofa, turned, and made her way back to her bedroom.

***

Miriam woke up the next morning to a pounding headache and the smell of fresh coffee. "What the—?" she muttered, and as she rolled over and hauled herself out of bed, the night before came rushing back to her. She groaned as her stiff muscles protested the movement, but she pulled on her robe and walked out into her kitchen, running a hand through her unkempt hair.

"Morning." Nelson smiled from where he was shoving a sliced bagel into her toaster.

"What are you doing?" Miriam asked.

"Making breakfast," Nelson replied, even though that was already clear.

She frowned as she noticed there were two coffee mugs sitting on the counter, including one that appeared to be untouched and freshly prepared. Greedy and needing all the caffeine she could handle, she picked up the untouched mug and took a sip.

"I really don't need you to take care of me," she reiterated as she lowered the mug and set it back on the counter. She'd said something similar the night before, but he obviously hadn't cared.

Nelson just shook his head. "I woke up, and I was starving. I'm taking care of myself and making enough for you, too."

Miriam rolled her head around her shoulders, her neck loosening up from the tension she'd been holding in. "Thanks, I guess," she said, taking a seat at the island. She picked the coffee mug back up and had another sip, hoping the caffeine would soon flood her veins and help her feel more human.

Blinking away the last bit of sleep from her eyes, she pulled over the map they'd enchanted last night. Her hand hovered over the streets and byways. There was a slight buzzing in her fingertips from the fresh magic that was trapped in the map. The entire city felt alive on the little map, and she could almost imagine people bustling around like they were in a real-life city.

"Let me know when you're ready to try again," Nelson said as he placed a plate with a bagel and fruit in front of Miriam. She knew for sure she hadn't had either of those two things in her refrigerator the night before, and there was no way he would have gotten back into her building without the doorman calling to announce she had a guest. That meant that there had been a small miracle involved in getting breakfast into her apartment.

Miriam took a bite of her bagel and then another. She was starving, and she would need to eat before she did anything functional, including scrying or going to work, which she would need to do very soon.

After she'd eaten about half of the bagel and taken another sip of coffee, she set her snow globe on the map. "Okay, ready," she said, and she snapped her fingers. The lights went out, and her shades closed, but her head thrummed with the effort. She was still light on magic, although she was pretty sure there would be enough to scry with. She placed her hand atop the snow globe, and it released a series of pinpricks across the map, just like it had the last time she'd tried. This time, however, only about a dozen locations were lit up, and with the more detailed map, it was easier to tell exactly where they were.

"So, one of these locations?" Nelson asked, frowning down at the magical pinpricks. His disapproval at how little they had narrowed down their options was fairly clear.

"Likely," Miriam agreed. "There's a pen and paper in the drawer. Can you hand it to me?"

Nelson pulled on the handle to the drawer, but it didn't immediately budge. "What's wrong with this?"

"Pull harder, and fast, before this all disappears." Miriam waved her hand over the map. They didn't have much time before her magic would run out and they'd have to scry again.

Nelson pulled a bit harder, and the drawer suddenly popped open. A mess of pens, batteries, empty ibuprofen bottles, chip clips, and other assorted pieces of junk came flying out, all over the kitchen. Nelson stood there, stunned, and then shook himself and searched around in the clutter for a minute.

"Here," he said, offering Miriam a pen and notepad.

"Can you take notes?" Miriam asked, her hand still hovering over the snow globe.

Nelson nodded, opened the notepad, and started jotting down the locations. "Wait, this one," he said, pointing to somewhere in East Harlem. "This is one of Housing Magic's buildings."

"You think we should start there?" Miriam asked, moving her hand and deactivating the snow globe.

"It makes sense. What if our things went somewhere familiar?" Nelson reasoned. "My medallion knows that building. We could go now."

"I have work," Miriam reminded him.

"Okay, then we go tonight," Nelson suggested.

Miriam shook her head. "I'm not going all the way to Harlem tonight."

"I could go today." Nelson seemed insistent, but although Miriam understood, she knew it wouldn't be a smart move for him to go by himself.

"It took both of us to get out of Chinatown, no reason to think this will be any different. We'll go on Saturday," Miriam stated.

"Friday afternoon," Nelson countered back. "Maybe at three?"

"That's early."

"Okay, so knock off work a couple of hours early. It's not that weird. Please." Nelson looked pretty pathetic when he was pleading. "This way, we can see if our stuff is there, and if it's not, we have all weekend to keep looking."

"Fine . . ." Miriam sighed. "But you have to promise to leave this alone until we can go together."

"Deal," Nelson agreed.

"Great. I need to go to work. I guess you're welcome to hang out, but I have stuff to do."

He nodded. "I'll see you later, Miriam Blum." And the way he said it . . .

Miriam wasn't ready to admit how it made her feel . . . and besides, she needed to go to work. "I'm going to get dressed," she announced, mostly to hide her own awkwardness, and she nodded towards her room and then retreated in that direction, leaving Nelson alone in her kitchen to decide how he wanted to spend his time.

"I need to head to work, too, but I'll see you Friday," he said, fumbling through his own announcement as she shut the door to her bedroom.

By the time Miriam emerged dressed and ready for work about a half hour later, Nelson had gone. Her kitchen, though, had been cleaned up, and Larry had gotten an extra helping of wet food. Nelson seemed intent on taking care of her, and she knew exactly how that made her feel.

It was an uncomfortable realization.

Chapter Nine

A T EXACTLY 3:00 P.M. on Friday afternoon, Nelson was waiting outside in front of Miriam's office building. He'd agreed to stay outside for the time being, which Miriam was incredibly grateful for after the debacle with her boss on Monday.

"I'll call us a car," Miriam said, starting to pull her phone out of her bag.

"No need." Nelson grinned and held up two distinct black and yellow MetroCards. "It'll take forever in a cab at this time of day."

"Thanks," Miriam grumbled, taking one of the flimsy plastic cards.

"The quicker we get our things back, the less time you'll be stuck spending on the subway," Nelson goaded her.

"Come on." Miriam turned towards the entrance to the nearest subway station, refusing to give in and take the bait. She navigated through the subway easily. She may be a witch, but she was still a New Yorker all the same, and she knew the subway system.

Even though they were a bit on the early side for rush hour, the subway uptown and ultimately to Harlem was already crowded. There were no seats available on their train, so they stayed standing but grabbed onto the rails to steady themselves.

"Don't you have work?" Miriam asked as the train got moving. "Why were you able to knock off early?"

"I'm sort of the boss," Nelson reminded her, easily adjusting himself as the train stopped and started and screeched. "And my schedule is weird," he continued. "I do community events in the evenings and weekends, so taking an afternoon to run errands is pretty normal. A lot of my social workers follow the same policy. If they didn't, they would never have time for anything but work."

Miriam looked up at Nelson as he spoke, noticing how mature he looked in his casual jeans and sweater. He *was* an adult, of course, and there was no reason for her to think he was in some sort of suspended animation, stuck in his teenage years from high school. He was in his thirties, after all, just like she was.

But there was something else about him. Perhaps it was just the self-assured, unbothered way he stood on the subway. Or maybe it was the fact that Miriam was still having a hard time not thinking about his arms as they flexed against the movements of the train car. They were muscular and strong without being absurd. And she could imagine them wrapped around her, holding her as he—

"I'm, uh, surprised you chose social work," Miriam blurted out, needing to distract herself from more lustful thoughts. "I always thought . . . actually, I'm not sure what I always thought."

"That I would be a doctor?" Nelson suggested.

"Actually, yeah," Miriam replied, thinking about his near-perfect grades in high school and his top university spot at UMass. "What happened?"

Nelson shrugged. "I wanted to help people."

"Doctors help people," Miriam countered.

"They do, but there are always going to be doctors. Every single spot in medical schools and residency programs is taken. There are a lot of people who want to be doctors. Social workers, not as much," Nelson explained, "I thought about nursing, like my mom, but then I realized there's a big need for social workers, and it's a way to help quietly."

"Quietly?" Miriam huffed a laugh. "You know how to help people quietly?"

Nelson ruffled his nose, the wrinkles around his eyes pinching in confusion. "You think that's all I am, right? Some savior just looking to be the better person?"

"I mean . . ." Miriam trailed off.

"Did it ever occur to you that I enjoy helping people and that I like helping you, especially?" Nelson asked.

"Right, but you have to get something out of it," Miriam proposed as the subway screeched to a halt and a large number of people exited. They were only about halfway to their destination, but a couple of seats opened up, and so they sat next to each other on the long bench in the middle of the train.

"Is that how you think the world works?" Nelson asked. "Everyone is just motivated by their own need for an incentive?"

"Humans need some reason to do what they do," Miriam argued. They may both be magical, but they were still very much human all the same.

"And I like to help people." Nelson shrugged. "That's my reason."

Miriam narrowed her eyes, unsure she trusted that answer. Sure, she had a pesky ethical compass she was currently navigating, and sure, she liked the problem-solving aspect of her job, but at the end of the day, there was a clear monetary incentive. One that allowed her to afford her apartment, and hopefully take care of her parents, and to give Larry his best life.

"What?" Nelson asked.

"You like to save people," Miriam reasoned. "You like to be a hero."

"Isn't that the same?" he asked.

Miriam shook her head. "I don't think it is."

The train screeched on and then stopped again, the doors opening wide. A mother pushing a double stroller tried to jam it across the gap. Nelson didn't hesitate, and in a moment, he was across the train, helping the mom push the stroller into the car. Nelson was smiling the entire time, offering words of encouragement as he guided the behemoth of a baby carriage into the rush-hour train car and then to its designated section. He made sure the brakes were secured before he left the woman to rejoin Miriam.

He really was one of those guys.

When he sat back down next to Miriam, she bumped his shoulder with hers. "You get your hero work in?" she teased with a smile.

Nelson rolled his eyes, and the train continued along, under the streets of New York City, under Times Square, through Central Park, past Columbia University.

Finally, Nelson motioned towards the door. "This is our stop."

They made their way off the train and up the stairs, exiting the subway. The gleaming glass skyscrapers and grand stone buildings of Lower Manhattan had been replaced with the efficient red-and-sandy brick buildings of Harlem.

"Just a couple of blocks," Nelson explained, leading the way.

"What exactly do you think we'll find here?" Miriam asked. Given how insistent Nelson had been that they check out this location, she assumed he had some reason for believing there was something here.

"Our things," he said with a shrug.

Miriam grumbled in frustration. "The magic? What do you think the magic is? What are we up against?"

Nelson gave a knowing smile. "I have an idea," he said, but he didn't offer Miriam any additional details. "This way." He made a left down a more residential street, and Miriam followed.

The restaurants and shops turned into the sort of utilitarian buildings that had defined New York's immigrant communities for generations.

"You feel like sharing?" Miriam asked as she matched his pace, definitely glad it was Friday, the one day of the week she dared to wear a more sensible pair of flat loafers and a casual dress and tights. It was the most comfortable she allowed herself to dress during the work week and probably most of the reason she was able to keep up with his long stride now.

Nelson shook his head. "I have a resident who has magic. I think he might help."

Miriam nodded, but they arrived at a bland-looking red-brick building before she could ask more questions. It was five stories high, and besides a small plaque in the brick that read "Housing Magic," the building looked like all the rest on the street.

"This was one of our first buildings," Nelson explained as he riffled through the pockets of his jeans and pulled out a sizeable key ring. He quickly selected one of the keys and used it to open the front door of the building. "This way," he said, leading her to the stairs.

"You *do* know where we're going?" Miriam asked suspiciously as they started climbing.

"I may have called ahead." Nelson gave his signature wink and a smile.

Miriam wanted to be frustrated by it, by the way her heart swooned at the skin crinkling around his eyes, just inside the rims of his glasses. She wanted to push the feeling away, refuse it, deny it. But the truth was, as much as she didn't need to be taken care of, she relished Nelson's competency. His ability to prepare. It was pleasantly different. The finance guys she usually ended up with (both professionally and in an "extracurricular" capacity) expected her to take care of everything, even though she worked an equally demanding job. It was why Miriam's romantic life was so . . . dead. No relationship ever went on longer than a few months. For Nelson to know where they were going and to have taken the initiative to do the work ahead of time was refreshing.

They stopped on the second floor, and Nelson led them down a shabby hallway to apartment number eighteen. He gave a polite but firm knock.

A man who appeared to be in his fifties or sixties opened the door. "Nelson, I'm so glad you stopped by," the man greeted, a hint of a Puerto Rican lilt to his speech. He gave a warm smile and opened up the door wider.

"Thanks for letting us come over," Nelson replied. "Alex, this is my friend Miriam, and Miriam, this is Alex."

"Nice to meet you," Miriam said, and she followed Nelson past Alex and into the apartment.

The space felt lived-in, but also tidy and cared for. Chunky furniture occupied the living room, each piece adorned with a thick knitted blanket. The floors had been freshly cleaned, and the coffee table was free from clutter. The apartment had a feeling of permanency that Miriam couldn't help but notice.

"How's your knee doing?" Nelson asked as Alex settled into an armchair.

Alex tapped his kneecap. "I'm bionic now. I feel like I could run a marathon."

A small tattoo on Alex's wrist distracted Miriam for a second, and she stared at it, entranced. The tattoo was just black ink, a simple outline, but it was clear what it was—two small entwined hummingbirds. What had grabbed her attention, though, was how realistically illustrated they were, as if they were about to fly up his wrist. There was a motion to the ink work that Miriam had never seen before. Although not many of her acquaintances had visible tattoos.

Nelson gave a laugh. "I'm glad things are better with your knee. Are you back at work?"

Alex nodded. "I am . . . but they're threatening to close the store and turn it into a Whole Foods. I don't want to work for Whole Foods . . . Not sure they'll hire me, anyway."

"Why don't you think they'll hire you?" Miriam asked, confused why Alex had already counted himself out of a job. Nelson gave her a sideways glare, and she grimaced inwardly. It was probably an inappropriate question; this wasn't exactly a social visit. Alex was one of Nelson's residents and didn't deserve to be interrogated.

"It's okay," Alex said, waving off Nelson's protective look. "I'm a felon. I've done my time, but it's hard getting housing and jobs. The only reason I'm not out on the streets anymore is because of Housing Magic."

"Oh . . ." Miriam's lips curled as she attempted to reconcile what this man was saying. She looked around, unable to meet Alex's or Nelson's gaze. The kitchen was mostly obscured by a wall, but she could see just the edge of a counter. A series of prescription pill bottles was lined up at the end.

"Pot . . . and being Brown." He shrugged. "I did my time. Two years at Rikers. Now I have a safe place to come to each night. That wasn't always the case."

"We can help you find a job close by," Nelson said, as if he had no doubt the perfect job would be there. There was a sense of optimism to him that seemed inappropriate to offer, but Miriam realized that she didn't know all the facts about getting a job with a felony on one's record. Nelson likely did. "In the meantime, I hear Thomas is looking for a bridge partner."

"Thomas, that old kook." Alex chortled. "He's not interested in me. I hear he has a new young boyfriend."

"I'm not asking you to date him, I'm just suggesting you play a round of bridge," Nelson countered with a laugh. There was something easy about the interaction, something friendly and familiar between them, and Miriam noticed how Nelson wasn't patronizing in the least.

"Hmm," Alex grumbled. "And how about you? Are you finally ready to settle down?" Alex motioned to where Miriam was still standing in his living room. "You finally found a hechicera you can keep."

Miriam's eyes went wide. She knew enough Spanish to catch his meaning, but she hadn't expected he'd immediately identify her as a witch. Although it made sense that he might be the source of the magic they were looking for. There didn't seem to be anything about him that was more or less unusual than for any other witch.

Not for the first time, Miriam wondered why her map had brought them here.

"Actually, Miriam and I are on a bit of a hunt. We've lost a few of our things and thought there was a chance they're here," Nelson explained. "And we figured, if there was something magical here, you might have an idea what."

Alex nodded and then pressed his thumb into the hummingbirds on his wrist. The little birds twirled and twisted up and down his arms. He closed his eyes for a moment as the birds disappeared up the sleeve of his shirt, and then there was a slight glow through his T-shirt, the birds seeming to settle over his heart.

Suddenly, Alex's eyes flew open. "You fool! You lost that damn enchanted medallion. The magic on that thing is unbelievable."

"It wasn't my fault," Nelson murmured.

"Your magic getting lost is always your fault," Alex scolded, and then closed his eyes again. "A broom . . . a little basic . . . but serviceable," Alex commented as he discovered what Miriam had lost as well.

"So, you know where our things are?" Miriam asked, feeling hopeful for the first time that afternoon. Maybe Nelson had brought them right to where they needed to be.

"Ha, no. Your magic has jammed itself somewhere in this city, but it seems to want you two to figure out how to find it by yourselves." Alex gave a snide laugh.

"Why?" Nelson asked, all the amusement gone from his voice.

Alex shrugged. "Who knows? Sometimes magic has its own sense of humor."

Nelson let out a long, exacerbated sigh. "None of this makes sense. How can our things even travel without us? I thought they were supposed to be conduits, channeling our own magic, not independently magical items," Nelson argued, running a hand through his dark hair. It came back rumpled, and Miriam's chest warmed at the sight. There was something she really, really liked about seeing Nelson all bothered, she realized. It wasn't exactly that she needed for him to be knocked down a peg, that wasn't it at all. She just liked these moments of vulnerability. He finally seemed like a real person rather than the knight-in-shining-armor front he often seemed to have.

Miriam responded to Nelson's question rather than waiting for Alex; she'd worked out the specifics long ago, and she thought she might be able to help. "Each day, we pump magic into our items. There is, of course, the seed magic—the original magic pushed into an item to turn it into a magical item, but then there is our continued use. Each time we use our objects, they become more like us. It's why my broom has a habit of chaotic adventures. I leave a little magic behind each time. Magic is . . . well, it's magic. It works without reason or logic. It takes on some of our traits, but it also doesn't follow rules."

"*Your* magic doesn't follow rules," Nelson fired back. "Mine, on the other hand, is very well-behaved."

"Excuse me!" Miriam exclaimed.

"Hey." Alex put up a hand. "Miriam's right. Magic is unpredictable. It is literally not a science. We can theorize about why and how your things ran away, but there won't ever be a definitive answer."

"So what now?" Nelson asked. "We're adults, with jobs and lives. We can't just quest through the Tri-State area looking for our things."

"Do you enjoy taking the subway?" Alex asked with a knowing smile.

Nelson sighed. "Not particularly."

"Then we quest," Miriam concluded. "But only after business hours and on the weekends."

"You told me 6:00 p.m. was 'the middle of the day,'" Nelson said, groaning.

Miriam scrunched up her face at the reminder that not only was she working on a big deal but that this particular deal was also one that was going to derail the Housing Magic project. She was going to be directly responsible for people like Alex, who struggled to find housing, being stuck out on the streets. *Five hundred* people. It was almost like Nelson knew she was working on the deal and wanted to pile on the guilt. Or perhaps it was just Miriam's own conscience that was making her feel that way.

In any case, she certainly needed to get serious about this. It wasn't just about her broom, either. Her bag was still missing too—her bag with the incriminating documents that would reveal just what she was involved in.

"We have the rest of the weekend," Miriam countered. "I can take tomorrow off, and we can find our stuff."

"Tomorrow's Saturday." Nelson was obviously confused. "Do you usually work Saturdays?"

"When I'm working on a deal," Miriam explained, even as she realized how hard this was going to be to justify to Charlie. She'd just promised earlier in the week that she would take the Pentacle deal, which meant putting in time over the weekend. "But the quicker we can get this done, the quicker we can go our separate ways."

Alex, who had been quietly observing the entire interaction, raised his eyebrows. "Seems you two aren't exactly friendly." He gave a hearty chuckle.

"You just got that?" Miriam asked, surprised. Sure, they'd spent the night together, but she and Nelson were hardly friends. How could Alex be so perceptive but have missed such an obvious thing?

Alex shrugged and then tapped his chest, where his hummingbird tattoos were still fluttering and glowing a bit. "The hummingbirds have a good idea about lovers, usually."

Miriam shook her head knowingly, and Nelson grimaced at the comment.

"Hahaha!" Alex laughed wickedly. "You two . . . and now . . . ! Magic sure has a fun sense of humor."

"Okay, okay, I think we're done here," Nelson said, motioning towards the front door. He seemed to have had enough of Alex digging into their sex life. "Alex, this has been—"

"—fun," Alex cut in with another chuckle.

Nelson groaned and shook his head. "Yeah, right." He paused and then changed the topic in an attempt to redirect the conversation back to Alex. "So, I think Lenor at the job center can help you find something if you're really worried about the store. I know there's this new big box store opening that we think will hire folks with a record. It might be a bit of a commute, but at least it's something," Nelson hinted.

Alex seemed to consider Nelson's words but then just said, "You kids have fun." And he nodded towards the door, hinting that Nelson and Miriam should continue their quest and leave him in peace.

Miriam gave him a wave and a "thanks" as they headed out into the hall. They made their way to the staircase, but before they could continue down the stairs, a glowing ball of light about the size of a softball materialized in front of them, twinkling brightly.

"What is that?" Miriam asked, reaching her hand out to the light.

"I'm not sure," Nelson replied. The ball of light winked once and then glowed steadily right in front of them. "I think it wants us to follow it." The glowing ball of light blinked quickly, urgently, as if to say Nelson had guessed correctly.

"We're just going to follow a ball of light?" Miriam asked skeptically. Had they learned nothing about just going into magical situations without a plan? They had no idea what this light was or whether anyone was controlling it.

The light blinked frantically and then zoomed up a couple of steps, waited, and blinked again.

"Just through the building," Nelson said, waving his hand in the direction the ball was indicating they should go—up further into the building instead of back out into the city. "It won't be a long detour, and maybe it'll be the answer to where our stuff is."

"Right," Miriam replied, but she was still skeptical. A random magical glowing light that appeared right when they needed direction? It didn't seem possible that it could be that easy, especially after Alex had told them they were going to need to quest together. It seemed unlikely that he'd meant for just fifteen more minutes. As someone who was used to chaos, taking precautions had always been the answer. Nelson seemed to live by a completely different set of rules.

"Fine," Miriam grumbled and then turned to the ball of light. "Lead the way."

Chapter Ten

T HE GLOWING BALL LED them up two flights of stairs until it turned down the hallway and guided them to another apartment. Oddly, the door was ajar, and the ball went in through the open door, leaving Miriam and Nelson standing in the hallway alone.

Nelson put a hand out, his palm open towards Miriam's face, signaling for her to wait. Then he raised his fist and lightly tapped on the doorframe. "Hello," he said, his voice strong and clear. "It's Nelson Copperfield, from Housing Magic. Are you okay?"

He paused and waited for a response. When there was none, he knocked gently on the door, announced himself for a second time, and pushed the door open a little farther.

In the middle of the room was a familiar-looking woman, and it took Miriam just a moment to realize it was the woman who'd spoken at the benefit last week. Now, though, she was slumped over on the threadbare sofa in the middle of the otherwise empty room. Unlike Alex's overstuffed, lived-in apartment, this place felt transitive and sparse. Miriam recoiled a step as she noticed a needle and spoon sitting on the sofa; they were things she'd only seen in documentaries and on *Dateline*, not the sort of thing she'd ever seen in person before.

"Talia," Nelson said gently, but with urgency. He placed a hand on her shoulder and pushed her up so he could see her face. Her lips were pale purple, almost blue, and her eyes were open, but her pupils were the size of pinpricks against the whites of her eyes.

"She's barely breathing. Miriam, call 9-1-1," Nelson instructed, his tone commanding and no-nonsense.

He pulled out a small white compact from his pocket, tugged the cap off, and carefully inserted it into Talia's nose. Narcan, Miriam realized. She only knew about it because of the signage plastered on every garbage can and bench in the city, signage with the slogan "You can stop an overdose." She'd never seen it in person, nor did she know how to use it. It always felt like it was meant for other people living in another part of New York she knew nothing about.

Miriam's fingers shook as she tapped on her phone to dial 9-1-1. She'd only ever used it once before, when she was in college and there had been a terrible wreck on Memorial Drive in Cambridge.

"Hello, 9-1-1, what's your location and emergency?"

"I would like to report an overdose," Miriam said into the phone, her voice wavering as she spoke the words. Talia suddenly inhaled a deep breath, but she still seemed unresponsive.

Nelson helped move her into a different position so she was lying on her side. He spoke loudly to her. "TALIA, I NEED YOU TO WAKE UP, I NEED YOU TO KEEP BREATH-

ING." Nelson's voice was firm, loud, and commanding, though he wasn't yelling.

"We've used Narcan, she appears to be . . ." Miriam paused. *Better* was the wrong word to use. She raised her voice so the 9-1-1 operator could hear her. "She appears to be breathing," Miriam explained, but she floundered, unsure what else to say. Nelson not only had Narcan on his person but also knew how to use it, which probably also meant he should be the one to talk to the 9-1-1 operator.

Nelson seemed to have the same idea, at least now that Talia had been treated. He stepped over and took the phone from her. Then he gave them the address of the building, something that Miriam didn't even know since she hadn't paid attention when they'd arrived. He explained that Talia had responded to the Narcan and that they would both be staying until the ambulance got there. He was efficient with the call and, within seconds, was back to encouraging Talia to breathe, to stay alert, to stay here.

Talia's eyes darted back and forth, but she didn't seem able to speak. Miriam wasn't sure if Talia even realized what was going on.

"Hey, it's okay," Nelson told her. "We're going to just wait for the paramedics, and I need you to stay with us." He remained calm and collected, even while Miriam was decidedly not. They'd . . . just saved Talia's life. Or maybe it was that glowing ball that had saved Talia's life.

"KEEP BREATHING, STAY WITH US," Nelson repeated, over and over, a mantra he seemed to know Talia needed to hear. And at the same time, he rubbed his hand against her sternum, encouraging her to breathe. He seemed to know exactly what needed to happen in the interim, in order to keep her safe, while they waited for medical help.

Talia appeared to relax, and Nelson continued encouraging Talia to keep breathing and to stay with them. It was not long before they heard the sound of sirens approaching through the thin windows of the apartment. Then, the loud clang of a stretcher being carried up the stairs echoed through the hallways and in through the still-open door.

"Paramedics." There was a bang on the open doorframe, and they came right in without waiting for permission to enter. Things went fast from there.

They asked Nelson a few questions while they examined Talia, stabilized her breathing with an oxygen mask, and got her loaded onto the stretcher. Miriam stood off to the side as everyone else had a job to do. Nelson explained how much Narcan he'd given her and approximately when they'd found her. He was smooth and experienced, detailing that they'd come over to the building for a normal walk-through and noticed the door was open. No one needed to know about the glowing magical blob that had led them to Talia's apartment.

The two paramedics who had loaded Talia onto the bright-orange stretcher expertly maneuvered her down the stairs to the waiting ambulance, Miriam and Nelson following behind them. Talia seemed panicked as much as she was aware.

"Can I ride with her?" Nelson asked. "I . . . I was her social worker for a while."

One of the paramedics shook his head. "No one but family."

"We'll meet you there," Miriam volunteered. She was unsure if that was an appropriate suggestion, but Nelson seemed determined to get to the hospital.

"We're taking her to Mount Sinai," the paramedic told them as he climbed into the back of the ambulance with Talia. Nelson nodded in acknowledgement, and the man shut the door.

As the ambulance drove off, Nelson sighed sadly. "She was doing well," he said, and Miriam gave him a gentle nod, then stepped off the sidewalk to hail a cab.

Thankfully, the first cab that drove by was unoccupied, and it pulled over for them to jump in. Nelson got in first, and Miriam was right behind him.

"Mount Sinai, emergency room," Nelson told the cab driver. The driver seemed to understand, and he took off from the curb right away, following in the ambulance's wake.

Nelson didn't look up. Instead, he buried his face in his phone, typing quickly. Miriam watched as they whirled through the city streets, going faster than they usually would, even though they were solidly in the middle of rush-hour traffic. Miriam suspected that following the ambulance was part of it, but lights magically turning green and pedestrians not darting out into traffic felt like the sort of small miracles Nelson excelled at. She assumed he was practiced at working them in a time of crisis, even while multitasking.

Miriam had always wished she could use her own magic to help, but without an intense amount of concentration, her magic always seemed to make things worse. Besides her broom and occasional small workings, her magic often felt useless.

When the cab arrived at the hospital, Miriam immediately tapped her phone against the credit card reader to pay for the ride, while Nelson tumbled out of the vehicle and hurried into the emergency room.

By the time she joined Nelson inside, he was already talking to a woman at the information desk.

"... she just arrived by ambulance ... Talia Lark," Nelson explained. "She OD'd ... I used Narcan on her."

The person at the information desk took his information down and then tapped something into her computer. "Take a seat," the woman instructed. "I've made a note for the staff to come get you once she's stable."

"Thanks," Nelson said with a sigh. Together, they made their way to a bench in a corner. The emergency room was crowded, which wasn't surprising. They were in the heart of the city, and it was likely always crowded here. Nelson took out his phone again and continued typing a bit more.

Miriam realized that this was probably a good time for her to bow out. Nelson was a social worker; he knew what he was doing. He ran an entire nonprofit that made housing available to people who used drugs. And yet, there was something about the way his shoulders slumped and his brow furrowed with concern that made Miriam wonder who was taking care of *him* when he was busy taking care of everyone else.

She'd always been so defensive about his insistence that he help her, and yet, she'd never stopped to wonder what weight he was carrying.

They sat in the waiting room for a long while as new patients filtered in from the backdrop of New York and others were finally called back to be seen by a doctor. She watched as triage sent exhausted and exasperated patients back into the crowded, uncomfortable waiting room.

And through all of that, Nelson stayed in his own fugue state, his eyes sometimes darting up to the analog clock on the wall, ticking away as time passed.

There was a soda machine on one edge of the emergency room, and after some time, Miriam got up and bought them both sodas.

Nelson let out a hollow "thanks" before placing his unopened soda on the floor, next to the leg of his chair.

Finally, when it seemed like the entire emergency room had turned over, a nurse stepped out of the double doors and talked briefly to the woman at the information desk, who motioned to where Nelson and Miriam were sitting.

The nurse made his way to them. "Nelson?" he asked.

"Yeah," Nelson sat straight up in his chair, giving the nurse his full attention. "How's Talia? Can I see her?"

The nurse nodded. "She's stable. She's upset, but it's been enough time that the Narcan has run out and she's not crashed again. We think she'll be okay for now without additional medication."

"She was sober," Nelson said solemnly. "It was a big deal. She was working with the career center to apply for jobs."

The nurse seemed uninterested in this young woman's relapse story. "You can see her, if you'd like. We gave her a sandwich and a soda to try to keep her in the hospital a little longer, so we can try to talk to her about help," he explained.

"We have a detox center we partner with," Nelson said, "and the funds to cover it."

The nurse gave Nelson a suspicious look, and Miriam understood why. Nelson hadn't introduced himself, and his appearance here seemed maybe a bit out of place, like he was some . . . well-groomed benefactor. He seemed to realize it at that moment, and he smiled tightly.

"I'm the executive director at Housing Magic. We operate judgment-free, housing-first apartments across the city. Talia is one of our residents. I was at the building for a routine walk-through, and her apartment door was open. That's how I found her," Nelson explained, obviously hoping to give the nurse some clarity. "I'm also a licensed social worker."

The nurse nodded. "I'll take you back to her," he replied.

They walked through the crowded waiting room and then into the emergency room proper. Talia was on a bed in the hallway. All the private rooms and curtained-off areas seemed to be full. Miriam followed because she wasn't sure what else to do. She'd already come this far, and it seemed to make sense to keep going.

Talia looked pale but was working on pulling apart a sad-looking sandwich on white bread. A can of soda was sitting on the bed, but she hadn't bothered to open it.

"Talia," Nelson greeted quietly, moving to stand at her bedside.

Talia looked up, and her eyes immediately closed again. "I'm sorry," she sobbed. "I . . . It was one time."

"It's okay," Nelson assured. "Part of recovery is—"

"Relapse," Talia murmured with a small nod as though repeating a familiar phrase, but Miriam could hear the disappointment in her voice.

"I have a spot at a detox ready to go. You can start again right now," Nelson offered.

"But I don't have to?" Talia asked.

"No . . . it's your choice," Nelson explained.

Talia nodded. "And my apartment."

"It's yours. Relapsing doesn't mean it gets taken away," Nelson said easily and softly.

Talia let out a sigh of relief. "Can I go home tonight?"

"I think you would be safer at a detox facility." Nelson was calm and collected, just as he had been talking to the 9-1-1 operator and the paramedics and the nurse. "But yes, you can if you want to."

Talia looked back down at her sandwich. "I think I want that."

Nelson nodded. "Talia, can you make me a promise?" he asked.

Talia's eyes darted up to him, but she didn't respond.

Nelson continued. "There's a safe use center two blocks from your building. They have fentanyl testing strips, Narcan, and clean needles. If you feel you need to use again, can you make a promise to do it there?" Nelson bargained.

Miriam watched as he maneuvered through finding the help Talia needed versus the help he very obviously wanted her to accept. He didn't try to force her into rehab or kick her out of housing. He did exactly what he needed to do to try to keep her alive—make sure she had the resources to survive, regardless of the decisions her addiction sometimes drove her to make.

Talia gave a shaky nod. "I can do that."

"Do you want us to take you back to your apartment? I can also call Shelly and see if she'll stay with you a while," Nelson offered. "Is there a friend we can call?"

Talia shook her head. "I was going to walk, get some fresh air."

"Can you please let me at least pay for a cab?" Nelson asked gently. "It would mean a lot to me if you would accept that."

Talia picked at her sandwich and avoided Nelson's gaze.

"I think I really just want to be by myself. It's just a few blocks home, right?" she countered.

"Yeah," Nelson said just as a doctor approached and stopped right next to Talia's bed.

"I have your release papers," the doctor said, handing a folder to Talia. "I've noted you've declined to speak to a social worker and any further treatment."

Talia took the paperwork without looking at the doctor and said, "I'll be fine."

"I can have a nurse give you a cab voucher," the doctor offered.

But Talia shook her head. "I'm going to walk home."

Miriam was surprised how routine it all seemed, as if Talia had not almost died. Everything with Talia had felt so traumatic to Miriam, and yet everyone here—the doctor, the nurse, Nelson even—was treating it like a nonevent. She kept her thoughts to herself, however, and watched as the doctor shot Nelson a knowing look. Yep, they'd both been here before, and Miriam quickly realized this was likely not the doctor's first overdose of the day, either. Both Nelson and the doctor looked exhausted at the prospect of Talia walking home alone, but neither of them had the authority to argue.

"I'll be fine," Talia said again as she swung her feet over the bed. She still appeared unsteady, but after just a little bit of wobbling, she seemed more than capable of making her way out of the hospital on her own. And she was obviously uninterested in anyone's help.

Miriam couldn't even begin to comprehend what Talia was thinking. Perhaps she just wanted to use again, or maybe she was embarrassed or ashamed. Perhaps there was no rational thought in Talia's mind besides just wanting to no longer be in the hospital. In any case, Talia had declined all the help offered.

Once Talia had left, Miriam and Nelson exited the ER and made their way outside the hospital. They stopped along the sidewalk, and Miriam shook her head in disbelief at what their afternoon had turned into.

"So . . . that's it?" she asked.

Nelson nodded. "That's it."

"You can't . . . get her into treatment or . . ." Miriam trailed off.

"I offered. I made sure she had the resources for safe injection. I tried to get someone to stay with her. But she's an adult. We aren't babysitters at Housing Magic, we just provide housing and make the services available that give the residents all the resources they need. Sometimes that's not enough."

"But what if . . ." Miriam shook her head, unable to finish her sentence.

"What if she doesn't make it through the night?" Nelson guessed, frowning. "We did what we were able," he said, "and sometimes we have to accept that is enough." Even as he said this, Miriam could see how much it was all weighing on him. She could see that the words had taken a long, long time for him to accept, that he'd repeated them over and over for years before he'd come to believe them.

This was her first time experiencing this, however, and she knew she would need time to process. She took a deep breath. "So what now?" she asked.

"I need to go home, make some calls, and do some paperwork," Nelson explained.

"Do you want company?" Miriam offered. She had a feeling that perhaps he should not be alone right now.

"Our things," Nelson said with a low groan, as though suddenly remembering their quest. "Can we . . . can we pause this for a night?"

"Oh, right. I . . . forgot about that," Miriam admitted. "It just seemed like maybe you might want company, rather than being alone."

"That would be nice, actually," Nelson admitted. "But Miriam, you don't have to. I'll be fine, really. You should go home and see your cat."

Miriam shook her head. "I want to stay with you," she said, because it was the truth. "I can call us a car to go back to your place."

"That would be . . . Thanks." Nelson gave her a small smile, and Miriam returned it, then looked down and started tapping on her phone. She never expected that she'd volunteer to take care of Nelson Copperfield, and yet, that seemed to be exactly what she was doing.

Chapter Eleven

T HEY RODE THROUGH THE city in a yellow cab, looping ads coming from the little TV that had been installed in the back seat. The cab driver expertly navigated the artificially illuminated city streets, lights flashing past them in a blur. The sun had set while they were in the hospital. Another day was gone.

Nelson had been quiet for a while, but he finally cleared his throat and spoke up, his voice not quite calm and collected anymore. "How about Larry? He'll be okay?"

Miriam nodded quickly, tapped on her phone, and then held it up to show Nelson a picture of Larry's furry little face, chowing down at the self-feeder. "He's fine," Miriam reassured him.

Nelson gave a tight smile and then started fidgeting with his phone again. Miriam noticed that the urgency with which he'd tapped away on his phone at the hospital had shifted now to more of an anxious scrolling, like he was trying to distract himself. And there was a slight tremor in his shoulders, like he was finally coming down from the rush of adrenaline that had surged while he was helping Talia.

Miriam reached over and placed a hand on his wrist, letting her thumb stroke the sensitive area just below his palm. "Hey," she whispered. This sort of intimate touch was not what she'd normally do with someone like Nelson, but he seemed to need something to break up the anxiety.

Nelson put his phone down for a second. "This isn't the first time I've dealt with this," he explained, glancing away from her and out the window. They were nearing his Brooklyn apartment, and he seemed itching to get out of the cab and into somewhere more familiar. "I'm really okay."

Miriam wasn't exactly sure who Nelson was attempting to reassure, her or himself. His shoulders seemed tense, even as he trembled, and he picked up his phone again and swiped across a few screens.

"I don't think this is one of those things that should ever become easy," Miriam said quietly. She wasn't actually sure what the right thing to say was, but she didn't like how Nelson seemed to be beating himself up over this entire situation.

"She was doing so well," he continued. "She . . . she's had a tough run of it. Foster kid, a series of abusive boyfriends, a lot of time spent on the street and all the horrible things that happened there. She was one of my last cases before I transitioned to executive director. I was the lead social worker, and I was still taking a few cases."

Nelson paused and rubbed the bridge of his nose. He took his glasses off and cleaned them with the hem of his shirt.

"She was so excited about speaking at the fundraiser last week. Talia's been doing a lot better, but she was still using a lot of Housing Magic's services, and she's around a lot at our offices. She always has a joke or some story to share, and it felt like maybe letting her be a success story could be a good motivator in her recovery."

"Do you think she'll go back to rehab?" Miriam asked quietly, still unsure if she was saying the right thing. It seemed a better question, though, than asking why Nelson thought Talia had relapsed again. She didn't want to say anything that might make him feel more guilty than he already did.

"I'm not . . . really supposed to discuss cases like this," Nelson said, as if only just realizing he'd said too much.

"Okay, yeah. But . . . who do *you* talk to when you need someone?" Miriam asked. His job had to be so hard to carry alone, and she hadn't really thought of that until just now. Her own work was simple in comparison, as much as it seemed to dominate every single moment of her life. She could usually go home and sleep easily, unbothered by consequences that were far removed from her role in anything. Well, that had been the case until her current deal, at least.

"I've been doing this for a while," Nelson said, reiterating that point without providing an actual answer. Miriam wondered if that meant he had a coping mechanism he was not ready to reveal or if he just spent his life burying all his emotions. Perhaps he was in therapy. Certainly, someone with this sort of job was probably in therapy.

Miriam nodded in acknowledgement and didn't question him further as the cab pulled up in front of the ice cream shop.

Together, they got out of the cab and made their way up to Nelson's apartment. As soon as they entered, he immediately went over to the kitchen and started rummaging through the cabinets.

"Can I get you anything?" he asked. "Water, coffee, tea?"

"Hey." Miriam stopped next to him in the kitchen. "I'm fine," she insisted firmly.

Nelson ignored her and then moved around her to the refrigerator. "How about dinner?" he asked. "I'm sure I've got something I can fix up really quick."

"Nelson," Miriam said with more force this time.

"Huh?" He stopped and looked up at her, confused.

"Come here," Miriam said, nodding towards his sofa. When he didn't immediately move, Miriam took his large, warm hand in her own, lacing her fingers through his. Then she gently led him over to the couch and pulled him down with her. In an act of obscene intimacy, she pulled his head into her lap and slowly ran her fingers through his hair.

"I'll handle dinner," she told him softly, pulling out her phone. "What are you in the mood for? Deli, Korean, dumplings . . ."

Nelson groaned at her last suggestion. "I'm not sure I'll be able to eat another dumpling for a while yet."

"Same, unfortunately," Miriam agreed. "How about pizza?"

Nelson nodded. "How do you feel about pineapple?"

"Would you hate me if I said I like it?" Miriam asked. She'd worked in a shitty chain pizza place in high school, and in a weird twist on normal, the Hawaiian pizza had been one of the best things on the menu. Her family had never been the type to keep kosher, even though they'd shipped her off to Hebrew school twice a week until she was thirteen. Pork had never been a restriction, even if it wasn't something her parents regularly bought.

"With ham?" Nelson asked.

"Yep. Classic Hawaiian. What do you say?"

"It feels like that kind of night," Nelson agreed.

"What kind of night is that?" Miriam asked while she completed the order on her phone.

"A weird one," Nelson deadpanned, but the joke fell flat.

When she was finished with the order, Miriam set her phone down and went back to running her hand through his dark hair. He looked different to her now, like this. It was that vulnerability again, though maybe it wasn't quite the same as what she'd seen before. And she was just now realizing how there was so much she didn't really know about Nelson, not back in high school and not now, since they'd started this outrageous trip to find their missing things.

"You're not used to this—being taken care of—are you?" she asked gently.

He almost laughed, though there was no humor in it. "That's not really my purpose," he said. "I take care of other people. I have the magic, the time, the skills."

"Even when they don't want help?" Miriam asked, but she immediately wanted to take it back; it was a low blow for a night that was already so depressing.

"I had to learn to get over that a long time ago," Nelson said with a shrug.

"Why don't you think you deserved to be taken care of?" It was another difficult question, but she asked it anyway.

Nelson looked up at her, his head still comfortably nestled in her lap. There was something so content about the moment, despite the serious conversation, and Miriam wasn't used to this feeling of safety and protection. Yet, she didn't dislike it. She touched his forehead gently and gave him a small smile.

"I never said I didn't think I deserved to be taken care of. I just mentioned that my job is to take care of others," Nelson corrected, but the way he said the words made Miriam think he was talking about more than just his job.

"That's why you were always trying to rescue me?" Miriam asked. She stopped running her hand through his hair long enough to take off his glasses and place them on the coffee table.

"I was trying to rescue everyone back then, especially the people I liked," Nelson said, the words slipping out of his mouth without effort.

"We didn't like each other in high school," Miriam reminded him yet again.

But he ignored her comment and changed the subject. "How about you, Miriam? It's not like you're one to accept help easily either."

"Says the man who has never had to compete in a male-dominated field every day of his life," Miriam countered back, deflecting so she didn't have to tell him the real reason she'd been so resistant to his help.

"I was talking about high school," Nelson replied. "In high school, you never wanted help."

"Right," Miriam said, and she closed her eyes for a moment.

It was too much to explain it all right now. In a lot of ways, competing in calculus and AP Physics was still competing in a male-dominated field. The teachers hated that she'd made top grades in her classes, and they'd hated that she'd done better than the boys, who were supposed to excel in math and science. It was hard to explain that she'd never wanted what felt like the pity of the golden boy. That she'd never wanted help from the kid all the teachers loved. Now though, she had to wonder if she'd read Nelson the wrong way. Perhaps it had never been pity. Perhaps it had been something else altogether.

It was also too much to explain that she'd fought so hard to not be the chaos witch. Her mom had never even tried to battle against it, and that had been all Miriam had ever wanted—a normal, quiet life, away from chaos. Yet, here she was, hunting down her broom, which had run away with Nelson's medallion. It was more chaos all the time. She had built a shell around herself because it felt like an injustice to make others suffer because of her own magic, and yet, Nelson had become a victim the moment he had let her in, even the slightest amount.

Miriam's phone buzzed, alerting her that the pizza had arrived at the door and saving her from having to explain any of it. Nelson got up from the sofa and jammed his glasses back on his face. Then he went to the door to grab the pizza, leaving her lap feeling cold and empty, and she realized just how much she'd liked the sensation of him being close.

She wanted to blame it on her lack of any sort of sex life. It felt so good to be close to someone, and she'd been craving this intimacy. But there was something more to it, too. As she watched Nelson open up the door to get their pizza, she realized how much she enjoyed the feeling of being needed and wanted. After convincing herself for so long that she needed to be self-sufficient, she'd forgotten what it was like to take care of others. It was such a weird paradox, this reality that shutting out help for herself had also robbed her of the joy of helping others. Miriam had never thought much of this being a two-way street, and yet it was.

Nelson placed the pizza on the coffee table, headed back into the kitchen, and returned a moment later with a couple of plates. "Do you want to watch a movie?" he asked, picking up the remote and flipping on a streaming service.

"Yeah, that would be nice, actually," Miriam said as she opened the steaming box of pizza. It was clear to Miriam that Nelson was not ready to be alone, and she hoped by committing to watch a two-hour movie with him, he would see that she'd be here as long as he needed her to be here.

"How do you feel about rom-coms?" Nelson asked as he flipped through a series of Nora Ephron movies.

"They're okay, I guess." Miriam had loved rom-coms as a kid. She'd loved the way they'd condensed New York into this magical land where everything was beautiful and where even kids could talk to random people on the subway. Now, though, she liked the unhinged chaos of reality TV. As an adult, romance felt too safe, too tame. She needed more drama, more chaos. She would have loved to recommend a season of *Real Housewives*, but she had a feeling that wasn't what Nelson needed at the moment. He probably needed something with less yelling.

"Is it weird to admit I love them?" Nelson asked, as the remote hovered on *You've Got Mail*. "When I was a kid, after my dad died . . ." He paused at the painful reminder of his father's sudden death when they were in middle school, only six months before his bar mitzvah. He'd received an unexpected cancer diagnosis, where he was fine one day and then the next day, he wasn't. A month later, he'd died. "This was all my sisters wanted to watch after it happened. I think it's because rom-coms are safe. They always have a happy ending, and no one is ever sad or dead. It got hard to watch other things. You never knew when something unexpected was going to happen."

His openness as he spoke about this difficult part of his childhood made Miriam's heart flutter and her stomach flip. It was the sort of vulnerability that made her want to hold onto Nelson and never let him experience hurt again.

She squeezed his thigh and then found the right retort, hoping it didn't undermine the memory of his grief. "Who needs toxic masculinity, anyway? It's been forever since I've seen that one," Miriam admitted. Actually, had she seen *You've Got Mail*? She must've, but all she remembered was something about the early days of AOL and that screeching dial tone from the dial-up days.

"It's a classic," Nelson said, selecting the movie.

Miriam settled into the overly soft couch with a slice of pizza as the movie started. The plot quickly came back to her when she saw Meg Ryan in an adorable little community bookstore. Meg Ryan's character owned the little bookstore, and Tom Hanks's mega company was attempting to open a large chain store right around the corner from where Meg Ryan's shop was located. The plot seemed quaint, given that there was another existential threat looming in the bookstore community, one that Nora Ephron couldn't predict. The point still stood. Tom Hanks's character and his mega corporation were the villains.

Miriam looked over at Nelson and tried not to wonder what his reaction would be when he found out that she was essentially the villain. Disappointment, anger, betrayal. Miriam's only defense was the jobs that were going to be on the line if this deal fell through. Sure, they were jobs occupied by investment bankers who all had minimum six-figure salaries and brand-name college degrees. And sure, the alternative was the most vulnerable people in the city losing out on free, no-strings-attached housing. But it was also her job.

She tore her eyes away as her stomach sank. Her arguments all felt so weak, so thin compared to the *actual* stakes, especially now that she'd been there and seen just what Nelson and Housing Magic did.

Miriam finished her pizza and placed her plate on the coffee table. She then nestled against Nelson's shoulder. She liked this momentary truce they had silently brokered, and she wondered if a hypothetical onlooker would think they actually liked each other in a way that was more than the superficial human need to be with another person.

Nelson wrapped an arm around Miriam and pulled her in closer. He placed a kiss on her forehead as the movie played on in the background. She hadn't been expecting something affectionate, but it only made her want to nestle deeper against his warm body.

"I could stay here tonight," Miriam murmured softly, drunk on the sensation of his arms gently holding her close. His shirt smelled like a familiar combination of must and spice that was not all that unlike a potions shop, old books, and used leather. It was familiar and safe, and Miriam liked that.

"Mmm," Nelson agreed, nuzzling into her hair.

"Just as friends, anyway. It's late and getting a cab home is going to be a whole thing," Miriam clarified, even as Nelson pulled her into his lap. "Or more than friends," she agreed, because the friends thing was a lie. She definitely wanted a repeat of their night together the weekend before. She could feel his rough jeans through the tights of the dress she was wearing—just a thin piece of spandex between her skin and the fabric of his pants. It would take nothing for her bare thighs to be against him, and she wanted that.

She wanted *him*. Nelson Copperfield, whom she'd been arguing with all over New York. Nelson Copperfield, whom she'd been enemies with since high school. Nelson Copperfield, whom she was about to sleep with for the second time in as many weeks. She wanted him in all the ways that were possible.

"I'd like that," Nelson said, as he pulled her closer. "However you want to stay."

"I like this," Miriam replied, settling further into his lap.

Nelson didn't immediately make the next move. Instead, he held her on his lap while the movie played. Every so often, when the movie slowed down, he would press his lips into her collarbone or on her shoulder. Slow and gentle, so soft Miriam wasn't sure they even qualified as kisses. More like his mouth just lingering on her skin, leaving a buzzing sensation in its wake.

And when the movie was over and Meg Ryan's bookstore had closed but there was still a bittersweet happily ever after, Miriam asked, "What do you need, Nelson?"

"This . . . you . . . here tonight. Not being alone," he whispered into her hair.

"I can do that; I can be that person," Miriam responded, because that was what she wanted too. She wanted to be that person. She wanted to be someone who was needed, wanted, desired.

She sighed against him but then let out a loud, unexpected yawn. It was now officially *late* late. Later than she usually stayed up. The long nights in the office were catching up with her, and she needed sleep. Although she probably also needed something else first.

"Time for bed," Nelson announced. Then, with a wink, they were floating just above the sofa, and he was carrying her.

Miriam knew it was not a long way to go and that he could only sustain this brief trip from the sofa to his bed. After such a human evening, and with all the feelings of helplessness that had come with it, it was almost easy to forget that they were magics. But then, there was no magical cure for Talia, no enchantment or potion or anything else that would just make her alright. There was only the glowing little ball of light that had led them to her. That one little piece of undefinable magic that had saved her.

It was a reminder that being a magic was a weird paradox. They had the ability to impact the mundane. To save time on a commute, to turn ordinary objects into something novel, to be forced to eat dumplings all day. But real-world things, the things that *mattered* . . . magic couldn't fix those things.

When they reached the bed, Nelson set her down and then kneeled beside her. "Are you sure you want to do this?" he asked.

Miriam reached up, pulled off his glasses, and set them on the table, and then she lay down, making herself completely available to him. "Yes," she whispered. Because she did. More than anything, she did.

His fingers seemed to know exactly where he wanted to start. They moved down her body, teasing along her sides and down her thighs. Then he reached up under her dress and found the elastic at the top of her tights. He hooked his thumbs under the waistband and gently rolled them down her legs. His fingers grazed her bare skin, sending shivers down her spine.

He stopped at her feet, letting the tights fall away. He then ran his thumb up the arch of her foot, pressing against the muscle that spanned across her sole, connecting her heel to her toes.

"Can I take your dress off?" he asked quietly.

"Take whatever you want," Miriam replied, already enjoying this. It was different from their night together last week. There was something about Nelson that was more present, less performative. He wasn't attempting to woo her with ice cream and a magical medallion (though he had still floated her to the bed); he simply seemed to want her and to be giving in to his own needs, just in this one moment.

Nelson ran his hands back up her legs, past her stomach, over the band of underwire supporting her breasts, past her bra straps, and he continued to work his hands across her skin, pushing her dress up her body with slow, tantalizing care.

Miriam raised her arms, anticipating his next step, and she was rewarded when he pulled the dress over her head, leaving her exposed in just her bra and underwear. When she looked back up at him again, her eyes were drawn to the bulge that had formed in his jeans. It was another thing she liked. Another sign she was desired, that she could make things happen to him. Sure, they'd been together before, but they were going slow now. It was no longer transactional. There was something more personal about this.

"Can I?" she asked, eyeing both the button on his jeans and the hem of his sweater.

"Mm-hmm," he hummed, and he nodded his consent.

Miriam sat up on her knees, and as she did, wetness pooled between her thighs. She placed her hands on his hips, and then, following his motions from before, she grabbed hold of the sides of his shirt and ran the hem up his abdomen. Her knuckles moved up his body, grazing his taut skin.

He threw his head back at the sensation, and a small gasp escaped him, sending a jolt through her. Without any more hesitation, she pulled his shirt off completely, and he quickly pressed his lips against hers. It was their first proper kiss of the night. It felt like so much more than a single kiss, and all the tension that had been growing in their slow, careful start simultaneously amplified and released.

Miriam's fingers moved with greater urgency to find the button on his jeans, and she unfastened it, finally releasing him completely. Her hands worked to undress him, as he'd undressed her, and when he was naked except for his briefs, everything seemed to slow down again. It was all soft touches and gentle hands. Nelson knew what he was doing, and even though they'd started out the evening with Miriam wanting to take care of him, Nelson was still as committed as ever to taking care of her. He went slow, drawing the process out, much to Miriam's consternation and finally pleasure.

And then, once they were both thoroughly taken care of, they fell asleep wrapped in each other's arms.

Chapter Twelve

W HEN MIRIAM AWOKE, THE weak early morning sunlight was trailing through the windows. Nelson was still asleep, and Miriam was entangled in his arms. She watched him for a moment, his face relaxed. She could make out the crow's feet at the edges of his eyes now that his glasses sat abandoned on his nightstand. There was a gentle smattering of stubble across his jaw that had grown overnight.

She desperately wanted to trace his jaw, to feel the coarseness of the stubble next to the warmth of his skin, but she also didn't want to wake him, either. He seemed peaceful, and she had a feeling that as soon as he awoke, he would be haunted by what had happened the day before.

Miriam was just about to close her eyes and enjoy the sensation of being wrapped in his arms for a little bit longer when his phone buzzed loudly from the nightstand.

"Hmm?" Nelson woke with a start, then lazily rolled over and grabbed his phone, pulling it up to his ear. "'Ello," he said, his greeting slurred with sleep.

Miriam watched as he sat up and put on his glasses, waking up more quickly now as he listened to whoever was on the other end of the line. "She has . . . Okay . . . That's . . . Okay. Tell her I can be there if she needs me," Nelson said into the phone. Then, after another moment of listening, he said, "Thanks." And he hung up and set the phone back on the nightstand.

He turned to Miriam. "That was a friend of mine at the safe use center. Talia came in this morning," he explained.

"Is that . . . good?" Miriam asked carefully.

Nelson nodded wearily. "It means she's alive and she's made a commitment to staying alive, even if she's still using. It means that maybe if she can keep showing up to a safe use center, she might actually accept help. Aside from a magical cure for addiction, it's as good of news as I could expect this morning."

Miriam nodded and gently rubbed his biceps. "So what now?" she asked.

"I thought we made an agreement to keep looking for our stuff all weekend," Nelson reminded her.

"Yeah, but that was before . . ." Miriam trailed off, not wanting to rehash everything that had happened yesterday afternoon.

Nelson nodded. "This is my job. I see this sort of thing all the time. It's hard, but I also can't freeze every time it happens."

"Oh." Miriam's mouth formed the vowel as she said it, and she studied him for a moment, thinking. He sounded casual, but she couldn't tell if she was hearing resiliency or callousness in his voice. "So, last night was . . ."

"Last night . . ." Nelson rubbed the back of his neck. "Last night was . . . not a mistake . . ."

". . . a truce," Miriam suggested, completing her own sentence.

She understood now. Last night, Nelson had needed comfort, and Miriam had indulged her own desire to be that person. But today, with the bright light from the sun illuminating everything, she could see things better. The only word to use was *truce*. They had taken care of each other in a moment of need. It had been a matter of convenience, really. Today, though—today, they needed to get back to this "quest" they'd been given, and they needed to find their missing magical items.

Nelson nodded. "Once we find our things, we can go back to our separate lives," he agreed.

"Right," Miriam said, and pulled herself out of bed. She was wearing a T-shirt of Nelson's that she'd slipped into after their activities of the night before, but she knew it left little to the imagination. She was still braless, and the shirt only went to her upper thigh. Feeling the tiniest bit exposed, she started around Nelson's bedroom, looking for the various pieces of clothing from her outfit. "We should go back to the map," she suggested. "It's still our best resource. And I should stop at home anyway because Larry probably wants some wet food."

"The journey continues," Nelson replied, as if he were attempting to talk himself into the same decisions as Miriam. He climbed out of bed to get dressed as well, and within just a few minutes, they were on their way out of the building.

After a minor argument about which mode of transportation to use, they headed down to the subway to make their way back to Miriam's Lower Manhattan apartment. Miriam, of course, thought they should have called a ride share, but Nelson liked the subway and claimed it was more practical.

When they got to her apartment, Miriam took a moment to feed Larry and freshen up, while Nelson made coffee and, for the second time that week, breakfast.

"Alright," Miriam said, leaning back over the map as she chewed on a warm, freshly toasted bagel. She snapped her fingers, and the lights dimmed and the curtains went down. It was a sort of magic she could do reliably, without having to worry about her chaos magic mucking things up.

She placed her hand on top of the snow globe, and again, the little pinpricks lit up the map. This time, there were only about half a dozen. Nelson stood over Miriam's shoulders, looking at the map.

"There," Miriam said, pointing to a spot on Long Island.

"Great Neck?" Nelson asked.

Miriam nodded, let the snow globe dim, and snapped her fingers to turn all the lights back on. "There's a jinn there, nice person," Miriam explained.

"A jinn?" Nelson's eyes went wide.

"Yeah, what's wrong with that?" Miriam said and then took a sip of her coffee.

"Miriam, we can't just walk up to a jinn?" Nelson shook his head in disbelief.

"Why?" Miriam asked. She popped a green grape into her mouth and stared at him, waiting for his response.

"Jinns are . . ." Nelson trailed off, as if unable to find the right words.

Miriam nodded. "They're fantastic at telling you things about yourself," she finished for him. "And that's what we need more than anything. We know our stuff is hiding somewhere in the Tri-State area, and we need to figure out a location with a personal connection. Maybe asking a jinn to reveal our most intense wishes will give us some insight into where our stuff has gone."

"I was going to say, dangerous beings who feed off of our own insecurities," Nelson corrected.

"I know this one," Miriam explained. "They helped with a deal I did a few years ago. Anyway, they're magics, just like us. I would hope that you don't think my chaos magic is dangerous."

Nelson nodded, as if considering his own magical bias. "A jinn helped with a business deal?"

Larry jumped up on the counter, and Miriam ran her hand down his back. "Sort of . . . Zari is also a tax accountant. They were the accountant on one of the deals the firm did," Miriam explained. "We worked a lot together."

"But we're not going in a professional capacity," Nelson countered, his skepticism clear. "We're going for magical reasons, and jinns have the sort of magic that can be disruptive." He seemed to be choosing his words more carefully this time, as if realizing he had his own prejudices to unlearn.

"Do you want your medallion back?" Miriam asked as she made her way over to the front door and picked up her replacement bag to pack for their adventure. "Because there's a train in thirty minutes, and I think we have just enough time to make it to Penn. I'm going, with or without you."

Miriam stuffed a final few things into her bag and then slipped on a pair of sneakers that went with the jeans and sweater she'd changed into earlier.

"Miriam," Nelson grumbled, but he followed her out her apartment door, down the street, and towards the subway station. Miriam slid her MetroCard through the reader, and the turnstiles unlocked, allowing her to go through.

She didn't pause and instead made her way down the stairs and headed straight towards the platform that would get them to Penn Station.

"I could use a small miracle," Miriam whispered to Nelson as she looked up at the wait times for the trains. If their train was late, which it currently looked to be, they'd miss their transfer, and they'd be out of luck. "If not, we have to wait another ninety minutes."

Nelson let out a sigh, gave a perturbed wink, and then, less than thirty seconds later, their train came barreling down the tunnel, a full five minutes ahead of its scheduled time.

Magic was such an odd wonder. Moving a train at speed would have been a big magic that needed an entire coven, but working a small miracle that somehow made a train arrive on time was well within Nelson's capability. It was peculiar that magic worked like that.

They boarded the train, and from there, it was a quick transfer to the Long Island Rail Road. Miriam watched the city fade, replaced by suburbs as they moved towards Long Island. In all her years in Manhattan, she'd only ridden the LIRR twice, and, curiously enough, both times had involved a search for her missing broom, which had been hiding on Long Island.

She'd flown over Brooklyn and Queens plenty of times, and the familiar contours of the streets and railways from above had been etched into her memory.

Miriam had spent most of her life above the rest of the city—either flying high on her broom or in her office building that was many stories up or in her apartment building, which seemed a distant oasis from the chaos of the city. This last week, however, she'd been grounded, in all senses of the word. She'd been forced to see things from a different perspective. And it was definitely making her think about things she'd always assumed she understood.

Her phone pinged, pulling her out of her thoughts. She looked at the screen; it was Charlie, sending a text, asking where she was. On a normal Saturday morning, she'd be at the office, working, and especially today, when everyone had just really gotten started digging into the specifics of the Pentacle deal, Charlie would have expected her to be there, in the office. All the associates were likely at their desks, and they likely had plenty of questions for Miriam on how to model the deal they were working on.

Miriam furrowed her brow, but before she could respond, her phone started ringing. She swiped to take the call and lifted the phone to her ear, thinking quickly about what excuse she was going to use.

"Hello," Miriam answered, her voice firm, knowing she was going to have to convince Charlie with her not-entirely-truthful excuse for not being in the office.

"Where are you?" Charlie asked just as the display on the train changed to the next stop.

"I had to go to my parents' house on Long Island. It was sort of sudden," Miriam lied. "There was an emergency."

"I hope everything is okay," Charlie said. Though his words were kind, Miriam could hear his frustration at her absence, and an uncomfortable wave of guilt bubbled up in her stomach. She'd never lied like this to get out of work. Usually, her magic, while a source of daily chaos, didn't impact her work to this extent. She could typically keep it under control.

"It's fine . . . My parents just had an issue with their house . . . I'll be back online tonight," Miriam explained. "But I'll be a bit out of pocket this morning."

Charlie sighed. "You'll be prepared to go over the model on Monday?" he asked. "The client wants to understand the deal better."

"It'll be ready," Miriam replied, and she hoped she was right. They needed to finish up with the jinn and find their things so Miriam could finally go back to work and put in the hours she needed to make this deal work. They *had* to be getting close to locating their things, even if Alex had warned they needed to go on this ridiculous quest together.

Miriam looked over towards Nelson, who was giving Miriam the illusion of privacy by staring down at his own phone. She wondered if maybe he was checking in on Talia. He seemed . . . not unbothered by it this morning, but he seemed to have healthy boundaries established to separate himself from his work. Still, Miriam had to wonder if he was struggling with how they'd left things with Talia. Miriam would have been, at least. Though, perhaps Nelson was built differently or had learned to cope in ways Miriam was unsure she'd ever be able to.

She finished her call but watched as Nelson remained focused on the little screen in his hands. For the second time that day, it was almost as easy to like him as it was to hate him. Miriam wasn't used to men who were so open about their feelings. The men she usually interacted with, both at work and in her coven, were constantly pressing forward in their careers, their goals, with little time to pause for things like this. They all lived in a world where emotion was a weakness. Nelson, in contrast, seemed sincere in his openness, and Miriam was unused to that. She didn't dislike it. Perhaps it was his ability to be so forthcoming emotionally that ultimately allowed him to cope with hard cases like Talia's. If he were the type to lock it away and push all those emotions down, then they would just bubble up inside him and eventually explode. Maybe it was this controlled release that allowed him to function.

"What?" Nelson asked, catching her looking at him.

"Was that about Talia?" Miriam found herself asking, because she also wondered what would become of the woman she'd helped the night before.

Nelson shook his head. "A big box store in Queens is having a job fair on Monday, and I was just finalizing the specifics to make sure we have transportation to get a few of our residents over there. It's the place I'm hoping Alex can get into."

Miriam nodded. "Jobs are good."

"Jobs are *great*," Nelson corrected as the train slowed at its next stop. "And this one is going to hire folks without immediately discounting felons. It means our residents with nonviolent felonies might be able to get jobs that are not only full time but also eligible for benefits."

Miriam didn't immediately respond to Nelson and instead let his words settle into the gentle whooshing of the LIRR. She couldn't imagine being thankful for a job bagging groceries. She couldn't even imagine Nelson's position, being grateful for something so humble as a minimum-wage position.

Their surroundings had slowly turned into dense suburbs, the in-between place between urban and truly suburban. She had little experience with these sorts of neighborhoods. Her parents lived in a much more suburban, picket-fence type of neighborhood.

Within just a few more minutes, they reached their stop and got off the train. They called a ride share that would take them to Zari's office. It was just a brief journey to the strip mall. Out here, things were farther apart and less walkable. There was likely a bus, but Miriam didn't have much patience for that level of public transportation.

The strip mall itself looked like it'd seen better days. The paint was flaking off the building, and about half the slots were open, the prior occupants having gone out of business, including a large anchor store that might have been a supermarket at one point. What remained, outside of the CPA's office, was a pawnshop, a rent-to-own furniture store, and a vape shop.

"It's a Saturday," Nelson stated as they approached the small storefront. Zari Jafari, CPA was etched on the frosted glass door. The halogen sign above the door, which only read "CPA," sputtered a bit before coming back to life. "They're probably not here." Nelson seemed more than happy to avoid meeting with the jinn.

"It's also almost April, which means tax time," Miriam reminded him. "They'll be in."

"They're probably busy," Nelson argued, and she got the sense he was getting cold feet.

However, any opportunity he would have had to convince her to leave was squelched when the frosted-glass door opened in front of them.

"Hello," the person on the other side of the door greeted. They were dressed in a sleek purple tracksuit, and their dark hair had been gathered in a neat ponytail on top of their head. It was slicked back in a way that made Miriam think they had spent a lot of time getting that style just right.

"Hello, Zari," Miriam said.

"Did we have an appointment?" Zari asked, opening the door to their office wider to welcome Miriam and Nelson into the shop.

"Not exactly," Miriam replied, tucking a curl of hair behind her ear. Miriam's business and magical contacts mingled occasionally. She'd done work with Derek's law firm before, and she, of course, worked with Hannah. Their coven had started out as a sort of girl boss, *who's who* in magical business. Then everyone's partners had joined, and their girls-and-gays power coven had become a bit more mixed.

What was rarer was for Miriam to meet an unexpected magic during the course of her job. Zari had been such a case. They had been a client's tax accountant, and Miriam had been introduced as she'd worked on the deal with her client. Zari had identified Miriam as a magic right off, although it had taken Miriam a bit longer to see the truth about Zari. Magic had a way of presenting itself to other magics, but Miriam found she was usually slower on the uptake than most. She'd always figured that was due to the interference caused by her chaos magic.

"I'm assuming you're not here for a tax return?" Zari's voice was lyrical and smooth, and they motioned for Nelson and Miriam to follow them to their office.

"No," Miriam said as she studied the office. While the office was in an unassuming, dated strip mall, the inside had been carefully designed and decorated. Plush cream carpets lined the floors, and the fixtures and furniture were all variations on the color purple. The wallpaper was a stunning gold pattern that circled the office. It was fairly upscale for a suburban CPA's office.

Zari took in that information and then led them to another door. Unlike the front of the office, which was well-appointed but still had the normal trappings of an office, including a desk, a computer, and so on, this room was entirely different. The purple extended into the carpets, and a lush purple sofa wrapped around the perimeter of the room. Gauzy purple curtains were on the walls, partially obscuring windows that looked out into a grimy back alley.

Zari directed Nelson and Miriam to sit on the sofa and then headed over to the small tea station in the corner. The teapot they picked up was different from the ones Miriam was used to seeing. It looked a bit like one teapot stacked on top of another.

Zari started working through the routine machinations of tea preparation, as if it were a ritual. "What brings you here?" they asked, placing the teapot and three small clear glass cups in the middle of the coffee table in front of Nelson and Miriam. They didn't immediately pour the tea and instead waited for it to steep.

Nelson looked at Miriam, presumably deferring to her judgment, given this was her contact.

"I've lost my broom," Miriam explained, "and his magical medallion thingy."

Zari nodded but wore a confused look on their face. "I'm not exactly the person you go to when things go missing," they explained.

"I'm aware," Miriam replied dryly. "It's been suggested that our things might have gone somewhere meaningful to us, but we can't figure out where that might be," she explained.

"And," Nelson added, "we think diving into our deepest desires might be a good place to start."

"I don't get many people volunteering to give me their wishes," Zari said, taking a seat on the sofa and tucking their feet underneath their body.

"My map pointed us in your direction," Miriam said. "And we've been on this search all over the city."

Zari nodded carefully, taking in the information with an amused look on their face. "Well, then . . . miracles do happen," Zari said dryly, and it was unclear to Miriam if they already had a read on Nelson or if they were just surprised to see two people walk in and voluntarily give their wishes to a jinn. "I have a lot of tax returns to do, but I've been low on energy. I can take a few hours on wishes," Zari decided with another nod.

"Energy?" Miriam asked, not entirely sure what Zari meant. She knew jinns could show you your deepest wishes and that there was a sense of danger associated with that, but she'd never stopped to consider the meaning behind it.

Nelson pressed his lips together and looked towards Zari as if waiting for permission. Zari gave a confirmatory nod. He then explained, "Jinns get their magical energy from other people's wishes. They don't take them permanently, but it is the act of witnessing them that allows a jinn to power up."

"So, it's inconsequential to us?" Miriam asked, unsure how she felt about allowing Zari to go that deep into her mind. Surely there were repercussions for such things.

"The further I go into your desires, the more energy I gain. And given you've come to me voluntarily . . ."

"You're going to go as far as possible," Miriam finished, understanding now what Zari was proposing.

But Zari brushed off Miriam's concern. "It sounds like you need this level of exploration, anyway," they said.

Miriam shivered at the idea of needing to have her desires explored so fully. She'd known there were risks coming here, but she hadn't quite understood what that would mean. What could Zari see that Miriam was missing? Perhaps they just meant that Nelson and Miriam needed to dig deeper to find where their things might be hiding.

Zari got off the sofa and reached over to the tea set that they had previously left on the coffee table. They poured the dark amber tea into two small glass teacups and then handed one cup to Miriam and one to Nelson. They didn't keep one for themselves.

"This is going to be fun," Zari said, taking their seat again on the sofa. "Drink up," they encouraged.

Nelson held out his glass to Miriam. "L'chaim," he said, as they clinked their glasses together.

Miriam took a deep breath and then had a sip of tea. Except for just a hint of an unfamiliar but not unpleasant spice, it tasted like any other cup of tea she'd had.

She looked at Nelson, waiting for something to happen. She took another sip of her tea and was about to take another when her phone rang. Charlie's number popped up on the screen, and she blanched. This was bad. She'd already told him she was away for the day, and the fact that he'd called instead of emailing or texting could only mean things had gotten critical.

With another deep breath, Miriam braced herself for the conversation. She was too deep into this now to turn around and head back to Manhattan, and she'd have to do her best to convince Charlie that she'd handle things when she could.

Miriam placed her cup on the table, held up an apologetic hand, and then answered the phone.

Chapter Thirteen

"M IRIAM," CHARLIE'S VOICE BOOMED through the phone speaker, louder than it should have been. It seemed audible to the entire room, even though Miriam hadn't turned her speaker phone on.

"Hey, Charlie. I'm still on Long Island . . . but as soon as I get home, I'll review the models so we have them for Monday," Miriam explained quickly. She realized too late that she should have made a commitment to stay in the office instead of heading out on this dumb magical quest. But that didn't stop her from peeking over at Nelson and thinking that perhaps he'd needed her more last night. Her heart squeezed at the thought. Then she chastised herself. There had been a real tragedy that had happened, and all she could think about was how much she liked that Nelson needed her.

"Hmm . . . Oh, yeah, the modeling." Charlie was dismissive, which was odd, given how adamant he'd been earlier. "That's not why I called, though," he explained.

"Oh, I'm sorry . . . I just assumed," Miriam said, and then she stopped to listen to why Charlie had called.

"I just got done with the board," he began. "And I wanted to be the first to let you know you're going to be a partner at Alchemy."

"I'm . . . What? I thought . . . I thought that was contingent on the deal going through," Miriam whispered, looking over at Nelson, but his face was buried in his phone, his eyes wide and intent.

"That deal's dead," Charlie continued, "but there's another one that you're going to take lead on, as partner. The board couldn't be more happy with your performance."

Miriam beamed at his words. This was excellent news. She could pay her parents' mortgage, and they wouldn't need to worry about anything ever again. As partner, she could choose the sort of deals she worked on, and she could avoid the ones that were morally gray, like undercutting a nonprofit whose altruistic mission was to provide unhoused people with housing options and resources. In the course of a single morning, she'd gone from stressing about losing a deal that was about to define her career to . . .

Her disregarded teacup caught her eye from where it sat on the coffee table.

"We've . . . just had one thousand units and ten million dollars gifted to Housing Magic," Nelson said into his own phone. When Miriam glanced over, all she could see on the display was the normal lock screen. He wasn't on a call at all. "That's incredible," he said, his voice lit up with excitement. "We're going to provide so much more housing."

He continued chatting with whoever he thought he was on the line with.

And Miriam realized exactly what was going on.

"It's not real," she said, shifting to look at Zari.

Zari nodded in agreement. "It's not. But interesting introductory wishes. You two are very invested in your work. That's not uncommon, though. A lot of those first wishes are about work or money or some combination." Zari then replenished the tea in both of their cups. "Drink up," they said, waving a hand at the full teacups.

Miriam lifted the teacup back to her lips, and a moment later, the door opened. She tamped down her surprise when Hannah, Maddy, Derek, Isabelle, and Heather all walked into the little parlor that Zari used to conduct their wish sessions.

"What are you doing here?" Miriam asked, playing along. She figured it was best to play out the wishes rather than try to resist them. The entire reason they were here was to explore their deepest desires, and fighting that wouldn't be helpful at all.

"Girls' night," Hannah announced, wedging herself in between Miriam and Nelson on the sofa. Miriam peeked over at Nelson, who appeared to be talking to a woman Miriam was pretty sure was his mom. She was handing him something, but before Miriam could see how his scene played out, Isabelle offered her a glass of rosé.

On the surface, Miriam knew what this wish looked like, but it was more than just wishing she could have a girls' night out. It was being with her coven, before they'd all coupled up and started having babies.

She looked over as Derek started to peel off one of those lotion face masks that you could buy from the drugstore, a reminder of when they used to have spa nights at someone's apartment.

"Now, Miriam, what were you saying about that deal?" Derek asked.

Miriam just smiled. This was how their Sundays used to be. They used to start at brunch; sometimes they would wander around the city, shopping or going to art galleries, and other times they would end up at someone's apartment, sprawled across the living room, drinking wine and gossiping. That was before anyone needed big magic. Back then, they'd just been a group of witches hanging out.

Miriam missed that—that feeling of being part of a group, a community. Now, the coven was less important. Everyone already had a partner, and their families were growing. It was a loss she hadn't even allowed herself to fully realize, let alone grieve. Instead, she'd slowly pulled away, throwing herself into her career.

She could feel a painful pull in her chest as she understood this thing she hadn't even realized she missed.

She looked over at Nelson, who was now joined by two other women in addition to his mother. Miriam squinted, and then decided they must be his sisters. Nelson had two younger sisters, Miriam recalled. After his dad had died, he'd spent a lot of his time helping his mom take care of them. They'd gone to different elementary schools but been in Hebrew school together longer than she could remember. It wasn't until they'd been in high school, when he'd started to become intent on taking care of everyone all the time, that Miriam had really started to find him irritating. Though, now she wondered . . .

Nelson let out a deep sigh. "I'll mow your lawn first, and then I can paint the living room, and then you need money for the electric bill . . ." He trailed off.

"Nelson, it's all taken care of," his mother explained. "We just wanted to have you over for dinner."

"But you needed a babysitter," he told one of his sisters. "I was going to take the train to Westchester to watch Olivia."

"It's all covered," one of his sisters said. "It's really just nice to see you again."

"It is?" Nelson asked. He seemed confused and then re-covered. "It's nice to see you as well . . ."

The room faded away, and Miriam realized that any semblance of all of this taking place in the real world had also faded away. Except for the door, the room had gone completely black, not unlike at a black box theater. It was if she were in some combination of a dream and a hallucination, though she was much more lucid.

This time, a new person walked through the door. Their face was blurry and obscured, like in a dream. Miriam felt a warm bubble of adoration settle in her stomach as the person walked over to her. They wrapped her in their arms and gently rubbed her back.

"I love you," they whispered into Miriam's ear, and she could feel their soft breath against her neck. "I missed you." The words made Miriam's knees go shaky. It was more than just the words, though. It was as if she had an entire bank of memories with this person. The time she'd gotten a stomach virus, and he'd stayed with her all night. That terrible day of work when Miriam had gotten home cranky and exhausted, and he'd ordered takeout and run her a bath. The feeling of his mouth between her legs. There was more, too. The time he'd sprained his ankle, and Miriam had lain in bed next to him all weekend and they'd watched bad reality TV.

It was if she saw an entire life that they'd had together—a life they could have together—in just an instant.

"I love you," Miriam whispered back to the faceless, formless person. "I need you." She could feel the tears that were starting to stream down her face. This was her deepest wish, the one she so vehemently denied. It made her feel weak to think she wanted another person, to admit that sometimes she was lonely. To admit that she could ever possibly need anyone besides herself.

"Let me out!" Miriam yelled, hoping to break through the wish. But instead, another memory or wish or whatever these things were started. It was Thanksgiving, and they were walking hand in hand through the autumn leaves. The air was perfectly crisp. He stopped and pressed her against a tree, then kissed her until her lips were swollen.

"Stop," Miriam cried out. "Stop." And she was unsure what she was upset about. She was stronger than this desire to need and want, and she could escape this.

Suddenly, Miriam was back in the purple room, and standing across from her, with his own damp eyes, was Nelson. Just Nelson.

She had made it out of the wish simulation.

She heard the clanking of a bell, and suddenly, Zari was standing in front of them.

"Your wishes are basic," Zari said. "But it'll get me through another tax season." Zari stretched their hands above their head and stood on their tippy-toes, releasing a loud groan, as if they had just woken up from a nap.

"Basic," Nelson grumbled. He sounded angry, but just shook his head. "I still don't know where our stuff could be."

Miriam let out a sigh. "Unless my broom went to a bottomless brunch in Midtown, I'm just as lost as you."

"Your greatest wish was bottomless brunch?" Nelson asked.

Miriam cocked her head to one side and looked at him. Did he really think she was so shallow to dream only of brunch? Did Nelson really think that her investment banker's life meant that the only thing she cared about was cheap sparkling wine and orange juice?

"No," Miriam said firmly, but did not elaborate.

Nelson gave her a look but didn't bother to ask more questions, and Miriam was eternally grateful for that.

"Well, I am so glad we did this," Zari said, breaking the tension that had settled between them. "But I have a pile of returns I need to get through." And with that, Zari left the parlor, went back out to the public-facing office, and sat down at their computer.

Miriam and Nelson shared a look, surprised at how suddenly Zari was ready to end things, how transactional it all felt. A silent conversation passed between the two of them, their eyes darting at each other frantically. But they seemed unable to reach a conclusion about what they should do next. And to Miriam, that was yet another reminder they didn't actually know each other that well.

Miriam decided for them both. She grabbed Nelson's hand and dragged him out into the main office area. "Thanks," she called to Zari, giving an awkward wave. "We'll . . ." She nodded towards the door, and she and Nelson made their way outside.

"What now?" Nelson asked as they stopped together along the walkway outside Zari's office without much of a plan.

Miriam let Nelson's hand go. "My parents are close by," she admitted with a sigh. She hadn't wanted to tell them about the whole missing broom thing, but now that they were already on Long Island and were running out of ideas, it seemed like a logical next step in their journey.

"You think they can help?" Nelson asked, although the question was not accusatory.

"They're the only other people who really understand my chaos magic," Miriam explained. "They might be able to help us make some sense out of where our things went."

"Hopefully," Nelson replied. Miriam could tell that he was trying hard to be patient with the entire situation but that everyone had a limit, even Nelson the Mensch was not immune. Hopefully, Miriam's parents could help.

Chapter Fourteen

A BOUT THIRTY MINUTES LATER, an old beat-up station wagon pulled into the parking lot of the strip mall. Miriam's dad, Josh Blum, a short, balding man with a soft smile and kind eyes, was in the driver's seat.

Miriam gave a little wave. "Hey, Dad," she said into his rolled-down window. "Thanks for coming to pick us up."

"Anytime! I just wish we'd known you were coming; I would have made lunch," her father said. "And who is this?" Her dad pointed to where Nelson was standing just behind her.

Nelson gave a little wave, and when Miriam started to climb into the front seat, Nelson got into the back.

"That's my friend Nelson," she explained, holding back a groan of frustration as she started to fasten her seat belt. She didn't want to sit here and answer questions. And more importantly, it felt strange to her to introduce Nelson as a friend. Mostly because they'd never been friends before. But also because they were sort of, kind of, sleeping together, or at least they *had* slept together and then continued to spend time together, all while they'd decided to maybe *not* sleep together anymore.

Their relationship was a bit complicated.

"Nelson?" her dad's eyebrows went up with amusement. "Copperfield? Wait, are you Lois's son?" he asked. "You didn't tell me this was Lois's son. How's your mom? We've missed her since she moved to Westchester."

"She's good," Nelson answered, but there was a strain in his voice.

Miriam wondered if it had to do with what they'd experienced in the jinn's wishing parlor. She'd been caught up in her own wishes, but she'd still noticed Nelson's relief when his family had told him he was not expected to take care of them anymore. Was Nelson's default *taking care of everyone*? For the second time, Miriam wondered who took care of the person who took care of everyone else. Had he been like this since his dad died? Had Nelson been unable to do anything but care for everyone else for the past twenty years?

"Well, I'm a bit surprised to see you two together. You two never seemed to get along," Miriam's dad noted.

Miriam grimaced at her dad's bluntness. "Dad, it's not like that," Miriam lied. "We went to high school together. We'll tell you and mom about it when we get home."

"Okay, okay," her dad said, his tone good-natured, as always. He shifted the car into drive, but it sputtered a bit and then died. Looking unperturbed, he let go of the steering wheel for a moment and put his hands atop the dashboard. The car immediately roared to life, the engine revving as though the car were ready to go. "Alright, just needed a bit of juice to work." He chuckled and slapped the dashboard again.

Miriam's dad was a house witch, which meant he could repair all sorts of small things, like the car. He was also a tailor by training and had owned a dry cleaning business Miriam's entire life. His humble career and not-so-reliable car matched his appearance. His clothes were in good condition but obviously well-worn, and the hair at the crown of his head had fallen out, though he still let the sides grow. They would frizz and curl away from his head. He looked . . . silly and like a bit of a mess.

He'd always been that way, and it never failed to make Miriam embarrassed. She loved her parents, but they didn't fit the image she'd always thought she wanted or the life she'd worked so hard to build for herself in the city. Her feelings about keeping them hidden away from her life were complicated, though. The only time she'd brought anyone home to meet them was when she was in college. She'd briefly dated this guy who was from *money*—a rich warlock from the suburbs of Massachusetts—and he'd joined her on Long Island one weekend. The entire two days, he'd made little jabs about her parents, their house, how chaotic their lifestyle was. She still remembered how he'd looked down on everything with an air of superiority and a hint of disgust.

When Miriam turned around to look back at Nelson, she half expected him to be grimacing at the tattered seats or frowning at how the old station wagon required magical assistance to start. Instead, he just gave her a kind smile as the car began to move along.

Miriam let out the breath she'd been holding. Nelson wasn't like those others—her college boyfriend, the bankers she worked with, the people she called her friends in the city. He came from this place, and he knew Miriam's chaos magic. And even now, even as they were on this frustrating journey, he didn't seem to judge Miriam for any of it. It was hard not to think back to high school and remember his insistence on fixing everything—that implication that Miriam herself was a thing that needed fixing. But Miriam now wondered if it had been something else entirely, something that had never been pity. Perhaps he'd just understood where Miriam was, and he'd met her there.

"You know, there's a jinn in there," Miriam's dad said, pointing to the little tax shop as the car sputtered onto the street. He sounded mildly concerned, which made sense. Jinns weren't exactly dangerous, but giving them your wish wasn't something most people did voluntarily, either. Typically, jinns traded in wishes. They traded to the lost, the despondent, people who had no vision for themselves and needed to find themselves again.

"We know," Miriam replied, glancing back at Nelson. Perhaps she and Nelson were not all that different from those others who might have sought out a jinn.

She still wished she knew what he'd seen. On the surface, at least, he seemed to want a break from consistently giving. But she hadn't seen his final wish, and she worried that even if he understood, he wouldn't hold back. His nature would always be to give all that he could, and that might mean he would give too much of himself for her if that was what *she* needed.

She didn't know what he was burying so deep down, though, and she may not ever know.

From his spot in the back seat, Nelson looked unperturbed now, maybe having buried everything back down like it had always been, and he leaned forward to address Miriam's dad. "We're fine," he reassured. "Just some business."

He gave Miriam a look, reminding her why they were here in the first place, and she smiled tightly.

"How's the dry cleaner?" Miriam asked, hoping to change the subject of conversation. She'd have to tell her parents about why they'd visited the jinn, but she would prefer to wait until her mom was there so she could just tell the story once.

Her dad shrugged, but a look of concern settled on his face—one that she'd noticed had become more and more prevalent. "No one needs dry cleaning anymore. Fast fashion, work from home, you know the drill."

Miriam gave a tight, stressed nod. She did. She knew the reality of the situation. Her parents were both small business owners, and there was a time when their business had been doing quite well. But now, they were aging, and so was their community. They had some savings but not enough to retire. It was part of why she wanted that promotion at work so much.

"But you don't need to worry about that," her dad said cheerfully as he navigated through the streets of Long Island, leaving the tight suburbs of Great Neck for the more open small towns. "How's everything at the bank going?"

"It's fine, Dad," Miriam said with a sigh. She hated talking about work with her parents. She knew they were proud of her. They loved that she had a fancy job in the city, and they loved that she could take care of herself. But she always found it hard to explain her life in a way they could understand. They'd only ever been a short broom ride away, but it was an entirely different world.

"Always fine." He chuckled, and Miriam saw him glance in the rearview mirror, pride in his eyes. "Nelson, did you know my Miriam is a big-time banker?"

"I've heard," Nelson replied politely, giving a sincere, amiable smile. Again, Miriam relaxed, realizing Nelson was more than happy to entertain her dad.

"How about you?" her dad asked. "Are you a banker like my daughter? I think she only dates fancy men, but she refuses to bring them home."

"Dad," Miriam grumbled. She'd already introduced Nelson and made it clear, she thought, that nothing was going on between them, even if that was technically a lie. "Nelson's just a friend from school. Lois's son," she reminded him.

True to his nature, Nelson took everything in stride. "I'm not a banker, sir, no. I work for a nonprofit," he explained. "Housing Magic."

Miriam's dad nodded and said something, maybe asking more about Nelson's work. Miriam had stopped paying attention. But the conversation continued around her as they turned into the subdivision where her parents had lived her entire life and approached their house. She took a deep breath, bracing for . . . for a few things. The first was Nelson's reaction, but the second was that she was also unsure what state the house would be in.

Miriam had inherited her chaos magic from her mother, but their approaches to handling their magic had been the opposite. While Miriam had spent her entire life fighting against her chaos magic, her mother had embraced it in its entirety.

They turned the corner, and Miriam's childhood house came into view. It was much the same as the last time Miriam had been here three months ago, though that wasn't a given. Her mom liked to change things on a whim. The outside of the house was still painted a vibrant pink. The yard was decorated with a combination of yard ornaments her mom had procured from garden centers and thrift shops over the years. There were the classics—the pink flamingos and gnomes—and then the more eccentric—the large, oddly shaped foot and the full-sized Frisch's Big Boy statue her mom had found at an estate sale and magicked to the roof of the station wagon. To make matters worse, her mom repainted the Big Boy every few months. Now, he was wearing full, classic drag, complete with sequins and a teased blond wig.

Her mom had probably sewn the clothing for the Big Boy herself. That was typical. She had an utter inability to sit still. During the day, her mom ran a fractional bookkeeping company where she did the books for a handful of small businesses. She was a CPA, but not the tax accountant kind. After work, her mom had an entirely different agenda that involved constantly redecorating their home. Of course, it was an excellent outlet for her mom's magic. Instead of suppressing it, like Miriam did, her mom embraced it. She often spent hours changing the colors of the inside and outside of the house, conducting paint rollers as if she were leading the philharmonic.

"I see your house is still as colorful as ever, Mr. Blum," Nelson said, addressing Miriam's father as if they were still in high school. Again, Nelson's voice was easy, without judgment. She had always just assumed he saw her as a project that needed rescuing rather than a fully realized person. Now though, he lacked any of that judgment she was so sure she'd always felt around him. He always seemed so put together, but something had broken that illusion for her last night. Perhaps seeing his own vulnerability was why Miriam could see his sincerity now.

"Thanks, and you can call me Josh, by the way. It seems so formal otherwise; we're all adults here," Miriam's dad said, giving an authentic smile. He looked to Miriam, and his smile turned into an apologetic grimace. "I think your mom attempted to cook lunch."

". . . Great," Miriam replied, not trying to hide her sarcasm. Miriam's mom was not one for the kitchen.

They made it into the house, and it was just as chaotic inside as it had been outside. It was neither messy nor cluttered; her dad had always been good at balancing that. And Miriam's mom never had an issue with keeping so many things that it became overwhelming. She never struggled to throw away garbage or give away things she was no longer using. But, like in the front yard, there was an eclectic maximalist collection throughout the house. The walls were all bright colors—yellow next to red next to lavender next to hot pink—and not in the pattern Miriam remembered from her last visit. Art and trinkets were everywhere, covering most of the surfaces, and the colorful, chaotic theme wove through all of it—from the art on the walls to the furniture.

"I'm in the kitchen," Miriam's mom called out as they entered the front room.

Her dad led the way into the kitchen, Miriam following just behind Nelson, and she braced herself again, hoping the kitchen was as it had always been—bright yellow, decorated with daisies. She appreciated that the kitchen had remained constant throughout the years, even as the rest of the house changed, and as they entered the room now, she saw it was still the same, even down to the fresh flowers sitting on the table and counter and above the cabinets. Her mom had enchanted the vases years ago, and the flowers always stayed fresh and dust free, despite their delicate petals. It was one of her mom's better spells.

Her mom, Zelda, was standing over the stove, watching over three different bubbling pots. She was wearing a *Kiss the Chef* apron, her curly hair loose and wild, like Miriam's when she didn't take the time to tame it. And like Miriam, her mom's body was soft and full. In some ways, Miriam felt like a carbon copy of her mother; in others, Miriam was exactly the opposite.

"Hey," her dad said, kissing his wife on the cheek while examining the pots and pans. "What are you making?"

"Well, I wasn't sure what everyone wanted, so I made a few things. I have a box of matzo ball soup in that one," Miriam's mom said, pointing to a pot covered with a lid. "Then this one is chili. I had most of the ingredients—well, except meat. It's vegetarian. And this one is tomato soup," she finished, indicating to each of the pots in turn.

"That all sounds great," Nelson said from where he'd stopped near the entrance to the kitchen. "I'm a big fan of soup."

"Well, I'm not sure chili is actually soup," her mom said, as if completely missing the point, especially given she'd prepared three things that could reasonably be considered soup.

Miriam's dad was usually the cook, but if he had to expend his magical energy to revive the station wagon midway through his outing to pick up Miriam, it made sense that Miriam's mom took care of the kitchen just this once. The tomato soup continued to stir itself, even as her mom stepped away from the stove to greet Miriam and Nelson.

"I'm so glad you came home," she said, pulling Miriam in and giving her a tight hug. "If you'd told us in advance, we would have had lunch ready to go, and I even would have made your father make it."

"Hey, Mom," Miriam said, hugging her back.

"Nelson, right?" Miriam's mom narrowed her eyes, as if trying to figure out why and how she knew him.

"Lois's son," her dad explained.

"And these two?" her mom asked, motioning between Nelson and Miriam.

"Just friends, Mom," Miriam replied with a long sigh.

"Hmm." Miriam's mom studied them carefully, as if she weren't so sure she agreed with that. Before she could make more damning comments, however, the lid on the pot with the matzo ball soup flew off and crashed into a light above the stove.

Thinking quickly, Nelson winked, and the light and lid fell harmlessly on the floor, unscathed. Miriam's dad gently tapped the edge of the stove with the heel of his hand, and the light flew back up to the ceiling and into the socket. The kitchen righted itself in a second.

Miriam's mom picked up the lid to the pot and then peered into the soup. "Well, looks like the matzo balls are floating," she concluded. "I think that means it's time for lunch."

Miriam watched as her dad took a seat at the table, winded by the little magic it had taken to repair the light, and she frowned. Her dad was tired, and her mom was less in control than she had been in the past. Normally, even in all the chaos, her mom wouldn't have been set off by making lunch. And her dad had always repaired things as quickly as her mom destroyed them. But it was obvious watching them now that they were getting older and that they were going to need more help. As an only child, Miriam had to figure that out. Her parents were in their early seventies, and they weren't getting any younger.

She stepped up to the counter and helped her mom search through the cabinets to find enough dishes for the trio of soups.

Then, once they were all seated, each of them with multiple bowls of chili or soup to taste, Nelson didn't hesitate to dig in. "This is fantastic," he said, pressing his spoon into a tender matzo ball.

"The secret," Miriam's mom explained, "is that you don't take off the lid, you wait until it explodes." She gave a cackle. Miriam wanted to cringe at her mom's propensity to cackle at her own jokes, but she knew she had a habit of doing the same.

Nelson gave a sincere chuckle and took another bite. "Don't tell my grandma, but I think it's better than hers." He gave a wink and a smile.

Miriam's mom placed a hand to her chest and waved off the compliment, obviously flattered. "You are too nice."

Once the soup adoration died down, Miriam's dad spoke up. "Now, what are you kids doing here?" he asked, glancing from Miriam to Nelson and back. "And do you want to explain why you were at a jinn's office?"

Miriam stirred her tomato soup, staring at the ripples her spoon made in the bowl.

"Miriam?" her mother asked earnestly. That was the thing about her mom. While she embraced the chaos, she also had an expert understanding of the exact sort of trouble that chaos magic caused.

Miriam took a deep breath. "My broom went missing again."

Nelson cleared his throat, giving Miriam the opportunity to explain the rest of the situation. She was unsure if he was attempting to do her a favor by not "telling on her," or if he had decided that it was Miriam's responsibility to explain her mistakes to her parents.

"And it ran away with Nelson's enchanted taxi medallion," Miriam added to finish the bare-minimum overview of the much-too-long story.

"And you can't find it," her mother said, putting the pieces together.

"Yeah." Miriam nodded and then shoved a large spoonful of chili in her mouth, using it as an opportunity to gather her thoughts.

She chewed the copious amount of beans her mom had put in the chili and listened as Nelson explained what they had done to try to locate their lost items. He gracefully navigated around the part where they'd been actively having sex when their things had decided to go on their own adventure.

Miriam jumped in on occasion with her own commentary as he described the map they'd created, the dim sum restaurant, Alex's apartment, and their trip to Zari's office.

When they finished, her dad nodded. "Well, try a finding spell here. Magic likes to go where it's familiar, and you two are both from this town," her dad explained.

Miriam looked at Nelson, and then they both shrugged in agreement. Miriam pushed her plate away and concentrated for a moment to cast a finding spell as wide as it would go. It certainly captured her parents' house and the rest of the block, and she was pretty sure it might have made it all the way to the high school just down the street and then past her childhood synagogue.

Everyone stopped for a minute, holding their breaths and waiting to see if the spell would yield anything. After a few seconds of silence, Miriam sighed and let her shoulders drop. Her finding spell had found nothing.

"Have you told your coven yet?" her mom asked. "They can help you with that map, with your chaos magic. It's no wonder you haven't had any luck scrying." Her mom paused and then added, "Our coven once had to pull our house out of a cloud. It was quite the event, but we had them to help us, so we got it done together. That's what you need now."

"Not yet," Miriam confessed. "They're so busy. They all have kids or are about to have kids, and they don't have time for this. You could help me, though." Miriam looked from her mom to her dad with a plea in her eyes. Surely they would help.

"Sweetie," her mom started, "we'd love to help you, but my magic will do nothing but create more chaos."

"And," her dad continued, "it's important witches have a community. Our magic relies on the help of others."

Miriam turned to where Nelson was avoiding her gaze. "How about your coven?" she asked.

"My coven doesn't know anything about chaos magic," Nelson deflected.

Miriam narrowed her eyes at him. There was something he wasn't explaining, but getting that information out of him in her parents' kitchen probably wasn't the best idea. If they didn't find their stuff soon, Miriam would have to figure out why Nelson was avoiding his coven. It couldn't be for anything good.

"So that's your best advice? Take the map to my coven and see what they have to say about it?" Miriam asked, stirring her spoon through her bowl of tomato soup again.

"That's it," her dad confirmed.

"And I thought you were going to help," Miriam grumbled in mock anger. Being here with Nelson and his judgment-free demeanor, watching him eat a bizarre assortment of soups with nothing but compliments, was . . . nice. She never thought that someone could appreciate this chaos, especially Nelson, who seemed so intent on counteracting her chaos at every step.

"We *are* helping," her mom argued. "We made you soup, and we gave you advice."

"Sure," Miriam muttered.

"And we have ice cream in the freezer," her dad said. "Which, I think, is very helpful."

"I love ice cream," Nelson said, and Miriam didn't even have to question if it was sincere. If there was anything she'd learned about this man during the past couple of weeks, it was clear that he did not mess around when it came to ice cream.

"Oh, I just realized, the ice cream is in the freezer in the garage," Miriam's mom said. "I could sure use some help." Her mom looked pointedly around the table, clearly attempting to motion to Miriam that she wanted to get her alone. If the act was meant to be subtle, she'd failed.

Miriam rolled her eyes, and Nelson and her dad stayed quiet, taking the obvious hint. With a sigh, Miriam stood up and followed her mom out to the garage. Her dad's car usually lived in the driveway because her mom used the space for her projects. They navigated around cans of paint and wallpaper swatches until they reached the freezer, which was right next to her mom's workbench.

"What?" Miriam asked, leaning against the workbench and glaring at her mom.

"I like Nelson," her mom said innocently as she rooted around the deep freezer.

"Mom . . ." Miriam huffed. "It's not like that."

"He's better than those finance boys you usually date," her mom continued, despite her protests.

"I never bring them home," Miriam reminded her.

"Exactly my point." Her mom raised her eyebrows, her frizzy hair moving with her forehead. "If you can't bring him home, then he's probably not a good fit."

Miriam sighed. "Is that what you wanted to talk to me about? Because Nelson and I are just on this dumb quest thing. That's all."

Her mom gave a little chuckle from her position over the deep freezer. "You think I don't have a good idea what you two were doing when your things ran away together?"

"MOM!" Miriam's eyes went wide.

Her mom pulled out a tub of ice cream and set it on the top of the deep freezer. She stepped in towards Miriam and pushed a strand of hair away from her face. "I'm worried about your magic," she admitted.

"My magic's fine," Miriam grumbled. She already knew where this conversation was going, and she was completely uninterested.

"You need to stop resisting the chaos. That makes it harder to control," her mom lectured.

"Mom, that's not an option." Miriam could feel her blood starting to boil at the idea. "I have my job, my apartment, my LIFE. Being a chaos witch is not conducive to any of those things."

"But it *is*, Miriam, because you are a chaos witch and you do those things. It doesn't have to be at the cost of hiding who you are."

Miriam shook her head. "Maybe this is who I want to be."

"But not who you are."

Miriam surveyed the garage with its mismatched holiday decorations, half-finished crafts, and spare cans of paint. This wasn't her future. She could overcome her chaos magic, push it down. Her broom going missing had just been because of one little blip in her control.

"It's not a curse, honey," her mom said. "And it's not something to be ashamed of. It's magic, after all. Your legacy, that you got from me and from my mother before that."

Miriam nodded but then slid past her mom and picked up the carton of ice cream. "We should get this inside before it melts."

Her mom gave her a firm squeeze on the shoulder and then pulled her in for a tight hug. "It's okay to be you."

Miriam pushed her face into her mom's shoulder. It was bonier, thinner than she remembered. And yet, this was still her mom, just as she'd always been.

"I am me," Miriam reassured and then pulled away and headed back into the house.

Chapter Fifteen

"W HAT DO YOU WANT to do for dinner?" Nelson asked hours later, as their train pulled into Penn Station. They'd finally left her parents' house after having ice cream, though Miriam couldn't help but feel the whole trip had been a waste of time.

"What?" Miriam asked, lifting her eyebrows at Nelson. Since when had they discussed eating dinner together? She still had work to do for her day job. Her laptop was at home, waiting for her to review the models the analysts had put together.

"I could cook. I do this great shakshuka. The key is to add chickpeas," Nelson explained as they made their way up from the platform to the station. "We could stop at the grocery store. I figured you'd want to go back to your place to feed Larry."

"Huh?" Miriam was still confused. She'd learned to tolerate Nelson the last couple of weeks, and she'd even accepted that he had uses beyond just being a nuisance. He knew his way around her body, and his mouth and hands did an outstanding job. He was more affable than she'd assumed. But they were still just . . . whatever they were, and it didn't involve talking about dinner. Or why he needed to go back to her apartment with her to feed her cat.

"We need to strategize how to get our things back. I know your parents said we should talk to your coven, but first, we need to prepare for that conversation. You promised we would spend all weekend on this," he continued, his argument firm as he seemed to realize why Miriam was confused.

"Nelson," Miriam started, "my coven meets tomorrow. We can talk to them then. We don't need—"

"Caesar salad, but a really good one, with fresh tomatoes and homemade croutons."

"Caesar salad?" Miriam asked.

"Your order from sweetgreen," Nelson explained.

"Oh . . ." Miriam paused as her heart fluttered a little. Had Nelson actually remembered her sweetgreen order from earlier in the week? That request had been sort of bitchy on Miriam's part, and yet he'd remembered it. Her wish from the jinn—the man taking care of her, that feeling of being both wanted and needed—bloomed in her chest. But with a start, she shoved it down. Romance was a myth perpetuated by the patriarchy to keep women in terrible relationships. Miriam was fine on her own. She had Larry, after all.

"Or we could get takeout if you prefer," Nelson said, continuing to entice her with the prospect of dinner. "There's this Georgian place I know that does these really amazing cheese boats."

Miriam sighed. "You're not going to give up on this, are you?" she asked.

"I'm tired of taking the train everywhere. I was late to work every day this week." He gave a crooked smile and then plucked his glasses off his nose and rubbed them with the hem of his shirt. "Also, I missed an entire meeting because I couldn't get there before it finished, let alone started. Tell me, sincerely, that you actually love having to take cabs and the train everywhere."

Miriam glared at him, but he was right. She needed her broom back. What was the point of being a witch if the best part of magic was just missing? And it was starting to get warmer out, which meant she could take a ride on her broom out to the Hamptons or Montauk. The Mers kept to themselves mostly, but she loved watching their No Moon festivals from the sky. The way the ocean would light up and the Mers would dance and swim and just disconnect from the world. None of it was visible to non-magics. It was just one of those special magical moments that she loved to take advantage of.

She *needed* to find her broom.

"Fine," Miriam grumbled, and she followed as Nelson led them to a nearby grocery store.

***

Nelson was competent in the kitchen, Miriam noted, as he expertly chopped an onion. She'd never really encountered that in a man before. All the men she'd dated were experts in domestic incompetence. They sent their laundry out, they refused to buy anything useful at the grocery store, and they didn't know how to dust. Not that Miriam did any of these things anymore, but the men she'd dated never seemed to have mastered these skills at all. She'd once dated a guy right after college whose mom had ordered his groceries for him and coordinated the laundry and the cleaners. Nelson, on the other hand, had started dinner prep in short order.

Miriam was sitting on a stool at her kitchen island, watching as Nelson pulled down rarely used pans and gave them a quick rinse and wipe down before he started to cook.

"So, the covens," Miriam started, knowing they needed to broach the subject.

Nelson stirred the contents of a pot and then placed a lid on top. He turned around to face Miriam.

"We should start with yours," Nelson replied quickly, as though not giving Miriam a chance to suggest the same about his.

"My coven is busy," Miriam said.

"What does that mean? Is there a big magic or . . . ?"

"They're all having babies," Miriam retorted, her expression sour. There was more to it, really, but she was uninterested in explaining how every other person in her coven had all entered a life phase that Miriam was sure was out of reach for herself.

"They're all actively in labor, right now?" Nelson asked with raised eyebrows.

Miriam huffed a laugh. "No, not exactly. How about your coven?" she deflected.

"My coven isn't used to dealing with your chaos magic," Nelson volleyed, repeating what he'd told Miriam's parents.

"And I think we have reasonably concluded that it's your magic that likes to take adventures." Nelson turned back around and opened the pot on the stove, then stirred the contents a few times. There was a certain finality in his actions, and his insistence that they meet with Miriam's coven first suggested to her—again—that there was more going on.

"Fine, we'll go to my coven meeting tomorrow," Miriam decided impatiently, uninterested in having a standoff with Nelson over their covens. She then pressed her hand into the snow globe that was still sitting on her counter, and a dozen little pinpricks lit up the map. A few of them were new locations, and none of them looked immediately promising. "I'll let them know I'm bringing you."

"We should bring the map as well," Nelson replied as he rummaged through Miriam's cabinets and found a few bowls. He seemed satisfied with the end results of the meal he'd prepared. He portioned the food out and placed a bowl in front of Miriam.

She just stared at him for a moment, her mind wandering again. Was this what it would be like to be with someone like Nelson? What it would be like for someone to make you dinner and go on adventures with you? She didn't *want* to like Nelson, that felt so against her programming, and yet they hadn't argued all day, not really. It had been so easy. Miriam wasn't used to easy.

"What?" Nelson asked, catching her looking at him.

"I was . . ." Miriam trailed off, knowing she couldn't tell him the truth. She smiled and then lied. "I was thinking about that thing you did last night. With your tongue." It was way easier to talk about sex than to talk about her brewing feelings.

Or that there was a part of her—one she didn't particularly like at the moment—that really wanted more of Nelson and not just his tongue.

His eyes lit up behind his glasses. "You're thinking about me?" he asked, setting his hands on the island separating them.

Miriam dug a spoon into the bowl of tomato sauce and poached eggs. "Just last night," she clarified.

"The truce?" Nelson asked. "Are we still in a truce?"

"I'm not sure," Miriam answered, refusing to look up at him. She was feeling uncomfortable with the entire thing and wasn't sure what all these emotions were. Nelson was supposed to be her long-time enemy, her competitor, and yet here she was, going weak in the knees over dinner. Amused by his masculine vulnerability. *Shit*, she needed to figure out why she kept going all goopy at the idea of Nelson taking care of her . . . and letting her take care of him.

Nelson disregarded his bowl and spoon and leaned across the counter, resting his elbows in front of his body. Miriam allowed herself to stare, admiring the way his arms flexed under his shirt.

"I . . ." Nelson started.

Miriam braced, because she had a feeling she knew what he was going to say. That he liked *her*. Could she stomach that—him acknowledging that this was more than a moment of weakness, a moment of human need? Could she admit she might be starting to feel the same way?

Before he could finish, Miriam's phone buzzed loudly on the counter, breaking the spell. She tore her eyes away from him and glanced down. It was *Charlie*.

With a tight smile at Nelson, she picked up the phone and headed to her bedroom to close the door. As much as the deal was shrouded in code names, she had literally just slept with the enemy *twice*, and she was sure they were just a few nice words away from doing it again. He didn't need to overhear whatever Charlie wanted to talk about.

"Hey, Charlie. I'm sorry, I just got home from my parents' house," Miriam said as she sat on her bed. "I was just about to log on."

"Huh . . . oh, sure," he said, brushing her off. ". . . Look, I wanted to talk strategy. We have a client meeting in a couple of weeks. And, as you know, there's a nonprofit that's bidding for the property. They have the backing of city council, and we really need to bring our A game. So I think we should talk through the strategy on how we can secure this for our clients. We need to figure out how we can get the zoning settled on the property."

"Yeah, I have some ideas," Miriam replied, rustling through her bag to get her computer. "Can you . . . Do you mind giving me a minute?" Miriam asked.

She put the phone on mute and peeked out of her bedroom. Nelson had finished eating and was busy cleaning up the kitchen. He looked up. "I have to take this call and get some work done tonight," she explained, holding up her phone. "Can we meet here tomorrow, before my coven meeting?"

Nelson gave her a nod and a thumbs-up, then turned back to the sink and continued to wash the dishes so she could get back to her call.

Miriam went back into her bedroom and closed the door. She'd just started to really run down the details with Charlie when she heard her apartment door open and close a few minutes later. She risked looking out her bedroom door, only to find her kitchen clean and empty, except for a single, fresh cup of coffee that had been placed on her counter and Larry, contently eating a bowl of wet food.

"Now, we really want to make sure this nonprofit doesn't think they have a chance at these buildings," Charlie said from the other end of the line. "The last thing we want is for the firm to appear heartless. This deal is going to provide a ton of luxury housing, and the price per unit makes this a really attractive deal."

Miriam nodded even though Charlie couldn't see it. She understood the strategy and approach from meetings with lawyers earlier in the week.

"It shouldn't be hard to get local officials on board," she said. "There's already some hesitation around the nonprofit housing from the community. The condos would raise property values, while the nonprofit housing would do the opposite." Miriam winced as she explained her logic. "We have a couple of meetings with contractors next week, and I think being able to show the community our plans ahead of the deal is going to be huge."

"Good idea," Charlie encouraged. "We missed you at the office today, but it sounds like you've been keeping up with the details and things."

"Thanks," Miriam replied. "I'll get you all the information this weekend so we can discuss on Monday." Miriam took a seat at her counter and sipped her coffee. It was perfect, with just a touch of almond milk. Just how she liked it.

"Alright, that'll work," Charlie agreed. "We'll catch up on Monday. Have a good weekend."

"Yeah, you too," Miriam replied, and then hung up the phone and placed it face down on her counter.

With a long sigh, she lowered her head into her hands. She was good at this work. She'd put in the hours, too—surpassing all the rich kids, the sort of kids with country-club connections and houses in the Hamptons. While they'd *networked* with their parents' rich friends, Miriam had worked around the clock to make connections, learn, build her skill set and knowledge so she could do her job.

And she *liked* her job. Sure, there were days it still felt like work, and sometimes her exhaustion won out over her joy. That was all true. But she enjoyed solving puzzles in spreadsheets and taking clients out and making deals. Her job was rewarding and challenging, and there was a certain excitement to it all.

Now, though, it felt disgusting, tainted. Miriam rubbed her temples. She'd always been this sort of harbinger of capitalism, the person who ushered in deals and helped facilitate them. But she'd never felt supremely evil. She'd always just been one cog in a machine. Alchemy Partners advised and facilitated, but it had always been up to someone else—to the companies buying and selling—to make the hard decisions. She was little more than an intermediary. That hadn't changed, even with this deal. She wasn't a partner yet, and it was the client funding this, not the bank.

Even more so, it was hard not to think of Alex—a magic, like her. A man who seemed like a good guy, who had paid for whatever crimes he'd committed, who was still stuck in a system intent on punishing him for his entire life. And it was even harder not to think of Talia, who was trying to get her life under her control and just needed another chance.

She thought of sweet Nelson, who had cleaned up her kitchen and had made her coffee, all while she was working on a deal that was going to make his life and the lives of his residents so much harder. Nelson, whom, if she let her guard down long enough, she could see herself really liking. Maybe even more than liking. Maybe something else entirely.

Miriam placed her coffee cup in the sink and then popped open the cork on the half-empty bottle of red sitting on her counter. She poured the wine into a large wineglass and then sat down at her island and opened her computer. What choice did she have, really? Miriam needed this job, and the firm needed her to do it well.

This was real life and the real world, and in real life and the real world, Miriam was an investment banker. She was a Witch of Wall Street. This was how business worked; this was always how business had worked. She did what she was told; it was someone else's responsibility, anyway.

Chapter Sixteen

"H EY, WHAT'S THAT?" NELSON asked as he arrived just outside Miriam's apartment the next evening. Miriam was carrying an oversized pastel gift bag with a friendly elephant cutout decorating the one side. In addition, she was also juggling a cardboard tube containing their newly enchanted map.

Both items made for an unwieldy load she was attempting to carry alone. The bag slipped from her hand, and Nelson grabbed it just before it hit the ground. Their fingers touched barely for a second, and Miriam felt a warm squeeze in her chest.

"Thanks," she replied, and a smile formed on her lips. She looked up at Nelson. He was watching her, giving his own toothy, sincere grin.

It was the smallest of gestures, him carrying her bag for her, but Miriam wondered what it would be like to share the burden all the time.

She also wondered what would have happened last night if Charlie hadn't called. They'd decided that Friday night was a sort of truce—the second time they'd done what was supposed to be a onetime thing. But Miriam had a feeling they might not be sticking to that truce.

She pushed away those thoughts as they started down the street. Obviously, their time with the jinn was still getting to her, and she was still attempting to reset herself after whatever had been dislodged. That, and the fact that they were heading to her coven meeting right now was messing with her head. It felt weird going with someone. She'd been the only single person in her coven for years now.

"So, I forgot until this morning, but this is also a combined baby-shower-slash-coven-meeting. Derek and Craig are adopting a baby, who's supposed to arrive in a couple of weeks," Miriam explained, still attempting to push down whatever feelings were churning in her stomach, threatening to sink her even lower. It didn't help that she was tired; she'd spent the morning finishing the last of what Charlie needed on the model and then the entire afternoon on 9th Street, combing through aesthetically pleasing but unsubstantial boutiques in East Village.

"You told them I was coming, right?" Nelson questioned, not unfairly so. Magics who were not members of the coven couldn't just arrive at a coven meeting unannounced. These were sacred spaces, and other magics were not automatically welcome. When others had introduced their partners, they'd done it slowly, a few members at a time, and then through more casual meetups before inviting the new magics to an actual coven meeting.

"I put it in the group text," Miriam mumbled, "and they're excited." She huffed in annoyance, remembering the cacophony of digital balloons and streamers that had flown across her phone screen when she'd asked if she could bring a guy to their meeting.

"They think . . ." Nelson trailed off and then nodded in understanding. "Sorry."

Miriam shrugged. "It makes sense that they would assume. Come on. We should hurry, so we're not late."

Derek and Craig lived only a few blocks from Miriam in their own Financial District high rise. It was a short enough walk that Miriam rarely felt the need to take her broom, even when she had it.

She felt a little guilty at having to bring magical business to this coven meeting. It was meant to be more of a celebration for Craig and Derek. The mother who was giving their child up for adoption was due in just a few weeks, and today was supposed to be about helping them prepare. But Miriam had been so busy and off-kilter the last week that she'd ignored most of the baby shower planning in the group chat.

"So, your coven's all Wall Street types?" Nelson asked as they approached the high rise.

"We are the Witches of Wall Street," Miriam declared dryly as the doorman, who recognized Miriam and expected her arrival, waved them through. "How about your coven? Are they all nonprofit do-gooders like you?"

"Something like that," Nelson replied, rubbing the back of his neck nervously. It was yet another reminder that there was something going on with his coven. It wasn't exactly her business to push, though. What was Nelson to her, anyway?

They took the elevator up a few floors and then hung a right down the hall. Even if Miriam hadn't known which apartment was Craig and Derek's, it was immediately obvious. Someone had decorated the apartment door in pastel baby décor, with streamers and paper cutouts of cherubic babies taped to the door. Miriam guessed it was likely Franklin. He was an advertising executive and by far the most creative in the group. He almost always took on these sorts of projects.

Unsurprisingly, Hannah threw open the door before they could knock, her clairvoyance at work. She was holding a full champagne flute.

"Miriam," she grinned at Nelson when she said this. "This is unexpected, but so exciting. We should have all expected you to be the type to just bring a new guy to the coven with little notice. It's chaotic."

Nelson gave a knowing smile, and Miriam rolled her eyes and then shook her head.

"It's not like that," she explained. "We have a big magic request. This is Nelson, a high school friend."

Hannah narrowed her eyes skeptically but then opened the door wider, welcoming them from the hallway into the apartment proper. The decorations from the door extended into the apartment, with more streamers and cardboard cutouts scattered throughout.

There was a pile of gifts off to one side of the living room, and the kitchen table had been covered with snacks and baked goods. It was more than they had at their usual coven meetings, and the atmosphere felt charged and exciting.

Yet the dread Miriam had started to feel earlier began to grow. Surely she didn't have a place here. She was an intruder, not part of the group. They were all the Witches of Wall Street, but her friends, her fellow magics, might as well be living on another planet with how closely their lives mirrored Miriam's. They were all starting families, and Miriam was carrying an enchanted map around to find her missing broomstick. They were all sitting here talking about affording parking if they bought a sensible sedan to drive their kids around, and she was living like a reckless twenty-something.

She took a deep breath and made her way through the apartment, greeting her coven with a series of hugs and smiles. Then, she introduced Nelson to the group. There were supportive handshakes, warm greetings, and a few sly looks at Nelson's butt from the less-discreet members of her coven. She let it go. Calling it out would have been more disruptive.

After all the fanfare was finished, Craig got everyone's attention. "Alright," he said, calling for the meeting to start. It was his and Derek's apartment, which meant it was their meeting to lead. "Any news?" he asked and gave a quick glance around the room. It was clear that he wanted this to be more of a formality than anything so that they could move on to the party. "And any big magic requests?"

Hannah and then the rest of the room looked to where Miriam and Nelson were sitting on the outskirts of the group.

Miriam raised her hand. "I have a request," she said. "My broom went missing."

"And my enchanted taxi medallion," Nelson added quickly.

"Together?" Derek asked with a perceptive press of his lips. He was certainly attempting to hide a giggle.

"Yes," Miriam admitted, and with a flush of embarrassment, she realized she was going to have to tell them exactly what she and Nelson were doing when their broom and medallion ran away together.

Taking turns speaking, Miriam and Nelson recounted their adventures over the last couple of weeks, including a confession that they'd been the ones responsible for releasing the Taotie in Chinatown. When they finally finished their story, Miriam could feel the eyes of her coven watching her, giving her the same look of pity she'd been used to her entire life.

The chaos witch who always messed up. That was her.

"Shit," Heather swore after the room became silent.

Craig glared at them. "You were the ones who let out the Taotie?! That's an ancient Chinese magic. It came over with my cousin's grandparents. It wasn't bothering anyone until you two yahoos stumbled in without a plan," he chastised.

"Sorry," Miriam mumbled.

"You should be. His parents pay good rent to keep it happy in that restaurant," Craig continued, piling on a little more guilt.

"Are you still sleeping together?" Franklin blurted out, redirecting the conversation. Heather playfully nudged him in the ribs at the comment, as if telling him he shouldn't have asked. Unsurprisingly, Franklin was one of the coven members who'd been checking out Nelson's butt.

Nelson and Miriam shared a look, and then Miriam attempted to explain. "It was just that one time and then one other . . . but we're done now." She avoided Nelson's gaze. They had agreed they were done, and this declaration gave it a finality.

"So the answer is yes," Isabelle decided.

Miriam closed her eyes and took a deep breath. She could feel her anger increasing, her chaos magic bubbling.

"It's not important," Nelson interrupted, which Miriam thought was an excellent answer and one she was extremely thankful for. It really *wasn't* important, and they were done sleeping together, anyway. The last time had been the last time.

"You brought the map?" Hannah asked.

Miriam nodded and then pulled out the cardboard paper tube.

Hannah took it from her, and Maddy rearranged the kitchen table so that there was room to spread it out. Dodging baby presents, Hannah rolled the map out across the table as the coven gathered around.

Derek was the first to examine the map. He cocked his head and then said, "You two made this, all by yourselves?"

"We didn't want to get the covens involved," Miriam explained. "Everyone is busy, and we figured we could just make the map?"

Hannah gave Miriam a smile and then squeezed her arm. "I could have helped," Hannah reminded her. "My magic works well with this sort of thing."

"That's why you have a coven," Maddy added.

Miriam felt guilt pool in her belly. While they'd ultimately been successful with the map, it had been at an extreme magical cost.

"Let's take a look at this." Derek stepped up and placed a hand on the map. He closed his eyes, and it glowed, just like it had the night they'd created it. The streets lit up little by little as Derek's magic worked through the map, and he studied it, examining the magic that Miriam and Nelson had bound to it.

"What happens when you scry with this?" Isabelle asked as Derek continued to examine the map.

"We've been getting a lot of different magical points in the area," Miriam explained. "So, we've been checking them off our list, but at this point, it'll take us months, maybe years, to find our stuff."

Derek took his hand off the map and nodded. "That's because the map just chaotically picks a couple of magical hotspots in the city. Honestly, it's a miracle it even works."

"Ugh," Miriam moaned, throwing her head back. "So, my magic has just muddied this whole thing up."

"It's still magic," Heather added encouragingly, "which means it's a good foundation for something usable. There are enough of us here that we should be able to put this together tonight. I vote Hannah take the lead on designing the magic."

Miriam and Nelson shared a look. They'd never discussed the architecture behind the map. Miriam knew that in theory, all magic, especially big magic, needed stability, and a plan, but that had never really worked for her. In her non-magical life, she worked very hard to stay organized, and it felt like a constant uphill battle. In her magical life, it was nearly impossible. She had a feeling that Nelson just worked a miracle and never worried about the specifics. People like Hannah, who were both organized and the type who had a lot of foresight, *literally*, were good at thinking about magical designs.

"I can do that," Hannah agreed, taking over for Derek. She placed her hand on the map, and it lit up once again. "I need magical backup from Maddy and creative from Franklin," Hannah instructed, and Maddy and Franklin each placed a hand on the map. "Heather for organizing, and Isabelle for power." They too placed their hands on the map. "Nelson and Miriam to guide, because this was your map to start with."

Miriam placed her hand on the map, and Nelson, reaching over her shoulder from behind, placed his hand on the map as well. He moved in to give everyone enough room. They were close. Her body was pressed into his. It was hard to focus on the magic with his firm chest flat against her back. She could feel the contours of his thighs against her, too, and his arm brushing hers. It was hard to focus. She was wearing jeans, and yet heat still came through.

"Miriam and Nelson, we'll need you to guide us," Hannah repeated.

"Right," Miriam said.

Nelson nudged her shoulder, as if asking for permission, and she nodded quickly. Then, he placed his hand on top of hers. She jumped a little at the spark that passed between them when they connected, but her hand was pressed under Nelson's and stayed firmly on top of the map.

From there, there were few words. Miriam could feel Hannah's sure magic following Miriam and Nelson as they retraced the same streets and paths. Behind Hannah was the rest of their coven, following Hannah's magic. Being in front of everyone, Miriam couldn't see or feel what they were working. Instead, it was just her and Nelson, leading the way through these paper streets of New York. It was almost as if they were strolling hand in hand through Manhattan. Miriam wanted to hate that idea of those disgustingly happy couples who did that each spring. Yet, it felt too good, too desirable to dislike.

With the entire coven working together, it didn't take long for the map to glow a brilliant yellow and then for the magic to start to shift and change. The yellow turned to blue, then green, then pink, and then the colors swirled together. First into a rainbow and then into pure white light. There was a flash, and then the map stopped glowing.

"It should be all set," Hannah explained, picking up her hand first.

"Should we test it?" Nelson asked. "Do you have anything to scry with?"

Craig nodded and then brought out a set of crystals. The scrying object was less important than the map, but Miriam still preferred the old snow globe she typically used. Craig handed Miriam a crystal, and Miriam gently placed it in between two fingers.

This time, the crystal only refracted on one spot on the map, a spot just a few blocks away from the dim sum place they'd started their journey at.

"That's a good sign." Maddy studied the spot. "Hopefully that means we matched your magic and that your things are motivation enough to send you to exactly where they are."

"Enzo's Custom Leather Goods," Henry read off his phone, having already located the address online.

"We don't have a connection, though," Nelson replied. "We're supposed to find places our magic has a connection to."

Miriam grimaced. "My magic doesn't like rules, so if we assigned a pattern to something . . ." She trailed off.

"Then that means we try this shop," Nelson said with a shrug. "It's close, anyway. We could go after work tomorrow."

"They aren't open again until Tuesday," Henry chimed in.

"Okay, Tuesday after work," Miriam decided. It would mean leaving the office earlier than she wanted, but if all went well, she could work from home after they got their stuff back. Surely the map had been rebuilt well enough that their stuff had to be there. It should be nothing more than a quick trip, and she and Nelson would be all set.

"Ah, well, they close at five," Henry added. "They're open Tuesday to Friday from nine to five."

"How do any stores make money with those hours?" Craig asked.

Derek shrugged and said, "If you can afford this sort of thing, you probably don't care about being in the office during normal working hours."

Miriam took out her phone and scrolled through her calendar. Tuesday was rough in terms of meetings, but she could block out Wednesday afternoon. It would mean more time out of the office, though, and Charlie was already upset about how much she'd been absent. But it was getting critical now. Their things had been gone for much too long, and it was never a good idea to let magic roam around free. Especially chaos magic. Besides, she and Nelson had a responsibility to find their things and keep them under control.

"I can do Wednesday after lunch," Miriam offered before Nelson could suggest they head to the shop first thing on Tuesday morning.

Nelson shook his head. "I have a donor lunch on Wednesday. How about Thursday morning?"

Miriam scrolled her calendar. "I can block out nine to eleven," she agreed, already tapping away on her phone. The coven stood by and watched them schedule out the next phase of their magical adventure with a scary amount of coordinated professionalism for something as whimsical as magic, and when they got everything all settled, Miriam looked up at them with a smile.

"Thank you, everyone," she said.

"Are you two going to need backup?" Hannah asked, glancing nervously from Miriam to Nelson and back.

"We'll be fine," Miriam assured. "Now that we've straightened out the issue with the map, we'll be okay."

There were more than a few skeptical looks, but Miriam brushed them off. "Alright, enough of me. We have a baby shower." Miriam lifted her hands to direct everyone's attention back to Derek and Craig. It was their big day, after all.

She settled back on the sofa as the party started around them, Nelson taking the spot next to her.

"Should I go?" Nelson whispered into her ear after a moment. His mouth was close enough that she could feel his breath on her neck, and she was nearly intoxicated for a split second.

Movement of everyone else around her as they transitioned away from magic and towards the baby shower portion of their get together helped her to reset herself, and she shook her head. "Only if you want to, but we should strategize after, so it makes sense for you to stay, and we can go back to my place after."

"That's a good idea," Nelson agreed, and although Miriam was sure there was something else to his answer, she didn't question him. It was just nice to have someone at her side.

The couch was crowded with the entire coven jammed into Craig and Derek's small living room. Nelson was sitting close, his leg pressed into hers. They weren't together, not in that way, but she didn't mind his closeness. There was something nice about not being there alone.

For the first time in a long while, Miriam didn't feel like she was fading into the background of someone else's story while she was at a coven meeting.

No, for the first time in a long while, she felt like she was part of the group again.

Chapter Seventeen

I T WAS NELSON WHO got a work call on the way back to Miriam's place Sunday night. Rather than be with her to strategize, he had to head to work and quickly find a replacement boiler that Housing Magic could afford. The boiler had blown at one of the nonprofit's properties, and although it was getting warmer outside, it still wasn't warm enough for the residents to go without heat for a night.

Monday morning, Miriam plunged back into her normal routine. Meetings, spreadsheets, meetings, spreadsheets. She got home a little before 10:00 p.m., greeted first by Bruce and his warm smile and then by Larry and his unending demands for wet food.

Then she woke up and did it all again on Tuesday. Back to her normal routine, away from her coven and, more importantly, away from dedicating energy to anything beyond completing her work and meeting her own basic needs. That routine allowed Miriam to mostly put Nelson and the wishes the jinn had shown her aside. Sure, having a partner sounded like good fun sometimes, but having to only worry about herself was easiest with her lifestyle.

Sure, the men in her office who were married to women who didn't work had it the easiest. They never had to think about things like groceries or like making sure their apartments were clean, even if that just meant coordinating with the cleaners. These things were taken care of, their wives providing full-time domestic labor while their husbands played businessmen in a skyscraper.

For Miriam, on the other hand, a relationship would just mean having to care about another person's laundry, having to shop for another person's groceries. More personal schedules to coordinate. More time that wouldn't be her own.

Or at least, that was what she'd always assumed.

And yet, when Miriam's mind drifted back to Nelson, she remembered his willingness to make her dinner and coffee, even when sex was off the table. It was hard for her not to wonder if it was possible for her to have a partner who wouldn't expect for her to be the only domestic one.

As soon as she thought about it, however, Miriam internally scolded herself. She wasn't weak; she didn't need another person. She was enough, and it was easier and safer to just be on her own. Even if someone like Nelson was willing to take her to bed and make sure she was satisfied and satisfied again, eventually, he would tire of her chaos. Or worse, he wouldn't, but her firm's actions would drive him away. There was still *that* aspect to consider.

On Thursday morning, Miriam marked a doctor's appointment on her calendar, taking a second half-day in as many weeks. And at nine, she skipped out of the office, opting for a cab rather than the subway to get her the few miles up to Little

Italy. She had agreed to meet Nelson at a cafe a couple of blocks away from Enzo's Custom Leather Goods. It made more sense to approach the shop together because they had no idea what was magical about it. After Craig had scolded them for bursting into the Taotie's restaurant, it made sense for them to be more intentional.

Nelson was sitting at a table, reading a copy of the *New York Times*, when Miriam approached. There were two cups on the table. "Almond milk latte?" he asked, holding a cup up for Miriam.

"Thanks," she said, and she took the cup with a soft smile. It wasn't *exactly* her order, but it was close enough, and it was pretty apparent that Nelson had been paying attention to her preferences ever since they'd started on their little adventure. He was trying.

Why was he trying?

Miriam was starting to suspect that they weren't at all on the same page about their relationship preferences. Although she hadn't exactly been setting clear boundaries, and Nelson seemed happy to oblige her lapses in judgment. She had to wonder if there was a reason it was so easy for him, how they'd fallen into this rhythm so seamlessly.

"You ready?" he asked, standing up from the table.

"Yeah, let's get this over with. I have a meeting this afternoon," Miriam said, her tone curt. She needed to tamp down whatever these emotions were that kept creeping up from her gut.

They walked two blocks to a little out-of-the-way alley, stopping right in front of Enzo's Custom Leather Goods. The shop was small and looked like something straight out of a storybook. The name of the store was stenciled on an antique glass window, and the window displays were expertly styled, with expensive-looking bags and boots propped up on sturdy dark wooden blocks. The light coming out of the shop was a warm buttery yellow.

Miriam pulled open the door and motioned for Nelson to go first. Then she followed him into the store. The inside décor and style seemed to match the outside. Dark hardwood floors extended up to thick, dark wood display cases. Around the room were deep-red satin chairs and couches. The entire aesthetic was the sort of quiet luxury that only the exorbitantly wealthy could afford. It was likely even more expensive than it looked, and it already looked extremely expensive.

The shop was empty, but there was a bell at the register. Neither Nelson nor Miriam immediately bothered with it.

Instead, they looked around the shop. Each item was in its own little display box, neatly organized on the dark wood shelving. Most items were sitting atop plush satin cushions that matched the chairs. The entire shop smelled like fresh, supple leather. It was fresher and sharper than the old leather smell that Miriam had gotten used to being around Nelson.

Miriam picked up a sleek-looking leather flap over. The leather was not the smooth, soft leather she was used to. Instead, it was rough and perhaps spiky, like it had come from something more exotic than a cow. Maybe something reptilian.

"Miriam?" Nelson hissed as Miriam opened the bag and looked inside. "We're not supposed to be shopping."

Miriam rolled her eyes. "I'm looking for our things," she replied as she closed the bag up. She couldn't help but run her hand over the unique leather. The bumps were just a smidge duller than thorns, and it was such a fascinating texture.

She was just about to put the bag on its shelf again and cast a finding spell when a female voice said from behind her, "That's Tatzelwurm leather. Very rare, and some very interesting properties."

Miriam jumped at the sudden voice and hurried to place the bag back on its cushion. She pulled her hand back sharply as her finger caught on one of the scales, puncturing her skin. A small dot of blood began to seep out, and she instinctively brought her finger to her mouth and sucked on it.

Miriam turned around just as Nelson greeted the woman.

"Good morning," he said with a small wave, and the woman nodded in acknowledgement.

She was an attractive woman, dressed head to toe in leather. Her sleek black leather pants and leather vest showed off her slender figure and contrasted with her lustrous silver-gray bob. At just past middle age, the wrinkles around her eyes made her even more attractive than she'd likely ever looked in her youth. She was a woman who had definitely aged extremely well.

"Welcome. I'm Sofia," she said with a smile that felt forced, and Miriam began to feel uncomfortable, as though maybe they were not supposed to be in this shop at all. "I would be happy to help you find what you're looking for. We have a great custom selection."

Miriam and Nelson looked at each other. They hadn't planned this far in advance. Should they be honest about their missing items? They had, after all, been holding that information fairly close. It wouldn't do for all the magics in the entire New York metro area to get wind of a broom and a medallion wandering the streets together. There were plenty of sinister things that ill-intended magics could do with other witches' magical items. When Miriam was a kid, she remembered a time that a malicious sorcerer had gotten a hold of an antique charmed dinnerware set. The sorcerer then found that with just a little enchantment, they could convince people eating off the dinnerware set to do things they'd never normally consent to. Like happily give up their entire life savings. She distinctly remembered that the scam had cost more than a few folks their retirement.

They certainly wanted to avoid having their items discovered and then used for any of that sort of riffraff, and she was pretty sure Nelson understood that, even if they hadn't specifically talked about it.

Miriam gave him a small nod, hoping he'd speak for them, and then she frowned inwardly as she rubbed the finger she'd pricked on the bag. It still hurt. It was like getting a paper cut; it was the smallest of wounds, and yet it hurt like hell.

Nelson acknowledged Miriam's nod with a half smile and turned to Sofia. "I'm Nelson, and this is Miriam," he said, introducing them both. Miriam gave a pinched-lip smile.

Sofia looked them up and down, as if assessing why they might be in her store. "We have more . . . personal items in the back room," she said with a sly smile, obviously insinuating that Nelson and Miriam were at the leather shop for something other than . . . flap over bags.

Miriam's eyes went wide. "We're not . . . together," she explained, but it was starting to feel like a lie she'd repeated too many times. He almost knew her coffee order. They'd slept together twice in the last two weeks. He'd made her dinner. By plenty of accounts, they were in the early stages of a relationship. Yet, she was *sure* they were not in any sort of relationship. They'd agreed to that much.

"Hmmm," Sofia hummed, long and drawn out and exaggerated. "That's surprising."

"But," Miriam recovered, realizing that they actually *did* need to see the back of the shop, "we're interested in what else you might be offering."

There was some secret code Miriam was trying to navigate, but she wasn't entirely sure what it was or where it was going to get them. And she wasn't entirely sure what Sofia was implying was in the other room.

She *hoped* it was their things, but she readied her magic just in case it was something more sinister.

Sofia gave a smile that crinkled around her lips. "I hoped you would say that."

She opened the back door and led them to another room, just out of view. The same rich interior design extended into this back room as well, but instead of the buttery-yellow lighting of the main store, the back room was cast in a much more telling stoplight red. The room itself was still soft and luxurious, but there was a definite change in the tone, suggestive, Miriam realized, of the shift in the intended audience.

As they walked through the room, the first thing Miriam noticed, besides the lighting, was that there was much more clothing available in this back room than in the more public portion of the shop. There were leather garments for all genders spread out on plush, clean dress forms. One was wearing a harness that was wrapped around its chest, and another had been fitted with a pair of leather riding chaps, in the same unique scaly leather from the flap over bag.

Instead of fancy gloves and boots, leather collars and handcuffs sat atop the velvety display cushions.

"This is . . . interesting," Nelson said, bumping into another dress form wearing a sleek black corset. His attempt at being respectful of the shop, even though this sort of thing was not his usual space, was so endearing, and Miriam smiled inwardly.

Oh, the sorts of things they might discover together with some of these . . . pieces.

Her thoughts immediately took off before she could shut them down, and she imagined herself wearing the corset, Nelson fumbling to figure out how to undo the laces. She was trying to be sexy, and all he could do was be sincerely perfect. When he didn't move fast enough, Miriam had him pinned against the bed. Her hands wrapped around his wrists. She straddled him. She could feel his hard length against her thigh . . .

"Miriam . . . Miriam . . ." She heard her name being called, and it pulled her out of the sudden fantasy she'd inexplicably found herself in. She shook her head and looked over at Nelson, who was watching her with concern. "What's going on?" he asked.

Miriam glanced around the room, her eyes landing on Sofia. The older woman seemed to be taking in the scene, a knowing smile on her face.

"Folks tend to get wrapped up in fantasy here," she explained. "It's part of the *magic*." She winked at them. "Though I pause to remind you that consent is, of course, at the forefront of everything we do here."

"We're not here for . . ." Nelson trailed off as an adorable blush spread into his cheeks.

His sudden shyness was both endearing and surprising. He seemed to have plenty of experience and few reservations when they were together. And yet, Miriam felt her heart flutter at seeing how coy he looked. She stared at him, her breath quickening as she thought about what she could do with him in this state, the sort of vulnerabilities she might expose further. She was ready to pounce, right here in this room.

Taking a deep breath, she closed her hands into fists and then opened them again, grounding herself in the moment. She didn't want to sleep with Nelson again, and yet, here she was, having *very* dirty thoughts.

"That's what you think," Sofia replied in response to Nelson's weak beginning to an argument. She picked up a leather whip and cracked it in the air with a flick of her wrist. "But so many of my customers are able to unlock their inner desires right here in this shop."

Miriam took another deep breath, finding temporary distraction in the pain pulsing in her finger again. The tiny wound from the bag was still hurting, and the pain continued to intensify. She hadn't noticed it when she'd been pulled into that fantasy, but she sure noticed it now. She could also feel the sweat that had formed on her brow.

They needed to get what they were here for and get out. Whatever magic Sofia was working was not in their favor at the moment.

"We're looking for something," Miriam replied. "Do you mind if we cast a quick finding spell?"

"You're not the fun type of magics, are you?" Sofia asked wistfully. "I miss when witches were all counterculture and had the ability to really enjoy themselves. I, for one, am still one of the fun ones. You should see my coven meetings. The magic we work is . . . exhilarating," she trilled, her tongue rolling suggestively.

"We can have fun," Nelson replied meekly, embarrassed.

"Being vanilla is nothing to be ashamed of if you can own it," Sofia taunted, and Nelson only blushed harder.

Which made Miriam even warmer.

Maybe they needed to take a detour after this. She had her own ideas about what she wanted to do with those blushing cheeks.

She was even warmer now. Almost uncomfortably warm, actually. She hadn't intended to be in the shop for long and had left her jacket on. It was starting to feel restrictive.

She pulled her coat off and then tugged at the collar of her sweater.

"I'm just going to cast the finding spell," Miriam declared, and then closed her eyes and snapped her fingers. She expected for their things to come whooshing out of the woodwork. Instead, Miriam felt the entire room sway. She braced against one of the wooden shelves as the sensation passed.

"Hey, are you okay?" Nelson asked, and she felt his hand set gently on her shoulder.

This wasn't normal for her. Miriam should have been able to cast a simple finding spell without an issue. Perhaps it was just whatever magic Sofia was using that was playing with her head.

Sofia had promised consent. Yet Miriam felt like she couldn't control her own thoughts. This felt like the *opposite* of consent.

Miriam pulled at her shirt again, the room suddenly too hot to bear. She needed to get outside to the cool air immediately. Ignoring Nelson and Sofia, she pushed through the dress forms and then out into the main part of the store and finally out through the entrance into the cool early spring air. Sofia was yelling something to her as Miriam ran out of the shop, but she didn't catch the older woman's words.

She stopped at the edge of the sidewalk and then, without even considering the expensive suit she was wearing, lowered herself to sit on the curb. She put her head in her hands and tried to take a few deep breaths, but her head throbbed and her stomach churned.

"Hey." There was a firm hand on her back. "Let's get you home," Nelson murmured in her ear.

Whatever thoughts she had in the shop had faded, and she was suddenly feeling entirely unsexy. All she wanted was to go home and fall into her bed.

Miriam nodded and started to stand, letting Nelson help her up. As he wrapped an arm around her waist for support, she frowned, remembering she had a meeting this afternoon. She couldn't just forget that she was lead on the Pentacle deal, and she couldn't just call out for the entire day.

She groaned. "Ugh, I need to go to work," she said, but she swayed slightly again, and Nelson's arm tightened around her.

"Do you feel well enough to go to work?" Nelson asked quietly as Miriam leaned into his shoulder.

"No," Miriam admitted, shaking her head. Nothing sounded more miserable to her right now than attempting to sit in front of her computer for the next nine hours. She shivered, suddenly freezing. Nelson seemed to know what she needed, because he slowly pulled away from her for a moment to pick up her jacket that had fallen onto the sidewalk, and then he wrapped it around her shoulders.

What was wrong with her? She'd been fine when they'd walked into the store, and now she felt like she had the flu. Realization struck, and she held up her finger to show Nelson the nick she'd gotten from the bag.

"Poison," Nelson noted.

Miriam nodded. "It was a Tatzelwurm bag, Sofia said, but I'm not sure what that is."

"Okay, we need to go back inside and figure this out," Nelson decided. He twisted his head back towards the shop and then gasped.

"What?" Miriam asked.

"The shop's gone," Nelson groaned, shaking his head.

"Huh?" Miriam turned around to look, mildly annoyed, but not shocked. It wasn't that uncommon for a shop to have been enchanted with this sort of charm. And sure enough, the shop that had been there just a few minutes ago was now nothing but a brick wall with ragged flyers plastered to the surface and a bit of graffiti for good measure. Sofia had obviously disappeared as soon as they'd left. Miriam's head was too foggy to comprehend why or to guess at where she might have gone.

"Come on. Let's get a cab," Nelson said, looping his arm around her waist again. He then led her away from the little alleyway and towards the main street. A moment later, he hailed a cab, and they headed towards Miriam's building.

She didn't remember much of the cab ride or the trip up to her apartment. But once she got home, unlocked the door, and let them inside, she felt a little better, maybe just because she felt safe here. "You can go," she said, waving Nelson off. "I can take care of myself."

Nelson's eyes went wide. "You've been poisoned. I'm not leaving you alone. Also, where are your magic books?"

Miriam pointed to the top of her closet, and then declared, "I'm going to bed." She wasn't sure she had any other option, really.

Nelson didn't follow her as she stumbled into her bedroom. He'd leave or not, she couldn't really worry much about it right now. She picked her pajamas up off the bed and went into her bathroom to change. When she was finished, she came back out, pulled out her phone, texted Charlie that she needed the rest of the day off, and then fell into her bed. The last thing she remembered was Larry jumping up next to her and nestling into her side. She pulled him in close and rested her head on top of his. Larry usually would have struggled against such a tight hug, but he seemed to know she needed him, and so he tolerated it.

Moments later, Miriam fell asleep to dreams of the shop, Sofia's taunting words, and her own complex feelings about Nelson.

Chapter Eighteen – Nelson's Version

NELSON PULLED OUT THE thick, leather-bound tomes from the top of Miriam's closet and settled at the kitchen island. He left the door to Miriam's bedroom open. She'd collapsed into bed almost as soon as they'd gotten back to her apartment, and Nelson was concerned. She typically seemed too put together, too controlled to show that amount of vulnerability. Watching her fall into bed with little decorum seemed so opposite her usual mannerisms.

Nelson rubbed his eyes and rested his elbows on the counter. It was hard to get a read on Sofia's magic while they were in the shop, but Nelson had pieced together that Miriam had likely been poisoned by something she'd touched. Magical poisons were difficult to cure, because, like all magic, they followed their own rules and preferred to be unpredictable.

Miriam's magic would only increase the expected volatility of whatever the poison was.

Nelson opened the first book, *Magish of the Homeland*. It was the oldest of the bunch, but it was familiar to him; he had his own copy at home. The book was written in Yiddish with Hebrew letters. Although his mom and grandma had taught him some, Nelson could only recognize a few words and phrases, and he knew he'd need a translation spell to get the true meaning of the words.

It wasn't uncommon for familial inherited texts to be written in a language no longer spoken by the descendants. Nelson's family hadn't spoken Yiddish for generations, and neither had Miriam's. Yet, their most familiar magical texts were written in this language.

Frowning, Nelson leafed slowly through the pages. He wasn't looking for the poison. It was unlikely whatever she'd encountered in the Italian leather shop would be found in a Yiddish magic book. What he was looking for was the entry for khaos magish. He needed to better understand Miriam's own magic, and he hoped he could use that information to help him find an antidote.

Finding the entry didn't take a small miracle, just a well-tread familiarity with this particular book.

Khaos Magish

Magical Illness and Poison

Chaos magics often find a heightened sense of chaos and uncontrollability when facing illness. The more comfortable and familiar the poison is, the less likely they are to experience chaotic symptoms.

Standard antidotes can be used for most poisons. It should be noted that ingredients should be double-checked before use, especially if they come from the khaos magish's own store. Random transformation and mislabeling is possible, both as a symptom of poison and as general chaotic workings.

Nelson nodded to himself and then got up and made a cup of coffee. The splatter of brewing coffee was disrupted by a loud clank and an outraged meow coming from Miriam's bedroom. Nelson peeked into the room and saw the pile of books that had previously been on Miriam's bedside spinning around haphazardly, some twirling around so fast they seemed dangerous, while others took a lazy spin around the room. Miriam was tossing and turning uncomfortably in her bed. He watched her for just a second before there was another loud thud as a book smacked hard against the wall, leaving a large dent in its wake. The book fell harmlessly to the floor.

Larry leaped across the room and huddled in one corner, his wide amber eyes following one of the books flitting about through the air. He stayed, though, as if he were Miriam's valiant protector, despite the clatter. Nelson moved carefully through the room to sit on the edge of the bed, and Larry snuck back over as well, jumping up on the bed next to him and then settling down in the crook of Miriam's arm while giving Nelson a suspicious look.

Nelson ignored the cat and placed a hand on Miriam's forehead. She was feverish, but not so hot he was concerned for her safety. It wasn't a good sign, but her symptoms made him think he had time to find the right answer rather than rushing and possibly coming to an incorrect conclusion. His mom was a nurse, so he'd picked up a little about magical and non-magical ailments growing up. The flu-like symptoms meant it was a slowly progressing illness, not something so rapid that every second was critical.

Miriam stirred and moaned. "Nelson," she mumbled. "I'm so sorry."

"Hey, it's not your fault," Nelson replied, and then turned his hand over and pressed his cool palm against Miriam's warm cheek. She seemed to settle a little at his touch, and she quickly fell back into a more comfortable sleep.

Nelson studied her face for a minute. She hadn't bothered to take her makeup off, and some of it had rubbed off on her pillow, smearing across her face. He was just able to catch a peek of her natural skin beneath. She was stunning, still, even in this state, with her hair mussed and her makeup smudged. Nelson couldn't remember a time when she hadn't been the most beautiful person alive.

His hand lingering on her cheek still, Nelson let his thumb brush slowly along her skin. She deserved to be taken care of, even if she'd always refused Nelson's attempts. He understood now that Miriam had always felt like she needed to overcome everything all by herself and that she hadn't truly realized how everyone needed a little help from time to time. No person was an island, no matter how much Miriam attempted to be. Nelson wanted nothing more to be that person for her. The person she leaned against when the world got too big. The man behind a force as powerful as Miriam.

Once she seemed a bit more settled, Nelson repositioned Larry so Miriam had enough room to move and then headed back into the kitchen, leaving her to get some rest.

He picked up his coffee, now full of fresh brew from Miriam's artisanal coffee pods. Then he settled back in his chair. It was going to take a while to find the answer he was looking for in the books. Even using his small miracle magic, these tomes were endowed with Miriam's chaos, and they would be very resistant to giving him a quick and clear answer.

Nelson set aside the first book and opened up a large volume called *Magics of Europe*. The book was less familiar than *Magish of the Homeland*, but it wasn't unfamiliar. The first chapter was a breakdown of magical creatures, including mermaids, werewolves, and vampires. These were creatures that were magical in nature but didn't work any of their own. Mermaids and werewolves transformed magically, but they themselves didn't work any magic. Vampires had been created by magic and received their life blood that way, but could not cast spells like witches. The second section was a long explanation of magical terminology, including a discussion of how the general term *magics* encompassed wizards, witches, mages, sorcerers, warlocks, and so on. Lastly, there were subsections on magics with specific types of talents, like the jinn they'd met and like Nelson's own specific type of magic—magics that were old and odd and worked in well-defined patterns passed down from generation to generation.

Nelson had inherited his talents from his father. His mom and sisters were all humble workers, but Nelson got the small miracle talent. It was why he'd been the one to step up and take care of everything when his father had passed away. He could do it easily. With just a little small miracle, dinner would be on time, lunch would be packed, and they would all make it to school before the tardy bell.

Small miracle magic was great for these small things, but for the big stuff, like the cancer that had killed his dad, there were no miracles, big or small, that could fix it.

He shook his head to push away the thoughts and remind himself of his task here and now. What Nelson could fix *now* was the poison that was currently coursing through Miriam's body. Even then, he needed a potion; his magic alone would not be enough.

Nelson flipped quickly past the section on *magics*, knowing it was unlikely to help Miriam. What he needed was a listing of rare and special creatures—magics that were so rare they could not be categorized into the other subsections.

He turned to the back of the book but frowned when he saw it was written with a clear bias towards English and Nordic audiences. There were plenty of chapters on fairies, one on unicorns, and another on goblins and ogres. While there *was* a chapter on dragons, nothing in that chapter seemed to match the poisonous creature he needed to find. Nelson recalled that Sofia had mentioned something about a Tatzelwurm. Wurm sounded German, and they had been in an Italian shop.

Not sure what that meant, Nelson pulled out his phone and searched for a map of Europe, quickly locating the two countries. Italy and Germany didn't quite border each other, but they were close, separated by a thin strip of land belonging to Switzerland and Austria.

Hoping for inspiration, he looked back through the rest of Miriam's books. There was one on the Chinese Wu (Chinese for *wizard*) and South Asian magics. Then there was a thick one that covered most of the African continent. She had a solid collection, which was unsurprising. Her parents had always been mainstays in the magical community, and Miriam was not the type to allow herself to go uninformed.

Nelson continued flipping through, finally locating a thin volume on southern European folklore. This time, he used a small finding spell to flip to the pages that matched his criteria. Magics had not bothered with documenting their happenings online, and this was part of the reason. A search engine paled in comparison to being able to flip instantly to the page he wanted in a book. That, and it wasn't exactly a good idea to put the entire magical community online like that. Security was too hard to manage. Books were easier to keep hidden and even easier to dismiss as fictional fun if the wrong person found them.

Finally, he found the entry he was looking for. The Tatzelwurm was a scaled, poisonous creature found in the Italian Alps. Miriam had stuck herself on the thorn-like surface of the Tatzelwurm bag. The entry noted that the Tatzelwurm hide was prized in some magical communities for its ability to bring out desires. The entry also explained that the leather itself would always contain some poison, but as long as it was properly sealed, it was not dangerous. Nelson wondered if the seal could be magically broken with some unintentional chaos magic.

And based on their strange experience, it was unclear if Sofia's shop was actually meant to serve the leather community or if there was something more sinister behind the entire operation. There were certain magics that fed off others' lust and desire, and Nelson had felt plenty of that in the shop. As much as he'd blushed, it had been hard not to think of Miriam when they'd been in that back room.

Feeding off of desire *was* a thing in the magic community, and Nelson even had a coven mate with a similar proclivity. One guy in his coven often headed out to bars as everyone was coupling up and going home together after last call. He would almost always go home alone, but he went just to enjoy the feelings of desire and want and need. It was how he fueled his magic. Pride events in June were another one of his favorites; he loved to go just to bask in all the unabashed joy and love and lust.

Perhaps that was Sofia's angle with her back room. More suspicious was the disappearing shop, but perhaps that was just providing her a level of protection, particularly given that she carried poisonous products made from Tatzelwurm hide.

Nelson turned his attention back to the book. It described how to make an antidote, and he was relieved to see that the ingredients were pretty straightforward: goat's milk collected on midsummer (it was sold freeze-dried these days), eye of newt, seawater collected on a new moon, and dirt from inside a forest on a full moon. It was a standard poison-remediation potion. Miriam likely had all the ingredients, but without her being able to sort through her own magic and determine what was good and what wasn't, Nelson would need to source them elsewhere. He could transport small things magically, but potion ingredients worked best if there were no other traces of magic in them.

That meant the ingredients should be sourced and delivered in person, without the use of magic. And that would be difficult because he didn't want to leave Miriam unattended.

He glanced towards the kitchen and nodded in approval at her gas stove, not surprised to see it. Magics typically found them essential. Potions were best brewed over a wood-burning fire, but the open flame on a gas stove was adequate when a wood-burning fire was unavailable. While there were certainly still apartments with fireplaces, Miriam's was not one of them. Her apartment was too new and too sleek for a dirty fireplace.

Nelson picked up his phone and scrolled through his contacts. He'd been absent from coven meetings for a while, but they were still his coven. *They were still his coven*, he reassured himself. They would pick up.

He chose Darrin, the potions expert in their coven. Unfortunately, Darrin was also the person who was least impressed with the most recent decisions Nelson had made. But all things considered, he was sure Darrin would still answer his text message.

Just a few minutes after the message was sent, his phone chimed with a notification of a text back from Darrin. Nelson was glad, but not unsurprised. This was still his coven, and he had been sure they'd still come through for him.

Potions tended to not travel well, so it made sense to brew the antidote at Miriam's apartment, given she had an adequate kitchen. Darrin agreed to come over and help and to bring the ingredients. Nelson took a minute to locate her caldron and prepare the kitchen for potion-making.

Then he checked on Miriam again, peeking into her room. She was much the same—in bed and feverish. Her curls hung limp against her forehead, and her face was pale and washed out. He tried not to let himself worry too much, after all, the entry in the book had suggested that while Tatzelwurm poison was sometimes deadly, it would take a matter of days or even weeks, not hours. Yes, she was ill, but they had time before the poison fully worked its way through her body.

Miriam rolled over in her bed, and the lights flickered. Then a series of stiletto heels flew out of her closet and wedged themselves against her bedroom wall. It was clear that the poison was affecting her magic *and* that using this much magic would inhibit her ability to heal.

Larry remained curled up against Miriam, and Nelson suspected the cat was attempting to protect her. He only hoped the feline's presence was providing Miriam with some comfort.

Nelson left the bedroom and sat back down in one of the chairs at the kitchen island, feeling useless now that he had an incoming solution but no immediate action items. He was saved only minutes later by a text message notification. Darrin was approaching the apartment building, and he needed one of Nelson's small miracles to get past the doorman without issue. That was something Nelson *could* do, and so, with a wink, he made it happen.

Another couple of minutes after that, there was a firm rap at the door.

Nelson hopped up to open it, relieved to see Darrin was on the other side, holding a reusable burlap shopping bag. He was dressed in a simple pair of jeans and a faded black hoodie, and his beard was a bit scruffy, as always.

"Thanks for coming," Nelson said as he opened the door wide and ushered Darrin into Miriam's apartment.

In lieu of a greeting, Darrin whipped his head around the apartment, surveying it. He took stock of the large windows that looked out on a stunning view of Manhattan, the grand stone island in the kitchen, and the open floor plan that dominated the space. The main living space was austere and minimalist except for a few family photos Miriam had displayed on a book shelf. It was a beautiful apartment, and in Manhattan, it also represented money. A lot of money. Nelson hadn't really thought much about it. It was Miriam's place, and Miriam was just Miriam, as she always had been. Despite the fancy clothes and the enormous apartment, the important stuff was still all the same.

"So, this is what you've been doing since you left. You've really sold out completely," Darrin remarked almost instantly.

"It's . . . it's not like that. Look, I can explain it all, but Miriam really needs the antidote first," Nelson pleaded. If this was his penance for the decisions he'd made, so be it. He would make the same decisions over and over again, regardless of his coven's view.

"Do you have a caldron to brew this in?" Darrin asked.

"Yeah, here," Nelson said, motioning to the large black pot he'd found in Miriam's cupboards. "I did a cleansing spell on it as well." He kept his expression even and smooth. Letting Darrin upset him would not be beneficial to anyone. He was going to stay calm and collected.

Darrin nodded and then gingerly set the burlap tote on the counter. He unloaded the ingredients in their sealed bottles and wax paper wrappers. It was a stark contrast—the archaic-looking vessels on the counter in Miriam's ultramodern apartment.

From there, the potion-making went quickly. It was simply a matter of combining the right ingredients, stirring them in the right order, and then letting it brew for about thirty minutes.

Once the potion was set and brewing, Nelson knew he couldn't keep avoiding the topic anymore, so he turned to Darrin. "The store," he said, referring to the big box store Nelson had been sending some of his residents to for jobs, "it's not what you think."

Darrin shook his head. "They're horrible to their people. They engage in egregious union busting. Folks regularly have to pee in bottles because they're not given enough time to use the restroom, and there've been at least two cases of people dying in the bathrooms from being overworked."

"I'm not arguing that it's an amazing place to work, and I wish there were more options," Nelson agreed, "but they're willing to hire felons with nonviolent drug offenses, and my residents desperately need jobs. A lot of them *are* felons. This is their opportunity to have health insurance, dental even. They'll be able to buy the groceries they actually want, when they want them, without having to depend on soup kitchens and food pantries. They'll be able to afford clothes beyond what they get as handouts. These jobs are going to be life-changing," Nelson explained as calmly as possible.

This was why he'd been avoiding his coven. The deal he'd made with the big box store to consider hiring his residents had been huge, but when his coven had heard the news, they'd gotten upset. They couldn't understand how he'd support a business like that. It was a broken system, sure, but it was one Nelson had to work within to make sure his residents got what they needed. He couldn't just be an activist while people starved. This was an interim solution, and a bad one, but it was what existed. It was what his residents had today, right now.

Before Darrin could debate Nelson further on his stance, there was a sudden clatter from the hallway closet.

"What is that?" Darrin asked, and Nelson shook his head as he went over to investigate.

He pulled open the closet only to see that the vacuum cleaner had come to life. It zoomed out of the closet on its own accord, its plug dragging behind it. Larry, who had been peacefully sleeping next to Miriam, scurried out of bed and started hissing at it.

"What in the world?" Darrin asked, standing back well out of the way as the vacuum spun around the living room.

Nelson caught the vacuum and flipped the On switch to Off. That was enough to stop the vacuum, and Nelson pushed it back in the closet.

"Miriam's chaos magic," he explained, trying to downplay the mess.

"A chaos witch has this apartment?" Darrin seemed surprised. "She must have done something . . ." Darrin trailed off, but his flippant suggestion, to insinuate that Miriam hadn't earned all of this on her own merit, made Nelson's blood start to boil. He *knew* Miriam, and he knew how hard she'd worked for this. She'd worked harder than anyone else to make this happen.

He pressed his lips together. "She's amazing, actually," he said. "She's accomplished so much, and she's been so determined to do it all on her own."

"I thought you said that you two weren't a thing," Darrin reminded him as he moved back into the kitchen to check on the potion.

Nelson frowned. The truth was, he wasn't sure anymore. He'd always admired Miriam, but she'd never seemed to have the same feelings, so he hadn't pushed her. He'd always just tried to be there for her. Then the last couple of weeks, when Miriam had actually wanted him, even for a night—that had been the best moment of his life. The second time had been even better. She'd been worth the wait, but he wasn't sure what was happening from here and whether he wanted to reveal even more to Darrin. So he deflected.

"We went to high school together," he said dismissively.

Unfortunately, Darrin didn't stop his interrogation.

"And you're hooking up?" Darrin asked, and he stirred the potion one more time, studying it, before looking up at Nelson for an answer.

"We've been on sort of a quest . . . It's a long story," Nelson said, once again sidestepping the question. While he didn't want to explain the missing broom and medallion, he was even less interested in explaining that he and Miriam had, in fact, been hooking up when it had happened.

"A quest?" Darrin raised his eyebrows and gave a condescending chuckle. When Nelson didn't elaborate, Darrin turned back to his potion. When he seemed happy with the look and consistency of the brew, he pulled a few clean bottles and an old, dented funnel from his bag and siphoned the potion into individual containers.

"Is it ready?" Nelson asked, noting that Darrin had filled about half a dozen small bottles and arranged them on the counter.

Darrin nodded. "You'll give her one now, and then you'll do one at sunset and one at sunrise until all the bottles are gone. She'll improve gradually, but she'll need rest through the end of the weekend to allow her body to heal. The poison takes a toll, even after it's been remediated."

"Thanks," Nelson said, picking up one of the bottles. "Look, I know things have been weird, but I really do . . . I miss the coven."

"You're always welcome back," Darren reminded him. "It's just going to be hard to accept our differences, and you may have to change."

Nelson nodded. "I appreciate that, but we're getting older, and we aren't always going to agree on everything, especially as the world gets more complicated and more nuanced."

Darrin shrugged. "A witch needs its coven, and I know your heart is in the right place. I think you'll come to your senses and understand why we need to take a hard stance."

Nelson inhaled a deep breath. Darrin wasn't going to try to settle their differences or understand the nuance of the situation. The rest of his coven likely wasn't ready, either. He was being offered an ultimatum. Change his views on the big corporate store, or leave the coven. Nelson shook his head. "I . . . should . . ." He held up the bottle.

This was it. He had drawn a line in the sand. This was the end of his time in his coven.

"Yeah," Darrin agreed, and to Nelson's surprise, he sounded disappointed. He gave Nelson a small nod—a somber, silent goodbye—and then gathered up his things and left.

Nelson only took a moment to regroup before he made his way back to Miriam's bedroom. Not much had changed. Larry had made himself comfortable again on the bed, and Miriam was curled up, shivering.

"Hey," Nelson said gently, brushing a curl out of Miriam's face.

Miriam stirred, stretched, and rubbed her eyes. She sat up and blinked at Nelson, wrapping her arms around her body.

"I need you to drink this," Nelson said, holding the bottle up to her lips. She nodded and then opened her mouth just a little. Nelson tipped the bottle slowly, and the liquid drained out, into her mouth and down her throat. She coughed and sputtered a bit, but the potion went down.

"Water," Miriam rasped, and Nelson obliged. With a flick of his wrist, there was a fresh glass of water in his hand. He carefully handed it to Miriam, and she drank thirstily.

And with very little fanfare or patience, Miriam handed him back the glass and said, "I'm going to go back to sleep now." Then she nestled back in her sheets.

Nelson let out a sigh of relief, and then he opened his phone and set an alarm for sunrise and sunset each day through the end of Sunday. He'd taken on this responsibility, and he fully intended to see it through. He would make sure that Miriam got better.

Chapter Nineteen – Miriam Again

AT FIRST, MIRIAM THOUGHT she was still stuck in a dream. The light was streaming brilliantly into her bedroom, making her head pound and her eyes sting. There was pressure on her chest, making it hard to breathe.

Before she could properly panic, she realized the pressure was from a giant cat sitting on her, staring her right in the face. It was just Larry. All seventeen pounds of him, perched right on her chest, his face just inches from hers. She tried to take a deep breath, but Larry seemed to have made his home in all the places that needed to expand for her to breathe easily.

Stretching, she carefully dislodged Larry and nudged him off of her. She felt dreadful, and except for a vague memory of Nelson waking her, the last thing she remembered was falling into bed after going to the leather shop.

She sat up, but that only made her head hurt more and the room spin. Groaning, she shifted to try to make herself more comfortable. When she turned, she saw Nelson slumped in the armchair in the corner of her bedroom. His glasses were askew, pushed up past his forehead, and his eyes were closed in sleep.

"Hey," Miriam said, hoping her voice was loud enough to wake him.

Nelson stirred, blinking his eyes open. When he saw her, he smiled. "You're awake," he said sleepily as he rearranged his glasses.

"And you look like you could get some sleep," Miriam replied, and then let out a few raspy coughs. Her throat felt like sandpaper, and she reached out for the glass of water on her bedside table. She picked it up and drank heartily.

Across the room, Nelson had straightened up in his chair, frowning as he watched her cough. "I'm fine," he said after she'd finished drinking. "I wanted to make sure you were okay yesterday."

"Yesterday?!" Miriam groaned. "I . . . Oh, shit . . . work." If yesterday was when she'd gotten sick, then that meant today was Friday, and she needed to call in. She reached for her phone, which was sitting on her nightstand. There was already a series of texts from Charlie. *Shit.* She tapped a quick email to Charlie in an attempt to explain herself and then swung her legs to the side of the bed, preparing to get up.

"What are you doing?" Nelson asked.

"I need to go to work. I'm already late," Miriam replied in a panic.

"Hey . . . Hey . . . Slow down now." Nelson stood up and within a second was hovering over Miriam. From this angle, Miriam could see that he had a spattering of stubble on his jaw. Perhaps it was the addled state of her brain or perhaps she was still under whatever magic Sofia had used on her, but she liked it. She wanted to touch it. She kept her hands to herself. "You need to rest," he insisted.

Miriam shook her head. "I'm fine. You gave me that potion. It made me better, right?"

Nelson seemed to study her. "Do you feel better?" he asked.

"I feel alive," Miriam mumbled. She felt the bare minimum of not dead. She attempted to stand up, needing to prove to herself that she could do it. But almost immediately, her vision blurred and her knees buckled. She felt Nelson's firm hand on her arm.

"You look like you need rest," he replied, and he gently guided her to sit back on the bed.

"I'm fine," Miriam argued, trying to brush him away. "You really don't have to stay."

"I'll make you a deal." Nelson snapped his fingers, not in a magical sort of way, but in more of an "ah-hah" sort of way. "Why don't I make you breakfast? You eat it right here, in bed, and then we can talk about how you're feeling."

"You're just trying to keep me here," Miriam grumbled.

"You caught me," Nelson replied dryly, giving her an unamused glare.

Miriam stood again, and this time, she was successful.

"Where are you going?" Nelson asked as Miriam hobbled a couple of steps.

"To the bathroom," Miriam replied. "Unless you think I need a bedpan." She made sure her tone clearly communicated that her using a bedpan would *not* be an option.

Without any more arguments from Nelson, Miriam excused herself to the bathroom. After she used the toilet, she looked at herself in the mirror. Her hair was a tangled rat's nest, and her face was pale, puffy, and broken out. She had pulled on possibly the homeliest pajamas she owned—an old, shapeless T-shirt that made her boobs flop around uselessly and a pair of Hanukkah pajama pants that had a small hole in the crotch. She groaned, wishing she could magic away her frumpiness. But she had such little energy that she didn't even trust herself to take a shower, much less use magic. There was no way she wanted to risk passing out and cracking her head open under the water. Nope. She was not dying nude in her own bathroom while Nelson was making her breakfast.

So instead, she splashed cold water on her face to rinse away some of the sweat that had accumulated and then attempted to run a hairbrush through her matted mane of hair. She was only moderately successful with the latter, and it was only just barely passable enough to squish her hair into a thick ponytail. She applied a bit of toner to calm down her face and then felt too weak for anything more in terms of personal grooming.

When she reentered her bedroom, she was surprised to see that Nelson had made quick work of not only breakfast but her actual bed as well. The bed had been made up, and on a tray was a full breakfast spread. Toast, eggs, fresh fruit, and a steaming pot of tea. Nelson could work small miracles, and there was certainly some of that at play here with how quickly it had all come together. But Miriam also suspected that Nelson had planned this while she'd been asleep.

"You should eat," Nelson said from where he was standing by the door. "You need to keep your strength up to fight the poison."

"I thought you gave me the antidote?" Miriam asked, because she vaguely remembered Nelson waking her up and tipping something slightly medicinal into her mouth. At least once, but maybe two or three times. He had already confirmed that much earlier, anyway.

Nelson nodded. "I did, and you'll need to take a dose at sunrise and sunset all weekend, but your body also needs a chance to recover. You need to get your strength back up."

Miriam took a seat back on her bed, sinking into the plush duvet and the pillows Nelson had fluffed up. She carefully avoided the tray of food so as not to spill it on her bedding. "Are you planning to just watch me eat?" Miriam asked. "Because that would be really awkward."

Nelson's eyebrows rose almost to his hairline, and his cheeks turned pink with embarrassment. "I can . . ." He tilted his head towards the living room.

"You could join me," Miriam replied, scooting over to make room for him on the bed.

"Oh?" he asked, and Miriam nodded.

Perhaps it was just the aftereffects of Sofia's magic, her moment of literal weakness, or maybe she was still ruminating on their time with the jinn from the weekend before, but Miriam really wanted Nelson there. She'd given him an out, and now that he'd chosen to stay, Miriam wanted nothing more than for him to be there. It felt like a weakness, but for a moment, she let it slide. She *was* weak. She would be strong later.

Nelson shuffled onto her bed, scooting until his back was against the headboard. He reached down and picked up the breakfast tray from in between them and then pulled his knees up so that the tray could rest on both their legs.

Miriam could feel just the whisper of his thigh against her soft cotton pajama pants. When she reached out to pour the tea, their hands touched, and Miriam felt that jolt of warmth that seemed to happen whenever their skin brushed each other's like this.

"I'm . . . I'm really sorry you got pulled into this whole thing," Miriam said after taking a sip of warm tea. It soothed her rough throat.

"You were poisoned. I wasn't going to leave you to die," Nelson replied, no question in his tone.

"No . . . I mean this entire adventure we've been on, looking for our things, having to travel to pretty much every magical location in the city," Miriam explained. The admission felt quite out of character for her. She didn't like to admit when something was her fault, and even worse, she hated to admit when she was wrong. Now, though, something about Nelson spending the night taking care of her—actually, really taking care of her instead of just pitying her and moving on—made her want to open up. It made her want to share the vulnerabilities she thought had been trained out of her long ago thanks to the cutthroat nature of investment banking.

Nelson set his teacup on the tray. Had Miriam been in a better state, she would have realized much sooner that Nelson had set the tray for two, as though he'd hoped she would invite him to join her. Actually, maybe she *had* realized it, but hadn't been able to admit it to herself. Maybe she'd wanted to give him an out first, see what he'd do. Her brain was still foggy enough that she wasn't entirely sure.

"This isn't only your fault, you know." Nelson seemed to turn all of his attention on her. "Actually, it's not really your fault at all. You didn't ask your broomstick to run away with my medallion, and you certainly didn't ask for your chaos magic, which you keep in exceedingly excellent control, by the way."

Just as Nelson finished his sentence, Miriam sneezed, and the breakfast tray went flying. She cringed, ready for everything to crash everywhere in a giant mess of eggs and fruit and tea. But it suddenly stopped in midair. Nelson waved his hand, and the entire breakfast tray righted itself and then reappeared back on their laps, where it had been before Miriam had sneezed.

"What was that you were saying about me being an *in control* chaos witch?" Miriam asked, picking up her mug again and taking a sip. The warm liquid felt soothing to her throat and helped to break up the congestion she'd been experiencing from the poison.

"You're going to be a little out of control as you recover from the poison," Nelson explained as he picked up a piece of toast.

Miriam sighed and leaned back against the headboard. "I guess you're back to taking care of me."

Nelson shook his head. His hair flopped around just a little, no longer neatly styled after the day they'd had yesterday and then whatever his night had looked like last night. "I think we've taken care of each other plenty on this adventure."

"You mean last week, after Talia?" Miriam asked quietly, not exactly sure how to word her question. It seemed awful to bring up someone else's trauma like that, but she didn't know how else to say it.

Nelson nodded weakly. "And you had all the scrying stuff, and your coven and your parents when we were on Long Island." He took another bite of toast.

"But . . . you feel that burden of having to help people all the time," Miriam said gently. "At Zari's office, your wish was to no longer have to take care of everyone all the time. This has to be too much work for you . . . just another emotional load that you can't escape from?" It was a pitiful question, but Miriam pushed through it anyway, needing to know.

Nelson placed his toast down and stared at her for a long time. Miriam waited, giving him time to formulate his response. Finally, he blinked and nodded a little and said, "When you were at the same point in your wishes, you wanted your coven to be like they were when you were younger. But you don't *really* want to go back in time, or for your coven to give up their families, or anything like that. Right?"

"No," Miriam admitted, but she didn't elaborate. Nelson seemed to have a fairly good understanding of the deeper meaning of her wish.

"That's not the case for me either. I love helping people, most of all, my family. It's just a lot sometimes, being that person all the time. Sometimes I wish I could just *be*," Nelson explained. "Not all the time, not even most of the time, but sometimes."

"You must hate spending time with me," Miriam huffed. "Talk about a person you can never stop helping."

"That's not true," Nelson said quickly. "Miriam, you're the one person who's easy to be with. You know what you're doing all the time. With you, it's like we're sharing the same burden. We're in this together. It's not just me doing small miracles all day and hoping I make a dent."

"You really think that about me?" Miriam asked.

"I've always thought that about you. Back when we were in school, you were so determined to do everything on your own. You were fiercely independent, and I admired that about you. I still do."

Miriam took this in. She'd never thought that Nelson might see her like this. She'd always assumed that he only saw her as someone who needed an excessive amount of help. And to her, it had always felt like Nelson was trying to one-up her, to be the golden boy. Now, though, with everything they'd been through, it was starting to seem like there was something else going on entirely.

"Is that what happened with your coven? You needed a break from being the caretaker?" Miriam asked carefully. She'd sensed that something had been going on with his coven, some reason he'd been avoiding them, but it had always seemed too personal a subject. Now that they were talking about what they had seen at the jinn's office, and now that he'd met her coven, it seemed like it was fair game to ask.

Nelson inhaled deeply. "My coven and I have a difference of opinion about a new chain of box stores. They think I need to take a stance against some of the inhumane work practices, but I'm looking at it from a different angle and appreciating the fact that they're willing to hire my residents with felonies."

"But don't you want your residents to have a decent place to work?" Miriam asked, confused.

"More than anything. If I could snap my fingers and immediately eliminate all the policies that make it hard for my residents to get jobs and all the things that made jobs bad, I would. But I'm only one person, and a large store that offers health insurance and decent hours and pay that is above minimum wage feels like a small miracle. I just wish I could work big ones."

Miriam was about to respond, to ask what he was planning to do about it, but an enormous yawn slipped out instead. She'd only just woken up, and yet she felt like she'd done an entire day's worth of work.

"Alright, I think it's time for you to take a nap," Nelson decided for her. He organized the breakfast tray, stacking the dirty dishes and piling up the leftover food, and then, with a snap of his fingers, it disappeared back to the kitchen. "I'll give you some privacy." He turned and started to scoot away towards the edge of the bed.

"You don't have to . . ." Miriam said.

"Huh?"

"You don't have to give me privacy. Um, you look like you could use some rest as well, and I have this entire bed that's way more comfortable than my couch." The words spilled out of her mouth in a chaotic jumble.

"Miriam Blum, are you asking me to come to bed?" he teased, his eyebrows raised mischievously.

"I'm asking you to lie down and get some rest. I would send you home to sleep in your own bed, but you're way too determined to take care of me for that to happen."

Nelson cracked a smile. "Do you mind if I take off my jeans? I'm wearing boxers," he explained.

"Please," Miriam encouraged.

She was unsure if she should divert her eyes as Nelson stood and pulled down his pants. It wasn't like she hadn't seen all of him already, and fairly recently. But there was something that felt exceedingly intimate about this moment. Before she could decide where her eyes were going, he was standing bare-legged in front of her. He had turned away, and his boxers were short enough that she could see the shadow of muscle that connected his thighs to his ass. She wanted to run her finger up the taut line. She wanted to feel his muscles, and she wondered exactly what it would do to him. They'd been together before, but there was something so incredibly comfortable about this moment.

And the more vulnerability they each shared, the more Miriam wanted him.

Nelson turned back around, and his eyes narrowed at her. "What?"

"It's nothing," Miriam said as she pulled down the covers and made room for him to slide in next to her. For good measure, as soon as they had gotten settled, Larry sauntered in from the living room and jumped up right between them.

"Well, looks like we have a chaperone," Nelson said as he ran a hand down Larry's back. Larry circled a few times, taking advantage of the back scratches. He let out a few long purrs before finally settling right between Miriam and Nelson.

"Larry's kind of protective." Miriam smiled, though a part of her was also disappointed that her cat had intruded on their intimate moment.

Nelson gave a single, hearty laugh. "Is that right?"

"Mm-hmm," Miriam replied, settling down into the bed. Suddenly, her eyes were heavy, and all she could think about was sleep. Maybe it didn't matter what Larry had done; she was too exhausted for anything much, and she was still wearing her very unsexy pajamas.

"Get some rest," Nelson said, and then he turned out the lights.

The bed shifted as he made himself comfortable, and the last thing Miriam felt before she fell asleep was Nelson's soft lips on her forehead. Her lips turned up into a content smile at his gentle touch, and she drifted off into a peaceful sleep thinking about that tender kiss.

Chapter Twenty

WHEN MIRIAM WOKE AGAIN, she was nestled in Nelson's arms, and Larry had moved to the foot of the bed. The sun had shifted, suggesting she'd been asleep for a long time. She moved a bit, and Nelson's fresh stubble scraped against her cheek, which was enough to wake him.

"Mmmm," Nelson hummed, stretching. He buried his face into her hair and murmured, "How are you feeling?"

"Better," Miriam replied, and it was the truth. Her head felt less floaty, and while she hadn't tried to stand up yet, she had a feeling that the pervasive lightheadedness she'd experienced earlier was likely gone. She stuck her nose down her T-shirt and inhaled. Then she grimaced. "Also, like I desperately need a shower."

Larry popped his head up and let out a long meow.

"I can feed Larry," Nelson offered, and Larry looked at him and blinked a few times as though the cat knew exactly what Nelson had said.

"You . . . you don't have to stay. I'm sure you have things you need to do this weekend," Miriam offered, even though she so desperately wanted him to stay. "At a minimum, get some clean clothes."

"Do you want me to leave?" Nelson asked earnestly, and Miriam snuggled up in his arms and shook her head.

"No," she said, her voice small and almost inaudible. She followed it up just a little louder. "I want you to stay."

"Okay," Nelson replied. He snapped his fingers, and a moment later, there was a small pile of folded laundry on Miriam's chair. "No need to worry about clean clothes."

"Thanks," Miriam replied, shifting so that she was leaning on one arm.

"You don't have to thank me. I've always wanted to be here for you," Nelson reminded her.

"I feel so stupid." Miriam groaned as she rolled over in her bed, burying her face in the sheets.

"Why?" Nelson asked.

"The entire time we were in school and the entire time we've been on this adventure, I was so sure you were just . . . pitying me. But all this time, you really just liked me as an actual person." Miriam stared up at the ceiling, unable to meet his eyes.

Nelson propped himself up on one elbow and then said, "It's . . . That wasn't entirely your fault. I had . . . a bit of a hero complex."

"Had?" Miriam popped up and looked him in the eye, one eyebrow raised inquisitively.

"Recovering," Nelson amended. "When I first became a social worker, it was easy to feel very superior in that decision. Then reality snuck in. Sometimes the people you try to help . . . just suck. They're just bad people. Sometimes there're good people who can't stop making that one mistake. Others are just victims of the system."

"Oh . . . so you *were* a self-righteous asshole," Miriam teased.

"Ouch, right for the jugular, Ms. Witch of Wall Street," Nelson said, closing the gap between them so their lips were almost touching.

Miriam nodded and then said, "I'm going to take that shower now." And then she pulled away, rolled out of bed, and headed to the bathroom without looking back at Nelson.

She gave a wicked cackle as she closed the bathroom door behind herself.

***

Thirty minutes later, Miriam was feeling renewed and refreshed from her shower. She was far from one hundred percent better; her head still ached behind her eyes, and she felt like she needed another nap in order to keep her eyes open and stay upright. But at least she could walk without swaying, and she'd managed to stay on her feet in the shower.

She wrapped herself up in a fluffy white towel and headed out of the bathroom, more than disappointed to see that Nelson wasn't there. She was starting to really appreciate their intimate moments, these exposed vulnerabilities.

However, she noticed that the sheets on her bed had been changed, and that was almost as good as Nelson taking the towel right off her body. She could hear Nelson in her kitchen doing something, which meant he was still here, but rather than head out to meet him, she walked over to her dresser to find some clothes to put on. Sure, their relationship was progressing in some intimate direction, but entering the kitchen in just a towel still felt much too forward. The bedroom was fine, but the kitchen was one step too far in the narrative Miriam had built in her head.

Miriam pulled on a pair of yoga pants and an oversized sweater and made her way into the kitchen. Nelson was sitting at her kitchen counter, typing away at his computer. He must have magicked it from his apartment, like he had with his clothes. Magic was funny like that. It had its own nonlinear, nonsensical rules. Nelson could magic small objects around, no problem, but when it came to moving himself, or Miriam moving herself, even, they needed their enchanted objects—his medallion, her broomstick. Sometimes, Miriam wondered if magic had a sense of humor. After all, its inconsistent and unfollowable rules made being magic a consistent exercise in *is this worth it?*

In a move that felt a little overly intimate, Miriam wrapped her arms around Nelson's neck and kissed him on the cheek, his stubble brushing against her lips. He smelled worn in, like a used book and soft leather. She was starting to really appreciate that smell. She pressed her nose into his neck and hummed with contentment.

She . . . liked this. Really, really like this.

Their relationship so far had been a series of *just for tonights* and *truces* and *not agains*. But earlier, something had changed. When she'd invited him into her bed and then he'd kissed her on the forehead, something had changed. Miriam . . . no longer wanted this to be an exception. It no longer felt like an exception.

"Hmm, what was that for?" Nelson asked, turning around to look at her.

"Just because," Miriam explained. "And for changing my sheets."

"Just because?" Nelson asked.

"Because I like you," she clarified. She hadn't meant to say it, and yet, she realized, she didn't regret the words. It felt right, it felt easy.

"Is that so?" Nelson smiled and grabbed her around the waist, pulling her into his lap.

"I do." Miriam laughed a little, giddy that she could still feel like this, dizzy that Nelson Copperfield could make her feel like this. The laughing, however, quickly morphed into a cough—a reminder she was still recovering from the poison.

With her cough, a burst of magical energy jumped out of her, and the burners on her stove suddenly roared to life, the flames licking high above where they usually stopped. Miriam was able to nod her head and turn the flames off, despite her hacking.

"Okay, it looks like that was too much excitement all at once," Nelson concluded, helping her off his lap and back to her feet. He stood too. "I'm thinking we do ice cream and a movie marathon. That sounds a little calmer."

"More rom-coms?" Miriam asked.

"You're not a fan?" Nelson pulled out two pints of ice cream from Miriam's freezer, along with a couple of bowls and spoons. Miriam was very sure she hadn't had ice cream in her freezer before she'd gotten sick.

"Too predictable. They always end up together," she complained, leading Nelson over and settling onto the sofa.

"They're safe," Nelson explained. He took a seat next to her on the couch and placed the ice cream on the coffee table. "When you're in the middle of a terrible week and you don't know how it's going to turn out and it may turn out horrible, no matter how hard you work, no matter what you say or do, rom-coms can always be trusted to give you a happy ending." He paused, picking up one of the ice cream pints. "But this isn't about what I like. What do you want to watch?"

"Reality TV," Miriam replied. "No one knows what's going to happen, and it's the most amount of chaos possible. What I like about it is that no matter how chaotic it gets, no matter how much drama there is, the stakes always seem so low. A party doesn't go over well, or a cake falls apart, or someone yells at another person," Miriam explained as she turned on her TV. "And there's an entire season of *Drag Race* that I haven't watched yet."

"I see," Nelson said, nodding. "Well then, I think we're watching *Drag Race*." He gently pulled Miriam into his arms, and she allowed it, leaning into his warm, secure embrace and laying her head on his firm chest.

This was nice. Relaxing. She didn't usually have many opportunities to just stop for a minute. She worked a lot, and the last few weeks, they'd been on this quest to find their things. Perhaps she needed to learn to slow down, even when she wasn't being forced to because she'd been poisoned.

They cuddled like that and ate ice cream, and then Miriam took her next dose of antidote once they made it to sundown. Afterwards, she only lasted through two more episodes before she fell asleep on the sofa, comfortably cradled in Nelson's arms.

***

Miriam woke up in her bed, and she could feel Nelson's weight on the mattress next to her. She vaguely remembered him helping her to bed and her asking for him to stay yet again.

She stretched and then dozed for a bit. The fresh sheets enveloped her in their smooth threads, and she felt even better than she had the day before. Her bedroom was cool, but she no longer had the feeling of being overly hot or cold that always came with being sick.

Sometime later, Nelson's alarm went off, a reminder that her next dose of antidote was due. Miriam rolled over towards her nightstand where the vials were being stored and poured a dose into her mouth just as Nelson turned off his alarm.

"We should get back to looking for our things," Miriam suggested as she sat up in bed. It was Saturday, after all, and soon, they'd have to go back to work. It would be next weekend before Miriam could start up the search again.

"You need more rest," Nelson told her firmly. "The potion works, but only if you allow your body and, more importantly, your magic to rest. Scrying with the map uses magic, and you'll need your magic for when we head out to whatever new place we end up going to look for our things."

"So what, are you suggesting we just stay here and watch *Drag Race* all day?" Miriam folded her arms indigently.

"We could," Nelson suggested, and then he leaned over Miriam and placed a long kiss on her lips. He was slow, and he kept his hands to himself, and Miriam realized she didn't want him to keep his hands to himself. She very much wanted his hands everywhere. "You're beautiful," he whispered in her ear, and he pressed another kiss to her skin, this time right along her jawline.

She let out a little giggle at her disheveled-ness. Her hair was a mess, her boobs were flopping in a weird, saggy angle across her sheets, and yet, hearing those words come from Nelson, she'd never felt so utterly beautiful before. She pulled away, breathless.

"Are you trying to distract me with sex?" she teased.

"Maybe, if it'll work," Nelson hinted.

Miriam stopped to consider that for a moment, and then, without any more hesitation, she peeled off the oversized, very unsexy pajama shirt she was wearing. She liked how she felt right now, wild and free and chaotic. Her curly hair was a thick, frizzy mess. She hadn't properly brushed it since before she was poisoned. Her breasts hung free and exposed, and her nipples puckered both from the chill in her room and in anticipation of what was to come. Her face was makeup free and puffy, and yet she had never felt more like herself in that moment.

"Yes, I think it might work," Miriam replied. "And you really think I'm beautiful?"

Nelson nodded with a low growl of approval and then pushed her back down to the mattress, straddling her thighs. He leaned over her and started at her mouth, trailing kisses down her neck, between her breasts, and then one on each nipple. He continued down, shifting back as he went, and he pressed his lips against her stomach and then the top of her hip in slow, sensual kisses that left her hot and wet and needy.

When he got to the waistband of her pajama pants, he scooted back more, and she lifted her hips as he slowly, gently rolled the waistband down just past her thighs. She wanted him, badly, the bulge in his boxers driving another wave of arousal, and she reached out to him, trying to pull him back down to her. But he stayed just out of her reach, and he bent down again and placed a kiss on her inner thigh, ignoring the part of her that was in most need of attention.

"I'm supposed to be distracting you," Nelson reminded her. "Which means, I think we have to go very, very slow."

The cotton fabric of her underwear felt wet and heavy, and she could feel each and every movement acutely. Every nerve felt exposed in the best way possible, even though Nelson was only moving farther and farther away. No longer was his mouth on her thigh. It moved to the back of her knee, then her calf, and finally the sole of her foot.

"Please," she begged.

"Not even close," Nelson murmured, but he started to slowly work his way back up. His lips on her calf, his tongue behind her kneecap, a nip on the outer edge of her thigh.

Then, finally, he made it to the hem of her underwear. He moved his hands back down and looped a finger in the cotton, then pulled them all the way off.

Miriam raised her hips in anticipation, but Nelson just sat back on his heels and admired her, splayed out on the bed, fully exposed. Miriam could see that he was withholding his own pleasure, his erection fully on display through his thin boxers.

"I wonder how long I can do this before you come," Nelson said, and then he looked at her with a curious smile as though he really was contemplating exactly how he would make that happen.

***

They did a good job of distracting themselves the rest of the day. Miriam stopped bringing up the need to find their things after Nelson's fingers hit the perfect spot.

When they weren't tangled up in Miriam's sheets, they were back on the couch, finishing the season of *Drag Race* they'd started. And when *Drag Race* ended, they watched *Pretty Woman* and *Runaway Bride*, and they ordered takeout.

It was easy to get caught up in the bliss and easiness of it all, and Miriam began to wonder if she could stay like this forever, suspended in a nest of takeout and sex and bad TV. They weren't honeymooners, not exactly, but it had been a long, long time since she'd let herself hole up with someone all weekend. She'd forgotten how reckless, how easy it could be. And maybe she'd never had it this easy before. Maybe no one had been this effortless in the past.

Everything was perfect right up until Sunday morning, or maybe it was already Sunday afternoon, when Nelson finally broached the subject. They were lying in bed, the sheets rumpled, having returned there after take-out brunch from Miriam's favorite bakery. Nelson was gently running his fingers up and down Miriam's bare arm. One of her legs was hooked over his, and they were both content in their postcoital bliss.

"So what happens when we find our things?" he asked, his voice somehow both soft and raspy. "To us, that is."

Miriam considered the question for a moment. She almost said, *We should keep doing this. We should be together, see if this goes anywhere, because I really, really like you.* But then she remembered the little factoid that she'd conveniently forgotten all weekend—the fact that her firm was currently brokering a deal that would undercut the housing project Nelson's nonprofit was working on. When he found out, whatever was happening between them would end. That inevitable breakup would only get harder the more time they spent together.

So instead, Miriam gave him a half smile and said, "Oh, I always figured this was just while we were still looking."

"Umm, yeah. That's what I thought as well," Nelson agreed a little too fast, his voice a little too high.

Miriam gave him credit when he didn't immediately leave. He took his time, first getting up for a trip to the restroom and then spending some time tidying up her kitchen. When there was really nothing else to do, he turned to her and mumbled something about needing to prepare for a meeting on Monday.

And just like that, the bubble they'd been living in all weekend broke.

"I'll . . . um, I'll text you," Miriam said as Nelson was nearly out the door, "about coordinating time next weekend to look for our things."

Nelson nodded slowly, his eyes wandering over Miriam until they suddenly snapped back up, as if he'd just remembered their little tryst was over and they needed to get back to work. As if he'd just realized that this could never really be real.

"Yeah, that's a good idea," he said. "I'm going to do some research this week to see if I can find us any new leads."

"That . . . that's . . . thanks . . ." Miriam said. The awkwardness and dead air between them felt almost painful after everything had been so easy all weekend. After they had created their perfect little lover's nest.

She should have known it would eventually lead here. Their relationship was always going to be broken. She only wished it had never started in the first place.

Nelson left, and she was alone for the first time in days. She turned the TV back on and thought about preparing for Monday. She needed to focus. There was no time to get lost in Nelson, anyway.

But even as the oversaturated colors of her favorite reality TV dating show played in the background, she couldn't keep her thoughts off him. Of all the things she wanted in life, somehow, he'd become the thing she wanted the most.

She pulled the blanket on her sofa around her shoulders and breathed in his familiar scent of used books and old leather, and she wished it was him, his arms holding her, his face against her cheek. But it was just a blanket, and she knew that the scent of him in it, the feel of him surrounding her would eventually fade.

It hurt, more than she cared to admit. It was the only possible decision, though. The only thing that would protect both of them when it all came crashing down anyway.

Chapter Twenty-One

MONDAY MORNING, MIRIAM WAS late for work. She lived close to the office, but she had spilled coffee on her blouse on the walk in and had to go home to change. By the time she sat down at her desk, the bullpen was already full, and the workday was already well underway. Her colleagues—all the analysts and associates working under her on the deal—had already put on their bulky noise-canceling headphones and were buried in their spreadsheets, hard at work.

The first thing she did was check her email. Unsurprisingly, Miriam's inbox was full. There was a massive fifty-five-email-long chain about a change in the financial model they were working on. By the fourth email in the chain, the discussion had turned to an issue with estimating the property taxes and a resulting error in the model that made the deal more expensive than previously thought. She was already frustrated because the taxes were properly calculated. Her model was just a little messy, and that error was easily fixable. She'd planned to clean it up.

She was not even halfway through the email chain when she got to a seven-email thread about how her color coding was not exactly in line with the firm's standards. She was getting more and more frustrated when suddenly, a spark erupted from where her fingertips met her mouse. It traveled up through the thin cord connecting the mouse to her computer and straight into the hardware that made the computer function.

And the screen went black.

Miriam sighed. She had mostly been in control of her magic for the last twenty-four hours, but the frustration with her emails and possibly the lingering effects of the poison meant she was still struggling sometimes. She no longer had Nelson's calming presence to help her stay settled or to keep her magic in check.

She'd only just started to unplug her computer from its docking station to take it to IT when Charlie and Gregory, the other SVP on the account, both walked into her office. They entered without knocking and without any greeting, and they both looked sour.

"Good morning," Miriam offered, trying to be optimistic. But the knot in the pit of her stomach grew, and she placed her computer back on her desk, knowing IT would have to wait.

"We need to talk about the models," Charlie started, completely ignoring her greeting.

"I was going through the emails now, but my computer sort of blew up," Miriam said, waving a hand over the dead laptop.

"You left us last week and all weekend with a bad model," Gregory cut in. "The team had to work overtime this weekend to make sense of it."

"The property taxes weren't wrong," Miriam explained. "I had just done the calculation a little backwards . . . Well, not really backwards, it was right . . . it was just a weird walk through on the logic."

"It wasn't just the property taxes," Gregory continued. "It was also the interest rate modeling, and the entire format wasn't something we could give to our client. It was a lot of work to get it ready, and you disappeared on us halfway through."

"Look, I'm really sorry. I was sick." Miriam tried to explain, but the little lies left a bitter taste in her mouth. She'd spent all weekend with Nelson, doing things that had nothing to do with being sick. Then, right as she'd had to make any sort of commitment, she'd sent him packing, all in the name of this job. This job, which was already starting to give her a headache even though it wasn't yet ten o'clock.

"You didn't even log on from home?" Charlie scoffed. "Surely you could've taken a look at a few emails."

Miriam sighed; she could have. She'd been feeling better most of Saturday and Sunday, but rather than work, she'd watched trashy reality TV, that was, when she hadn't been cuddled up with Nelson in bed.

"I'm really sorry. Let me get my computer to IT, and then I can fix the model," Miriam pleaded. This was the part she hated the most about her job—the pleading, the groveling, asking for forgiveness. She'd never seen a man do this, though it often felt like she was the only person in the whole office who ever made mistakes. Perhaps she was. The entire thing made her feel small and incompetent.

"The model's already fixed," Gregory explained. "We need you to start preparing for the client proposal next week. They're coming in to run through the details before we start the negotiation process."

Miriam nodded, but it was becoming increasingly clear from this conversation that she'd lost the privilege of being lead on the deal and had been relegated back to a simple staff member. They'd never say it. She'd still take the lead at the client meeting, but they obviously felt she could no longer be trusted to put the information together and effectively direct her team.

"I'll get to work as soon as my computer's fixed," Miriam huffed. She wanted nothing more than to get out of her office and away from these two. But they didn't seem to be finished with scolding her yet, and Charlie remained in her way, blocking her exit.

"You need to close this deal," he warned. "This is a big one for the bank, and the client is treating this like a trial run. If we can get this deal done right, then it means more business. A lot more."

"I know, I know," Miriam whined, though it did nothing to make her feel better. She'd messed up; she knew she'd messed up. The models were flat wrong, and she'd spent all weekend ignoring work, and now she was trying to shrug off responsibility like she was an insolent child.

No wonder they'd demoted her from lead.

"You need to take this seriously," Charlie continued, his tone firm and almost threatening.

Miriam took in a deep lungful of air, steadying her breathing. She didn't appreciate the feeling of being double-teamed, and it was making her anxious. The last thing she needed was to cry, right here, in this office. "I . . . am," she insisted, putting a frustrating amount of space between the words. She continued, though her words sped up and got more emotional. "Look, I'm sorry. I got really sick this weekend, and I didn't pick up my computer. I'm sorry. I'm here and I'm focused now. Can I please go to IT to get my computer fixed?"

Charlie glared at her for another second, but then conceded and stepped aside. With an obviously-still-unhappy nod, Charlie turned and motioned to Gregory, and they both left her office.

It didn't take IT long to conclude that Miriam's computer was fried. They ended up giving her a loaner, but it was someone's old, bulky castoff. On her way back to her desk, Miriam stopped in the kitchen for a coffee. Hannah was there, making herself a cup of tea.

"Oh, good, you're alive!" Hannah said. "You've been missing from the group chat."

"Yeah," Miriam nodded. "It's been a weekend."

"We should go to lunch. Maybe catch up," Hannah suggested, her enthusiasm bubbling. Despite her clairvoyance, she didn't seem to have caught Miriam's foul mood.

"Today?" Miriam asked, frowning as she glanced down at her computer. It would take her at least a couple of hours to set up before she could work again. "I really don't have the time."

"Please," Hannah begged, and it seemed important, but for the second time in so many days, her job needed to take precedence over the people in her life.

"I'm really, really, sorry. I just—I can't today. I have a ton of work to catch up on, and my computer's crashed. Rain check?" Miriam pleaded.

"Tomorrow?" Hannah leveled her a look, but Miriam was just glad Hannah hadn't asked to go out in the evening for afterwork drinks or something. She likely already knew Miriam wouldn't get off at any reasonable time.

"Tomorrow," Miriam agreed. "I promise."

Miriam spent the rest of her day hunkered down in her office, mostly cursing at her computer for going slow and not being configured the way she wanted it to be. When she finally got in to take a look at the model for the client, nothing seemed right. It was worse than a mess, and she quickly realized she was probably going to be working all night to figure things out.

She slipped on her headphones and turned on her favorite podcast, needing the background noise to help her focus.

When she finally finished her work for the day, she was the last person left in the office. The lights had already been shut off in all the main areas, and everyone else had already headed home some time ago. She gathered her things and headed to the elevator.

Bruce greeted her when she got back to her building not long after. She smiled at him, gave him a curt good night, and then went up to her apartment. It felt empty and sterile, even though Larry was meowing loudly for his dinner. It was way past the time he'd decided he deserved his wet food, though he'd eaten his fill of dry food thanks to the self-feeder.

When Miriam fell into bed, she could still smell Nelson—old books and worn leather—and it filtered through her bedroom like thick perfume. She hadn't made a mistake, not really. She knew it was best to cut things off with Nelson now, rather than have it happen later. She'd been vulnerable, and he'd been vulnerable, and certainly, being vulnerable and raw was a terrible reason to start a relationship. A trauma bond wasn't exactly love. They both deserved better. Even so, lying here in bed, smelling him on her pillows and remembering what it felt like to lean against his chest, she was having a hard time convincing herself of that. And her realization days ago that he hadn't ever been judging her or her family or her magic or even her job made this all hurt that much more. How could she ever find someone better than him?

Even though it was late, and even though Miriam was tired, she tossed and turned all night. Larry gave up at one point when she almost rolled over him. He leaped off the bed with a yowl and sauntered out into the living room to sleep.

By the time she made it to work the next morning, her inbox was already full again, despite having only been gone for a handful of non-working hours. The first email she noticed was from a fresh analyst who had sent a poorly written, not-well-thought-out email to someone at her client's office late last night.

"Gabe!" she called from her doorway. "My office, now!"

Gabe was a thin kid, no older than twenty-three. He'd graduated from Columbia and was an ace when it came to building out models in Excel. He was obviously much less proficient when it came to emails.

Gabe poked his head into the office and gave a little wave to Miriam. "Hey, good morning."

Miriam nodded a curt greeting and got right to the point. "You emailed our client last night and told them they needed to provide a hundred years' worth of *puberty* records," she scolded, reading the words directly off her computer. Her tone was harsher than the analyst deserved. In fact, given her own poor mood that morning, Miriam really should have left this discussion to one of the associates on the project. They were only a level above Gabe and would have been much gentler. Instead, she'd made yet another bad decision and had taken her own frustration out on this kid.

And it's only Tuesday, she thought, watching as Gabe quaked a little, standing meekly just inside the doorway to Miriam's office. His eyes widened, and then he looked down at his shiny black dress shoes.

"I'm . . . sorry . . ."

Miriam gave a frustrated huff. "No emailing a client without asking an associate first," she instructed, and he gave a nervous nod. Then he carefully peeked up at Miriam. She must have still been glaring because he looked right back down at the floor.

She sighed and then cocked her head. "It's fine, you'll get it, but for now, I need you back to work. We've got the client meeting to prep for."

Gabe nodded one more time before shuffling out of her office, continuing to avoid looking at her.

She threw her head back and ran her hands through her hair. She hadn't meant to be so witchy about it, but that was the reality of working in investment banking. To get any respect, she had to be tough.

***

In the afternoon, she got pulled into an extended strategy session. The receptionist ordered in lunch, and there was no escaping once the bland sandwiches had been delivered.

It was only when the meeting broke much later and Miriam went to use the restroom that she ran into Hannah.

"Hey," Hannah greeted as they both stood together at the sink to wash their hands. "I saw you got stuck in a meeting during lunch."

"Shit . . . Hannah, I'm so sorry. We've got meetings and more meetings to prepare for this upcoming client meeting, and it's just—"

"It's okay," Hannah cut in, her tone making Miriam think it was not, in fact, okay. "Can we try again tomorrow?"

"Yeah . . . I'll put it on my calendar," Miriam agreed. "I promise, tomorrow,"

***

Miriam went home late again. She was greeted by Bruce, she fed Larry, and she slept on top of sheets that still smelled like

Nelson. She would have to wash them eventually, and she was already dreading laundry day.

***

It was raining when she stepped out of her apartment Wednesday morning. The heavy, cold, soaking kind of rain that made her want to curl up with a book. The sort of rain that she didn't want to walk to work in, even with an umbrella. If she'd had her broom, she could have cast a protection spell and flown the short distance, avoiding the rain altogether.

It was another morning of emails and meetings and analysts, and she felt absolutely miserable. It was all her own doing, she knew. She'd dug herself into this bad mood, and it only seemed to continue spiraling through every interaction.

At twelve thirty, Hannah walked into Miriam's office. She was wearing her coat and holding her purse.

"Lunch," Miriam sighed. "I forgot . . . I have"—she grimaced—"stuff to do."

But Hannah wouldn't accept no for an answer today. "Please," she begged. "I know you've been busy, but I have something I want to tell you."

"And you can only do it at lunch?" Miriam huffed, frustrated. She needed to put all of her effort in here, at work. She needed this deal to get back on track, and *she* needed to be the one who made that happen. It might be her only big chance.

"Miriam, you know I love you, and I understand the whole 'girl boss' thing, I really do, but you've been off all week.

Actually for a while. Can you please just take forty-five minutes and get a salad with me?"

With a sigh and then a nod, Miriam conceded. Hannah was right; she could take a forty-five-minute lunch to grab a salad.

She slipped on her coat and followed Hannah out of the building and down the street to sweetgreen. The line was long, but it didn't take too long, and after just a few more minutes, they settled together at a table with their standard sweetgreen orders.

"Okay, so what did you want to talk about?" Miriam asked as she plunged her plastic fork into her salad, spearing a piece of romaine lettuce coated in Caesar dressing.

"Can you please just pretend to care about me for two minutes? I know you've been on *this woe is me, I'm a mess* thing for a while, but for just two minutes, can it be about someone else?" Hannah snapped.

Miriam dropped her fork, taken aback by her friend's blunt words. "Hannah, I didn't realize—"

"I know, and I really want to share this with you, and I want you to be here, for me, for just for a second."

Miriam nodded and let Hannah's words settle, the uncomfortable pull of guilt churning in her gut. With all the time she'd spent in her own little world of self-pity, upset about her friends and their growing families, she'd forgotten that her friends needed her just as much as she needed them.

"Yeah, sorry, Hannah . . . I want to hear your news. I should've come to lunch on Monday."

Hannah nodded to accept Miriam's apology, and then her lips turned upward into a wide smile. Whatever news she had was too exciting for her to stay mad at Miriam any longer.

"I'm pregnant!" Hannah exclaimed. "I've known for a few weeks, but we're just telling close friends now. We didn't want to tell the coven yet. Everyone else had news, and we'd figure we'd wait until Craig and Derek had the baby, and we wanted to give Isabelle a while with her news. But I really wanted to tell you. I kind of need a friend here at work who knows. Maddy knows I'm telling you."

"Hannah, that's . . . that's amazing," she said, pouring as much enthusiasm into her words and her smile as she could, and then she stood up and moved around to the other side of the table to hug her friend.

It wasn't exactly a surprise that Hannah was pregnant. She and Maddy had been sharing secretive glances every time babies came up in conversation. The firm also had pretty good family-planning support to help couples get pregnant, and Hannah and Maddy were at that age and stage in their lives that it made sense. And it was fine. There was no world where Miriam wanted a baby anyway, and she'd just ended the closest thing she'd had to a relationship in years. She just didn't want to feel so left behind anymore.

"We're still not technically out of the woods yet, in terms of getting through the first trimester, but each week we get a little safer," Hannah babbled on as they both sat back down. "Maddy has already started to think about nursery designs, and I'm going to try to take a six-month leave from work. It's longer than standard, but I really want time to bond with the baby."

Miriam gave a forced smile and then stabbed her salad again with her fork and shoved a large bite of Caesar salad into her mouth. "This is so exciting," Miriam mumbled, her mouth full.

"And you—you're with Nelson?" Hannah asked. "He could join our coven."

Miriam immediately shook her head but avoided meeting Hannah's eye. Hannah meant well, but she was trying to plan a life out for Miriam that would never exist.

"I don't think things are going to work with Nelson," Miriam said, pushing around the lettuce in her bowl. She didn't bother to elaborate. There wasn't much to explain, and she couldn't go into the specifics of the Pentacle deal, not before it closed. And certainly not in a busy, fast-casual chain restaurant in the middle of the Financial District.

"I'm sorry," Hannah said. "It seemed you might have finally found someone."

Miriam shook her head. "It's fine. I haven't really been looking."

Hannah's expression morphed into that look of pity Miriam hated so much, and Miriam felt her stomach drop. Sure, at one time, they'd all been young and living in the city and hooking up and casually dating. But then the casual dates had slowly started becoming more and more serious, which was exactly what Miriam hadn't wanted. Now, she'd stopped dating altogether, and she would be what? The chaotic aunt who worked all the time?

"Look, I have to get back to the office," she said abruptly. "I need to get some stuff over to Charlie this afternoon."

"Sure," Hannah replied. Her face fell, and Miriam knew what she was thinking. She was sure Hannah had decided that Miriam could only make everything about herself and her own problems. She'd said as much already. But she just couldn't stay here any longer and have Hannah look at her like that—with all that pity in her eyes.

Miriam gathered her trash and threw it away, not waiting for Hannah to follow. She really just needed to get back to work and away from this . . . whatever this was.

Feelings of emptiness and loss and chaos swirled around inside of her, and Miriam felt off again as she left the restaurant. The entire week had been frustrating, and nothing had seemed to go her way. And worse, it all felt like her fault. It was like she couldn't help but keep making the sort of mistakes that disrupted her life even more. The same mistakes, over and over again. She was one of those people that even Nelson couldn't help, which was another reason they needed to stay away from each other. He would eventually figure out that she was one of the helpless ones, even if he still liked her.

She was doing him a favor.

Well after the sun had set, she finally wrapped up at the office. It was another late night followed by another few hours of getting lost in reality TV on the sofa. She made it through half a bottle of wine and several episodes of *House Hunters* before even her own self-doubt couldn't force her eyes to stay open any longer.

***

By Friday morning, Miriam had shut herself in her office with a coffee the size of her head. She was determined to end the week better than it had started, which should have been a low enough bar, but Miriam still wasn't sure she could clear it.

She was making good progress on the deck, and her magic was finally under control. But she was still in a sour mood. Larry had thrown up a hair ball right as she'd walked out the door, and her hair was sticking up in all directions. No matter how much hair product she'd used, it had refused to cooperate. She'd finally given up and shoved it into a clip, hoping for some sort of organizing force. Yet, even that had failed.

At least things at work seemed to be moving in the right direction, and by the afternoon, Miriam was finally seeing a light at the end of the tunnel.

That was until she got a text from Nelson.

We're going to Jersey, meet at the Oculus tomorrow, 9 am

"What the fuck is in New Jersey?" Miriam swore to herself, and she lowered her head to her hands with a deep breath.

It would be another Saturday wasted on this ridiculous quest of theirs. Another Saturday when she was supposed to be working. She'd promised Charlie that she was going to do better, and she couldn't keep skipping out on work—especially to go to New Jersey.

Somehow, she needed to figure this mystery out and find their things. Fast.

Chapter Twenty-Two

NELSON WAS WAITING AT the entrance of the Oculus, an ultramodern white whale of a building, when Miriam approached the next morning. His jacket was pulled up high to shield him from the worst of the spitting rain that seemed to have taken over the city the last few days. He was holding two paper coffee cups, and Miriam's heart broke a little.

He'd still brought her coffee after Miriam had sent him packing.

She didn't deserve him, not even now, in what was hopefully the final throes of their quest.

"Morning," Nelson said curtly, business-like, thrusting one of the cups in front of her.

"Hey, good morning," Miriam responded, accepting the cup but keeping a reasonable distance between them. "What's in Jersey?" she asked. She wasn't particularly excited to go to New Jersey, of all places. Long Island was fine. She was from there. Brooklyn was still in the city, and Staten Island was fine too. Anything was better than *New Jersey*.

"Our things like going places that are familiar, right?" Nelson asked as he led them to the entrance for the PATH train. "Well, I decided to call my uncle, who helped enchant my medallion, and he mentioned he got it off someone in Hoboken."

Miriam looked at him suspiciously. "How did your uncle come into possession of a taxi medallion?"

In high school, Miriam hadn't thought much about the worth of a small piece of metal. But as she'd gotten older, she'd learned about the economics of taxi medallions. It seemed odd that Nelson would have something so valuable when plenty of common objects could be enchanted. Or at least, something that had had a high value when they were in high school. The rise of ride share services had crashed the New York taxi business and the medallion market. Miriam remembered reading that taxi medallions were sometimes sold for over a million dollars at auction as recently as ten years ago. Now, their worth was only a fraction of that.

"It's not real," Nelson said with a shrug. "It's not registered with the city. It was a defect, cast off from a factory that minted them back in the 1930s. My uncle got a tip about it and thought it would make a cool magical item."

"So, what, we're just going to walk around the place your uncle bought a magical medallion twenty years ago?" Miriam prodded, poking at all the holes in his plan.

"The map hasn't been working," he replied bluntly. "And you almost died the last place we went." His tone was firm, and he didn't look at Miriam as he spoke. It felt like even more evidence of the wall that had been erected between them. And given how this felt right now, it was hard to believe that they'd spent all of last weekend together, so happy and content.

It was her own fault. It was always her own fault.

"Anyway, we still have the finding spell," Nelson added. "So, once we're there, we can cast one."

"Yeah," Miriam agreed, and then looked down the track, waiting for a train. She didn't want to see whatever knowing expression was inevitably plastered across Nelson's face. That little jab at her map had just been another reminder of her awful week—the awful last few weeks, really.

After a few more minutes, the train finally arrived, cutting through the uncomfortable silence that had settled between them. They boarded and found seats in a mostly empty car. The number of people who wanted to go from Manhattan to New Jersey on a Saturday morning was limited. Miriam didn't blame them. She also had zero desire to go to New Jersey, of all places.

The train zoomed out of New York, and once they were well on their way, Miriam mustered up the courage to broach the subject, wanting to make sure they both had clear expectations. "About this weekend . . ." she started.

Nelson put a hand up to stop her. "We were never anything," he stated, as though he'd known exactly what she'd planned to say. "You never owed me anything."

"You took care of me," Miriam argued, surprising herself. She realized she sort of wanted him to be mad about what she'd done. She was mad at herself for what she'd done.

"Okay, but you're still a friend, and I'm still going to take care of you."

"Oh." Miriam sank back into her chair. His gentle words and his insistence that he would take care of her, even if they were just friends, made her feel small, all of her guilt bubbling back up.

Nelson cocked his head and looked at her, his eyes sharp, like he could see right through her. "Did you want us to be more?" he challenged.

He was probably waiting for her to concede, to break down and spill her guts right here on the train. And that was something she certainly wasn't going to do.

"Nope," she answered quickly, but her voice sounded weird and hollow. It had to be the least-convincing lie she had ever told.

Nelson nodded. "So, we find our things, and then we go back to our lives."

She'd repeated that phrase both to herself and out loud so many times in the last few weeks. And now, he matched her conviction, like he too had decided it was best for them to move on.

"Yes, and with any luck, your New Jersey idea will lead us right to our stuff. Maybe it's been hiding there all this time," Miriam said.

"Sure," Nelson agreed.

They rode in an uncomfortable silence, Miriam distracting herself with the thought that even though she kept saying their relationship needed to end, she didn't *really* want to give it up. She didn't *really* want New Jersey to be their final adventure together. But there was no way she was going to tell Nelson that.

When they finally reached their stop in Hoboken, they got off the train. The rain had intensified, and the sky was a dark, stormy green. Miriam pulled her jacket tighter and the hood up.

"It's just a short walk," Nelson yelled over the sound of the strengthening rainstorm.

Miriam gave him a glare but followed his lead. This was his idea, after all, and so she would let it be his mistake if and when it failed.

They slogged through soggy sidewalks for what felt like hours, even though the time could have been better counted in minutes. The Manhattan skyline was just barely visible in the distance, almost completely lost in the weather.

Finally, Nelson stopped at a large park that included a wooded section, swing sets, and a couple of baseball diamonds. "Here," he declared.

"A park?" Miriam said, looking around. "We're going to search an entire park?"

Nelson shrugged. "This was where my uncle bought the medallion. He met someone in Nishi Park to buy it off them. So, here we are in Nishi Park."

"This deal sounds shady," Miriam opined.

Nelson shrugged. "My uncle wanted to make my bar mitzvah special, after everything with my dad . . ." He trailed off, his gaze far off and unfocused.

Miriam pressed her lips together in sympathy. On her bat mitzvah, she'd been given the broom her parents' coven had enchanted for her when she was a baby. Maybe Nelson had a broom somewhere, or maybe the magic was too tied to his dad's and too unstable to have been gifted to him after his dad's death.

Either way, it was clear the memory still pained him. So she stayed silent for a moment out of respect for his loss. Then, she asked quietly, "So what now?"

"It shouldn't take that long to walk around the park and cast a few finding spells," Nelson explained. His plan wasn't exactly sophisticated. Nor was it any different from how they'd already been approaching this quest.

"We should divide and conquer," Miriam suggested. "That way, we can each take a section of the park and cast our finding spells."

"I'm not sure that's a good idea," Nelson cautioned. "We've been in some pretty tricky situations looking for our things so far."

"Yeah," Miriam replied. "But all the other times, we'd followed the map into areas that had a high concentration of magic. And you were the one who said that wasn't working," she reminded him. "This is just a park. Anyway, the weather is bad, and I need to get some work done tonight. I'm still behind from last weekend. I can take any non-magic threats, and I need to get this done." She waved a hand at him and started to walk away, studying the park to decide where to begin.

"Miriam," Nelson called over the rain.

She ignored him, having already chosen which side of the park she'd search first. "I'll take anything left of the baseball fields, and you take everything else," Miriam shouted as she headed into the wooded area.

"Wait, Miriam!" Nelson called out again, but Miriam was already trekking ahead, scanning for a suitable spot to cast a finding spell. Nelson could go search his own area of the park.

The trail through the forest was muddy, and her sneakers were already soaked after the walk from the train station. She walked a little faster, hoping they could get this over with quickly so she could go home and change into warm, dry clothes. She was alert, and she had readied her magic. She didn't expect to encounter any malicious magics, but she was cautious as she made her way through the secluded part of the park, careful to not disturb any magical goings-on. If this journey had taught her anything, it was that magics were present in all nooks and crannies of the city.

Once she was a good bit into the woods, she cast her first finding spell. She waved her arm and then waited to see if their items magically revealed themselves. When nothing happened, she walked farther into the park. Unlike when she cast the finding spell at her parents' house, she wasn't familiar enough with the area to know when her magic hit the outer bounds of the park or even how big the park was. She'd need to cast a few more and see what happened.

She treaded deeper into the woods, and the rain, which was already bad, seemed to take a turn for the worse. Even though it was still only late morning, the sky had gone dark, and it was getting difficult to see. Because she was the only one in the forest and she didn't want to risk getting her phone wet, Miriam conjured a small orb of light in her hand. She let it go so that it could float in front of her to light her path as she walked. It bounced and bobbed chaotically around her, but it felt good to let her magic out. She spent so much of her life attempting to keep her chaos magic in check that it was a relief when she was truly allowed to let it out.

The wind whipped through her hair, and it got colder the farther into the park she got. She was just about to stop and cast another finding spell when she heard her name.

"Miriam," a male voice called out. It sounded like Nelson's, although it was coming from deeper in the woods rather than back towards the baseball fields where they'd started.

"Nelson?" Miriam called back, and she started walking towards where his voice was coming from. He must have looped around to the back of the park and was coming up to meet her. Maybe he'd already located their things.

The trail ahead eased slightly downhill and was even muddier than the trail when she'd first entered the forest. She took careful steps, but the ground was slick, and she slipped suddenly, losing her footing. She landed on her butt, and her little ball of light flickered out entirely, leaving her muddy and on the ground and in the dark.

It was even darker than before. So dark that it almost felt like dusk.

"Miriam, come on," she heard Nelson's voice call again.

"I slipped! Can you come meet me?" she yelled back as she pushed herself up and wiped her hands on her jeans, attempting to get some of the mud off.

"I need help! Miriam, I need help," the voice called.

"Are you okay? I'm coming," Miriam shouted, and she started running towards the voice, glad she hadn't twisted an ankle or anything. She could feel branches and leaves cutting at her legs, trying to slow her, as if the forest didn't want her to find Nelson. She cast another orb, but it quickly fluttered away in the storm, off on its own adventure. It wouldn't get far without her—the magic no longer had a source, and the orb would extinguish on its own once it was just out of sight. But that left her in the dark. Again.

"Miriam . . . !" Nelson called again. His voice sounded strained, as if his situation was dire. Miriam needed to get to him. She needed to save him.

"Where are you?" she asked, raising her voice over the wind and rain. "Just stay where you are, and I'll find you." It would be impossible for them to find each other if they were both running around each other in circles.

She pushed her hair out of her face, but the wind and the rain quickly whipped it back. Her entire body ached from the cold, and rain soaked through her coat now, but she kept running. She had to get out of the park, and she had to find Nelson. She called for him again, hoping he would call back. But she could barely hear her own voice now.

She tripped on a tree branch and fell in the mud again, only this time when she tried to stand back up, her shoe had lodged itself in a root. "Nelson!" she yelled, pulling her foot to try to dislodge it. "Where are you?"

She was about to give up and just take her shoe off when the root suddenly extended up her leg, imprisoning her. Her heart raced as she felt panic rising in her chest. Nelson needed her. She had to get to him. He'd stopped responding, and something was wrong, and she was about to lose him.

Pausing, she took a deep breath in while she thought about what she was going to do next. She needed to calm her magic enough to find a way to get out of the branch's hold. Maybe . . . a scatter spell would work? It usually caused a boom that made pesky raccoons and ruckus teenagers scatter without doing any real harm. It could be just enough to call off the tree.

She concentrated for a moment, focusing to put just a bit of power behind her magic. Then she forced her magic outward. The magic connected with the tree in a loud boom. But when she tried to move her leg, the root just held on tighter.

The scatter spell hadn't worked.

And worse, the branches of the trees above her had splayed and bent, almost as if they had come alive and were slowly closing in on her.

She needed another idea, and quick.

Trees hated fire, and it was wet enough that she was unlikely to start a forest fire in the park if she tried to use fire against it. Her decision made, she balled her hands up into fists and then let out a very controlled fire ball—or at least as controlled as a chaos witch could manage. It was about the size of a beach ball, but even so, it dissipated harmlessly against the tree. Everything was too wet for any fire to have an effect.

Panic rose again as she could feel her magic attempting to escape in a chaotic mess. She did her best to push it back down so she could stay in control. What she really needed, though, was a small miracle from Nelson. She hated herself for that thought, to think she needed Nelson. But it was true.

She was about to take a deep, calming breath in to gather her control, when she suddenly remembered how she'd freed herself and Nelson from the dim sum restaurant by making the dumpling cart crash. Perhaps control wasn't actually what she needed.

Exhaling, she let out all the magic she could muster. The ball of chaos that had settled in her chest burst out in an unpredictable mess.

There was fire and fireworks and flowers and rainbow balloons and sparkly confetti and music and screaming and everything, everything all at once in a chaotic mess. Her magic roamed free and unrestrained in a way she had not allowed it to in so, so many years. It was a release unlike anything she had felt in so, so long.

The tree released her from its grasp, and the dark sky lightened. It was still raining, but Miriam was no longer stuck in an inky-black storm with spitting rain. She pushed herself to her feet, tucked her hair back behind her ears, and took another deep breath as she started walking down the hill again.

"Nelson!" she called as she continued in the last direction she'd heard Nelson yelling from before the tree had grabbed her. "Nelson!"

"Miriam!" The voice came from behind her this time, opposite the direction of the voice she'd been chasing.

And when she spun around, there he was, standing in the rain, his hair slicked back and water dripping down his face. There he was, whole and alive.

She ran to him and wrapped her arms around his waist and buried her head in his chest. "You're okay," she sobbed.

Nelson rubbed circles on her back and then pulled away so that he could look at her. He brushed a rain-soaked curl from her face. "What happened?"

"You were calling for me . . . and then I fell, and the tree . . ." She wanted to explain everything that had happened, but her body shuddered with another sob.

"Okay, hey, slow down," Nelson said soothingly. He touched her cheek, and it felt reassuring. "I was on the other side, over at the jungle gym, casting a finding spell. I came when I saw your magic explode. It was quite a show. We should probably get out of here before non-magics come down to see what the ruckus is."

"You . . . you weren't in trouble?" Miriam asked as she tried to wipe a tear away from her face only to realize that the rain kept coming and there was nothing she could do to dry her eyes. "You weren't calling for me?"

Nelson shook his head. "No . . . but if that's what you were hearing, we should get out of the woods now," Nelson replied as he swiveled his head around, his eyes wide and searching. He put his hand out for Miriam, and she intertwined her fingers with his, feeling a security that was all emotion.

Together, they hurried back up the hill, helping each other over parts of the trail that were slick with mud. Even when they reached the open section of the park, they kept moving. It was almost completely empty, given the weather, and the only person there was an older man. He sat on a bench right next to a sign that read "Nishi Park."

The man glared at them as they approached the egress of the park. "You fools," his voice rang out in the familiar accent of a native English speaker from south Asia. "You two have no respect for magic."

Nelson glared back at him and then wrapped a protective arm around Miriam.

The man narrowed his eyes and gave an understanding nod of his head. "Never trust two magics who are falling in love," he grumbled. "It brings out the worst in the Nishi."

"Nishi?" Nelson's voice was some combination of skeptical and defensive.

"Our community built this park to give it a home and keep both the Nishi and our community safe, and then you two murkhs disturbed its peace."

"Oh . . ." Nelson rubbed a guilty hand across the back of his neck, while Miriam just watched the interaction, still too stunned to interject. "Why is it here?" he asked.

The man's eyes went wide. "Because we're here, and magic follows its people," he said, without giving more context.

Miriam understood, though. Magic would always be where its people were, just like language, food, and culture. And she knew that made the world richer, even though there was some danger in it.

"We should . . ." Nelson trailed off but tilted his head towards the exit.

"Go," the man agreed, and his voice had a notable fatigue. "We'll clean up your mess, but you should go. You're not helping."

Without another word, they left the park and continued walking through the rain, straight back to the PATH station.

They arrived right as a train was pulling up, which Miriam assumed was from the help of a small miracle.

"So . . . in the woods, you heard my voice?" Nelson asked quietly once they were on the train back to Manhattan.

"Yes, you were in trouble." Miriam trembled as she recounted what had happened. "I'm not sure exactly what the Nishi was doing, but I heard your voice, and you sounded scared, as if something had happened."

"Hmmm." Nelson frowned. "Must be because we had been together . . . I mean, in the park . . . not like together, together . . ." He stumbled over his words, but it was clear he was avoiding bringing up what the man had said about them falling in love.

"Hmmm," she agreed with a nod. She sighed and looked out the window, watching the water trickle down.

She had another theory, but she wasn't sure she was ready to share it. When she'd thought Nelson was in trouble, she hadn't just been worried about a random person; she'd been worried about *Nelson*. She'd been overcome with the feeling that she didn't want to live any part of her life without Nelson. And even now that they were back on the train to New York, safe from the Nishi in the park, she still felt the same way.

"But you're safe now," Nelson said. "We just need to figure out the next place we're going to look."

She turned back to him, but he'd already opened up his phone and pulled up a map, obviously ready to move on from the incident in the woods.

"Hey, Nelson," Miriam said, because she felt both too scared and too brave, and that was a terrible combination.

"Yes," he said, and he looked up from his phone patiently.

"Do you remember on Sunday, when I said that this, us . . . was just for the duration of looking for our things?" Miriam asked him.

"Uh-huh," Nelson replied, his expression unreadable.

"I . . . I was wrong. I don't actually want this to just be a thing until we find our stuff, and I understand if I blew my chances and I understand if you have no interest in someone who can't seem to make up their mind . . . but when I was in the woods and I thought you were in trouble and I couldn't get to you, and the thought of having to be here . . . without you . . ." Miriam finally stopped her ramble, and she pursed her lips and held his gaze. She'd just said so many truths, and yet, she hadn't told him the real truth.

Even if he accepted her now, everything would still collapse once he found out about her work.

Nelson just turned to her in his train seat, placed his hand under her chin, and kissed her. He kissed her right there, on the PATH train, in soaking-wet clothes.

"World Trade Center," the voice announced over the speaker, signaling that they'd reached their stop. Nelson broke the kiss and pulled back.

"My place," Miriam said, and when Nelson nodded in agreement, she took his hand. Together, they stood, exited the train, and then made the walk back through Lower Manhattan to her apartment.

As soon as the door was closed and they were in Miriam's apartment, he had her pressed up against the door. Their wet clothes were likely making an imprint on the pristine white walls of Miriam's apartment. But she didn't care. His lips were on hers, hard and hungry. She pushed out of her dripping jacket and slipped off her shoes, and Nelson did the same, without ever taking his lips off her hers.

Miriam could already feel him hard and ready beneath his jeans, and her own desire was pooling between her legs. She didn't want to go slow, and she hoped he didn't either. She found the waistband of his jeans and quickly unfastened the button and pushed his pants down off his thighs. At the same time, he ran his hands up underneath her shirt, unclipping her bra as he moved up her torso. When her top was off, his fingers deftly unbuttoned her jeans, and then his hands began working them down her legs. He was efficient, pushing her down underwear with her jeans. With a smirk, she realized it was a small miracle that they were able to get out of their wet clothes so easily. She'd have to remember to thank him for that later.

Nelson kept moving, clearly feeling the same urgency she was. He turned them around, backed them up, and then hoisted Miriam onto the edge of the kitchen counter. He spread her knees apart and then reached down into the pocket of his discarded jeans and pulled out a condom.

"Always prepared?" Miriam hummed as he rolled the latex over himself.

He laughed a little. "I carry a lot of things just in case."

Then he was back in front of her and then inside her, moving fast. The pressure grew with a delicious intensity, and she held on to the edge of her island and leaned back as Nelson moved with her hips.

And then Miriam let herself unravel with a release that rivaled the one she'd had earlier in the woods.

Breathing hard, she leaned her head onto Nelson's shoulder and let out a sigh of relief and pleasure.

"I'm glad you want to keep doing this," Nelson said, "because I'm pretty sure you've ruined all other women for me."

Miriam laughed and then pressed a kiss into his collarbone. "We've ruined each other."

Nelson kissed her forehead. "Now that we've decided we are allowed to keep seeing each other after we've found our stuff, we should probably go back to trying to find our stuff."

"Hmm, I have an entire bed," Miriam offered. "And I bet we can top what we just did."

"Or we could let the tension build, make it a reward for when we finish our quest," Nelson taunted.

"After all that mud, I could really use someone to help me wash my hair."

Nelson cradled her chin in his hand and then brushed his fingers through a strand of her hair. "I think it could wait," he teased again.

"You're evil," Miriam said, and she scooted off her kitchen counter. "I'm going to change first, and then we can figure out our next move."

Miriam left Nelson alone and naked in the middle of her kitchen as she made her way into her bedroom to change. Larry followed her.

Chapter Twenty-Three

"Okay," Nelson said. "Let's go over the facts again."

They were clothed now, sitting on the stools at Miriam's kitchen island—the same island that Miriam had been sitting on just a few minutes ago. Now, however, Nelson was all business.

"Your broom usually ends up in places with a high concentration of magic, and we think that there might be a personal connection to the magic?" he asked.

"The personal connection is a theory, but it's a good place to refocus," Miriam agreed. "Maybe we figure out where our connection overlaps."

Nelson nodded. "You already did a finding spell near your parents' house, and that covered our high school and the synagogue," he ticked off, reminding Miriam that they had also gone to Hebrew school together as kids. Their childhood synagogue had only been a couple of blocks from the school.

Miriam nodded. "Maybe we share the same dry cleaner or something." It was a stretch, but they were running out of places to look for their things.

"I own two suits. I go to the dry cleaners approximately twice a year, and it's in Williamsburg," Nelson explained. "So, unless you're going all the way to Williamsburg for dry cleaning, I don't think it's a good place to start." He paused and then seemed to consider his next question. "Do you go to shul?" he asked, using the Yiddish term for synagogue.

"High Holy Days, with my parents back on Long Island," Miriam said. "You?"

Nelson shrugged. "About once a month, a reconstructionist temple near my apartment and for my father's yahrzeit."

Miriam nodded at Nelson's explanation that he went to synagogue for his dad. He probably only belonged to a synagogue so he had a place for yahrzeit. Miriam hadn't lost a parent or a spouse, and so she had never considered how she would mourn. Would she cling to the traditions that had come to this country along with her magic? Or would she bury them away in passive assimilation?

Nelson broke through Miriam's thoughts as he continued problem-solving. "I'm only in Manhattan for work and to visit our Harlem building."

"I'm never in Brooklyn, I guess, except to see you." Miriam smiled and gave his arm a quick squeeze.

"A cross-borough relationship," Nelson considered with a chuckle.

"Which won't be an issue at all once we find our things," Miriam reminded him. They were finally on the same page about that, at least. Although she still needed to come clean about the deal her firm was working on. For now, though, she pushed away that thought. She could be selfish and let herself have this, just for a while.

Nelson got up from his seat and started wandering around Miriam's living room as if to help himself think. He did a lap, looking at the books on her shelves and then some of the expensive abstract art she'd purchased to make the place feel more sophisticated. Finally, he turned to the family photographs she had on her walls. They were the one thing in her apartment that had not been carefully curated to match the elegance she'd worked so hard to foster in the space, and she'd only put them up at the insistence of her dad.

At first, it didn't seem like Nelson was looking at anything in particular. He seemed more lost in thought, just needing to move a bit to think better. But then he stopped and picked up a photo and brought it over to Miriam.

"This photo?" he asked.

It was old-timey, going back to the twenties. At least Miriam thought that was the right time period. It was a black-and-white photo of a man and a woman standing in front of a shop. The full name of the shop had been cut off in the photo, but it ended with "field."

"My great-grandparents," Miriam explained. "They lived on the Lower East Side. They met after they came over to America," she continued. "Before they met, my great-grandmother worked as a seamstress. I think that was outside the apartment they lived in." She was referring to the classic tenement buildings that had been so popular in the Lower East Side for an entire generation. They were not all that different from the buildings of Harlem, which had welcomed other groups of immigrants from other places in the world.

"That's Copperfield's Butcher Shop. My great-grandfather opened the shop, and my grandfather ran it. My dad grew up under that shop. It was only when he met my mom that he moved to Long Island."

"Do you really think our things have gone back all the way to where our great-grandparents lived?"

Nelson shrugged. "If our grandparents lived on the Lower East Side at the same time, they were inevitably in the same coven."

Miriam nodded; he was right. There were few Jews living in the Lower East Side who were also magical, and they would inevitably have run in very close circles. It was why Miriam and Nelson had known each other for so long. They'd gone to the same school, their parents had been in the same coven, and they'd gone to the same synagogue. They might have been rivals, at least in Miriam's eyes, but their lives had intersected for a very long time. Maybe even longer than they'd realized.

"Wait, what if we're cousins?" Miriam asked.

Nelson shook his head. "That's probably a question best left unexplored."

As magical Ashkenazi Jews, their ancestry almost certainly overlapped at some point in the last five hundred years. Given they had never identified a shared relative, that meant they were no more or less connected than any other Jew they might meet in the wild. It was a very odd reality of being Ashkenazi. Everyone was likely your cousin, just many generations removed.

Miriam nodded. "Do you know the address of this place?" she asked.

"I have an idea. I think it's pretty close to the leather shop, actually," he said, and then he typed something into his phone. "It's a pottery studio now. The sort that does classes open to the community."

"Book a class," Miriam immediately decided. "Something for this afternoon, if possible. It'll be easier if we're supposed to be there. We can cast a quick finding spell. The restrooms will likely be in the basement, which means it'll be easy to look around. It's not much of a waste if we don't find anything, and it's something else to check off the list."

Nelson shook his head as he browsed the website. "Nothing this afternoon, but there is a class tomorrow with slots available. It's a brunch-time pottery class with a mimosa bar," he explained.

"That sounds horrendous," Miriam replied. "But I'm in if that's the next class available."

Nelson tapped away on his phone and then looked up. "All set. We're booked for tomorrow."

"Good. Worst case, we drink a cheap mimosa." Miriam let out a long breath, hopeful that she might *finally* get her broomstick back. It almost felt like she could have everything she'd ever wanted . . . if only she could be sure the thing between her and Nelson wouldn't be ending after she told him the truth about Pentacle.

"So, then tonight . . ." Nelson gave her a soft smile. "What do you think about a proper date, if we're going to try this for real?"

Miriam grimaced. "I need to work tonight," she said. "I'm still really behind on this work project."

Nelson's gaze lingered on her for a moment as though he were considering something. "Actually, I need to review about a million grant proposals our grant writer sent me. What if we both worked, here, together?" he suggested.

"Oh, yeah, sure. That sounds good. Perfect, really," Miriam said with a nervous nod.

It *would have* sounded good, that was, except that she had to work on THE deal. But she also wanted to spend time with Nelson.

Nelson grinned broadly. "Okay, what if we had a working date? We could order takeout, put on some music, but also get all the work done we've been putting off since we've been on this quest," he proposed.

"Oh, hmm . . ." Miriam frowned and trailed off, unsure how to respond. The concept was nice, but if Nelson got a glimpse at her computer screen and saw exactly what she was working on, the "working date" would probably be cut short prematurely. Sure, most of the things she had had been anonymized, and if she was careful and kept her computer locked when he wasn't looking, she'd probably be pretty safe.

But it was a risk.

Her hesitation was long enough for Nelson to notice. His eyebrows pinched together, and his grin faded. "You don't want to?" he asked, and the look of disappointment on his face made Miriam's heart melt into a giant puddle.

She couldn't help but wonder what would happen when he found out about the deal. Really, finally found out. Eventually, there would be press releases, and everything would be public, and Nelson would know. He would know, and it would be over between them. What would kill her the most would be seeing Nelson so disappointed in her. Really just disappointed. He didn't deserve that.

"I do, actually," Miriam agreed. "That actually sounds really nice."

He grinned again, and it seemed to brighten the whole room. "What about dumplings?" he asked, and he looked back at his phone, presumably to find a place for takeout.

"Too soon." Miriam scrunched her face, a bit disappointed as the thought made her stomach roll. She liked dumplings, or at least she used to, so it was unfortunate to not be particularly interested in them.

Nelson gave a little chuckle as he continued scrolling through menus on his phone. "Oh, how about Indian?" he asked. "I could go for a saag paneer."

"And garlic naan and a mango lassi?" Miriam nodded enthusiastically and added, "And if they have a chickpea curry, that too."

Those were just a few of her favorites, and she was glad when Nelson seemed to agree with her.

"Okay, what else for the perfect work date?" he asked.

"Coffee," Miriam decided. "I can't drink while I'm doing this modeling, or it will be all wonky."

"Same with the grant proposals. I'm bad enough at this part of the job, and yet the grants are how we keep operating. With the new facility we're about to open, these grants are going to be especially important."

Miriam tried to smile through that absolute gut punch. *Shit.* How could she do this deal knowing what it would do to Nelson? And worse, knowing what it would do to all the unhoused people in New York who needed the opportunity Housing Magic was trying to provide? She might be an investment banker, but she wasn't unaware of the issues her city faced and the best way to solve them.

"I'll make the first round," Miriam said with another strained smile, and she turned away from him and headed over to her fancy pod coffee maker. Her hands shook a bit as she inserted the pods into the machine.

She could do this, she told herself. And there were a lot of really solid reasons why she needed to get this deal done. All the jobs at the firm was a big reason. Folks losing their livelihoods wasn't something Miriam wanted to see happen. Sure, the investment bankers would be fine, but there was also the clerical staff and Hannah's entire accounting team, all the employees working in HR, IT, and all the departments that made the business run. The jobs of all of these people might be at risk if the deal were to fall through and it got out to the public just what had happened.

There was also the matter of being able to really take care of her parents. Sure, she could probably downgrade her apartment or figure out how to cut back in other ways so that she could send them money, but she still wanted them to have comfort and security. She still wanted to be able to cover it, no problem, if they got sick or needed more care as they got older.

Of course, all of those reasons felt small compared to the monumental battle the current and future residents of Housing

Magic were facing every day. If her deal succeeded, all of those people who would have benefitted from the Housing Magic project would no longer have that opportunity for a roof over their heads.

How would Nelson even be able to look at her when the truth about what she did came out? How could she even look at herself? She liked Nelson a lot, and she was going to lose him. There was no way he was that understanding. There was no way he'd be able to see her as anything but a very wicked witch.

She set down the mug of coffee she'd just prepared and turned back to Nelson.

"Hey," he said with a gentle smile. He pulled her into his arms and kissed her forehead. Then he looked down at her, his blue eyes shining through the fringe of his shaggy, dark hair.

Miriam could get used to this. Actually, she was already getting used to this. It had been years since she'd been in an actual relationship, way back when she was in her mid-twenties and in school for her MBA. The relationship had ended when Miriam had wanted to move back to New York and get back to her investment banking job. Her boyfriend at the time had taken a job in Boston, and even though they hadn't been that far apart, it had been too much with the amount of hours they had both had to work.

Miriam had looked him up online once. He'd gotten married to a very blonde woman, who spent her time taking care of their very blond kids. She'd been some sort of marketing associate or something in her past, but after they'd gotten married, she'd become a housewife.

That would never have worked for Miriam. She'd never been interested in giving up her career. Kids had always been something she'd given little thought to. And on top of all that, she'd never wanted her identity to be reduced to "so-and-so's wife." Even if she were to marry and even if she were to have kids, she still wanted her own identity above and beyond that.

Nelson leaned back in and kissed her forehead again, and Miriam sighed.

"What's that for?" she asked as she savored the feeling of his lips on her forehead.

"Just because," he said, and he placed another kiss on her temple. He then turned to his computer that had literally just magically appeared on her kitchen counter.

"Just because?" Miriam smiled. She liked *just because*. She liked this man who brought her coffee without being asked and who seemed hell-bent on making sure she felt cared for. She enjoyed taking care of the man who took care of everyone else. She liked this man who watched rom-coms because they were safe and understood that sometimes their dates needed to be work dates because Miriam had a job that required her to work a lot of hours.

She sat down behind her own computer but didn't hit the power button to start it up yet. "You know I work a lot?" she asked after a moment.

"Me too," Nelson said with a shrug. "I've put a lot of time and energy into my work."

"You don't think that's going to be a problem?" Miriam asked. "A woman who's so focused on work?"

"I like that you have things in your life. It's probably not healthy that work is an identity, but we're also Americans, and that's sort of how we are," Nelson reasoned, his words confident as though he'd had this argument before. "If work is who you are, then I want to love that part about you. It means you're passionate about what you do, and you have meaning in your life, even if it is just a lot of spreadsheets."

"You want to love me?" Miriam asked, grinning as she knocked his sock-clad foot with her own.

"I do," Nelson said. "I want to."

"Me too," Miriam said.

They hadn't said the actual words, but seeing as they'd only been doing this together for a few weeks and they'd only agreed to give an actual relationship a try earlier that day, it was too soon to decide they loved each other, even if they were already imagining it.

It was a nice evening, an easy evening—the sort of evening Miriam could imagine having the rest of her life. Being with Nelson felt right. She wanted this. She wanted this more than she wanted anything else.

A bit later, their food arrived, and they ate over their computers, sorting through emails, reading through documents, being together but taking care of the things that had gone by the wayside during the last few weeks of their magical quest.

When it got late, they went to Miriam's bed together, as if they did this sort of thing every single night. They'd already rooted out the awkwardness, the formal dance of seeing each other in the unmade vulnerability of sleep. Now, they could just be together, the newness almost gone in the best way possible.

Chapter Twenty-Four

T HEY ARRIVED RIGHT ON time for their pottery class. They made it a priority, even when Nelson brought Miriam coffee in bed and then they spent the rest of the morning trapped in the confines of Miriam's sheets.

The pottery studio had a vibe that could only be described as *1990s art teacher*. The décor was all warm yellows and maroons, with a healthy number of sunflowers scattered about. The shop was warm even though it was cold outside, and Miriam wondered if there was a kiln somewhere in the basement.

There were a few participants already milling about and taking advantage of the mimosa bar that had been set up in the back of the shop.

A woman wearing a pair of paint-stained overalls met Nelson and Miriam near the entryway. "Good morning. I'm Shawna, and I'll be teaching this class this morning. I am so glad to have you. What are your names?" she asked, her voice and tone only building more on the elementary art teacher vibe of the studio.

"I'm Miriam, and this is Nelson," Miriam said, and Nelson gave a little wave of his hand in greeting.

"We're so glad to have you," Shawna replied. "Please help yourself to a mimosa and then find a pottery wheel. We'll be starting soon."

"We should cast a finding spell," Miriam whispered as they made their way across the room to the mimosa bar.

Nelson nodded, but before either could make a move, Shawna was back in front of them, as if she had not just dismissed them to go find a spot. "Have you done a pottery class before?" she asked, backing them into the corner near the mimosa bar.

"Have we?" Miriam repeated the question. "I haven't . . . you?" she asked Nelson. They hadn't gotten to the part in their relationship where the topic of previously attended pottery classes had come up.

"I took a pottery elective in college," Nelson explained. "But it's been awhile." He was sincerely invested in the question, which made Miriam want to laugh a little, in a good way. She missed sincerity. The investment banking world didn't allow for it much of the time.

"We were going to take our seats," Miriam said, directing that declaration to Shawna, who still seemed intent on hovering. She needed a moment away from the instructor so she could cast a finding spell and see if anything happened.

"Great, I'll show you the setup," Shawna replied, and she turned and led them to two pottery wheels right in the front row. They were in a position where they would be a major distraction for the entire class if they got up from their seats.

Exchanging a knowing look, Miriam and Nelson sat down in their spots. Shawna then proceeded to show them how the pedals operated the wheels and the different tools they would use to work the clay.

Miriam wondered if Shawna was attempting to distract them from something. She wouldn't leave them alone long enough for Miriam to consult with Nelson.

As soon as Shawna finished her demonstration of their wheels, she made her way to the front of the class, just a few feet from where Miriam and Nelson were sitting. Then, she officially started the class. She went through the entire lesson again, this time addressing everyone, not just Nelson and Miriam. Something was certainly going on.

Miriam tried to catch Nelson's eye, but, like a dutiful student, he was paying attention and following instructions on how to load his clay onto the wheel. She thought about excusing herself to the restroom, but the last time they'd split up, she'd ended up alone in some sort of nightmare-fueled adventure in the woods. She was not interested in a repeat.

"Hey, babe," she whispered. She'd never called him *babe* before, but something about it felt right in this situation. Perhaps it was just the act she needed to pull him away so they could cast the finding spell, or perhaps she was testing what the word would feel like if she were to actually use it, outside of a potentially dangerous and magical playacting situation, that was. "I need your help . . . in the restroom . . . for that thing," she whispered when Shawna seemed to finally be distracted by another student who couldn't get their wheel to spin properly.

"Huh?" Nelson asked, looking up at her and then back down at his hand, which was thoroughly coated in clay.

"Just, come on," Miriam hissed. She tugged at his sleeve and nodded to a door marked "Restrooms" near the back of the building.

Before they could disappear through the door, Shawna's voice called out from across the room. "Where are you going?" she asked with a forced sweetness.

Miriam groaned but kept moving. "I have a thing that, um, Nelson needs to help me with," she explained, already pushing open the door.

"We were going to learn how to spin," Shawna argued.

Miriam glanced back at her, and she was watching them with an oddly expectant expression, obviously waiting for them to return to their seats.

"It's an emergency," Nelson said, and Miriam turned away and pushed the door open, revealing a staircase that led down to a basement bathroom.

Miriam went first, and Nelson followed behind. The door closed behind them as they stumbled down the stairs.

"She probably thinks we're having sex in the bathroom," Nelson said suggestively.

"Or she's part of hiding whatever magic is down here." Miriam glanced around as they entered the basement and then motioned to Nelson. "She's been staying close to us since the moment we walked in."

They continued through the basement, passed the door to the tiny single-person bathroom, and forged straight ahead to the basement proper. The room was a combination storage unit and kiln, as Miriam had suspected, given the heat in the shop above. There were large stacks of clay bricks stored in plastic bags to keep them fresh, other pottery-making supplies, and then a stack of cleaning supplies and a bunch of brooms and mops pushed up into one corner.

"Do you think it will work?" Nelson asked as he looked around the bland basement.

"I hope so, because at this rate, we'll never find our things," Miriam said. "The least we can do is give it a try. It's not like this was much of a hassle." Miriam waved a hand and then waited. Much to her surprise, she felt a familiar ping against her magic, like when the doctor hit her knee with a reflex hammer. It wasn't entirely comfortable, nor was it painful, just unusual. Miriam paused, looking around the room.

"What?" Nelson asked.

"It's here," Miriam replied with cautious excitement. After all the places they had searched, she hadn't really expected this to be the end. "Something is here."

She put a hand on Nelson's shoulder, holding him in place. If their things were here, there was also something magical here, and they needed to be prepared for whatever was coming their way.

His eyes widened in understanding, and then he looked around. "What do we do?" he whispered.

"I'm not sure." Miriam's heart was pounding loudly in her chest, and she readied herself for a fight or for whatever was coming.

But there was nothing she could have done to really prepare herself.

In a blink, the stacks of clay in the corner started to shake and rumble. Miriam and Nelson looked at each other and then both raised their hands, ready to work any magic needed to combat whatever magical creature they were about to meet.

The wall of clay came tumbling down, splattering loudly on the concrete floor of the basement. There, standing along the wall of the basement, was a gigantic creature that seemed to have been made of clay. It was taller than either Miriam or Nelson, its round bulbous head grazing the ceiling. It had a cracked, dried look as if it had been constructed a long time ago but had never been put through the kiln.

Its eyes were just two divots above a thin-lined mouth, little more than a crude drawing in clay. Its forehead was wide and thick and had three Hebrew letters etched into it. Miriam squinted as she tried to remember her aleph bets. She managed to make out an aleph, mem, and tav on top of its head.

The creature stood there, staring at nothing with its blank eyes, and with a start, Miriam realized her magic was coming from its stomach. That was where their things were, she could feel it—some combination of the finding spell and her own magic wanting to come to her. She could also feel her own chaos magic swirl dangerously in her belly. She shoved it down; this wasn't the time. She had to stay in control to fight off this clay golem.

"It ate my medallion," Nelson said as the clay monster seemed to straighten up even taller in front of them. "I can tell it's in that thing's stomach."

Miriam nodded; they were close enough that the magic of their things was calling to them. The finding spell Miriam had done had only heightened the feeling.

The monster suddenly took a step away from the wall, and Miriam and Nelson both instinctually stepped back.

"What do we do?" Nelson asked. His eyes were trained on the monster as though waiting for it to drive forward and push them farther back against the wall.

"It's a golem," Miriam stated. "Do you remember the story from Hebrew school?"

"Was it in Chelm?" he asked calmly—too calmly. He was thinking of a different story their teacher in Hebrew school used to read them.

"No, it's a clay monster," she explained as the golem took another step towards them. Miriam's back hit the cold concrete wall behind her.

"Okay, but what do we do?" Nelson asked. "Because unless we figure something out first, I think we might be its next victim. I want to think it won't hurt us, but those hands look like they were made for crushing."

Nelson was right, Miriam realized. Its hands were disproportionally large relative to its body. They looked strong, as if they could crush bones. Miriam couldn't quite remember the specifics about the golem from her Hebrew school classes, but she was sure it was meant to be a monster, and a scary one at that.

Miriam thought for just a second, searching her memory for anything she could use to help them. With a start, she remembered there was a way to make it retreat. But Hebrew school had been so long ago, and she hadn't ever been given a lot of information about defeating magical Eastern European clay monsters. She stared at the creature, frowning.

Then, the memory came to her, and her eyes widened.

"The head! The letters on its head! We need to erase the aleph," she stated with maybe a little more certainty than she had.

The monster took another lumbering step forward, the floor rumbling with its footfalls. Getting rid of the aleph was the key. It had been in a picture book she'd had as a kid. To defeat the golem, they needed to erase the first letter—the one on the right.

"How?" Nelson asked.

"A small miracle?" Miriam proposed.

Nelson shook his head. "I'm not sure what sort of miracle can help us right now."

The creature took one more step towards them, and Miriam grimaced as she worked hard to control her chaos magic. In her fear, it was attempting to escape, nearly screaming to be let free. But that was the last thing she needed. The situation was already precarious enough.

"Miriam," Nelson called, nervously reaching out for her hand.

Miriam grabbed it and squeezed tightly, fear bubbling up more in her chest. The golem loomed over them, threatening and massive. And when it began lifting a hand towards them, she just knew they were going to die.

In an instant, her fear grew more and burst out, releasing her magic with it.

The clay bricks that had been lying motionless on the ground suddenly went flying. The lights flickered, and the doors opened and closed with a slam. It was noisy and messy and chaotic. She couldn't control it anymore; all she could do was yell "duck!" as a large block of clay came straight for them.

They dodged the block just in time, and it smashed against the wall. Then another came flying towards the back of the golem's head, and the golem went down. The monster started struggling, trying to stand again, but Nelson waved over a gigantic pile of clay, pinning the monster to the floor.

"We need to erase the aleph," Miriam yelled, and with a courage she hadn't known she possessed, she hopped over the golem's body. She licked her finger and then placed it on the aleph—the first letter on its head when reading right to left. The clay was still just tacky enough to smear, and the letter became too blurred to be recognizable. She'd done it. She'd erased the letter.

There was a giant shudder, and the golem stopped struggling. Then, within a matter of seconds, the clay dried up, turning to dust and falling into a pile on the floor. In its place was Miriam's bag, dusty but intact. It fell over onto the floor, and the contents came spilling out—Miriam's lipstick container-sized broom, Nelson's tarnished taxi medallion, and the printed-out slide deck that revealed all the details of the deal Miriam had been working on.

Everything was scattered across the floor, and the top sheet of the slide deck showed the address and the name of the property, written clearly and in large, easy-to-read letters.

Nelson bent down to pick everything up, and Miriam watched as his hand grazed the paper. He stopped for a minute as a look of recognition passed over his face, and then he turned, wordlessly, and handed the papers to Miriam.

Before she could respond to Nelson's schooled, unreadable expression, Shawna appeared at the bottom of the stairs. Her eyes were wide as she surveyed the mess. Then she let out a sigh of relief. "You've finally done it!" she breathed.

"Huh?" Nelson asked, though his eyes were still fixed on the printouts Miriam was holding.

"It's been here ever since I bought the shop. Hasn't bothered me much, but in the last few weeks it's been an absolute menace."

"You knew this was down here?" Miriam asked. "Were you protecting it?"

Shawna shook her head. "No. Well, not intentionally . . . but I did get cheap rent because of it. No one wanted to deal with a golem created nearly a hundred years ago. I think I heard something about immigrants dealing with their shop being vandalized back in the 1920s." She babbled on a bit. "It's mostly left me alone, a bit of rumbling when I fired up the kiln, but certainly not bad enough that I'd needed to worry about it. Then a few weeks ago, things got weird, and it put me under some sort of spell or something. It wanted me to do its bidding."

"It's gone now," Miriam said with finality.

Shawna laughed lightly. "Hmm, well don't tell my land-lord; I can't afford to pay market price for this place," she joked, still staring at the dusty mess on the floor.

"Wouldn't dream of it." Nelson gave her a half smile, but he seemed quite distracted.

"You're welcome to come back to class," Shawna offered. "I'll even throw in a free class if you want to come back another time."

Miriam and Nelson looked at each other, but Miriam spoke up first. "Thanks, but, um . . ."

Shawna seemed to get the hint, and she smiled and nodded. "I should get back to the rest of the class."

Shawna disappeared back up the stairs, leaving Nelson and Miriam alone in the basement amongst a pile of dried-up golem dust.

"I can explain," Miriam said, holding the papers up stiffly.

Nelson shook his head. "Not here," he said, gathering Miriam's bag and shoving the papers and the broom that looked like a lipstick container inside. "Let's go somewhere we can talk." He took a last look around the basement. He then put out his hand for Miriam to take.

Reluctantly, she wrapped his fingers in his, and for just a moment, she savored the feel of it. The warmth of his skin. His gentleness. His strength. This would be the last time, after all—the last time they would touch, the last time they would have the opportunity before the whole truth came out.

He would be done with her. She just knew it. And she deserved it. More than anything, she didn't deserve him.

Chapter Twenty-Five

T HEY APPEARED IN NELSON'S apartment in just a blink of an eye, thanks to the magical taxi medallion. The warm, cozy little one-bedroom deep in Williamsburg still smelled of spices, old books, and worn leather. And it felt like Nelson—the Nelson she'd gotten to know the last few weeks.

"I can explain," Miriam said again as Nelson let her go and stepped away. She wasn't sure what she was going to explain. The company she worked for was attempting to buy out and rezone the building that Nelson's nonprofit had committed to for a steal. Once the rezoning was complete, the current owners would sell to Miriam's client instead. It would be one of the biggest deals Alchemy Partners had ever facilitated in their entire history.

And it would rob so many unhoused people of the opportunity to have a bed to sleep in at night.

Nelson put a hand up to stop whatever explanation she might have tried to give him. "I knew," he said bluntly.

Her stomach dropped, and she stared at him for a moment before she spoke. "What exactly did you know?" she asked, realizing she needed to make sure they were on the same page. Surely, he hadn't been aware this whole time. Was this all fake? The thoughts swirled through her mind as she watched his expression tighten.

"That your firm is facilitating the deal that would rezone the property Housing Magic currently has under contract," Nelson started, his tone flat. "Then, once everything is rezoned, your client is going to buy the property up for more money than we could ever fundraise. We'll lose the new units and the giant expansion, and there will be less housing for the most vulnerable New Yorkers." He laid it out as concisely and painfully as possible. It felt a bit unnecessary to include that last part about the most vulnerable New Yorkers. But it did the trick.

Her stomach twisted again, and she thought she might be sick.

"That's . . . about it?" she said, her mind still racing. How could he have possibly known? "Is . . . that why you took me home from the fundraiser? You thought you could sleep with me, and then I'd change my mind? But then our things went missing, and I never got a chance?"

Nelson shook his head. "I didn't know until after that night . . . when we lost our stuff," he replied, his voice still level and calm. "I'd known for a while that the property was at risk. We have a donor who fed us that information to try to help, and I had some notes on the folks working the deal, but I didn't put two and two together until I googled your office when I needed to come talk to you."

"Is that why you took me to your building, to make me grow some sort of heart?" Miriam asked. "Because, even if I step down, Alchemy is still going to finish the deal."

It wasn't a threat; it was the truth. Miriam sat down on the sofa and ran her hands through her hair. She might be a part of this, but she wasn't sure there was anything she could do to make it right.

Nelson shook his head. "That's not it at all."

Miriam glared at him; she could see through him. There was no way that hadn't been his intention in taking her to see Alex.

"Okay, that might have been part of it," he admitted, "but your magic map really led us there."

Miriam sighed and let herself look up at Nelson. This was the last time she was likely going to see him, at least like this. "We should . . . This should be it," she said quietly. "Because I don't know how to stop this deal. I . . . I had never thought much about the outcomes of the deals we worked on until this one. This one has always felt evil. I tried to bring a six-figure donation to the fundraiser that night, but Hannah wouldn't let me," she added, and then she shook her head. "That probably wouldn't have made it better, either."

"Then stop it," Nelson challenged.

"But what if I can't? Does that mean we're done? Because I wouldn't blame you if you couldn't look me in the face again."

Nelson sat next to Miriam on the couch and placed his hand on top of hers. "I understand that very few things are black-and-white," he said. "You know that big box store I've been working with to get jobs for the folks who live in Housing

Magic's buildings—the one my coven is upset with me about because the store has a horrible labor record, a history of union busting, doesn't allow breaks or offer paid vacation? Despite those awful things, they'll hire felons, and that is extremely hard to find."

"Your residents need jobs, and it seems like this opportunity is a godsend, even if it's not ideal. I don't think that's the same," Miriam argued.

"No?" Nelson asked, and she got the sense he'd been purposefully leading her down this path. She wasn't particularly impressed, but she understood the intent.

"You know damn well it's not. You're about to lose a lot of potential housing so a few rich fucks can have luxury condos," Miriam swore. She was angry. She was angry at herself. She was angry that this was a deal that had ever been brought to her firm. She was angry that she felt like a cog in a big, giant, evil machine. If she lost this client . . .

"This wasn't your idea," Nelson pointed out. "You aren't the company actually buying the buildings. You're just the bank—the advisors on the deal, right?"

Miriam nodded, but she could feel her gut twist with guilt. She still felt responsible, but recusing herself would only mean she'd lose her job. Charlie and Gregory would manage without her. They'd proven that when they'd managed the team in her absence.

And it still didn't feel right.

"But you still think I should try to figure this out for you?" she asked, because that was the kind of sacrifice she should have to make for Nelson. It felt like something he would do for her.

Nelson shook his head. "No, I can't ask you to do that. I understand a lot about what having a job means. Remember, I work with a lot of people who get their first job, sometimes ever."

"I don't deserve you," Miriam said. It was not a compliment; it was the truth. How could she possibly be with this man if her job was about to destroy something he'd worked so hard for? Even if Miriam had been rivals with Nelson for what felt like her whole life, she realized now that she could never, *would* never want to hurt him in this way. He was creating these false equivalencies, and that was just as frustrating to Miriam. It only intensified her guilt.

"You do—" he started, but she cut him off.

"I . . . Nelson, can I think about this? I had . . . I had assumed this would be the end of us when you found out. I didn't tell you because, selfishly, I didn't want it to end . . . but now that it's not ending, I'm not sure how to process everything."

His eyes narrowed with confusion. "Miriam, are you breaking up with me?" he asked.

"I'm not . . . I don't want to. I *really* actually don't want to," she answered with more honesty than she'd had in weeks. "But I feel like I need a bit of time to think through what I'm going to do next."

"I understand. I'll be here when you're ready," Nelson replied with a weak nod.

"Thanks," Miriam said. She leaned over and kissed his cheek, and then she picked up her bag with her broomstick and made her way out the door.

Before she'd even reached the bottom of the stairs, she snapped her wrist, and her broom extended to its full size. She smiled as her fingers traced the familiar knots on the smooth wood. At least, as a small consolation, she had her broom back.

Once she was outside and alone, she took to the skies. It had warmed up outside since she'd lost her broom a few weeks ago, and it felt good to see the city below, to feel the wind ruffling her hair. She'd learned a lot about New York during their quest—the magic that held the city together, the little things that happened each and every day while Miriam was up in her ivory tower, looking down on Manhattan.

She'd known the Pentacle deal had been bad from the moment it had been introduced to her, but she'd been riding along, an accomplice to capitalism. Sure, maybe she was just one part of that, but maybe there was a chance she could do something—anything—to help fix it.

She continued soaring above the city as she ran through her arsenal of magic. But except for her broomstick and a few party tricks, she mostly kept it in check. Her magic was never cooperative, and, if anything, it was something she was constantly fighting with.

Although, Miriam realized, that wasn't necessarily true. They'd escaped the Taotie when Miriam's magic made the cart crash. She'd escaped Nishi Park when her magic chaotically and unpredictably released everything. And she'd disarmed the golem when she'd lost control of her emotions.

Maybe she was thinking about this all wrong. She'd been approaching it in the context she'd lived her whole life—thinking about how it could all be controlled. But perhaps there was an acutely chaotic solution she was missing all together. Perhaps her mom was right about not running so far from her own magic.

Chapter Twenty-Six

I T HAD BEEN THREE days since she'd left Nelson's apartment and put their relationship on hold. Now, it was Wednesday—the day of the big client meeting where they'd discuss the plan to buy up the property after the rezoning was complete.

She'd been busy these last three days. When she hadn't been at work, she'd still been working, and she'd managed to formulate a separate plan—a plan to make sure that this deal fell apart. She'd come up with an idea that she hoped would make this entire thing go chaotically awry. In a lot of ways, it was best if she didn't plan too carefully. The whole point was not being entirely in control, and a plan was control.

So on Wednesday, Miriam was ready to go, her half-baked, chaotic plan already in motion. She sat in her office, clicking a pen manically while waiting. Right on schedule, Hannah poked her head in the office and gave a thumbs-up and a smile. She had backup. She wasn't alone in this, and for that, she was glad.

A moment later, she got a call from reception, letting her know the clients had arrived. She stood, straightened her skirt, and headed out of her office to meet them just as they all stepped off the elevator. They were a group of men—all real-estate developers, all dressed in sleek black suits. It was hard not to think they looked a bit like pallbearers at a funeral.

Miriam greeted them, as did Charlie and Gregory, who would also help to present Alchemy's proposal. Allowing the presentation to go off without a hitch was going to be the hardest part of this. Miriam had to be in control just enough for that. Her coven would lend her the extra magic she needed.

Once the niceties were out of the way, she led them to the conference room, and Charlie started the meeting.

"Let me start by saying thank you for coming in today. We're all very excited here at Alchemy Partners to have the opportunity to work with Pentacle on this deal . . ."

Miriam tapped her thigh under the table. She could have worked this magic without any prompting, but a signal, a motion, a small movement to start was always nice. She could feel a buzz through her body, and she knew the spell was in motion.

". . . our collaboration on this deal will mean . . ." Charlie continued.

Miriam could hear the words echoing in her head, a clear sign her magic was working. It was uncomfortable, but she was willing to tolerate it for the results.

The meeting continued on for a few minutes until one of the suits interrupted Charlie to ask, "And you're sure that no one knows about the building purchase at five-one-five Edgewood? One of the most important things we need at this stage is a guarantee of confidentiality."

Miriam interjected here. She knew exactly how she wanted to phrase this; she was going to be publicly tied to this deal already, so her voice on the record would not be an issue at all. "We understand that there's a lot of sensitivity with this deal. Housing Magic, a nonprofit organization, has the intent to purchase five-one-five Edgewood. But we're working diligently to have the property rezoned, and once we do, we'll be able to procure it for your condo project," Miriam summarized succinctly. She didn't mention the name of the developer, but it didn't matter. Her goal was to stop the project, and once this piece of information got out, that should be enough.

The suits nodded in approval, and then Miriam opened the deck, ready to walk them through the deal in full.

She'd just gotten through the first three slides when there was an urgent tapping on the conference room door. *Just in time*, Miriam thought as an entire horde of analysts burst into the conference room, Gabe at the front of the group.

"Your meeting is being broadcast all over the city!" he announced, holding up his phone. The words Miriam had just spoken rumbled through the phone's speaker, sound muffled and distorted, as if it had been recorded from the grainy audio of a subway speaker. There was a good chance it had been.

Miriam was unsure how many PA systems were in lower Manhattan, but there were a lot, and, for just a few minutes, all of them had projected this meeting through their speakers. Everyone south of Houston Street had been privy to their very confidential meeting.

"How?" one of the suits asked, looking at the speakerphone system that sat in the middle of the table. It was off, and

Gregory reached under the table and grabbed the unplugged wires, holding them up for everyone to see. This meeting had been fully in person, and there was no good explanation for how everything had been broadcasted.

Miriam did her best to act just as alarmed as everyone else, but mostly, she was preparing for what was about to be an endless day of crisis PR management.

She had figured out how to derail the deal. It had simply been a matter of exposing the deeds of everyone in the room.

Chapter Twenty-Seven – Three Days Earlier

MIRIAM FLEW AIMLESSLY THROUGH the Manhattan skies, her mind racing. Nelson had known. He'd known her firm was working on a plan to rezone the building Housing Magic had secured and then outbid them. He'd known, and yet . . . he still wanted her? She didn't quite understand how that was possible.

Even though she hadn't originally set out to, she ended up at Isabelle and Henry's apartment right as the coven meeting was starting. She'd thought about skipping the meeting, but an idea had formed while she was flying, and she knew if it was to be successful, she'd need the help of her coven. She'd probably still feel like an intruder at her own coven meeting, as she had for a while now, but she needed the help. She needed them.

She flew into the large apartment through an open window and landed in the middle of the single room, which had been broken up with screens and furniture to give it dimension. No one paid her much attention. Hannah and Isabelle were deep in conversation, probably talking about babies and their pregnancies. Heather was watching Franklin chase Chloe around the apartment, and Derek and Craig had opted to stay home and take care of their new baby. It would be a few weeks before they had the wherewithal to make it to a coven meeting.

Heather waved her over when their eyes met, smiling. "Hey, you found your broom?" she asked as Miriam approached the couch and sat down next to her. "Where was it?"

Miriam blew out an exacerbated sigh that made her cheeks puff. "Short story, in the belly of a golem in the basement of a Lower East Side pottery shop."

"Why don't you seem relieved?" Heather asked, narrowing her eyes thoughtfully. "Why do I think this has to do with Nelson?"

Heather was intuitive like that, even if she was more inclined to physical magic that could be used to turn things into other things—animated things and other stuff like that.

"I'll explain once the meeting starts," Miriam said. The whole coven would need to know, and she'd rather not have to repeat herself.

"We're here," Heather reminded her.

Miriam smiled and gave her a small nod in acknowledgement. Heather and Franklin had gotten married first, and they'd had a kid first. They'd leaned on the coven with all of their firsts. In turn, Heather had been a sort of mentor to everyone else as they'd taken their own steps right behind her. Miriam had mostly been left out of that, or perhaps, Miriam had just decided a long time ago that she didn't need help. After all, she'd never had a wedding she needed bridesmaids for, or a baby that needed clothes, or an engagement that needed photographers, or any of the other milestones that all of her friends had hit.

It didn't take long for everyone to settle in, and then business started.

"Does anyone have any big magics they need worked?" Isabelle asked.

Without Nelson, Miriam felt exposed, vulnerable. She had to do her least favorite thing—ask for help and plead for someone else's time and energy.

She took a breath. "I . . . need help," she said. The words almost felt foreign on her lips. She really didn't like having to rely on others. And yet, that was what her coven was for. That was what Nelson had been there for. Perhaps it wouldn't be as hard as she thought.

She started at the beginning, explaining the Pentacle deal and then what it would do to Nelson's nonprofit. More importantly, she explained what it would do to the people of New York who most needed the housing.

"It'll impact the firm?" Hannah asked, with her brow furrowed in concern.

Miriam nodded. "I understand if you don't want to be involved . . ." She trailed off, guilt rising in her chest. But Hannah shook her head.

"Oh . . . no . . . I want to be involved. More than anyone, I want to be involved," Hannah confirmed. "That firm makes more money than God, and I can barely get my accounting staff enough money to pay rent. They'll be fine. Worst case, I'll find a new job, give my staff stellar recommendations, and take who I can with me."

Maddy gave Hannah's hand a squeeze of support and then nodded towards Miriam. "I'm on board too."

"Good." Miriam smiled and looked around the room. "Is everyone else in? I know it's a little unethical, a little chaotic even, but I think we have an opportunity to do something to help our city, and I want to do that."

It didn't take long for her coven to agree to give her their support and promise to help with the more complex magical components.

For the first time in a really long time, Miriam remembered what it felt like to be supported, to be part of something. There was this part of her that had felt so empty for so long. But now, here working with her coven, relying on her coven, leaning on them for this thing she needed, felt good. She'd let herself forget that she'd been surrounded by her own community this entire time.

By the time Miriam left to go home, they'd designed a complex spell that would project the meeting with Pentacle, which was taking place at the Alchemy office in three days, to every PA system in a twenty-block radius. The entirety of Lower Manhattan would know all about Alchemy Partners' plans to facilitate a buyout of the buildings intended for Housing Magic. Alchemy would become the enemy—the evil corporate entity attempting to displace the most vulnerable of New Yorkers.

It would be a PR nightmare, one that would force the firm to backtrack.

She finally felt confident that she'd found a way to stop the deal.

Chapter Twenty-Eight - Present Day

MIRIAM'S MOM WAS THE first person to call when the news broke. The suits had already left in a huff, mumbling about their lawyers calling or maybe that they needed to call their lawyers. Miriam wasn't entirely sure in the cacophony and panic and upset that followed.

Everyone at Alchemy was in a holding pattern, waiting to see what was going to happen, and when her phone rang, she slipped away into her office to take the call.

"Hey, Mom," Miriam said wearily. She rubbed her eyes and rested her elbows on her desk.

"You okay, sweetie?" Her mom's voice was gentle and easy, and it reminded Miriam that there had been a time when her mom had been the one taking care of her. She'd been so focused on her parents' retirement that it was easy to forget that they had raised her and that they could still be there for her.

"I think so," Miriam responded, because despite the absolute chaos going on around her, things felt like they were finally right. "You've seen the news."

"Mm-hmm . . ." her mom confirmed, and Miriam figured she was nodding, even though Miriam couldn't see her. "That was quite the magic, very chaotic," her mom added, confirming that she had not only seen the news but had also figured out Miriam was behind it.

"I . . ." Miriam inhaled slowly and ran a hand through her hair. She wasn't actually sure what she wanted to ask her mom or even how she wanted her to react.

After a pause that felt way too long, her mom said, "You did good, kid."

"I . . . exposed important business secrets in the most chaotic way possible. I'm not sure that is good," Miriam argued in a low whisper so no one could hear her through the office walls. There was a part of her that wanted her mom to be disappointed. To tell her she did the wrong thing. To punish her in a way her bosses would never. Not that anyone at Alchemy would ever figure out what she'd done.

"Okay, but it seems like now, there's a chance your firm won't be responsible for cutting off resources for a nonprofit run by a certain handsome, available, totally-smitten-with-you man."

"MOM," Miriam gasped. "It wasn't about him, at least, not completely. I wanted to help, to make sure the housing project went through."

"Sure . . ." her mom goaded. "But you did good with your magic. That was quite the event."

"It wasn't elegant, was it?" Miriam said, and she was surprised that when talking to her mom about it, she felt no shame. Her magic was loud, bombastic, and chaotic, but that was exactly how her magic was meant to work.

"Who needs elegance when you have the right kind of magic to get the job done?" She could almost hear her mom beaming with pride in the background.

"Thanks," Miriam said, but then she continued. There was more she wanted to say. Her thanks wasn't just this, it was everything. "Thank you, Mom, for showing me that my chaos magic wasn't something to be ashamed of. I've been so embarrassed about it, but you never were."

"Miriam, I've told you before. Our magic is nothing but spectacular. You just had to learn to use it, make it work for you."

"It took me long enough." Miriam laughed a little. "But, I'm glad I've had you."

"Me too," her mom said. And Miriam looked up to see Charlie waving through her office door. It was time to get back to work. Another meeting, probably. They would have a lot to do to recover from what had just happened.

"Bye, Mom. I'll call you later," she said with a nod at Charlie.

"Bye, sweetie. Love you."

"Love you, too, Mom."

Miriam spent the rest of the day in a series of crisis PR meetings. There were calls from every single news outlet in New York and a few national ones. There was a visit from the Department of Homeland Security and the NYPD. Not so surprisingly, one of the cops was a member of the Mages of Manhattan. She gave Miriam and Hannah a knowing wink and then moved the investigation towards something about satellite internet connections.

There was nothing particularly unethical or illegal, magically speaking, that Miriam and her coven had done. Magics had a healthy respect for chaotic happenings, and this was just another in a long line of unexplainable events.

***

It was well past midnight by the time Miriam took to the skies and made her way back to her building. It had been a long day. She'd made herself scarce when Charlie and Gregory had attempted to figure out how their meeting had been magically broadcast to a section of Manhattan. They'd ended up turning that over to IT and law enforcement and shifted their attention to crisis management. Miriam made sure to be part of those meetings. The deal with Pentacle was already dead, but she needed to make sure it was buried as well.

She landed in the small courtyard outside her building. It was discreet enough that Bruce wouldn't notice, and it was easier than landing in an alleyway. Her broom retracted into its lipstick-sized case, and she slipped it into her bag.

Nelson was already there, sitting on a bench and waiting for her.

"Hey," he said softly as she took a seat next to him. "So . . . that was a lot."

"It was," Miriam agreed.

Nelson placed his hand on top of Miriam's and gave it a warm squeeze.

"You didn't have to do that for me."

"I didn't," Miriam replied firmly.

"Oh?" Nelson asked, confused.

Miriam shook her head. "I did it for the people who need housing, and I did it for myself, because I'm part of the community and I owe them this."

Nelson cocked his head to one side, his expression curious.

"Okay, and maybe . . . maybe I did this a little bit for you, but that wasn't my main motivation." Miriam smiled.

Nelson nodded and then laughed. "So what now?" he asked.

Miriam shrugged. "We're trying to figure out what the firm is going to do. I think the entire phenomenon has been pinned on satellite internet, cell phones listening in, and crossed radio frequencies. Most of the public is focused on that, reasonably, so when all they hit are dead ends, there will be less involvement of law enforcement and everything. But there are enough people who care about what the firm was trying to do—the bad stuff, that is—and now we'll need to make some changes, I think, to save face."

"That's all great, but I meant tonight," Nelson joked, and warmth rushed to her cheeks.

His words sure made it sound like he was here for her. Just her. Not the firm or the housing project or anything else. And she really liked that response. She also liked that he'd given her the space she'd needed to decide on her own and fix things on her own.

It felt like he'd grown in his own way, just as she'd grown in her own way.

"Oh . . . tonight. Well, I was going to feed Larry, and I have my taxes to work through. There's also this documentary on tortoises I was thinking about watching."

"That sounds—"

"—riveting, I know." Miriam laughed and then leaned in and kissed Nelson on the forehead. "But . . . I could always change my plans, you know, for the right person," she said.

"For the right person?" Nelson asked.

"I'm thinking dark hair, blue eyes, tall, a bit of a golden boy . . ." Miriam looked up at him and smiled.

"And what would you do if you found someone like that?" Nelson played along with a silly grin.

"I am a witch, you know. And I have a broomstick." Miriam batted an eye suggestively. "Have you ever seen the top of the Statue of Liberty up close?"

"Are you trying to charm me with magic?" Nelson asked, avoiding the question. With his medallion, she was sure he'd gone to all sorts of places that were technically off limits.

"I am, in fact, attempting to charm you with magic," she said, standing up and putting a hand out for Nelson. He took it and stood up next to her. Miriam took her broomstick back out of her bag, flicked her wrist to extend it to full size, then got on, giving Nelson room to sit behind her.

Moments later, they were flying above the New York City skyline. New York might be the city that never slept, but this late at night, it was certainly a city that was just resting its eyes. The theaters had long since emptied, the subway was on its limited overnight schedule, and the bars were nearing last call. If there were stars in the sky, she couldn't see them; the lights from the city sparkled high up into the stratosphere.

Nelson wrapped his arms around Miriam's waist and rested his head on her shoulder, looking forward towards New York. She navigated over the Hudson Bay and between the spikes of the Statue of Liberty's green crown. Nelson's feet grazed the copper first, and then Miriam touched down next to him. She flicked her wrist, and her broom went back into its little metal case.

They sat down in the space between the spikes, and Miriam didn't wait. She kissed him first, wrapping her arms around his shoulders. Their kiss was long and soft and lived-in. It felt like the culmination of everything they had been through together and the beginning of a life they would share. For the first time, there was nothing standing between them.

Chapter Twenty-Nine

"Alchemy Partners strives to do the best thing for our community and our country at all times. The deals and the clients we take on should align with our values. The agreement to facilitate the buyout of five fifteen Edgewood, when Housing Magic was already set to procure the space, was not in line with the ethics of our firm and our partners," Charlie recited, addressing a sea of journalists outside of Alchemy's office two days after their confidential meeting had been broadcast to the world.

Charlie continued. "While we respect the sensitive nature of the deals we accept and will continue to use the utmost discretion with our clients and partners, we also understand the value of making sure that every decision we make is one we would feel comfortable ending up on the front page of the *New York Times*. That is why, today, Alchemy Partners is establishing an ethics and morality committee to review all of the deals we work on. We will no longer do things that could be detrimental to our community."

Miriam had never attended a press conference before, and she had certainly never spoken at one. And yet, here she was, standing just behind Charlie, holding her rumpled note cards that she'd read and reread so many times. She was as prepared as she could be.

"In addition," Charlie said, "we've formed a new group, the Alchemy Partners Foundation. Our newest partner, Miriam Blum, will lead the foundation. Miriam stepped up and proposed this idea to our partner group. She was the voice that made sure our firm did enough to make amends with our community, and we are very pleased she is leading this initiative."

There was polite clapping as Charlie stepped aside for Miriam to take the podium. He gave Miriam a firm handshake, and she moved in front of the microphone to address the journalists.

"Thank you so much," Miriam said to Charlie. Then she started her own speech. "Alchemy Partners is recovering from its darkest day. Our IT team is in coordination with law enforcement officials and is working around the clock to understand how this breach could have happened. But I am here today to address the other issue: our commitment to our community. Alchemy has always been a part of the greater New York community, and today, we are making a promise to uphold that commitment, always. Going forward, we will endow three percent of all gross revenue to fund community programs across the city. I am pleased that much of my day-to-day activities will be focused on making sure the most funds possible reach the people who need it most in New York." Miriam smiled tightly as she finished her short speech. "I'll take questions now," she said, and she paused as journalists raised their hands.

Charlie hadn't misspoken when he'd mentioned that the endowment had been Miriam's idea. The firm had been dealing with the dual crises of the leak and how they were being perceived by the city, and so, she'd easily wedged herself into the latter. She had conflicts of interest with both crises, of course, given she was the reason the leak had happened and she was dating the man who ran Housing Magic. Even so, Miriam wanted to be part of the solution. Her proposal for the endowment had been a hard sell; she'd started by asking for ten percent, and when they'd agreed to three percent, she'd ultimately been happy. The firm made enough money that even three percent was a sizable amount.

It wasn't exactly the job she'd been hoping for. She'd been working towards a top spot in leadership, and this was certainly a hedge. But it was a job she could feel confident about. She liked the ability to take the firm's money and redistribute it. She would never be like Nelson, who lived his life to help people, but she could use her very specific skill set to make sure that Alchemy at least tried to do better. She could work within the system currently available and be the reason it was less bad. Maybe there would be a future where really rich people didn't make life even harder for those who had so little. But for now, this was the best opportunity Miriam had to make a difference.

She was a witch and an investment banker, and from her position looking out over Wall Street, she'd finally found her community and herself.

Epilogue – One Year Later

"BABE, WE'RE GOING TO be late," Nelson called out to Miriam. She was in their bathroom, trying to tame her hair. Nelson walked up behind her, fiddling with the cuffs on his jacket. "You look beautiful," he said, leaning down to kiss her neck.

"I could use a small miracle to get my hair under control here," she said, frowning up at him. It was early spring, and the humidity was already doing its worst. The situation would be even more dire once summer started.

"Miriam Blum, are you asking for me to help?" Nelson turned to sit back against the bathroom counter, his eyes tracing down her body seductively.

"Just with my hair," Miriam begged. "I love you," she added with an overexaggerated plea.

Nelson gave a nod and then just continued to lean against the counter.

"We're going to be late," Miriam reminded him, hoping the threat of showing up a few minutes after they were supposed to would get him to actually do something.

"I just need to take in this moment—the very time and place Miriam Blum asked me for help."

"You're enjoying this way too much." Miriam shook her head and then hopped onto the bathroom counter.

"I do like making you ask." Nelson gave a suggestive wink, and Miriam knew exactly what he was talking about. She'd have plenty of things to ask for when they got home later. For now, though, she just needed her hair to be fixed so they could actually get going. And thankfully, when she glanced in the mirror, she was glad to see that her once-wild curls were tamed and sleek. "For the record," Nelson added, "I think you are beautiful both ways."

She smiled up at him. "You make this too easy," she said as Nelson held out a hand. She took it and hopped off the counter.

"I know," Nelson replied. "You ready to go?"

Miriam nodded, and they walked into the living room of their shared apartment together. They had moved in six months ago. It seemed fast, but New York rent prices and the impracticality of maintaining two residences in such an expensive city made the decision easy. In all honesty, though, she'd been ready to move in with Nelson as soon as her lease was up, and they'd decided on a new place together.

He was easy and supportive to live with. He sent her out the door with coffee each morning and picked up the dry cleaning. When she worked later than any reasonable person and got home way after he'd gone to bed, he would sleepily pull her into his chest and kiss her forehead. She also liked being there for him. When his job became too much tragedy and heartache all at once, she was the person who supported him, the person who helped distract him from whatever he was dealing with. She liked to curl up on the couch and watch rom-coms with him on Saturday evenings. She liked that he never made fun of her love of reality TV.

She loved him.

Nelson held out his hand, and Miriam wrapped her fingers in his. In an instant, they were in the alleyway behind 515 Edgewood. Housing Magic was opening their largest property to date.

They slipped into the fray of the waiting crowd and then worked their way to where Miriam's coven—their coven—was waiting. Hannah and Isabelle were both holding their infants in baby holders that were strapped across their chests. Craig and Derek were hunched over their child's stroller, and Chloe was hanging on Henry's leg while Heather rubbed her very round and pregnant belly.

"This is so great," Maddy commented from where she was standing next to Hannah. "You've done a great job," she added, addressing Nelson.

"It was really the entire staff at Housing Magic, but the extra funds from Alchemy to get the project done have been monumental," Nelson said.

"So, what's next for you two?" Heather asked, giving them an expectant look.

"Well, we're going to Lithuania on a vacation. We think our great-grandparents knew each other and made the golem our stuff got stuck in," Miriam explained. "We want to understand why they made it, what was happening in their own community. We've searched what we can in New York, but we think it might be something older. Maybe the golem was even created there. We thought it might have been made in New York, but everything suggests that it came over with them."

"That's not what I meant," Heather clarified, tapping her belly to hint at the true meaning behind her question.

"Not right now," Nelson replied.

"We're still new," Miriam reminded them. "And we're going to take advantage of the honeymoon phase for a while."

"You should definitely take it at your own pace," Hannah agreed with a nod.

The conversation faded, and after a moment, Nelson seemed to glance around at the crowd nervously. Miriam took his hand and laced her fingers through his.

"It's their loss if they don't come," she said. "You've done great work and helped a lot of people."

"They aren't happy I took the Alchemy money," he reminded her. "They think that it's encouraging billionaires to govern on their own. But I miss them. I may have left the coven, but they're still my friends, and I just wish they would support this."

Miriam nodded. "Look, I don't deny that it would be a better world if tax policy and social services and criminal justice all aligned and if everything could be done free from the shackles of capitalism, but right now, in the world we live in, I think you've done a pretty good job with what you have. And yes, that means accepting money from an investment bank. But it also means that five hundred new families have a place to live, no matter their work history, or their criminal record. You are the reason five hundred people have a second chance."

Nelson gave a toothy smile. "You are really good at this," he said, and then he kissed her on the cheek. "And I think I know exactly what I'm going to do to thank you when we get home."

"What could you possibly be thinking?" Miriam asked suggestively.

Nelson winked, but didn't offer an answer. He made his way to where a podium was set up to deliver all the pomp and circumstance that came with this sort of event. And Miriam stood with her friends and watched.

She did wonder what Nelson had in mind for their evening, but she liked that he did that sometimes—made her wait for his surprises. She never would have thought she'd appreciate someone allowing her to give up control. And sure, it wasn't a one-way street. Miriam had had her own thoughts after that initial visit to Sofia's back room. She had her own surprises for Nelson, and she liked that he let her feel like she could do these sorts of things with him. She liked that it made her feel needed, powerful, feminine, and competent.

Things were good with her and Nelson—better than good, actually—and she was excited to see what happened next.

Things were good with her life, too. Her coven, her community, was standing beside her, there for her when she needed them. In turn, she was there for them, too. And the man she loved was doing what he did best—helping people.

She looked up to where he had taken the stage.

"Thanks for coming," Nelson greeted the crowd. "Today is only the beginning."

Acknowledgements

I can't believe I am already writing acknowledgments for a second book. First of all, a big thank you to my first readers, Ashley and Cooper. You took the time to read this little book and offer feedback and encouragement. Also, my stepmom, Jill, who helped with the parts on substance abuse, both adding comments and discussing standard care practices with me. I cannot forget my sister Aliza who is always willing to talk through ideas and books. Also, Sam, because you should be thanked too. To Marc and Dixie for hosting me in their New York apartment over the years and for taking me to NYC Dim Sum. To my editors Sara and Courtney over at Mild Mannered editors who allowed me to work with them a second time, and once again transformed this book into something that felt real. Truly, there would be no book without them. My team would not be complete without a shoutout to Miblart and the amazing designers and project managers that worked together for this truly stunning cover art.

To the Boston Romance community, specifically Lily and Hannah at Read My Lips Boston and Rachel at Lovestruck in Cambridge. Thank you so much for buying my books for your stores and welcoming me into the community as a romance author and reader. And to all the independent bookstores across the country that have taken risks on indie authors and have stocked their shelves full of romance. Thank you for including us as part of the author community.

Thank you to all the powerful women in finance I have worked with over the years. The ones who helped me write this story just by existing in the industry.

And lastly, thank you to my readers, especially my ARC readers who take such care and dedication to writing reviews and posting across social media. As an author, being read and knowing you are dedicating your valuable reading time to my stories is such a humbling experience. I am forever grateful to you.

And of course, a big thank you to Izzi, the CEO of Izzi House Books. She's a hands off executive, but she runs a very robust health and wellness program, that requires multiple, long walks every single day. She is the best supervisor, even if she does have four legs.